Declanii

Nathan Daniel Davini

Declanii Part One: Ideclan

Main Edit: Laura Fister

Final Edit, Formatting, and Map: Nathan Daniel Davini

Published by Ravenborne Publishing

www.Declanii.com

@sagasoftheravenborne

Cover Art: Illustrations by Jana Westabrooks @silvansense

ISBN# 978-0-578-49279-7

First Edition: 2019

Revised: 2024

Acknowledgment

I thank Cole Henry Hampton Jr., my great friend, who helped me with many things at the beginning of this quest. I will always remember going to you for advice after I'd gotten stuck with just a map, some names, and an idea. I asked you what to do next and you said, "Well Nate, you need an outline." And the story took shape from there. I hope your travels treat you well, brother, and that our paths should cross again.

Table of Contents

Declanii

Part One: Ideclan

Declanii

Prologue

The Wizard's War

Five Thousand Three Hundred Years Ago

Lightning coalesced into spheres and soared across the battlefield. Tornadoes of fire anchored to wizards' hands and scorched scars in long arcs across the plain. Cold wind and water combined to throw forth destructive ice. Sand flew wildly and trees splintered, beaks punctured and teeth ripped. Earth shook as wizard fought with wizard and Ancient fought with Ancient.

Segais, a human, studied the struggle while wind tore at him and Ancients worked to get to him. He was leader of half the wizards there and founder of the order to which all wizards on the battlefield once belonged.

Krovin, leader of the rebelling half, looked out from across the plain, constantly resurrecting his fallen followers. Sandlions, Shadowhawks, and wizards of all abilities protected the necromancer. None could get close enough to end his majic.

"Segais, if Krovin isn't defeated he'll continue regenerating his army until ours is no more," Hardolf, eldest of all Treewolves told him.

"I know!" the old wizard snapped back before looking toward the sky, scanning with anxious eagerness.

The Treewolf towering next to him stood fifty two feet

tall. When not rooted in place, all Treewolves' trunks split at the bottom to form two legs. Their roots reached up, wrapped around and came back down the legs creating sinewy muscles and claws. Almost every branch wrapped around two main ones forming strong arms and claws. Their heads always looked like wolf heads with saplings for hair, but when uprooted they were alive and unhidden by branches. While taking this shape they could run like wolves or also walk upright. And never did their anatomy of the tree of origin change.

"I will lead the Alrukalkrinn in a final assault. For with him his cause also dies," Hardolf declared.

Segais continued searching the sky, seeking with all his might and finally glimpsed what he sought. He yelled to Hardolf, "Hold your people! The Heavens are here!"

"We must draw on Krovin if you are to defeat him. I bid you well, wise human."

"I can defeat him! You must hold!"

But it was too late. The Treewolf bound away with others to attack the main part of Krovin's army in an attempt to reach him. And Segais looked hesitantly to the Heavens again.

"It is time!" Bailart, also a wizard and his greatest friend yelled. "The Heavens are here but they will pass!"

Segais inspected the battlefield. His existence paused as he took in every detail. The old wizard knew that if he didn't act now they would lose this battle and the world would eventually be destroyed by the path on which he set it. So he looked toward Bailart and nodded.

Bailart yelled, "Protect Segais!" then threw a ball of lightning at a large Shadowhawk and tore it asunder.

Those near them formed a perimeter and guarded from the consuming threat.

Segais directed his intent toward the sky. His intense concentration didn't break as malicious collisions killed many around him.

The Treewolves clawed through Krovin's men, yet because they were resurrected behind them the Ancients became surrounded. The Alrukalkrinn continued forward and battled with a group of Sandlions, pushing them back to the point Krovin could only focus on where they were, and where Segais was located eased because of it.

The old wizard continued his intention uninterrupted while the battle raged. Sweat poured down his contorted face as every muscle strained to the point of pain.

Thunderous roars came from the sky as nine balls of fire fell forth from the Heavens. Segais held his concentration, every muscle flexed to its peak as his intent stayed on them, pulling them down while directing their paths. He paid attention to nothing but the fireballs, not even the thralls who broke through his protecting line and charged. The old wizard aimed each fireball at Krovin, but focused on three. On those he gave more intent and let the others go. When Segais felt their trajectories were accurate he sped them up. Freefall began working with him. And soon the three took little force to guide as they flew down with a sound that split the sky.

All nine had been called in by Segais but five headed toward parts of the world unknown. Across the battlefield, thousands stopped to watch or run. When Krovin became aware, the resurrecting ceased. He searched his mind for a counter, something to save himself but it was too late, even though his thralls were almost at Segais. And the old wizard let go of the last three fireballs just in time to fight the thralls off with his staff.

Four fireballs impacted the battlefield and destroyed everything in their paths. Two obliterated Krovin when they crashed into each other on his exact spot. As he died, all beings resurrected by Krovin fell to the ground, leaving Segais the opportunity to watch the last five fireballs fly far and away, much farther than he'd anticipated. And the other two that hit the battlefield pummeled Hardolf, eldest of Treewolves, as well as many more who'd considered the old wizard a friend.

Segais stood there, motionless. When he could move again he rushed for an impact site, ready to heal. Tears filled his eyes and streaked down his face.

He stopped running when he saw a Treewolf carrying two humans, and his heart sank as he changed direction to run for them.

"Wife! Son! How are they?"

"There is no more of Hardolf, nor Gidolf, Tindolf, and Grekdolf. They are all dead because of your fireballs," Wardolf told him as Segais reached them. "Heal your wife and son if you can." He set them on the ground next to each other. "Now that this is over, the Alrukalkrinn have other matters to attend."

Then he bound off.

Segais asked his son, "Are you alright?"

The boy tried answering but blood came from his mouth. And his wife wasn't moving at all.

The old Ariek wizard held his palms over their chests and said the ancient healing words, *"Palratas seero yunovik, kalratas heerlox sunovrim!"*

Both his wife and son died instead of healed, and Segais the Long Lived was drained of much of his own life force as well. He looked at his hands with great anguish and confusion. And though the Wizard's War was won because of his actions, he still entered the darkest phase of his life.

Declanii

Chapter One
Midwinter, 333'rd Year of the Ninth Age
Present Day

"Ashnayn!" her father yelled while storming up the stairway to her room. "Ashnayn!" he growled again as he entered. "There you are. You cannot leave the Gathering of Chiefs it is forbidden. Get back there now!"

"I will not!" she yelled while holding tight to a small stone figurine her mother gave her before she died.

"You will do as I say! I have chosen your path!"

"Why would you promise me to that cruel man? He isn't even Hobaru and yet, you would give him leadership of the Twenty Tribes?"

"If you don't marry him I will *lose* leadership of the Twenty Tribes!"

The All Chief, Nuadhu, said that louder than he meant to and looked around to see if any of their servants overheard. He was a big man with a big belly and his voice always carried.

"It doesn't have to be this way," Ashnayn said, misunderstanding his true meaning.

"This is the way I have chosen and this is the way it will be. Now, come back to the gathering."

"But it doesn't have to be," she pleaded. And after a short pause, Ashnayn said with innocent conviction, "I can lead the Hobaru," while putting a lock of blonde red hair behind an ear.

The tall Nuadhu looked at her for a moment. His jet black hair fell loosely around him, covering his tan broad shoulders and some of his big belly. Disgust formed on his face as he ripped the necklace of seashells from himself and threw it to the floor at Ashnayn's feet, a necklace she had made for him.

He spit on her and said, "A woman will never rule the Twenty Tribes of Hobaru."

Then he walked over and grabbed her wrist to forcefully bring her back to the gathering. Tears escaped the Princess' eyes as she returned the stone figurine to one of her diving vest's pockets, and then pulled a cloth from another so she could clean off the spit.

The walk back wasn't pleasant. Nuadhu held her wrist tightly as they made their way through Date Palm, Totara, and Pomegranate Trees. The Gathering of Chiefs met within an elaborate temple made from bamboo and located at the center of a sacred grove. When the All Chief and his daughter returned, the other chiefs waiting outside moved into the temple with them. And each gave Ashnayn disapproving looks.

Nuadhu let go of her wrist after they entered and she massaged it gently while studying everyone in the room. Ashnayn knew exactly where Gowgluni was, the man she was just told she'd be promised to, but the Princess wouldn't look at him directly. For the last three years of his being on the Hobaru Islands she had never liked him.

Most of Ashnayn's blonde red hair was gathered in a long braid that fell down her back. She was dressed in a blue sarong with leather sandals and her black linen diving vest with many pockets. In one of those pockets she had the stone figurine her mother gave her. And the Princess put a hand on it to make sure it was still there; an old and nervous habit.

The Hobaru claimed mastery over four abilities: running, swimming, climbing, and diving. Therefore most were fit with great endurance and Ashnayn was no exception. Her muscles were toned and lean with shoulders slightly broad. And she moved with the grace of a dolphin, strong and sure.

"We're all here. Everyone, take your places," the All Chief ordered. Yet many looked to Gowgluni and waited for his nod before doing so.

"All Chief Daughter, you may take your place," another reiterated once everyone settled.

The Princess moved to the center of the room. And a different chief held the sacred wreath of shark teeth and bones above her head.

Then her father said, "All Chief Daughter Ashnayn, under the rights of teeth and bone it is declared…"

Ashnayn stepped out from under the wreath. Nuadhu looked astonished as his voice trailed off and almost everyone there was offended.

"All chiefs hear me," she asserted before any of them could speak. "I am my father's daughter. I am the best climber of all Twenty Tribes, among the best runners, often the best diver, and up front with the best swimmers. There's no need for an All Chief's Son because the daughter is better than all the men. *I* will lead Hobaru."

The chiefs went into an uproar as Nuadhu menacingly walked over to Ashnayn and forcefully held her under the wreath.

He yelled, "Under the rights of teeth and bone you are now declared promised to Gowgluni! You are his and he inherits the All Chief Seat and all it claims!"

He let her go and she fell to the floor with fear. Then Nuadhu looked at Gowgluni who nodded with the thinnest of smiles. And the All Chief let out a breath of relief as he walked back to his chair.

Ashnayn was up quick and ran through the door before anyone could grab her. She didn't care to find out what else was going to be declared under teeth and bone. Tears ran down soft cheeks while strong legs carried the Princess to her favorite lake faster than anyone who would think to follow her could go.

The lake was ringed with tall trees and grasses, and when she got there she sat down near the water's edge while crying heavily. Ashnayn pulled the stone figurine from her diving vest and held it close as she continued to cry.

"Mom, I need you," she pleaded toward the sky.

The cherished wooden cart traveled many miles during its short life, fulfilling its purpose more than was ever hoped for. It had become a great comfort to Cristin and his son,

Elasus, doing much to serve them during the last three years of fleeing from their homeland. The cart had seen its fair share of wear and tear along the way and now, every rock or crevice not avoided underneath the snow made it creak and groan. Splinters stood out from each piece of wood, looking like small pikemen ready for a cavalry charge. The axel at the center of the cart was on its last repair, all leather needed mending or replacement, and both wheels were rickety to the point one of them would fail soon.

The mule pulling the cart reflected her charge perfectly. She was a good mule and like the cart she'd become a great comfort, but like the cart she was nearing the end of her days. Cristin gave her a light tug of encouragement as they walked South toward Ideclan.

"Come on old girl, just a few more days," he assured her, half assuring himself.

Cristin was a young man at twenty one and a big man for any age. He was easily over six and a half feet tall with a chest as broad as a tower shield. His hair was dark brown and kept short so it stayed out of his hazel eyes, both of which were Edemarian features he passed down to his five year old son who slept in a bundle of blankets at the front of the cart.

When Elasus fell asleep during midafternoon, Cristin chose not to wake him, knowing that a rest wouldn't ruin his night. But now if he continued letting him sleep it would, so Cristin decided to wake his son. He reached inside the cart to gently shake him just as one of the wheels hit a rock covered by snow.

Elasus awoke and sat up, wrapped in all the blankets they had except for the one around his father's sheathed two handed Edemarian Sword lying in the cart with him. The young boy looked in every direction, trying to discern where he was through the cavern of blankets, and then looked straight at his father with half open hazel eyes.

After checking the wheel for damage, Cristin chuckled when he saw him and said, "It was only a rock, son."

Elasus nodded as the world started making sense again. "Are we close to Ideclan?" he asked, his voice crackling from the sleep.

"A few days still, perhaps more."

"Wake me when the bed is near," the boy said, then laid back down.

Cristin laughed as he shook his son to keep him awake.

The father wore two pairs of brown pants and three coats of varying green and gray to keep warm. And if he hadn't been walking for so long that might not have been enough. He too, was looking forward to a warm bed. And to take their minds of their struggles, he resumed telling tales about Ideclan, the land that could accommodate them, now that Elasus was awake.

Elasus didn't know the true story of his family. He often wondered why they constantly moved around, always changing their names. So much so that he didn't know his middle or last names. But he did know they were from Edemar. And it had been getting harder for Cristin to keep the truth hidden from him. His questions were increasingly more intelligent. Traveling and being exposed to different cultures made Elasus a critical thinker for a five year old. And his father felt the learning taught by the Philosians at Ideclan would serve him well because of it.

"Remember, son. When we arrive we'll continue saying we're from The Gray Forest."

"Alright, but I'm only five and I can easily tell we're not from Fwynndarlanai."

"Yes, but we do know it's called Fwynndarlanai, among many other native customs few have heard of. We'll keep to the original story. Which is?"

"Our ancestors were travelers and settled in The Gray Forest four generations ago."

"Very good."

Someday you'll know who we truly are, I promise, Cristin thought.

"Do you think it'll be warmer when we get there?"

"There's no roof over the city. But I can assure you our room will be warm. Ideclan has many inns and all of them are said to be of quality."

He wrapped his three coats tighter as he thought of the warmth.

"You know a lot about Ideclan, father, a lot of stories. How come?"

As an adolescent, Cristin was taught of many lands. It was the only other subject he paid attention to besides his favorite, the Edemarian Sword. He'd never told these stories about Ideclan to his son before, and up until recently, Elasus had only known of the place as a name. Cristin's memories of his studies came flooding back as they neared the city. Many had been suppressed by three years of constant struggle for survival, but being so close to Ideclan caused them to return.

"When I was young, starting from the age you are now, I began a school for people born into our position."

"Our position?"

"Just listen. I learned many things in this school. But at Edemar they withhold this knowledge from almost everyone, and only people born like us get to learn it. You see, Elasus, just as physical strength can separate us in some ways, intelligence does so in many more. Knowledge is the true power of this world. And at Ideclan, not only are the teachers from Philos more knowledgeable, but I'm sure they teach everyone, which is a better setting for learning and a much better place for you to grow up."

"But that isn't the real reason why we left Edemar, is it?"

How do I tell you why you're forced to grow up without the love of your mother, your aunts and uncles, your grandparents? Cristin asked himself.

He was searching for the right words when Elasus asked, "It hasn't all really been a game, has it? All the hurrying and hiding, the constant running and changing homes?"

"No, it hasn't. We had to leave Edemar because those who rule there wish to harm us."

"Harm us... Why?"

"We threaten them."

There was a different kind of fire in Cristin's eyes as he answered, and Elasus chose not to question about their home any further.

The young child wasn't surprised, the sense of danger had always been present. Elasus was aware that games were supposed to be fun, and almost nothing they'd gone through over the last three years had been fun.

"Will we be safe at Ideclan?" he asked.

"We should be. Once there's a tournament I'll join and become a soldier in their army. After that, we get a house of our own and you can start education with the Philos, meet friends, perhaps even Clanii. And before you know it our descendants will be true Ideclaners," Cristin said with hope to his son.

"You've said those names before. Who are the Philos and the Clanii?" Elasus continued.

"The Philos are a wise people who live close to Ideclan and teach the schools there. The Clanii, with their Ravenborne Kings, are the people who founded Ideclan. And they are the bearers of the *nifu ellwulle* for this Age."

"What is the *nifu ellwulle?*"

"Another time perhaps, Elasus. I wish to think of other things."

Declanii

Chronicle One

The following is transcribed from a stone tablet carried with the Clanii on both exoduses. It is translated from Old Clanii into the Common Tongue.

At the beginning of Gynne, First Breath was life and first life was breathed. That is when Space, Time, and Form were first perceived. Another breath was breathed and the Earth formed. On it there were mountains, oceans, rivers, lakes, grasses, valleys, canyons, and streams. Trees grew tall where wind blew wild, fires transmuted while water provided, this continued for a time unknowable. Then another breath was breathed and trees began to walk, water began to swim, and the air began to breathe. The whole of the Earth gently rose and fell, the mountains swayed, large oceans and lakes sloshed with the heaving of a breathing Earth. The first forms to arise from this world were beings of nature in motion, beings breathed of both nature and movement. They walked and flew across the whole expanse of the Earth, mastering their ways of being. When the ancient animals of element and form grew, expanding into more breath, a fourth breath was breathed by the First, and out of the misty smoke of the transmuting fires walked the Thirty Three, all of whom are sprung from the same spring...

This is where the tablet ends for the rest is broken off. The Clanii have with them a manuscript of the entire transcription of the tablet, but this was taken from the stone and is therefore dated to the Seventh Age.

Translation by Siras of Philos for Turas of Philos' manuscript: Histories of the Clanii

Declanii

Chapter Two

"ORAKAL, MAY I ENTER?" A HEAVYSET MAN OF SEVENTY asked. He was completely bald and wearing silk robes of light blue and purple.

"You may," the child answered without turning from her window.

He walked into the room and then bowed by putting his forehead on the floor four steps before her.

"Rise," she commanded.

The man rose while favoring a knee and then looked toward the young girl with auburn hair. She turned and he beheld green eyes that understood more knowledge than he knew he could hope to achieve. To the old man who was her wisest advisor, the young oracle looked very wise.

"The cavern vaults are prepared for the people. Emperor Camulus' army will not find them. And they'll have enough provisions to last one year."

"Thank you, Binc. Please tell Captain Higada and the Shogin that instead of their training they will dine with us this evening."

"Yes, Orakal," Binc said before walking out and seeing to her wishes.

The Orakal gazed back through her window overlooking the holy city of Saddeye. Her heart was resolute but hesitant.

She'd found the path that would save her people and now it was time to tell them.

When the dinner bells rang, the young girl put on a mantle of thick white cloth across her shoulders over her brown dress and then walked toward the dining hall. She noticed every crack and crevice in the walls. Her ancient city deteriorated faster then they could repair it but there were other matters to attend.

When she arrived at the hall, everyone stood. The Orakal held up her hand so that all would sit back down except for Captain Higada, who walked over and put his forehead on the floor four steps before her.

"Rise."

He sat on his knees and drew his short katana, then slid it across his upper forearm until blood dripped, then sheathed it after wiping off the blood before completely standing. When the Eastern man rose he saw a youth younger than she was. To him her hair was black and cut straight at just past the ears. Her eyes were brown and full of knowing. But to the man who was sworn to protect her, she looked like she needed protecting.

To each soul in the room, the Orakal looked different than how the next soul perceived her. Some saw red hair and blue eyes, or yellow hair and gray eyes. The differences of her appearance were as many as there were people in the room. To each she looked unique, according to what their perception deemed the Orakal should look like. The only consistencies were her clothes and her age of twelve. She was indeed the one prophesied by their faith.

The Orakal and Higada sat at the long table full of

simple foods. The meal was uncomfortably quiet as all waited to hear the child's decision. And when they finished eating she finally stood.

"Thank you for being patient. I know this is difficult. But I've found the way through without death or bloodshed."

Everyone at the table cheered, only the Shogin remained silent.

"Do as I say in the exact manner I say it, and all shall live. My faithful Shogin, you shall draw no blood when Camulus brings his army here."

Higada rose while saying, "My lady, it is for us to protect you with our lives."

"You are fifteen men. He has more than one hundred and sixty five thousand. If you truly wish to protect me you will not fight, and instead let me be taken prisoner."

They expressed their outrage so she held up her hand, and the Shogin fell silent.

"The Robed Priests and Corded Masters will stay with us when Camulus arrives, but that is after all pilgrims and supplicants have been led to the vaults and sealed in. Camulus will take me away, but also bring me back for he is going to leave the bulk of his army here to plunder and feed. The Emperor knows we keep enough provisions to supply all that arrive and he means to exploit that fact.

Robed and Corded, he will not harm you. And his men will be ordered not to harm you. Camulus Erra'Aulius wishes for me to name him and therefore will follow the customs required."

Many spoke but she held up her hand again.

"Of course I will never name him. Robed and Corded, take all care to keep hidden those in the caves. Camulus' men are brutal and bloodthirsty, but they are disciplined and do as commanded. None of you will be harmed so long as you remain true to our way. Then, you may rejoice once you've freed the people in the cavern vaults after the Emperor has left for the second time.

To my Shogin, I ask the most difficult of you. While with Camulus, before he returns for his army I'll go through many hardships. And when we return, he'll hand me over to those who are going to torture me." She held up her hand once more while continuing, "You must do nothing. You must not attempt to rescue me until you've crossed paths with the Ravenborne. Try before the Ravenborne is among you and we'll perish. Force the Ravenborne to cross your path and we'll perish. Wait... and I'll be free again."

Her legs and lungs burned as she ran to her fullest ability, faster than almost anyone else on the islands. There was no wind but the Princess' speed caused her sweat to cool her down. The path was wide and well worn so she ran without worry. The faster she went the less she thought about anything, and that was the intent. Her muscles ached and lungs screamed but that didn't matter; nearing the limit of her ability she still ran perfectly. Ashnayn wore a dark green sarong and her black linen diving vest. And her long blonde red hair bounced behind her in a thick braid.

The All Chief Daughter of the Twenty Tribes completed a long bend in the path and slowed as she entered the capital city of Hobaru, then started walking. Intricate bamboo structures covered by flowers with large red and purple petals adorned both sides of the roads she followed.

Upon arriving at her family's estate, she went back to where her pull up bars, sand pit, balancing beams, and free weights were located. Next to them was a small bamboo hut she often used to change clothes. Ashnayn walked directly for that hut, then stopped when Gowgluni exited its door.

What's that bastard doing in my changing room?

"You're not allowed in there!" the Princess yelled forcefully.

"Um, well, yes, correct. But only for so much longer. Then we'll be married, as it should be."

"As it should be? That's your problem, you and most other men on these islands. You think it's your place to decide for another."

"I give you full respects, Ashnayn. You're the strongest woman I've ever seen, both internally," Gowgluni paused as he looked up and down her body, "and externally," he said in a way that creeped her out. "I understand why you wish to be above others, because that is your true place."

"I never told the chiefs I wish to be above others. I said I wish to lead Hobaru. Being a leader and being above are two separate ideas."

"But you will be above others."

"What do you mean?" she asked, completely revolted by his presence.

"After I become ruler of Hobaru there are far greater tasks to accomplish. My associates and I, well, all in good time. First we wed, now that you've finally reached the marrying age of twenty two. I wish your father was allowed to promise you sooner. We could've married on your birthday."

He tried holding her hand but she pulled away.

"Tell me, how did you persuade my father and the other chiefs to hand over leadership to you? Because I've been thinking about it and can come up with nothing."

"Your father and the other chiefs know wisdom when they see it. You, not always, that's why your choices are made for you."

"Tyranny is why choices are made for me. Now answer my question. How did you do it?"

"I'll see you at dinner," Gowgluni stated as he started walking off.

"Stop!" Ashnayn commanded with a force she'd never felt before. "Answer me!"

He stopped and turned involuntarily, trying to resist but couldn't. He almost blurted out the complete truth due to the force of her voice except he was able to recover just before, somewhat surprised and said, "Such power, when we're joined it'll be the greatest ecstasy."

Then he turned and left.

We're never joining, she thought.

Ashnayn entered her hut and dried herself off with a towel while searching for clues of Gowgluni's intentions. After finding none, she felt the pocket holding her small stone figurine before quickly walking to the main house and up toward the second level so she could grab a blanket to have while sitting at dinner.

When the Princess went back downstairs she crossed paths with her father. He was dressed in a woven grass skirt and his long black hair covered most of his torso. After a short pause he was the first to speak.

"I want to apologize if I hurt you."

"Physically, or emotionally?"

"Physically. Is your wrist alright?"

"Yes. Tell me, All Chief of the Twenty Tribes of Hobaru."

Nuadhu stood taller as she used his full title.

"What does it feel like to be the first All Chief to barter leadership?"

He looked at the floor.

"Because that's what you did isn't it? What did he give you? Leadership of your own people, to someone who doesn't even care for those people; you are officially the worst All Chief in the history of the Twenty Tribes."

Declanii

Ashnayn's vision went black as she fell to the floor. Her jaw throbbed as it never had. She sobbed while her father walked away with his fist still clenched. And a handmaiden ran to her once Nuadhu left. The handmaiden had known Ashnayn since she was a child and cared for her very much. After her mother died, the old handmaiden did what she could to fill that role.

"Dear, dear, it'll be alright."

"What do you know?" the Princess asked between tears.

"I know you're going through hard times. But something tells me you'll swim through."

"I wish mother were here."

"So do I."

"She had a way of getting father to listen."

"The only one who could."

"Except Gowgluni," Ashnayn said with disdain.

"He's an odd man. I'm sorry you were promised to him."

"It doesn't make sense."

"What?"

"Whoever I marry becomes leader of the Twenty Tribes."

"Yes?"

"So why would twenty men, all of whom want the All Chief's Seat, freely give it to someone they've known for only three years and is not even Hobaru? We run, swim, climb, and dive. This man does none of these!"

A group of eight Hobaru men interrupted their conversation by walking into the house with spears tipped by shark teeth. Gowgluni had set up his own policing force on all five islands. They were mercenaries, bought and paid for, and now they were paid to bring Ashnayn to dinner so that she could sit next to him.

"All Chief Daughter, you're coming with us," the leader said.

"Where?" she asked incredulously.

"To the dinner tables. You'll be sitting with Gowgluni from now on."

"Better go with them dear," the handmaiden said as she helped Ashnayn off the floor.

"Fine," she answered, and then dried her eyes and rubbed her jaw.

The Princess thought she might feel more comfortable at dinner. But when they arrived at the impressive pavilion she realized how wrong that thought was. Hardly anyone looked at her and no one spoke to her. She was stunned.

"Are all of you blind?" she yelled. But no one acknowledged.

"To me," Gowgluni said forcefully, and the eight men made Ashnayn walk and sit beside him. "Do you like them?" he asked, gesturing toward the eight.

"Why would I like them?"

"They're to protect you from now on. They'll be with you always, except for when we want our privacy of course."

"Always?"

"I don't want anything happening to you, Ashnayn. I have too many plans for us."

Ashnayn looked at her father but he didn't look back. Then she looked at the other chiefs but none of them looked back either. They were all focused on the honeyed pineapple ham in front of them.

"All of you are cowards," she said loud enough so they could hear her without her having to yell.

Gowgluni chuckled.

I need to figure out how to get away from this whale's ass, she thought.

Chronicle Two

Tenets of the Ancient Clanii

Humility is Honorable
Kindness is more powerful than Rage
Wisdom is cultivated through Integrity
Positions of acquisition are positions to Give
Gifts are special when they are special to you as you give Them
No being has say over any Other
What is acquired through deceit is truthfully not Acquired
They who owe nothing earn Everything
Eradicate the guarding of Knowledge
Forgiveness sets the forgiver Free
What is true for one is true for All

Three texts accompany the stone tablet from which this translation was taken. These texts speak of many more tenets lost from the tablets. The Tenets here are approximate based on the fact that they are translations, but the intent is clearly transferred from Old Clanii into the Common Tongue. These tenets are translated straight from one of the stone tablets brought with the Clanii on both exoduses, so their authenticity to the time of the Seventh Age is believed confirmed.

Part of the manuscript: Histories of the Clanii.
Written by Turas of Philos

Declanii

Chapter Three

"FATHER, I'M COLD," ELASUS PRONOUNCED.

Cristin came out of his deep thoughts and saw the Sun almost completely set. "Sorry. We can stop there," he answered while pointing toward a thick grove of Ponderosas.

As they made their way into the grove, Cristin searched the ground for wood of any kind, and his anger grew as he saw none.

"What? Do people come and clean up the forest?"

"What do you mean?" Elasus asked as they stopped at the center.

"I don't see any firewood."

"We have to have a fire."

"I know. We also want to eat." Cristin looked at the cart and then walked over to it and looked inside. "We'll use this," he said.

"For what?" Elasus asked while shivering.

"To get the fire going, unhitch Ella."

Cristin slung his sword across his back and then started breaking the cart apart. It was so worn it broke into pieces easily.

"Here's the flint, father."

Elasus gave it to him before unhitching the mule. It was Edemarian tradition for their sons to be responsible for something important.

"Thank you."

When the fire pit they'd found was ready with a little log cabin made from the broken wood, Cristin ripped strips from his inner coat and placed them within. He looked around in the growing dark and saw a large boulder, then got up and walked over to it. He cleared the snow away from the edge and dug at its base. Cristin figured there'd be dry pine needles there and he found some at the bottom of the thick layer of duff. He grabbed a few handfuls and walked back.

"Father, I'm freezing," he heard Elasus say in a weak voice.

"Where are your blankets?"

Cristin hurriedly placed the needles on top of the cloth strips then ran to his son.

"They fell off when I was unhitching Ella, and they're wet with snow now," he answered through chattering teeth.

Cristin rubbed his arms, then picked up Elasus and put him in his coats against himself and rubbed his back, having to adjust his sword sling while doing so.

"Are you getting warmer?"

"Yes," the child answered.

Cristin walked back to the fire pit and waited till his son stopped shivering before setting him down, then arranged his materials and struck the flint. His proficiency had the fire going within a moment and Elasus hunched over it closely while putting on two of his father's coats with growing glee.

"Now for some food," Cristin said as he went to grab the blankets and dry them by the fire.

Elasus looked at the mule and yelled, "Not Ella!"

"No, son. We won't eat her." *Not yet.* "But we have to eat something."

"There was lots of rabbits."

"Yes, but…" Cristin looked at his son and then his boots. "We can live without boots but not food."

Cristin used his sword to cut a piece of leather the size of his palm from his right boot. From his left boot he cut the lace into two even pieces. After poking holes at the corners of the piece of leather, he thread the laces through them and then tested his new sling. Rocks had not been hard to find, a few were located near the boulder where he'd dug for the pine needles and for that, Cristin was thankful.

He threw a few more pieces of cart on the fire and said, "Stay close to the warmth, I'll not go far."

Elasus nodded.

When Cristin made it out of the grove he checked for how well their fire could be seen. Not well was his decision. With that off his mind he began searching the ground for tracks and game.

His skill allowed him to hunt a brace of rabbits in little time. And he returned to find Elasus still next to the fire with Ella right beside him. Cristin was pleased he'd gotten the rabbits this late and without losing sight of the grove. These were the only times he'd ever left Elasus over the last three years and they were always the most anxious for him. When he got close to his son and mule, he held up the brace and the boy cheered, which caused Ella to raise her head in his direction.

"We have enough wood to cook those," Elasus said. "But do we have enough for the night?"

"I saw a few dead and downed trees while hunting, we'll have enough."

"This is gonna be tasty," the boy proclaimed.

Cristin smiled as he skinned the rabbits, cut them up, then placed each piece on the stones by the fire.

Elasus looked warm next to the mule which eased Cristin's mind. He'd acquired the mule and cart three years back, when Edemarian politics forced him to flee his home. Since then; trained murderers, hired assassins, and the feared Edemarian Executioners had tracked the young man and his son to no end. But Cristin defeated all of them. Including the teams of three or four. Though, he did have a long scar down the front of his chest from one such group of four.

As he rested by the fire, Cristin thought of when he first fled from Edemar with his son. He'd chosen to go North into the lands of the Runidareeans. But after eight long months he decided that place could no longer keep them safe. So he directed his son, mule, and cart even further North into The Gray Forest. It was a land not known very well by non inhabitants, but home to many villages nonetheless, some of them quite large, Cristin found.

Eventually they were able to evade detection in The Gray Forest. After a year and nine months of moving around in the extensive woods, constantly changing locations, it seemed the pursuers finally lost their tracks. It was then that Cristin was able to direct his thoughts toward their further futures instead of immediate ones. The two of them, along with the old mule, had been on the run for two years and five months by that time, most of it in The Gray Forest, and he knew he needed to change this. The men they fled from would stop at nothing. The Gray Forest was their last known location so more assassins would eventually come. Cristin contemplated with great care on where they could go and he thought of one place that might work: Ideclan. He figured Ideclan had a large enough army he could slip into it safely.

He knew Edemar sent word to all the lands that he was already captured and put to death, as having it known that he was still alive was the last thing the ruling elite wanted. Because of this, he figured getting into Ideclan might not be that difficult. Much time had passed since they fled Edemar and their travels had changed them. Yet he was aware of how cautious they needed to be. Cristin knew the extent to which Edemar went to with its coin for informants. And the crimes he was accused of would encourage anyone to hunt him down if they thought him alive.

They'd been making their way to Ideclan for seven months since leaving The Gray Forest, scrounging to save and pay as they went, hunting, foraging, or trapping where they could, hiding when they thought they had to. And after seven long months on a road between the Lefwynn Mountains and the Tyrdan Mountains, then the Haltcla and the Brimmgards, they were almost at their destination. It was very near to the three year anniversary of their flight from Edemar. Cristin hoped there'd be a tournament soon so he could join. If not, he'd have to find a trade to keep his little family going until there was one.

As they'd gotten closer to Ideclan over the past few days, Elasus talked more about his excitement for a real bed. Cristin, no matter the location, was weary and ready for a greater sense of security. The only other thought he had besides getting to Ideclan was turning the cart around and heading back to Edemar so he could kill everyone who had anything to do with his current situation. And though the latter appealed to him more, he figured if he went to Ideclan and joined the army, he might get to do both.

Cristin was also aware of the hardships Elasus had to endure. He was going to make sure he did well in the next tournament so his son could experience something more stable. They'd eaten their last grain stores with the mule earlier that day and as Cristin looked at Ella lying next to Elasus, he gave her soothing voice remedy while patting her neck, letting her know that soon she could rest properly; soon, they all would. Then he put his attention back on the rabbits roasting near the fire.

"Lady Orakal, I humbly ask for your wisdom," the forty eighth supplicant received that day requested.

"You have it. What do you ask?"

"My lady, our well has run dry and our village is without water. Our ale will soon run out as well. We ask that you tell us what to do, or where to go?"

"Have you looked for another water source? Or asked your neighbors for aid?"

"No," he answered.

The old man looking at the child saw a young girl, well fed and unkept, with tangled brown hair and droopy eyes.

"Why not?" she asked.

"I am the youngest of our village and I'm old. Our youths were taken away, by war or slavery. Most of us need assistance to survive. Taking the journey here was a risk, my lady."

"You're from Halat?"

"Yes."

The Orakal sat back in her chair and focused on the people from Halat. "About sixty at your village?"

"Correct."

"Hrija."

"My lady?"

"Have Jal and his men drive carriages to Halat, bring those people here, and then lead them into the caverns with the others."

"Yes, my lady."

To the old man she said, "It'll be cold but it'll be safe, and you'll have all the food and water you need. I don't know precisely how long you'll stay. But it will be safe."

For most of you, age will take some.

"Thank you, my lady!"

"Follow Hrija to the stables and meet with Binc afterward so he can give you further instructions."

"Yes, Orakal!" the man said enthusiastically, and then left her presence with Hrija.

"Next!" Binc yelled.

A young man close to the Orakal's age stepped forward before her. When he looked at her he saw a beautiful girl wearing a golden crown.

"Lady Orakal, I humbly ask for your wisdom," he said.

"You have it. What do you ask?"

"My mother is sick. And others in the village are sick too, especially the elders. My father says to ask for medicine."

She closed her eyes and focused.

"You must ride from here with all haste. Find the herb crowned with many gems ruling over where the winds play."

Then she opened her eyes.

The young man thought for a moment before a smile

creased his lips and he began to nod.

"Thank you," he said with a slight bow, and then ran out of the vaulted room.

"Next!" Binc yelled again.

A woman of forty stepped up. She saw a heavyset little girl with blonde hair, pimples, and uneven legs.

"Lady Orakal, I humbly ask for your wisdom."

"You have it. What do you ask?"

"Love, my lady. I seek love."

"Do you love yourself?"

"How can I love myself when no one else loves me?"

"To find love you must be love. That is your way."

"Are you sure?"

"Are *you* sure!" Binc yelled at her. "More than ten thousand and all have been correct!"

"Binc, your self righteousness," the Orakal told him.

"Yes, my lady," he acquiesced as he bowed and stepped behind her.

"The key is for you to be sure," the child explained to the woman, who then walked off disappointed.

"Next!"

A grizzly man with a black beard and three small scars on his face stepped forward before the Orakal. He was dressed in full plate armor with a relief design of a castle on his chest. To him, she was a spoiled little girl with everything handed to her. He neither believed she was raised the way they claimed nor that she could see anything worth knowing, and her appearance reflected that to him.

"How can I help you, General?" the Orakal asked. She knew he wouldn't observe their traditions.

"My Lord would like an answer."

"He would like a different answer?"

"A proper answer," the General returned with a growl.

"Saddeye has never fought for a nation, nor shall it. We are a city of peace," she declared loud enough so all in the large vaulted courtroom could hear.

"You are a city who harbors the most dangerous army this side of the Bodokin!"

"Fifteen is not an army. Long ago are the days when the Shogin numbered that many."

"But that fifteen can still turn the tide. Now is when they are needed! My Lord will *have* their aid!" the General yelled as he stepped forward aggressively.

The Shogin were between them before he could react with their weapons already drawn.

"Hold," the Orakal ordered peacefully. "General, I understand your plight. But it has taken you two months and three days to return from your home to here, yes?"

He shifted uneasily due to the fact that fifteen Shogin now had their weapons drawn on him, and that she knew his time of travel exactly.

"Yes," he answered.

"I'm sorry to tell you but your home is lost. Five weeks from the time you left it, Emperor Camulus took it."

The General shook his head fervently. "No, no, I was told I had plenty of days to reach you and bring the Shogin back!"

"Everyone can be wrong at times," the Orakal told him. "Return," she commanded the Shogin.

Each turned to her and presented their weapons, then drew them across the part of their arm that was bare until blood dripped, then wiped and sheathed them before returning to her side.

That put a rapid end to matters and many shuffled out of the vaulted room. Soon it was just the Orakal, her Shogin, and a few Robed and Corded. Among them was Binc, her High Advisor, and he was the first to speak.

"My lady, as time draws closer to Emperor Camulus' arrival, many of us grow nervous."

"Is that why you snapped at that woman for questioning me? Because you wish to question me?"

"You just said so yourself. Everyone can be wrong at times."

The Orakal smiled.

"At times; as in noon, midnight, weeks, or months. I didn't mean in general, Binc. I was speaking of time specifically. Rest assured, we must wait for the Ravenborne. If I wish to stay alive I have to be tortured."

Chronicle Three

During the last pilgrimage I had the pleasure of journeying upon, it came to my attention that many are beginning to mix up certain words belonging to the Clanii. This is not an affront in and of itself except, as a man of language I cannot help but try and rectify this. So what follows is my humble attempt to render clear these definitions for those who do not know.

Clanii is the oldest word used to distinguish the people, history, language, and all other facets of its culture. In their ancient tongue it means: 'The Clan of One.' Both men and women of the lineage refer to themselves as Clanii. It is a genderless word, and also both singular and plural.

Declanii means 'Of the Clan of One.' Originally, this is how the Clanii sailors referred to themselves when out at sea, and this is known to be true since before the Ages were recorded. Ridec O'Ronan knew his lineage well and suggested this be the name of the new protecting power when it was formed at Ideclan. All agreed.

Ideclan, which Jossilan O'Ronan proposed they name their city, translates into 'Lord of the Clan,' a name that weighs with their ancient heritage. When I is used as a prefix in Old Clanii and is not a part of the root word, it will always mean 'Lord' or 'Lord of.'

Sunil is another word brought over to the Common Tongue from their language. To the Clanii it refers to the color affectionately known as, 'the deepest blue in the black of a raven.' It's a magnificent color, the dye of which comes from a plant known to the Clanii since their beginning and brought

with them on both exoduses. The plant is known by the name
Sunila.

Ahroo is used in many ways and has a number of translations. Its main usage, however, is in greeting at any time, and
its closest companion in the Common Tongue would be 'hail'
or 'honor to you.' To say this word correctly, the h is fully pronounced after the a, and the r is trilled as in most Clanii words.

nifu ellwulle. The knowledge is common among
language scholars and friends of the Clanii that this is actually
more than two words, but the phrase is still mostly translated
into 'willed intentions' or 'prophecies.' What either of those
means is another writing entirely, but this is the label given to
what Ridec and his companions accepted from the Treewolves
to start the Ninth Age. And it is for reasons unknown to myself
why they never capitalize it.

For a more complete list of vocabulary and precise
pronunciation, please refer to my: Book on Languages: Old
Clanii.

Written by Siras of Philos
Pard, the Seventh of Midfall, 28th Year of the Ninth Age

Chapter Four

THE CLANII KING OF IDECLAN, ACILLUS O'RONAN, crouched under the winter bare canopy of a large Larch, as did eight others belonging to his contingent of the hunting party. He kept a close eye and mind on two ravens flying some distance from them, high above a prominent ridgetop covered with forest.

Three other contingents worked together pushing a large herd of deer down the mountain toward them. One of those groups kicked up snow as they chased the deer under the late morning Sun, exerting much of what energy they had.

Acillus and his men couldn't see the runners. But they each stayed mindful of the two large ravens flying above the herd, shadowing their every move.

A group farther down the ridge readied themselves as the herd bound their way. They filled their lungs and set their stances. When the deer passed by, each leapt for their middle, splitting the herd in two. Then they followed the slower, weaker half, as did the ravens, corralling them down a smaller ridgeline toward Acillus.

The last group positioned themselves more accurately along the herd's new path and waited, hidden behind Aspens while listening to hooves and timing their approach. As the herd reached them they sprang in a manner that split them again, coaxing the slowest deer directly toward King Acillus' contingent at the base of the mountain.

A hunter from this last group found himself in the path

of a buck who wouldn't be frightened again, and the collision between them knocked the man to the ground in severe pain, gasping for air. Those from the group who'd been running the longest fell behind and stopped due to exhaustion, and they helped the hunter on the ground who worked to retrieve his breath.

The rest ran furiously around trees or jumped over rocks to keep up with the agile chase.

Raven and man pursued the whittled down group toward the valley floor, the men running to their fullest extent the entire way. The deer almost escaped the runners to the left because of a thick stand of brush but the large ravens, Acillus' close companions nearly his whole life, swooped down and helped with loud caws and flaps. The deer were frightened by the black flyers and dashed to get away, putting them right back in the hunt.

The male raven let out a loud caw, signaling to Acillus the time was near. The King judged the path of both ravens and marked where the deer should exit the forest covered mountain. As they continued being corralled toward him, he chose the best course and commanded his men.

"Now."

They sprang from their hiding place and ran fast, aligning to intersect the path the deer would most likely take. When the deer broke the thicket with runners close behind, the King saw they were in perfect position and ran faster without changing course. Then all in his group laughed as the Admiral of Ideclan tripped over a rock and put his face into the snowy ground.

Sprinting fast, closing in the last bit of distance up an alluvial fan, Acillus and the Veterans of the Sunil let loose a volley of spears. And their projectiles soared through the air before hitting their targets with exact precision.

"Ha ha!" Seamus laughed and roared, his grin was one worn by a light heart. "Is it the snow slowing you down, or are you starting to age, Acillus?" he joked between breaths.

"I do believe I hit my target, Seamus," the King said to his old friend.

"Aye, that you did. But it wasn't your spear arm I was referring to."

"No, it wasn't, and neither did you refer to my sword arm, lad. But I'd be happy to show you how that too, still strikes just the same."

"Soon enough!" Seamus the Old Bear replied while walking over to give thanks to the animals.

Seamus had been jesting with the King all morning and was loving every bit of it. Others of the hunting party chuckled at his antics as they united with the group while still catching their breaths as well. Everyone there had contended to best Acillus a great many times during the tournaments at Ideclan without success. So they all knew Seamus had little hope of defeating their King in the tournament that was less than a week away. But they all knew that wasn't the real reason why Seamus had been antagonizing him the entire day, either.

"The Festival of Four Fires is nearly upon us, and… do we have enough?" Seamus asked, referring to the deer specifically for the festival.

"Almost," Finnian answered. "Normally I'd think this amount sufficient but there's talk of more people coming to this festival than any other. We should hunt more after we load these and rest."

"Agreed, Finnian," Seamus said. "And what of you my King? Do you think your legs can carry you on another hunt?"

Acillus' laughter could be heard throughout the entire area.

"Seamus!" he bellowed. "You're throwing more words than spears today! I've seen your spear hit its mark, now tell me what your words are hunting."

The men around them exchanged glances caused by a thought only shared amongst themselves or other ranking Veterans of the Sunil, a thought they'd never discussed with the King. None of them expected they ever would. But Seamus' smile stayed broad on his face as he gave voice to what each in the King's company were now thinking.

"Sire, the lads and I know that you've been undefeated since after your first tournament."

Everyone turned toward them with curious smiles.

"But we believe you'll be defeated this tournament," Seamus said in his most venerable yet mirthful tone.

"Ah, so that's it. And who is this champion that will defeat me? Who is this vanquisher my spear cannot reach?"

As Acillus studied each man's face, Seamus gave their answer. Though the King had long already known what all this day's jesting had been about.

"He is Cael, your son, Sire."

Acillus regarded them collectively as he nodded. The right corner of his mouth creased with a smile. He knew they all respected his boy and this, he thought, was a good showing of it.

"He may indeed," Acillus agreed.

"Speaking of the lad, where is my nephew?" Quinnlan Mullquane asked as he pulled his spear from the old doe lying at his feet. His spear throw was the farthest.

The last of the hunting party rejoined them to hear Acillus answer his wife's younger brother. And one of them was clutching at his chest where an antler nearly punctured it.

"He and Segais are up at the mountains outside of Philos. Roxgrin and Binneen also went with them. I think Cael wished to be away from the excitement surrounding this festival. The whole realm is expecting him to do well."

"Not training, eh?" Marchann asked in a doubtful yet joking tone while still clutching at his chest.

Corcc smiled as he finished their unified thought with, "Well, if the lad isn't training hard, then he probably won't defeat you, Acillus."

"Oh don't you worry," the King assured them, and they laughed. "Cael's ravens are considerable opponents. Segais knows truths about combat I've yet to perceive. And I know Cael to be a good opponent even for himself."

Many chuckled. The Prince was known for his anger at times.

"So he won't be lacking in practice," the King continued. "One fact that remains certain, however, the young lad is going to trounce every last one of you."

All laughed as they agreed. Then they hauled the deer over toward the wagons where two ravens waited. When they reached the wagons, Acillus thanked them through his thoughts. Every Ravenborne could develop their own unique ways with ravens, but all could speak with them through thought.

"Dugan, Fey, thank you for your help on the hunt."

"It is our pleasure, Ujiriff," Fey, the female answered, calling Acillus by the raven name they gave him many years ago.

Acillus nodded before looking back toward the others.

The hair and eye color of the men with him varied, but each wore nothing save the color sunil: the deepest blue in the black of a raven. All had the tunic and cloak but many wore other variants of clothing as well, or had them draped over a wagon or draft horse.

The King studied the actions of his finest warriors as they prepared the animals for their journey home. All with him were brothers to him by bond. Some he'd known more than fifty years. And he knew they'd serve him well in time forthcoming.

Almost every one of them had begun their service in

the Ideclan Army at age twenty, customary for descendants of Clanii after education. As their rite of passage into the army, almost all Clanii had to complete four years of rigorous training throughout The Kinned Lands before earning the right to compete in a tournament back home, which, along with voting, told the young Clanii their first rank.

Everyone there had fought their way and were voted into the army during the first tournament they participated in. Each had been commanders and soldiers for multiple units in the Ideclan Army, as well as commanded Talons of one thousand soldiers, including their archer and scout contingencies. Some were recipients of the Oak and all had earned the Corvid. Seamus Weynahar was General of the Twelve Talons and Finnian U'dinry Captain of Declanii. Many formed the first shield wall of Declanii known as the King's Ravenline. Most of them were there, above the Cliffs of Quenie, fighting by Acillus' side during The Last Battle of the Runidareeans. And all of them, having never fully contested against his son, Prince Cael, were still fairly sure the young boy could best any of them, and blindfolded if he chose.

Acillus gave a light laugh at the thought as he went back to task. He knew they were right to think highly of what Cael might become. He also knew they had no idea of what the hidden nifu ellwulle, only shared with the O'Ronan line, foretold he would.

"You've been running a lot lately," Ashnayn's hand-maiden said to her while combing the All Chief Daughter's hair.

"The Moon Race is approaching," she responded.

"You've won it before haven't you?"

"Twice."

"You'll win it a third time if you keep up your running. I saw your stride, it's beautiful."

"Thank you."

"You're welcome, dear. But there's something else."

"What?"

"You've also been spending a lot of time in here."

"This is my room."

"I know that. But you're usually not in it. Lately, if you aren't running, you're either in here or somewhere else on your grounds. You haven't spent any time with your friends."

"People aren't acting friendly to me since I was promised to Gowgluni. I don't even know if I have friends anymore."

"Nonsense. Now you're just feeling sorry for yourself."

Ashnayn stood from her chair and turned. "Get out," she commanded.

"Ashnayn."

"Get out, now."

The handmaiden left the room without saying anything more.

She is right, Ashnayn thought as she finished combing her hair. *I haven't been away from this house except for running or eating. That's because no one is treating me the same though. Everyone's been different since I was promised to Gowgluni. Some won't even acknowledge me. Except for my diving friends. They should be at the clear cliffs right now, and I need to practice my diving and swimming at least once more before the race. I'll go to the cliffs then. That's away from most people anyway. And I can take the narrow path to outrun my guards quicker.*

Ashnayn exited the house and found her guards having their leisure near the front gate, who all looked up as she walked toward them.

"I'm going to the clear cliffs," she announced.

To which many of her guards groaned.

"You just ran this morning," one of them complained.

"And now I'll run to the cliffs."

The Princess didn't wait for anymore argument and the guards had to get up quickly. Ashnayn kept an even pace, not her fastest but faster than them. And for all their best efforts, when she reached the cliffs they were far behind.

There was an unexpected crowd of people at the clear cliffs when she got there. A few of them were training for the Moon Race but most were there just for the show.

Everyone turned to look at Ashnayn when she greeted them as she arrived, and then they turned back without returning her greeting.

No greeting by anyone? Not even my friends? There's Aynbay.

"Aynbay," Ashnayn called out while walking toward her.

Those around Aynbay walked away and Aynbay tried walking away too, until she looked at Ashnayn and felt sympathy.

"What's going on?" the Princess asked as she reached her. "Why are people not speaking to me, or walking away like them? Is this some game?"

"Ashnayn, please, I have to go with my friends."

"I'm one of your friends!" Ashnayn yelled.

"My friends don't yell at me. Good day."

"What?" Ashnayn questioned as Aynbay turned and walked away.

The All Chief Daughter looked around and realized no one would look her in the eyes.

It's as if some majic has come over you all, this is absurd.

Then she saw Lindhee, an elderly woman who was nice and talked to everyone. Ashnayn walked quickly toward her and the people around Lindhee got up and left. The All Chief

Daughter stopped and looked at them with confused sadness as Lindhee stood up and hobbled over to Ashnayn.

"Lindhee," Ashnayn said, doing her best not to cry. She put her hand on her diving vest pocket that held the stone figurine as she asked, "What's going on?"

Lindhee reached her and whispered, "Go home, Ashnayn. Be with who you are promised. Gowgluni is all the companionship you need."

Then she turned and hobbled away from the young woman.

Ashnayn's guards arrived and slowed to a walk. Each breathed heavily as they reached the All Chief Daughter. She looked off in the distance as they tried chiding her for running ahead and they couldn't get a response; until the Princess looked at them, then turned and walked all the way home without a single word.

Declanii

Chronicle Four

65

Rone watches over the darkness of Turs, Rone is first and Mard is third. Bran and Pard come after these, then following all is lastly Nees.

Nees wished more for light on land, but discouraging Nees was always Bran. Pard between them felt alone, so Mard and Turs both turned toward Rone.

Rone then felt the plight of Pard, to light the land Rone called on Mard. Bran didn't like it as much as Nees, Turs hated it more than both of these.

Mard warmed the land as Nees preferred, to scorn the gift was always Turs. Bran and Pard then created the sown, to order it all is always Rone.

A Clanii Myth Poem

Declanii

Chapter Five

Aғᴛᴇʀ ᴛʜᴇ ʟᴀsᴛ ʜᴜɴᴛ ᴏF ᴛʜᴇ ᴅᴀʏ ᴡᴀs ᴄᴏᴍᴘʟᴇᴛᴇᴅ, King Acillus and his party spent the rest of the evening giving thanks and preparing the animals for their journey home. And as night descended upon them, so did the wind.

"I'd say that about does it," Seamus affirmed.

"Indeed," Finnian agreed. "We have enough."

"Alright, lads," the King called out. "Let's head back."

To the ravens, Dugan and Fey, he asked, *"How do you feel about a scout fly?"*

"Are you worried?" Dugan questioned.

"Cautious," he thought back.

Then the ravens flew up and South.

Acillus led the wagons to a Southward road that'd take them toward Ideclan. With a fast horse, the voyage home lasted little time from this location, but directing draft horses who pulled loaded wagons through the snow extended the voyage considerably. Thus, they chose to travel at night as well as day because the festival was fast approaching.

"Well, Acillus," Seamus said to his lifelong friend as they led everyone on under the waxing moon.

The King shook his head because he knew some sort of

banter was heading his way.

"Are you tired?" the General asked.

Acillus smiled before answering, "Seamus, if we fight again this tournament, I'm going to put you to sleep."

Seamus laughed fully from his heart. He was a tall and broad man with lots of undefined muscle. His eyes were brown and he wore a bristly blonde beard that was longer than the short blonde hair on his head.

Acillus and the lads continued walking throughout the night, laughing and conversing as they went. They led the horses instead of riding them, assuring the footing in front while giving the work animals their complete strength for the task at hand.

Everyone wrapped their sunil cloaks tighter from the wind as they thought of warm hearths and walked South, leading the horses around big snow drifts or digging straight through them when they needed to.

Nearing the end of that first night of traveling and just before daybreak, Acillus' party was rejoined by two other hunting parties of Declanii.

"Ahroo, lads. Looks like you were successful," the King said to them. Many of whom were Clanii and family to those with him.

The hunting parties formed one column with Acillus at the front and continued on. Leading their draft horses through the cold Midwinter snow, they'd reach their beloved home two mornings from this one.

Only members of the Declanii, or Veterans of the Sunil, went hunting for the Festival of Four Fires. It was tradition that they hunted for this festival, but more importantly it was they who knew how to hunt en masse without damaging the local animal kingdoms. The Declanii worked hard to help them grow stronger by thinning out the slower deer and rotating hunting sites.

It was believed that by hunting the slowest from the herd they made the herd faster. Acillus had long been enthused with this program first introduced by the plant eating Philos, and even spent much of his own resources to further its study. When he could, the King went over detailed notes and observations he'd made for a Philosian as they continued South with the biting wind that hadn't left them since they began their journey back.

"Hey, Finnian," the King called out while looking at his notes.

"Yes, Acillus?"

The Captain of Declanii was a calm and collected man of average stature who wore his dark hair long and kept his face clean shaven. His right blue eye looked at the King while the left one remained hidden and scarred underneath a cloth and leather eye patch; a souvenir from the Last Battle of the Runidareeans.

"What were the numbers for that second group?"

"The herd was forty two and the hunt took eight."

"Thank you," Acillus said as he recorded them.

"It would've taken nine but Finn had to trip and put his face into the ground. Luckily there was snow to break his fall," Finnian continued.

The King looked directly at Finn and said, "You're unparalleled as an Admiral. But your sea legs do you no justice on land."

"Agreed," the Admiral said in a manner that brought chuckles from all.

"Can we stop for the night?" Elasus asked through bluing lips while riding Ella.

"I'm sorry, little bear. We can't. There's nowhere to get firewood. We have to walk through the night to stay warm."

"Can we build a snow cave?"

"It's too late for that."

"Ella is starting to feel cold."

The waxing moon made it easy for them to see, and Cristin did his best not to get snow in the boot he cut. But he and the mule walked side by side and they didn't always fit on the path that had been worn into the snow.

"Even I'm getting cold," Cristin said.

"You're never cold."

"Almost never, but it feels like tonight will bite with this wind. Do you remember the last time we were caught in a cold like this?"

"Yes. Fwynndarlanai had never seen a Winter like it,

and we were traveling between villages."

Cristin looked at his son. "You do remember."

"I remember being cold, and then being warm."

"That's what's going to happen now. Shed your blankets and hop inside my coats."

"Shed my blankets!" Elasus exclaimed.

"And take off your shirt."

The child laughed. "You're joking, father."

"I'm not. With your body against mine we'll keep each other warm while I walk."

"On the count of three then," Elasus surrendered.

"You count," Cristin told him while he unbuttoned his coats.

"One, two, three!"

Elasus quickly shed his blankets and shirt. Cristin grabbed him and put him inside his coats before buttoning them back up. He left one of the wool blankets over Ella and put the others around himself, his sword, and Elasus.

"Getting warmer?" he asked.

"Yes, very."

"Good. We won't have to deal with things like this

once we reach Ideclan, I promise."

"That sounds nice."

"Oh, cac."

"What is it?"

"I got snow in my boot."

Two and a half days had passed since King Acillus' hunting party started their voyage home. And as the Sun rose behind a newly formed blanket of clouds, the column of Declanii caught their first sights and smells of smoke from the fires of Ideclan. The previous night had been intensely cold with the wind. But morning brought warmth to the air for them, as if the heat of the Ideclan fires had been trapped by the blanket of clouds.

"Always a beautiful sight," Seamus remarked as he took a deep breath and continued walking on.

The wind that'd been howling over the past few days stopped this morning as well, making it necessary for them to shed a few articles of thick clothing. After doffing their cloaks and coats, the Declanii watched their beloved city grow closer. And though they were without rest the entire trek, being so close to home gave them renewed vigor.

Soldiers manning the North Gate of the outer wall recognized them long before they reached the city. When Acillus and his men came close enough for the sentry captain to be sure, he gave the order for the oak and iron doors to be pulled open from the inside.

Seamus Weynahar, General of the Talons, raised the Horn of Ravenborne and blew three loud blasts, signaling the return of the King.

"Ahroo, Acillus!" the captain called down to him from the wall walk above the gate.

"Ahroo, Dekard. How fares your day?"

"It fares well," he answered, then turned and yelled, "Bring the King's horses!"

Acillus led his column through the gate and between two large dirt piles on either inner side of it, then past a smaller wooden wall thirty feet back from the stone wall. When the last of the loaded wagons cleared the wooden wall, Acillus gave his men their orders.

"Alright lads, bring these wagons to their designated butcher shops and ice houses. Then you're free until the festival."

They said their farewells and led the draft horses on. The sentry captain's subordinates brought three horses to Acillus and handed one to the King, one to Seamus, and one to Finnian, all who mounted and then rode for Ideclan's Hall at the center of the city.

When the Horn of Ravenborne was sounded by Seamus, those who had pressing business with the King knew it as the signal to make their way for the hall. Acillus had been gone nearly six days, leaving much that needed attention.

Declanii

The Clanii were originally a gift and trade people. And never throughout their ancient history did they use coin. But allying with Gisspor not long after the onset of Ideclan and The Kinned Lands' existence made it practical for them. So since then they'd been saving it. Ideclan's underground treasuries were vast due to the Clanii's proclivities. And the workings of the city required a great deal of collaboration.

The King, General, and Captain made their way on horseback toward Ideclan's Hall, waving back at some of the people working on the fields as they got closer to the middle wall, or second wall. When they rode past the fields and through the second wall into the middle part of the city, they had to slow because Middle Ideclan was populated with the most inhabitants. Many streets were lined with Ideclaners coming and going from this shop or that craftsman. And a great many travelers were already around for the festival.

When tavern doors swung open, loud cheers and songs could be heard coming from each, along with the traditional foot stomping. Acillus recognized one of the songs as they rode by a particularly crowded tavern. He smiled at it before continuing past blacksmiths, leather workers, bath houses, tailors and textile dealers, markets with numerous vendors, butchers, bakers, herb shops, cobblers, and more.

Wagons and carts filled the streets, taking turns to go next with one another. More than ninety thousand people called this section of the city their home. And those who became aware of him, cheerfully greeted their King as he rode past on his way to the hall. Acillus nodded and waved to many people before smelling the pleasant scents of a soap and candle shop as the three rode on.

The land rose ever so slightly as they arrived at the

third and innermost section of the city, the oldest part of Ideclan; a square mile of land with fortifications that served as the inspiration for the two defensive walls the three had just traveled through.

The first square mile of Ideclan, or Old Ideclan as it was called, no longer housed the main population like it used to. In Ridec's day, everyone lived inside the first wall. And even when the second wall stretching five miles on each side was built, many still lived inside the first. It wasn't until the number of people swelled and the third wall stretching nine miles on every side was constructed that the majority started making their homes inside the second, and the descendants of Clanii took up Old Ideclan.

The hall they rode for was the oldest building in the city. Before the city was founded, a Treewolf named Wardolf had given four saplings to Ridec and the Clanii, and instructed them to use the trees as corner posts for their new hall. The Clanii voyaged for a number of years after that and the saplings mysteriously stayed the same size throughout their journey.

When they arrived at what would later be Ideclan, they planted the saplings as instructed. Ridec then formed an alliance he called the Tribellion, and went to war. When they returned in less than a season, the saplings had grown to be forty feet tall with enormous canopies of both deciduous leaves and evergreen needles.

Long round logs were cut into thick planks and notched from tree to tree, enclosing the new hall. Carved logs were staked into the ground vertically, connecting the thick horizontal planks at synchronistic intervals along each wall. And then gradually, the four trees grew to roughly one hundred feet tall and fifteen feet in diameter, swallowing the thick plank framework and causing numerous repairs to the roof as they did.

The entrance was cut from the North wall of the hall. It arched at the top and was tall enough for someone to ride through on horseback. The door had been replaced recently, and this new one had the Rockraven symbol of Ideclan carved upon it. The raven was dissected down the middle every time the doors were pushed open from the outside or pulled open from within. The wood used for the original door had been the inspiration for the gates in the outer walls; thick vertical oak planks tempered by fire with thin iron paneling. This new door was close to the same except it wasn't tempered by fire but kept beautiful and away from decay by the natural oils Ideclan used to sustain the wood of its structures.

Acillus and his two friends reached the hall and dismounted with tired ease. There were three young stable hands waiting for them. And they greeted the young lads as they took their horses. Then the men walked the rest of the way. Acillus O'Ronan pushed the hall doors open. Seamus and Finnian closed them, keeping out the Winter cold.

More than eighty people were waiting for the King inside. And among them was Conail of the Cailian Family, now Acillus' main advisor. Conail used to be co counsel with Arakkus of Philos, but Arakkus died a few years back, and Acillus had yet to refill the position; in part because Conail possessed the full trust and respect of the King. He was very wise and skillfully performed all his duties. He had everything ready and in order when the King, General, and Captain stepped into the hall.

Ideclan's Hall was expansive and filled with four rows of long wooden tables accompanied by many benches and chairs. Near the entrance there were eight circular tables with twenty chairs each. And there was no specific seat for the King, no throne. Hides covered almost every bench and chair. The walls were adorned with carvings of mostly animals and

Ancients. And at the very Southern end of the hall was a large obsidian stone sculpture of Ideclan's symbol; an Ancient known as a Rockraven.

The hall had the feeling of a large, comfortable den. And when anyone would meet for any reason inside it, they all chose the table they'd sit at together. This day, like most Winter days, everyone thought it best to sit next to the large fire burning at the center.

Above the fire, a wide conical chimney made of thin obsidian stone caught and released the smoke. It was supported by eight iron chains anchored into massive beams that were a part of the roof. The hearth encircling the fire was also of black obsidian, each stone weighing twenty to thirty pounds and a purity of such that if looked through at just the right angle, the fire could be seen as though the stones weren't there.

Acillus grabbed a chair from one of the circular tables and started moving toward the fire. An elderly woman warming herself by the flames with her grandchildren, noticed the King leading a mass of people toward the warmth and it caught her by surprise.

Was the King due back today? That's why all those people are here. I must not have heard the horn, she thought.

Acillus greeted her with a smile and nod. Then the woman, half shy all of a sudden, made a gesture with her hands, asking him if he'd like them to leave so they could have privacy. Acillus lightly shook his head and held his palm flat to the ground, letting her know they could stay if she wished. Her choice to stay surprised her even more when everyone proceeded to sit down beside her and her little family as though they'd been saving seats for them the entire time.

After cordial hellos and a few brief pleasantries were exchanged, Conail Cailian pulled out a leather bound notebook and the council began.

"Sire, the Northern and Southern scouts have reported back no disturbances. However the Caibre Scouts report there was an attack by Camulus' men at the pass again, which was a diversion for a scouting party that was found just South of there within the Brimmgards," Conail stated.

"What are the numbers?" Acillus asked.

"The attack at the pass was done by five hundred. We lost nineteen before they sounded their retreat, and the fallen's rituals have been performed according to their customs. The scouting party had twenty three people and we lost no scout in the dispatching of them."

"Have the nineteen families been put on the List?" the King continued.

"I wrote them in myself just yesterday morning."

The List was a document with every Ideclan soldier's name on it. If a soldier served for twenty five years and almost all chose to serve for fifty, partly because the average life span for all humans at this time was one hundred and twenty, then their name was never taken off the List when they left the army.

Every name on the List was paid the same wages from the end of their service all the way up to their last breath. If a soldier died while on the List no matter the cause, then their closest relative's name was put on the List under their own, and subsequently they were paid the soldier's wages till their last breath. If the soldier died while in battle then the pay was doubled. This was true for both the King's Army and the Queen's Army; a program instituted by Acillus' great grandfather, Kyndirial, and a very popular one. The majority of the Clanii's disregard for coin allowed them to spend it in such ways. And the competition to be among the limited number of Ideclan's elite military ranks was great because of it.

"What's next then, lad?" the King asked as he thought of the good soldiers and moreover good people Ideclan just lost. He felt for the families of each under his command who passed, and it saddened him.

"Advanced parties for all The Kinned Lands have arrived, placing everyone here in time for at least the war council if not the festival. The Edemarians confirmed they won't make it for the festival. But they'll be here soon enough."

"Very good," Acillus approved. "And what of the festival itself?"

"Everything's on schedule and progressing smoothly. Also, upkeep for the defensive ditches in front of the Northwest wall have been completed and the work crews are moving on to the Southwest. The fresh drift snow is being removed from the outer walls as well. And the engineers are about to enter into the final stage of the underground aqueduct."

At mention of the aqueduct, the elderly woman sitting by the fire with her grandchildren let out a small and almost imperceivable sigh as she put her head down. Acillus was the only one who noticed because he was the only one paying attention. He was keen on gauging citizens' reactions to conversations of the realm, and he was curious with hers.

"Excuse me, miss," he said to her.

She lifted her head and saw that Acillus was looking directly at her, so she answered, "Yes, my King?"

"As one of the people of this city, would you please tell us your thoughts on the new aqueduct?"

Everyone in the council directed their attention toward her without hesitation, as all were used to Acillus' ways by now. Realizing she was about to address the King she straightened her back even though she didn't have to.

"It would be an honor, Sire. I think, like most others that more water in the city is a good thing, and underground is smart, too. I'm grateful for the Prince creating this. His reasons why we need an underground one cannot be challenged. But the new gathering spot isn't going to be any closer to our home than the others. And they're all too far for us. We live in one of the districts without the aqueduct systems, and so we'll have to continue walking there every day because we cannot carry enough water to hold us for longer."

Acillus breathed deeply with sympathy while thinking before saying, "I'm sorry this wasn't started sooner. The sewage and aqueduct programs are running behind due to the underground project. But there's another program that will help. Conail."

"Yes, Acillus."

"Institute the public transportation system using draft horses and wagons so that everyone has access to every part of the city. And put the maximum weight of goods allowed at twenty bricks."

Conail acknowledged the King and wrote down the

notes with a smile. Then the elderly woman thanked Acillus as she smiled her appreciation as well.

"We shouldn't be so frivolous with the coin, Acillus," Fehurin Cailian said. "In these coming times it might not be wise to spend it on such things," he continued with little backing from the crowd.

Fehurin had his long dark gray hair tied in a horse tail and each of his many layers of robes were finely embroidered. Over his robes he wore an Ideclan Amulet that was made of gold and embedded with precious gems.

"Your position is noted, Fehurin. However, this program was to be instituted some time ago, and will be delayed no further. The coin is for the people, the city, and their defense."

"Spare us the justifications, Acillus. All here know if the Clanii don't change our warring ways we'll destroy ourselves like other bearers of the nifu ellwulle in the past. And that starts with not spending so much coin on things like the army. We need to use the coin for trade and growth, not military might, or, helping people who can't help themselves. In truth, I'd say the reason why people wish to attack us in the first place is because we have such an army!" Fehurin declared as more than a few gave him odd looks, while a small group of others cheered him on just enough to give him confidence.

Fehurin was Councilor Conail's cousin, the man who advised Acillus. They were never close and the rift between them now was expansive. Fehurin was part of a growing movement among the Clanii who wished to return to their ancient and peaceful ways due to a concern that they as a society had become too warlike in accordance with the nifu ellwulle. Except Fehurin reminded people more of the greedy

Clanii Ridec left behind, rather than the noble and peaceful Clanii from their mythic past. Fehurin was one hundred and sixteen years old and every bit of his adult life had been devoted to the accumulation of wealth and influence.

"This isn't a war council, Fehurin," Seamus told him. "And Acillus just instituted a civil project where no coin will be going to the armies, and likely benefit trade. So shut it."

"The posterity of the Clanii people is the most important thing to…!"

"Enough," Acillus said calmly. "This isn't the time."

Fehurin calmed reluctantly while Seamus raised his eyebrows at the man. And then discussions continued.

Once Acillus and Conail finished the main business, everyone else began voicing their reasons for being there. It was well into the afternoon and the elderly woman had long left for home with her two grandchildren by the time the others started exiting the hall.

After most had left, the large doors were pushed closed and only four men remained: Acillus, Conail, Seamus, and Finnian.

"Conail, has Aislin returned?" the King asked.

"I don't think so. But we have until tomorrow before we start sending out search parties."

"Aye, well, the lads and I are going to get some rest. Please instruct our city planners on that public transportation project. I want to see wagons on streets by three days after the festival."

"It is done, Acillus," Conail assured him.

"Oh, and check on their progress of planting more trees in house patterns outside of the middle wall as well."

Conail nodded. Then the four walked through the doors and stepped out into the afternoon air.

Councilor Cailian said farewell as he headed toward the City Planners' Offices. And they who returned from the hunt headed home for some much needed rest.

Declanii

Chronicle Five

The Edemarians didn't lie and the plan has moved forward. Entering into Ideclan was a success and the ease of it urges me to recommend more spies to infiltrate. I'll inspect the walls and send details in my next report. But the gate is no barrier. I've not seen anyone turned away from this city, even peasants are allowed access. This place is a trough for the low-born and below.

The teams have been deployed. Team One already thieves and sabotages while Team Two awaits until I leave in one more week for Hinturan. Each team will continue with reports from this location upon my departure.

As for whether the Northerners believe in beings such as Treewolves; it is fully a part of who they are. They live as if these beings existed and still exist. Whatever other ignorances they believe, we will also learn and exploit. All indications favor the plan.
Hrajat alat iston ko romus dar klarsin.

First Report on Ideclan
Sent by Jexra, Master Spy of the Ophal Circle
To the Council of The Sovereign's Lords at Aguptah
The Great Empire in the Southern Lands
Year 4919 of the Dawning Sun

Chapter Six

WHEN ANDRASTE AWOKE BEFORE SUNRISE SHE BUILT a cooking fire that also served to warm her. After cleaning up, she donned her warmest riding dress and thickest sunil cloak, then headed toward the stables and set out.

Among the many things she needed to accomplish this day, she still made time to visit with her mother, Saraid. While visiting they heard three echoing blasts sound from the Horn of Ravenborne, signaling the King's return. So the daughter said farewell to her mother as she continued on with her busy schedule. And before leaving Old Ideclan, Andraste Mullquane rode for the underground treasuries because an inventory was taking place.

Throughout the Clanii's history they'd been fond of diving deep underwater. They dove deep around their old island and into Ideclan's surrounding seas as well. Shortly after Ideclan's founding, Clanii divers discovered unique pearls of many colors which they traded with Gisspor, who, over the years had turned them into valuable commodities abroad. Most of the stones used for Ideclan's defensive walls and city buildings had been brought back by Gisspor's large ships because the Philos were protective of their mountains. When the stone wasn't needed, Gisspor brought back silver and gold, bolstering Ideclan's economy.

A great many of the Clanii still had such a lack of interest in the personal accumulation of coin, that it was easy for them to fund the two Armies, the Navy, Homeguard, Vanguard, and much of the workings of their city. The treasuries were vast, well organized, and protected. And besides pearls of rare beauty found by the divers; there were rooms filled with ingots of gold and silver, gems of emerald and sapphire, and coins in abundance from many lands. All of which had to be accounted for down to the smallest Dranlian Penny.

After the treasuries, the rest of Andraste's tasks were quick. And her last task for the day took her to the site of three new stone buildings located within a half circle of seventeen oak trees planted thirty years before. The three rotunda structures were hexagons with a window in each side and doors to the East. They were made in the traditional Philosian style for rotundas, with domed roofs and ceilings, and would serve as another center of education at Ideclan.

Two of the buildings were there for teaching the first three levels of education, the third was for teaching the fourth. And the Philosians enjoyed taking their students on field trips no matter what level of education they were in; some of them quite far due to the Philosians' love for going on pilgrimages themselves.

As many worked to get the large classrooms ready. Andraste stood outside of the rotundas at the center of the courtyard overseeing their progress. And after she was satisfied with the current status of this project, she began making her way home.

While Andraste rode back to Old Ideclan, she gazed at the city's architecture. To her it displayed a beautiful mixture of earth, stone, vine, plant, and tree; that even when looking at it closely, it was hard to distinguish where one building began and another ended after years of growing together. Especially within Old Ideclan where everything was so close, it was more like a forest than a city at times.

Almost every building was made using four to seven

living trees, with either wooden or stone walls notched into them. The Clanii had taken the stone working of the Philos and the tree working of the Teker Ren to create a unique combination when they founded Ideclan.

As Andraste made her way home she appreciated the Winter bare flora that mixed with the stone and wood and tree. After years of traveling through Ideclan she'd never gotten tired of it. And as she grew older, so did the view, making the city feel like a grove that had grown with her.

Much went on around Andraste while she rode back. People trained in groups with swords, spears, or bows. Others practiced swinging their swords down and stopping before hitting an iron bar, strengthening their wrists and control. Some practiced falling down and getting up, catching small pebbles quickly for reflexes and hand eye coordination, or holding shields and swords up for as long as possible, and many other exercises.

Every day when possible, Clanii man and woman trained together. Seeing the Ideclaners and Clanii train as she rode past them, made Andraste think back to the beginning of her own courtship, when she and her husband sparred with spears many times. And it brought a smile to her face as a sudden wind whipped her long black hair back.

Andraste entered Old Ideclan and rode to the stables. After her horse was settled in she walked toward home and the path taken went right by Ideclan's Hall. She knew the King would be in there discussing matters and wondered how tired he must have felt after the long hunt.

She continued home and moved inside quickly to shut out the cold, then started a cooking fire that again served to

warm her. While waiting for some good coals to form, she prepared a few ingredients for a slow cooked, thick potato soup.
When the coals were sufficient she pushed them aside and set
the pot of water with the ingredients over them.

The soup had been cooking for almost an hour when
she went to stir it for what must have been the tenth time.

The front door opened and even though she felt
eyes upon her, Andraste kept her back to it while stirring the
soup. By the steps she figured it was a man and could tell he
closed the door fast but soft. She didn't say a word and kept
stirring. She knew by sound that the man put his sword and
spear down, but must have kept his shield as he started walking
toward her.

He paused for a moment to gaze at Andraste. And
when he started walking again, she discreetly grabbed an iron
pan that was in front of her with her left hand, then brought it
up to the ready while stirring with her right.

By listening to the man's steps she judged his location
and waited, acting the whole time as if she didn't know he was
there. Andraste listened until he was almost upon her, then
turned to her left and struck for his face. As she did, the man
moved the shield strapped on his left arm to his right side and
brought it back across his body over to his left, deflecting Andraste's strike. His block knocked the pan from her hand and
it hit the stone wall. She turned back around and reached with
her left for another pan while still stirring with her right.

The man quickly moved in behind her and grabbed her
left wrist with his right hand while reaching under her right arm,
keeping her close and backing her in toward him. He wrapped
his right leg around hers to hinder her from spinning. She let

go of the wooden spoon and grabbed the pan with her right hand, then swung it over her left shoulder. The man let go of his shield but it stayed against his arm because of the wide leather strap that cinched across his forearm. With the newly freed hand he grabbed Andraste's wrist that guided the make-shift weapon as it clanged against the inside of his shield, and he pulled her in tightly, crossing her arms in front of her and somewhat cocooning them inside of his three foot in diameter circular shield.

The Warrior Queen, Andraste, let out a light giggle.

"Ahroo my wolf," King Acillus said.

"Ahroo my lion," said Andraste.

"Please forgive me, my lady," Binc pleaded to the Or-akal.

"It's not your fault, Binc. You're not accountable for the actions of others," she told him while they walked through her garden at the ancient city of Saddeye.

"Still, they shouldn't have spoken to you thus."

"They were only words. Everyone is afraid of Emperor Camulus, and I don't blame them."

"He's absolutely succeeded in taking enough of the East."

"As he always said he would."

Declanii

"Are you ready for your Shogin?"

"Send them in after you've eaten."

"Yes, my lady," Binc affirmed, and then walked out of her garden.

The Orakal continued through Winter bare flora, grabbing and letting branches slip through her fingers. During Summer, this garden was lush with life and color, and hummingbirds could be found in abundance. It was her favorite place to be, especially whenever she needed solitude. No one could disturb her here without permission.

As she walked, to her right was the reflecting pool, a perfect equilateral triangle. It was always still and the Orakal had never looked in it. She wasn't allowed to look until her seventeenth birthday; dictated by her ancient faith.

The young girl continued walking toward the Stone Throne, the seat from which she addressed only those closest to her, such as the Robed, the Corded, and the Shogin. For tonight it was the Shogin's turn to demonstrate.

The Orakal sat on the Stone Throne and closed her eyes. Binc was a heavy eater so she knew she had time before they arrived. The child breathed deeply and slowly, and as she did a smile spread across her face, then serenity became her demeanor. She stayed this way until hearing the Shogin enter her garden, and waited with her eyes closed while they stood before her in a line, with Captain Higada between them and her.

Then she opened her eyes and they bowed instantly.

Higada and eleven other Shogin were adorned in

armor indicative of the East. Many different sections of their armor were put on ceremoniously, and connected by different colors of silk cording. Each individual section had many small plates that were connected by silk cording as well. Not one part of their bodies was left unprotected, including their faces which were covered by masks carved into horrific demons with wide eye holes and open, snarling mouths.

The masks were connected to the helmets and the helmets were called, kabuto; and twelve of the Shogin placed their kabuto in front of them as they bowed. Five wore two katanas, four wore long bows with quivers, and three wore nodachi across their backs. One of them with a nodachi was their captain.

Two of the Shogin were dressed in loosely fitting black silks with two kamas each. The only things uncovered on them were their eyes. They bowed by touching their heads to the ground and every movement was silent. The last Shogin was dressed in white and brown silk robes with five wine gourds tied around him by silk cording, and he bowed in the same way.

"Rise and be proven," the Orakal commanded.

Captain Higada rose first and drew his long nodachi from his back. "My life and honor are yours," he said.

Then he opened his armor on his arm and drew the long blade across it until blood dripped evenly. Within moments the blood ceased and his cut healed.

"Your honor is proven. I accept your life," the Orakal stated.

Higada moved to the back of the Shogin, and the next rose.

His name was Rokomu, and he pulled an arrow from a quiver while saying, "My life and honor are yours."

Then he drew the arrow across the part of his arm that was revealed until blood dripped evenly from the wound.

When the bleeding stopped and the cut healed, the Orakal said, "Your honor is proven. I accept your life."

Each took turns proving their faithfulness. Their cuts would heal only if their intentions toward the Orakal were unwavering, and each cut healed within moments.

The last Shogin with the wine gourds tied around him stepped forward.

His name was Nakuta, and he said, "My life and honor are yours."

Then he cut his arm using friction from one of the silk cords until it bled evenly.

When it healed, the Orakal said, "Your honor is proven. I accept your life. And I thank you all for your unwavering dedication. Because of you, I will live long. As will you all, as we stay unwavered."

Captain Higada stepped forward as he said, "My lady?"

"Yes?"

He looked uncomfortably at the other Shogin before looking back at her and saying, "Our way of being commands us to never allow you to be taken, harmed, or touched. Our trust in you puts us against everything we've been taught at Kentaro."

"If you will remember, Emperor Camulus won't harm or touch me since he wishes to be named. Because he thinks there's a chance, neither he nor any among his army will break our laws. Know this about Camulus, inside his heart he doesn't feel being named is necessary. He only marches for Saddeye because his father always told him to. Camulus' army is now considerably stronger than his father's and he knows it. If any of you make any attempt to defend me, he'll decide he no longer desires to be named and will kill us all."

"As you say, my lady. The Shogin will not interfere when he arrives," Higada confirmed.

"You must go further than that. When Camulus' patience is pushed to its edge, he'll give me over to the Drouknen who'll perform tests and other tortures. No matter what you hear, what you see, what you think, as I've said before, you must wait until your path crosses the Ravenborne, then you'll rescue me."

"How can we stand by while you're being tortured?" Nakuta asked.

"If I cannot go through this with grace, and if you cannot do the same, then we have no business going forward; as everything we do is preparation for the next."

Acillus awoke next to Andraste the morning after returning home from the long hunt and rose from their bed, then walked toward the hearth to get the fire going again. Once he had the wood sufficiently combusting he went to an Eastern window of their second story room, raised the heavy cloth and pushed open large wooden panels to look for the Sun. It hadn't yet risen but its rise was only moments away.

Andraste awoke and watched him. The way he stood there reminded her of years past when Acillus had just distinguished himself in battle at Caibre Pass. After that battle, she remembered fondly, watching him fight to the top of his first tournament where he achieved youngest ever Captain of Declanii, and also remembered his calm and collected reaction when he lost to the then General of the Talons, Arkben Rorourke, the only person to ever defeat Acillus in a tournament.

Tournaments had become a frame of reference for how well an O'Ronan Prince did in their debut compared to the Prince before them. And true to the nifu ellwulle, Acillus had made it further than his Da, who made it further than his Da before him.

Andraste's thoughts drifted to when Acillus' father, Ailither, marched his army North for a campaign lasting four years. And she thought of how after they returned home victorious, the army was celebrated like no others before them.

At that grand event, Acillus looked out across the cheering people and his attention was caught by one. Andraste remembered well the gaze they shared while he was up on that platform and she in the crowd. Even when the people hailed him singly as champion of the realm and the honors of Corvid and Oak were presented to him, the only other person he saw amongst the masses was her.

Andraste's father, Aislin Mullquane, was one of the men standing with Acillus when the honors were presented. And it wasn't long before Acillus was over at Aislin's house asking permission to see Andraste. Aislin knew she was near, listening in on the conversation, so he called his daughter over to ask of her thoughts on the matter. His questions received no answer as the two young ones looked into each other's eyes and smiled. Aislin and Saraid gave Acillus and Andraste their permission to see each other and just short of three years later, the two were married.

Three and a half years after that, Cael was born. The time must fly, thought Andraste.

She watched her husband while thinking of the past when Acillus turned and their blue eyes met, interrupting her memories.

"Good morning," he said.

"Come back to bed and warm me," she commanded lovingly.

Acillus shut the Eastern window, walked over to stoke the fire, then lit a dried herb known as silversage, an herb introduced to them by the Teker Ren, then put it into a small ceramic bowl. He blew it out so that it smoldered and smoked tremendously before walking back to their bed and climbing under the covers to complete her request.

"I don't have much time," he said in his softest voice reserved only for her.

"What place is the Sun?"

"Just beginning to show itself."

"Are you off to find my Da?"

"Aye, but I'm off to the roost first."

"Sending out some of your raven scouts?"

"Indeed."

Andraste lightly laughed and said, "When you see my Da, tell him ahroo. Oh, and here!"

The Warrior Queen got out of bed and hurried to a large chest, then Acillus got out again as well. After retrieving something from the large wood and iron container, she turned around and held it up with a smile. The King recognized it the instant he saw its color. It was a long, hooded, sunil cloak; the deepest blue in the black of a raven: a color that had been with his ancestry for a vastly long time.

More than five thousand years ago, when the fishermen of Clanii went out to brave the sea, their wives made them sunil cloaks to keep them warm and somewhat dry. Through many generations the cloaks became tradition, and took on much symbolism between Clanii woman and man. When the Thirteen of Old left with Ridec and the Clanii became warriors, the cloaks took on an even deeper meaning. They were made to be sturdier, and began serving multiple functions that protected in battle or aided on voyages. And they were also coveted reminders of loved ones back home.

Acillus took the cloak from Andraste and held it close to his heart.

"You finished it," he said.

"Aye, two days ago. Try it on."

The King changed from his nightclothes into a sunil tunic. Then grabbed his old cloak from a wooden spiraling

Clanii Clothes Tower, unfastened its Oak Brooch, and attached it to his new cloak. The Oak was a silver brooch in the shape of an oak leaf pointing down, awarded to the soldiers who out thought the enemy. The Corvid was the battle honor given to those who out fought the enemy in such a way as to require recognition; and it was an Ideclan Raven's feather that hung from the brooch.

With his new cloak ready to wear, Acillus spun it around his shoulders and clasped the Oak Brooch at his neck, then hung his Corvid from the Oak, which rested over his plain iron Ideclan Amulet.

"I'm surprised our enemies don't stop and stare when they see what that color brings out in your eyes."

"They're too busy staring at the rest of the army," he replied.

Andraste laughed as Acillus pulled the hood over his head and wrapped the cloak fully around himself, testing its dimensions.

It's perfect, he thought.

"How many tasks do you have today?" the Queen asked.

"More than I'd like. But I want to come back and eat prior to checking on the festival this afternoon."

"Cael returns today. Why don't we all eat midmeal together? Then we can discuss what my Da tells you."

"Agreed, and we can also plan more of what we'll say at the war council," Acillus stated while pulling on a fur boot.

"Speaking of plans, my lion, it happened again. Thieves struck while you were away."

"Ah, yes. Conail briefly mentioned that. What did they take?" he asked while pulling on the other boot.

"A few houses were cleaned out. The people are being reimbursed from the treasuries but this is growing into something more than just thieving."

"There's increasing reports of piracy on the sea as well. People might be getting restless in anticipation of Camulus."

"I don't think it's that simple, Acillus. I think it's coordinated and funded. My first suspect is Edemar. Their behavior during past councils causes this suspicion."

"Edemar has made leaps and bounds since joining The Kinned Lands."

"They still push for slavery."

"I know they're not the most advanced in ways of peace. But who are we if we do not work with all to make the whole of Terr'ah peaceful for all?"

"Do not let your kind heart blind you to truths. Edemar may be behind this, or at least working with those who are."

"Conail said the City Scouts haven't found anything."

"Edemar is good at intrigue because intrigue is what they do. They hide it from one another so I'll not be surprised if they can hide it from us. I'm not saying we need to expel

Edemar. I'm saying be watchful, Acillus. You know the treasuries are sought after."

"I do, and I will. My hope for Edemar has blinded me in the past. May it not do so again."

"I'll deal with the thieves. And if they turn out to be Edemarian, then we'll deal with them together once you've dealt with Camulus," Andraste smiled.

Acillus gave her a kiss before agreeing, then left the house and set out for the roost.

The roost was where the Ideclan Ravens lived, the large ravens of the Ravenborne Kings. It was a site built much the same way as Ideclan's Hall except it had no roof. And the living trees used for corner posts were not given to them by the Treewolves, but transplanted from four local forests. Inside the roost there were many different trees and rock formations for the ravens to rest upon. And the first water gathering source from the first stone aqueduct was built near the roost as well.

As Acillus walked toward the ravens' home he said ahroo to the people gathering at the ice cold water being brought down from the Philosian Range. Past the water source, he noticed three children lingering in front of the roost's entrance, and so he listened to their excited voices daring one another to go inside. None of them did however, because their excitement overflowed and caused them to run away once they saw the smile of their King walking toward them.

Acillus entered the roost and hundreds of ravens turned to inspect their guest. Some cawed a greeting and he bowed his head in return while walking past them to a favorite resting place of the two ravens he bonded with when very young.

Unique thought patterns and emotions were associated with everyone, and when a Ravenborne would meet a male and female pair of ravens who'd think and feel along the same patterns as themselves, then they'd connect with each other on this level and the bond solidified, allowing them to speak with one another through thought. Meeting a pair of ravens like themselves, however, could be the difficult part.

Acillus' ravens were a reflection of himself; strong, decisive, and kind. The King found his close friends where he thought they might be, nestling next to each other up on a Pine Tree limb in the far corner.

"Ahroo, Hra'ahven," Acillus thought to both.

"Hello, Ujiriff," they both said as one.

Acillus had been with them for almost three hours, discussing in detail where he wanted scouting before he heard the large wings of two other ravens swoop down into the roost, and then the cawing of their return. Some of the ravens, including Dugan and Fey who were conversing with him, cawed back at their two friends whom they hadn't seen in at least a week.

When the cawing quieted down the King heard a low whistle come from behind him, followed by a voice that asked, "Did Ma just finish it then?"

Acillus turned to see his son. The King was just under six feet tall while Cael stood a bit taller. The Prince had his Da's golden blonde hair worn down past the middle of his shoulders. But what separated him from being a close image to his father were the qualities and features he received from his mother. At first glance most would say Cael took after his Da. But those who knew the family well, could see the underlying

Andraste in Cael's looks and demeanor.

The two walked toward each other and grabbed the others' forearm with their right hands and embraced with their left arms, the traditional greeting dating back to the olden days of Clanii.

"She finished it two days ago," Acillus answered after the greeting. "How was your time at the mountains?"

"It was the peace I wanted. But you know what happens when we get what we want."

"What's that?"

"We begin wanting something else," Cael answered.

"Ha! To be sure."

"What do you have planned for today, Da?"

"I was just finishing the scouting details with Dugan and Fey. So now I'm off to see if Aislin has returned."

"He has. I spoke with him at the second gate."

"Then I need to catch him before he rests. What are your plans?"

"Getting something to eat first. Then I have a few people to see here. And I'm off to the bay for more training with Segais later. But most importantly I have a question for you."

"Ask it, lad."

Declanii

"I ask that my three friends be allowed to skip the four years of training abroad and go straight into the tournament."

Acillus thought for a moment. He regarded his son very highly, never taking his questions lightly, and he likely knew the reasons for this one.

After thinking it over he answered, "I'm not so sure I have the authority to grant such a request."

Cael responded, "I know every Clanii except we O'Ronans are supposed to pass four years of training. But I ask the Tournament Council that this tournament be their test. That if they make it high up enough to be voted Declanii, then those votes will be considered seriously. Because it'll prove I've trained them well past what the four years can. I want them experiencing the battles we have coming."

"Said with great confidence. I can assume I know of whom you speak?"

Acillus knew his son's answer before he gave it. They'd been Cael's three best friends since childhood.

"Ohelathe, Irhanach, and Anrahan."

"I'll address the council."

"Tell them I'd consider it a personal favor."

"I will."

They embraced once more in the traditional Clanii way, then Acillus went to exit the roost and find Aislin.

On his way out he turned back to his son and said, "Go and see your Ma before you do anything. She has midday meal planned."

"Aye, Da."

Acillus walked for a distance and then exited Old Ideclan while considering where Aislin might be. He knew his wife's father had been away with the Silent for almost three months, gathering information. So he decided to go and check an ice house that belonged to him.

The upcoming festival, compared to others, wasn't going to consume much ice. But one of the ice houses owned by Aislin had been converted into a personal den, and that seemed a likely place for him to be since he hadn't been seen entering into Old Ideclan by any sentries.

Acillus walked a half mile through the middle part of the city before hearing, "Ravenborne," come from a deep and clear voice off to his left between two wood and stone buildings. The figure who'd spoken was clouded in shadow but the voice was unmistakable to Acillus.

"Aislin," he said.

Aislin Mullquane stepped out from the shadows toward the King. He was Captain of the Silent and considered by many who knew him to be the most lethal man alive.

The Mullquanes were adorned with something no one else possessed. High up on the adult men's and women's cheekbones, just below the outside corners of each eye, they had small dark blue markings forming a design, the meaning of which could only be discerned by them. The tattoos were known as the Mark of the Mullquanes, and every single one of them who'd reached the age and passed the rites had received the Mark, including Andraste, the Warrior Queen.

As Aislin stepped out from the shadows the sunlight revealed his black Mullquane hair and the Mark of the Mullquanes on both sides of his weather chiseled face. He was seventy five, still in the good part of fighting age. And his hair was lightly streaked with strands of gray that had succumbed to the stresses of time faster than the others.

Aislin walked toward his King and the two men greeted the Clanii way before speaking.

Acillus asked, "Have all the Silent returned?"

"Aye, and each has given me their full report."

"And?"

"It's just as you thought. Camulus' Western Army has taken Teranim."

The night air cooled Ashnayn as the cliff rushed by and the sea rushed up. She was perfectly straight as she dove, hands leading the way, ears protected by her arms, and she entered the water with almost no splash.

The All Chief Daughter stayed in diving form until she glided her body upright and starting floating upward, then she kicked to help. After surfacing and her first breath, the Princess swam for the cliff and climbed.

Ashnayn didn't climb fast, the Moon Race was only one night away so conserving her strength was the game she played.

At the top, all but one of her guards slept. None of them had earned the right to compete in the Moon Race and so none of them had thought to train.

When Ashnayn reached the top she turned around and looked out across the sea. She loved how the moonlight danced across the water like a shimmering mirror. Then she leapt, silent as she fell, and again barely any splash. Over and over she dove deep into the night.

That should be enough. I'm ready. I'll win the Moon Race and with the Champion's Request, I can reclaim my freedom.

She sat down on the ledge and drank water from her gourd. It was peaceful now because all her guards were sleeping. And she looked out across the sea again, feeling ready for the race.

Then two large ravens flew by not thirty spans away. She watched them, their flight pattern, their grace, and the moonlight playing off their wings. She was thankful her guards slept so she could enjoy this moment alone as the ravens did a loop back around that made her smile. And before they left her view around the island completely, each cawed like she'd never heard before, and then they were gone.

Chronicle Six

Mother,

Father has become more distant every day. In truth, all fatherliness has left him. He exhibits no care and has even promised me under teeth and bone to a man not of Hobaru. Nothing is making sense. If he loved me he wouldn't treat me this way. So then, does he not love me? My life is moving in a direction I can't control. I don't want to marry this man, Gowgluni. I fear he's manipulated the chiefs in some way. For who is as power hungry as the chiefs? And yet they're giving that power to a stranger. I need your help. Please, visit me in my dreams or give me a sign, and watch over me during the Moon Race.

A letter from Ashnayn, All Chief Daughter of the Twenty Tribes of Hobaru, to her late Mother. Ashnayn put the letter in a cylindrical envelope and then buried it under the floor of her favorite lake.

Declanii

Chapter Seven

Segais looked out across Ideclan's Bay. The great conflict known as the Wizard's War happened more than five thousand years ago, and yet the memory of it was still fresh for him. The site of that battle had been a great distance away. But the fireballs Segais let go of, knew no boundaries when they flew their great arcs across the sky. The fireball that created Ideclan's Bay was one of the larger ones Segais drew in with his intent. Though his intent was never to destroy the peaceful civilization that had once lived where the bay was created. He couldn't help but grow saddened every time he reflected upon the devastation caused by his decisions.

The loss of life caused by my carelessness, he thought.

The Treewolves had long forgiven him in their own way. They didn't hold Segais accountable for the death of their eldest. But the wizard did hold himself accountable for the loss of his own wife and son. It'd been many years since he visited the site of that carnage. But Ideclan's Bay was forever a constant reminder of it all, and the old Ariek knew the bay well.

He saw it when it was first just a crater and the Hilernian Sea was slowly eroding its edge away. He remembered the moment water came down into it and the first tree that sprouted. Everything else around was dead. The force of the fireball cleared a great radius. But slowly, Segais watched the flora make its comeback and the fauna start to test the waters. Until great trees eventually took their place amongst the landscape and the bay looked like it had been there the entire time.

Segais stood there, on the same beach he stood almost

every time he came, contemplating it all.

His student, Prince Cael O'Ronan, practiced with the staff in a small clearing encircled by pine trees up a short distance from the bay. The moon would be full in one night's time and more darkness was given by snow holding strong to the sturdy branches' needles than not. The clearing was just wide enough for Cael to maneuver a few paces in each direction while still spinning his staff. He often preferred the closeness of trees when practicing without an opponent. His long golden blonde hair was tied behind him and his dark green cloak whipped about. And he was as quiet as possible while exerting himself to the fullest extent.

The wise man down by the bay was a tall, lean man, with eyes as gray as heavy clouds. His long and thick bronze hair grew down to his lower back and was kept as long as his curly copper brown beard, both of which he often oiled and braided. His many layers of robes had the hues of maroon and gray. But the innermost robe was black.

The calm lapping of the sea soothed the old wizard as he looked out across the bay. And when he heard hoof steps from a mule far down the beach, Segais turned his head. He saw down the shore, a giant of a man with a small boy covered in blankets while riding on a mule next to him.

"Ah, finally," the wizard said with a change of mood.

"Will you rub my back, father?" Elasus asked from atop the mule.

"Of course," Cristin answered.

He rubbed the blankets on his son's back, chest, and arms while walking as close to the mule as possible, trying to keep his child warm.

"I don't see anything to eat," Elasus stated.

"Nor me."

"You said we'd be there by now."

"I thought we would be. But I must've chosen the wrong path because this is Ideclan's Bay."

"Will we reach Ideclan tonight?"

"I hope so. Except we need help. Perhaps we can talk with that man up there."

"If he's here then maybe he's lost also."

"Maybe," his father smiled.

Cristin, Elasus, and Ella made their way toward Segais. And the wise man displayed no signs he was aware of their approach.

"Excuse me," Cristin called to him.

"You are excused," Segais said back with a smile they couldn't see.

"Forgive me, but I must ask for your help. My son and I are trying to reach Ideclan and I've obviously taken a wrong road."

Cristin and the mule stopped just short of Segais, who turned to give them his full attention.

"What are your names?" the wizard asked.

The Edemarian instinctively lied. His habit was strong.

"I am Raddox. And this is my son, Ryker."

"Raddox and Ryker, the famous twins from Lore," Segais remarked with a smile.

Cac, he's Philosian, Cristin thought.

"Our ancestors settled in the Gray Forest, but I feel my blade would better serve at Ideclan."

"That may be," the wizard agreed. "And what of your bellies?"

"Our bellies, sir?"

"The Gray Forest is some distance from here. You must be hungry."

"Incredibly," Elasus answered.

Segais grinned as he turned and walked toward a pile of rocks. "Well then," he said while grabbing a basket from behind the pile. "It's not much farther, just up the road there, a few more hours and you'll reach Ideclan. This should keep you company."

The old Philosian handed Elasus the basket and the young boy looked inside.

"Cheeses! Bread! Berries! Apples! Nuts! Crackers! Butter! Pastries!"

Cristin humbly said, "Thank you."

His upbringing at Edemar should have caused him to reject anything from an Ariek, but his years on the run had taught him otherwise.

"Eat up Raddox and Ryker. Then rest well. That path leads to Ideclan," Segais pointed.

Cristin thought the man was friendly and a bit odd, yet still a blessing as they said farewell and then followed one of the many paths up from the bay.

"Want me to make you a cheesy cracker, or buttered bread?" his son asked.

"How about both."

"Yes!" Elasus agreed, and then started preparing what to them were delicacies.

As they walked, the father and son enjoyed the food given by Segais, and each was full for the first time in a long while.

"Are we almost there now?" Elasus asked after three hours of walking.

"Find out for yourself. Take a deep breath."

The boy took in the biggest breath he could through his mouth and Cristin interrupted him.

"Through your nose. *Smell* the air."

Elasus let out the air and then breathed in the cold Midwinter air of the night darkened sky through his nose.

"It smells like smoke from a fire."

"Yes it does. That's the cooking and heating fires of Ideclan. We should be there very soon," Cristin told him in heightened spirits.

"And then we get a warm bed to sleep in?"

"A warm and comfortable bed," the father answered before biting into a peanut butter pastry while tying the basket to Ella.

As they approached the city through low pockets of fog beginning to blanket the land, Cristin groomed his appearance, smoothing out any wrinkles that may have been in his clothes, and brushing off any dirt or dust or mud that could've accumulated on him. Elasus saw his father doing this and thought to do the same, except he quickly realized he was too wrapped in some of their blankets to do so.

While trying to loosen the blankets, Cristin tapped him lightly on the chest with the back of his hand and pointed forward after he had his attention. Elasus smiled when he saw what his father pointed at. To the front, just coming into view through the fog were the fortifications of Ideclan: the longest walls of smooth rock either had ever seen.

"Is that it, father?" the child asked in a whisper.

"Yes it is," Cristin answered with a smile.

"How tall are those walls and towers?"

"The circular drum towers on either side of the gate are thirty three feet tall. Every tower along every wall is thirty three feet. And the walls are twenty two feet tall. You were too young to remember our walls back home but these are thicker; nine feet thick at the top while twenty two feet thick at the bottom. When we get closer you'll see how the outside of the wall curves inward so that the top and bottom meet smoothly at two thirds height. One of my favorite paintings is of the first walls to be built like this, made famous in Ages past by the Williand."

Elasus grew excited while Cristin checked the Edemarian Sword slung across his back to make sure it was still covered and wrapped by a blanket. Only the lowest but largest hilt and crossguard remained revealed, somewhat disguising its Edemarian style. Then he checked himself and his son one last time to make sure they were presentable for their first interaction with the city. And as the two got closer to the gate that was the Northern most corner of the city, Cristin grabbed his mule's harness because he knew a halt would be coming soon.

"Halt and state your business!" a powerfully gruff voice called down to them.

He immediately brought Ella to a halt and said, "My son and I have come to seek shelter and work until your next tournament, which I wish to join."

"Hold where you are," the man commanded.

Within moments, the large oak and iron doors were pulled open from the inside, but only wide enough for one guard.

Declanii

The Edemarians saw a man walk through and Cristin figured him to be the same who'd yelled from atop the wall walk. He couldn't see him clearly but as he walked toward them, Cristin recognized what he wore. The man was wrapped in a thick cloak of the deepest blue he'd ever seen; such a deep blue it appeared to be swallowed by the night as he moved.

"What are your names, lads?" the man asked as he stopped just short of Cristin, Elasus, and Ella.

His voice was indeed the gruff one that called down to them. And it was evident this man felt comfortable being in command. He was just under six feet tall and stout. The hood of his sunil cloak covered his short dark hair. And Cristin noticed the man had a large raven's feather hanging from the brooch of his cloak.

Underneath the feather he wore an Ideclan Amulet Cristin saw many times in books. The amulet was fashioned after the layout of Ideclan's defensive walls; two squares surrounded by a diamond. The only wall not represented on the amulet was the wooden wall that incorporated many living trees along its distance, built thirty feet back from the outer wall that was nine miles on every side.

"You're a man of the sunil, you're Declanii," Cristin stated.

"Names lads, then we can start with the pleasantries."

Cristin didn't recognize it at the time but this meeting was highly irregular. The man in sunil was long past ever having to perform gate guard. He was there because his sub commander and great friend needed the night off to be with his wife while she gave birth.

Cristin did think it was unusual that only one man had come out to check them. But he didn't notice the group of Ideclan Scouts walking silently up behind him.

"My name is Raddox, and this is my son, Ryker. We're from The Gray Forest," he replied.

"Do you know when the next tournament is, Raddox of The Gray Forest?"

"I do not."

"Well then, boy. First Breath surely smiles upon you! Will you be ready to fight in the morning?" the stout, gruff man asked with a wolfish grin.

"The tournament starts tomorrow?"

"Ha ha, aye, lad! And it's the three hundredth and thirty third Festival of Four Fires this tournament belongs to! Your timing is perfect!" he answered with his arms wide open. The man was getting a real kick out of what was otherwise a dull night.

Cristin had been caught by surprise. He was grateful but also familiar with important numbers to the Ideclaners. And it was possible this could be the biggest festival ever held by them thus far.

"Alright then lad, how's your mule? Is she friendly?"

"Yes sir, she's friendly," Cristin answered.

The man wearing sunil leaned in and gave Ella a reassuring pat on her neck and a sniff of his hand as he whispered soft words into her ear. His whispering seemed funny to Elasus, who thought it sounded more like grumbling than speaking.

The man leaned back from the mule and took a step around her. As he did, Cristin heard a sound come from behind. Turning around he saw seven scouts wearing white winter cloaks.

"Don't worry about them, lad. They've only been following you for about a mile now. Usually folks don't like traveling at this time of night during this time of year, not even for a festival. But you don't seem like you want trouble. We're just making sure you're not trying to smuggle anyone in," the man said with a sly smile at Elasus who was still covered by blankets, and the child smiled back.

Cristin had never caught any hint they were there. The scouts of Ideclan held a high reputation and already he was witness to it. The situation was surreal for him, being at the front gate while talking to a Veteran of the Sunil with seven Ideclan Scouts behind him and his son.

The whole of the last three years flashed before Cristin's mind in an instant. The choice to take his son and flee Edemar, the incessant running through Runidarees, the constant hiding at Fwynndarlanai, then the long, cold, and hungry road toward Ideclan. And now...

We're here, and the tournament starts tomorrow.

He looked at his son and grinned.

As the man in sunil continued walking around them, he saw the large two handed longsword wrapped by a blanket across Cristin's back.

"I suppose anything smaller would feel like a toy in your hands," he said, then made it all the way around the newcomers before looking toward Elasus. "Are you here to fight in the tournament as well?"

Elasus laughed and then the man directed them to follow him as he started walking toward the gate.

"Captain," the man in sunil called out to one of the scouts behind them.

"Yes, Commander?" the scout called back as the gate was fully opened and all walked through.

Cristin walked taller after hearing him being addressed as Commander. He knew what that meant in an Ideclan Army. Then he halted his mule as the Commander stopped them just inside the gate and in between two large dirt piles.

"What are the dirt mounds for?" Cristin asked.

"Cridolf and Bidolf? Win many fights tomorrow and you'll know first hand," the Commander said. "Captain," he continued. "Your shift is over. If you please, accompany Raddox and his son into Ideclan proper and help them find suitable lodgings. Raddox, may you find some. It's late and everyone from The Kinned Lands is here for the festival. It seems you're the last to arrive."

"Oh no, no bed!" Elasus groaned.

The Commander chuckled before saying, "No need to worry, little lad. You see Liadine right there?"

As the Commander pointed behind the boy, Elasus

turned around and saw an elderly man step forward. The old man didn't look as old as he was, but his wrinkles had the appearance of being chiseled there by the wind and rain, like the side of an eroding cliff. His hair was all white and barely reached his shoulders. And it was tucked behind his ears underneath the hood of his heavy white cloak.

"He's a Fourth Tier Scout and Captain of all scouts in the Tenth Talon; which is the best Talon, because it's *my* Talon. He happens to know about the finest establishment in the city. You'll have no trouble finding it with him. Might be some rooms with beds available there."

"Thank you," Cristin said.

"Get good rest, Raddox, lots of fighting come morning for you," he informed him as he sent them on their way.

Then the big oak doors were pushed shut by soldiers they hadn't seen, who went back up the walls with their Commander.

Walking inside Ideclan was much easier for the Edemarian and the mule. The roads were kept as dry as possible and most of them were cobblestone or gravel. The seven scouts also made the journey quicker by telling stories about the place, as well as answering the many questions Elasus asked.

"This land between the outermost wall and the middle wall is mostly farmland and pastures for livestock," Liadine told them. "Farmers, animal tenders, kennel masters, bee keepers, and others stay in houses out here but most of the population lives inside the middle wall. That being said, the quiet neighborhoods out here are growing faster than anywhere else, and more than a few communities are now villages in their own right."

When they reached the inside of the middle wall, Liadine said farewell to the other scouts and directed Cristin to follow him.

"Where are you taking us, sir?" the Edemarian asked.

"Name's Liadine, and I'm taking you to the finest establishment in town: The Fox's Hypothesis."

Cristin laughed loudly. He was in a very good mood having arrived.

"Must be a Philosian place then, right?" he questioned while grabbing Ella's reins to correct her path.

"Ah, you must be a student of thought then, right?" Liadine returned with charm.

"No, just read some books. Philosian literature is interesting."

Interesting is a man of your size, stature, appearance, and knowledge coming to us from The Gray Forest, Liadine thought.

"How young are you?" the old scout asked.

"Twenty five," the Edemarian answered with another lie.

"Come to fight in the tournament, then?"

"Yes," Cristin said with finality.

"May you do well," Liadine responded, getting the hint as he led them onward.

Prince Cael continued practicing with his staff in the small clearing down by Ideclan's Bay, spinning it every which angle and direction, knocking the snow that gave him shade from the moon off branches.

THWAACK!

His staff abruptly met two bit sticks held by Segais who now stood in the clearing with him.

Bit sticks or bits, both abbreviations for rabbit sticks, were two half staffs, each roughly the length of an arm, usually with knots at the end and wrapped tightly with leather after being fire hardened. Simple yet effective, they and staffs were what everyone assumed the Philosians protected themselves with.

"I knew you were there," the young Prince stated as he stepped back.

"How so?" Segais inquired.

"I heard you," he replied in a matter of fact way.

"I'm not so sure," the wizard chimed with disbelief. He wore a smile that warned the Prince and the young man took another step back. "Because if you heard me, then why did you follow through with your strike?"

Cael threw his staff like a spear at Segais. The old wizard thrust it aside with ease, hooking it with the small knots at the ends of his bits and then flinging it to the ground. Cael pulled his bits tied to his waist and then brought them up just in time to stop Segais' attack.

THWAACKACK!

"I thought you wanted to head back," the Prince said.

"We still have time."

The small clearing became enveloped with the sounds of their practice.

THWAACK DRAAACK THWAACK!!

They attacked and countered while circling each other, kicking the snow as they moved within the confined space. The sounds of the bits became fluid as the rhythm of the simple weapons took on the flow of music. The combination of their strikes along with the slicing through the air and the stomps of their planting feet became a beautiful song. A song that only a few who've mastered this art have had the opportunity to hear, or the few who've been chosen to witness its practice.

Segais, like all Philosians, had practiced with the staff and half staffs to the point of mastery. The wise people preferred these simple weapons, relying on patience, angles, and agility rather than lethality. And he showed these techniques to Cael at a young age.

Most teachers only taught one level of education out of four at Ideclan, but the old wizard had already taught Cael all of them, as well as much else he'd picked up during his long life, and still, what Segais the Sagacious had taught the young man to this point was fractionally small compared to the vast stores of knowledge within himself.

Cael quickly found a fondness for the Philosian weapons and was intrigued by how well they could overcome a blade if one were fast enough, they were used properly, and the bits or staffs not allowed to be chopped in half. He studied them as rigorously as he studied his own native battle compliment of sword, shield, spear, bow, and heavy throwing spikes.

Cael advanced in skill rapidly at each of these throughout his life, not only by learning from his father and mother, or from the teachings of Segais, though these alone would make a master of a warrior. But by taking everything he'd been taught and teaching it to his three best friends: Irhanach Fianna, Anrahan Aenenay, and his cousin, Ohelathe Mullquane.

After the Prince had taught them what he learned, he found he possessed a new understanding of the skill he was teaching. And when he went back to Segais or his parents, Cael would have the technique well understood. He was able to achieve the song he now practiced with Segais in less time than any Philosian ever had.

THWAACK DRAACK THWAACK THWAACKACK!!!

The symphony continued as they performed a harmony of balance, agility, and a hint of aggression. Only to be broken by the cawing of Cael's two ravens as they returned from acquiring a meal.

Each flew directly over the young O'Ronan and descended in counter but concentric spirals all the way down, until softly and simultaneously landing on each of his shoulders.

The Prince grinned as Segais raised a bit stick so the fire strengthened knot was a breath away from Cael's face and said, "Until next time, boy." Then he walked off toward Ideclan and Cael quickly grabbed his things to follow.

"Where's your basket?" he asked after catching up with him.

"I gave it to a friend. Are you prepared for tomorrow?"

"I am. But I must protest."

"Of course you must. Tell me your reasons."

"It's dishonorable to lie," Cael said assertively.

"Who are you lying to?"

"The whole city! This tournament of all tournaments you ask me to disguise and compete, the one where the whole realm will be watching me; my Prince's debut."

"That's the reason I ask. You are adept at moving through crowds without being seen. Now you must become the same while moving in front of them."

"What if someone recognizes me? Everyone will think it peculiar I joined the competitions under a false name."

"Indeed they would. Don't forget, I'd like your false identity to lose before the end of the second day."

"How could I forget? If I did, I might end up fighting myself at the end of the third."

The old wizard smiled as they continued walking back.

They walked for over an hour before it became apparent to Segais that something new was now troubling his young protégé. Cael had become more quiet and reserved than usual, and was angered by simple matters like tripping over a rock.

"What is it?" the old man asked.

"Many things," Cael answered as he adjusted his dark green winter cloak.

"You know of what I speak. It's the ravens, isn't it?"

Segais counted himself fortunate to have such a personal relationship with a Ravenborne. And to be witness to some of the truths behind this long unknown. Cael had once told him of his ravens' secret lineage, the reason why they and all Ideclan Ravens were twice as large as any other, and lived as long as humans. Once Cael shared this, Segais felt he was free to ask about the matter whenever he deemed necessary. So when Cael didn't answer, he continued to prod.

"Well then, what troubles you the most in this moment?"

The Prince looked up at the ravens flying above him and said, "Roxgrin and Binneen have given me an oddity and they won't speak of what it means."

There was more than a hint of frustration in his voice.

"Have they done this before?" Segais inquired as smoke drifted from his long stemmed pipe.

"Yes, but only a few times," Cael answered after looking back to the road.

"Exactly how many times?"

"This is the third time."

"What did the ravens give you?"

Cael raised his hand toward Segais and held up the source of his confusion tightly between his fingers, pointing toward the sky.

"A hawk's feather," he answered.

"An oddity indeed."

Declanii

Chronicle Seven

I did not kill you. I loved you. I loved all my family.
All of you were taken from me, all of your deaths are blamed
on me.
Everyone pursues Elasus and myself for a falsehood believed
stronger than truth.
I saw your bodies, I could not let Elasus see.
I know why they arranged you all in that way.
I know the ritual they performed.
I know what the people have been led to believe of me because
of it.
I will avenge your deaths. I will clear my name. And I will
smear their blood on my face in victory.

Written by Cristin and then burned in a campfire under the
canopy of The Gray Forest, also called Fwynndarlanai

Declanii

Chapter Eight

"How did you follow us for so long outside Ideclan without my father knowing you were there, Liadine?" Elasus inquired as they walked for The Fox's Hypothesis.

"Ah, but the fog and cloud hide many things, young one."

After passing by numerous inns and taverns, all of which were full of song, they walked past a few more and then left the lively area for a residential one. After a few turns, Cristin saw a building big enough he thought could be it.

As they neared the structure, Liadine said, "Follow me around back there's a small stable. Even though the Philosians mostly walk they still have it."

Cristin, Elasus, and the old mule followed him behind the inn. The stable was indeed small. When Cristin got Ella situated he noted not more than two horses could fit inside, and they'd be cramped at best. Cristin uncovered the oat box, then made sure the stall was secure and turned to leave. As he did he saw his son walking in funny circles outside the stable, still holding the blankets around himself.

"You lose your way, Ryker?" he asked while reminding him of his name.

"Both my legs fell asleep and I won't be able to walk soon. Please pick me up!" he pleaded.

Cristin adjusted the Edemarian blade across his back,

then picked up Elasus before his legs became pins and needles and followed a smiling Liadine toward the front of the building.

"Goodnight, Ella!" Elasus yelled to the mule who was all too happy with the oats she found.

They'd almost lost Ella a few times over the course of their travels. Once they searched for five days before finding her again after a specifically threatening attack from three Edemarian Executioners. Cristin was ready to leave her then, but Elasus had grown too fond of the mule and so his love forced them to reunite. Elasus and Ella's relationship continued to strengthen and the mule neighed when she heard her name on the young child's voice.

As they walked toward the front of the building, the large Edemarian noticed it appeared to be made of wood, which Cristin remembered from his studies was unheard of for a Philosian structure.

"Is it all made of wood?" he asked quietly, while Elasus giggled from his legs waking up.

"Just on the outside. Inside you have your usual Philosian stonework," Liadine answered equally quiet, then frowned when he got a look at the state of one of Cristin's boots.

The white haired scout started leading them up the wooden steps that met the door to the inside. There wasn't much light seeping out from within but there was enough from the moon for Cristin to read the sign: The Fox's Hypothesis.

On the sign, a red fox stood on its black hind legs while dancing with a pipe in its mouth. Cristin loved it because he remembered reading the Philosian fable of the same name when he was younger. He also loved how quiet it was. Every other establishment they passed was filled with raucous people singing and foot stomping. This quietness was exactly what they needed.

As Liadine led the two up the wooden stairs the old scout looked back and said, "You're both going to like this place." Then he reached the top and unlatched the iron catch lock before pushing open the heavy oak door.

They felt serene warmth as they walked in and Cristin quickly closed shut the door behind them. Lanterns warmly lit the room and both Edemarians were surprised to notice the building was more spacious on the inside than it looked on the outside. There were bookcases in every corner and all along every wall. Two of the three stairways leading up to the next floor were packed with stacks of books underneath them as well, giving the appearance it was the books that led one up to the next level. And a fourth stairway led down to storage.

Tables, chairs, and couches were aligned in disarray to accommodate a number of odd discussion arrangements on multiple sections of the main floor. Tea tables and small end tables, along with low wooden circular tables were placed throughout, and most had books upon them. All along the walls above the bookcases were big tapestries and paintings, some small, which covered almost every space the bookcases and bookshelves did not. There was also a table with the Philosian board game kijgin upon it, but Cristin had never learned the rules.

The inn was filled with people who for the most part were quiet. Almost all were local and discussions went on around the room at a level where no group competed with any other.

A number of the patrons looked to Cristin like they were just the age to be joining the tournaments, or perhaps this was their first year of tournamenting. But others were obvious veterans and the young ones listened to their every advice.

"For these first fights, stick with your teams," a veteran said. "It's too easy to get taken out if you don't."

"What Talon did you start your entry at?" Cristin overheard a rookie ask him.

"The one I'm in now, the Fifth."

"Do you know Phaedrus of Gisspor?" another questioned.

"Of course. You'll all know your Commanders well."

"What about the Vanguard Commander? You ever meet him?" an archer asked.

The veteran looked at his friend before turning back to the young group amassed in front of him. "What do you want to know about the Vanguard Commander?"

"Is it true he's from Aguptah?" was the first question asked but not the one everyone wanted an answer to.

"Yes."

"Is it true he sells the bandit leaders and pirate captains he captures into slavery?"

All the boys listened closely. Of everyone at Ideclan there was more rumor surrounding the Vanguard Commander than anyone else.

"None of us knows how Commander Rallin accomplishes what he does. But I assume King Acillus would exile him if he used methods such as that."

"What about his troops? Are they all murderers and thieves?"

"Not all, but it's true that *some* murderers get the choice of exile or Vanguard, and some choose Vanguard. All Vanguard are there by choice."

A man sat with his back to them while listening in, going through pages of a manuscript he pretended to read. Cristin noticed nothing extraordinary about him and neither did anyone else. He seemed to be by himself and no one in the room could've recognized him at first glance. But he was Commander Rallin, of the Vanguard himself.

Rallin was well aware of how few people wanted to join his Vanguard, and that's why he was disguised, so he could learn secrets to manipulate those he thought worthy into joining. The Vanguard was a new creation and far less desirable for those who sought to be among the might of the Twelve Talons. But under Rallin's leadership they were proving to be more than worth their weight in pearls. And Rallin knew the secrecy and rumor surrounding him and his men was serving them well.

He grinned as he listened in on the people talking about him. No one but he, his men, and the King knew how the Vanguard accomplished their missions. Rallin's methods were nothing like that of the Clanii's or even The Kinned Lands. They were all his own and they were effective. Bandits and pirates were beginning to fear the Ideclan Vanguard, and their place among Ideclan's ranks was solidifying.

Some of the most capable soldiers under his command were those Rallin had to manipulate to join. And his attention was caught by Cristin.

That young man has a deathly mobility to him. I wonder what secrets he's hiding, Rallin said to himself.

Cristin continued scanning the room. To his far left he noticed a lone man, an elder Philosian, sitting in front of the largest stone hearth he'd ever seen. The building didn't have a corner in that section, just the hearth, or more precisely the corner was the hearth. The large hearth ran from the basement through all four floors to five feet above the roof. The smoke from each floor's fire traveled up its own channel in the stone to be let out at the top. And the opposite corner of the building had a hearth just the same.

Sitting in front of the fireplace was the lone Philosian. And he stood up quickly once he saw them.

"See! I told you three more people would come in!" he shouted above everyone else. "Alistriana, will you please get me that ale? I think I am going to stay a bit longer."

"Yes," Alistriana sighed.

She rolled her eyes as she left the company of a young man with long, burning red and yellow hair that looked like fire, whose name was Irhanach, to grab her fellow Philosian another ale.

Alistriana was born far off but her father had moved her to the peninsula when she was very young, and opened up the first establishment of its kind: The Fox's Hypothesis. Since then it'd become a necessary stop for all Philosians about to begin a pilgrimage or just returning from one. Partly because the only true path that led to Philos was the Ideclan Philos Pass. So unless one wanted to do some climbing they likely walked through Ideclan to get to Philos.

The pilgrimage was in the heart of every Philosian. And the old man had just returned from such a voyage and was sharing his glee with many throughout the night. It was fairly late and people were starting to go home or to their rooms. Yet a good number remained on the main floor.

The old Philosian was invigorated by returning from his journey so he'd been going strong with the ale. Alistriana had expected no one else would come in and was about to finish with her responsibilities for the night, before Liadine walked in with a young man holding a child.

She knew the wayfarers would need a room so while going downstairs to get an ale, she also picked up the key for a room with some blankets, and while doing so she heard Ella through a window, neighing happily. When Alistriana came back up she quickly walked over and gave the man his ale, then walked to her desk.

The young man with red and yellow hair whispered something into her ear and she laughed.

Most who saw Alistriana couldn't help but notice her beauty. She had long black hair with the darkest eyes in the slightest shapes of almonds. She wore a long black dress that fit her form fluidly. And her gracefulness belied a confidence that was near intoxicating. Had she not obviously been in love with the young man with hair the color of flames, Cristin might have taken more notice.

"Father, I can walk now."

"Alright, Ryker."

As soon as Cristin set his son down the boy gave him their blankets and started making his way toward the old man by the fireplace. Then Liadine led the father over to the desk where Alistriana talked and smiled with the young man.

"Hello, Alis," Liadine said.

"Hello, Liadine. Bring them here for a room?" She turned to Cristin after he nodded. "We have one available. Just sign your name and pay the friend price of five coppers and it's yours."

Cristin thanked them as he handed her the weathered coins, then signed: Raddox. He was very grateful for the price.

As Elasus got closer to the old Philosian, the voices of his father and the others seemed to fade away. All he could hear was the crackling of the fire while quietly walking up behind him.

"Hello, child," the Philosian said without looking from the flames.

Elasus froze in his tracks for a brief moment, then walked at his normal pace to step between the man and the fireplace.

"How'd you know we three would come in tonight?" he asked with curiosity.

"What's your name?"

"Ryker, what's yours?"

"My name is Kandros, Ryker. And I didn't specifically know that you three would be coming in, just that some three would."

"How'd you know that? It's fairly late and cold for anyone to be arriving now."

"Do you think so?" the wizard questioned back with a smile. "Well, I knew because of synchronicities. Do you know what that word means?"

Elasus shook his head while the old man took a drink of ale.

"A synchronicity is a coincidence that is no coincidence at all. It is a mere, matter of perception of the events at hand, if you will." Kandros let out a drunken snicker.

Cristin watched his son from across the room while Alistriana put the coin away. He saw Elasus make a funny face at whatever the old man just said and chuckled to himself.

"Come to fight in the tournament then?" the young man with Alistriana asked him.

Cristin turned and answered, "I have. But I'm unsure where to begin."

"It's my first as well. Where are the sign ups this year, Liadine?"

"Why, or more precisely, how are you fighting this year, Irhanach?" Liadine asked.

"By personal request of our Prince," the young man declared proudly, while Alistriana looked at him with worry.

Liadine had to stop and think before he answered. It'd been a long time since he had to sign up for a tournament.

"They're just outside the district closest to the First Talon's practice field." Then he turned toward Cristin. "My wife and I eat breakfast here before every tournament, and we'll come a little early tomorrow so I can show you where they are. I'll see you in the morning, Raddox. Sleep well."

"Thank you, Liadine."

The old scout nodded and with that, he was on his way home.

"I'm off as well," Irhanach stated as he leaned over the desk. Alistriana leaned in and they kissed. "See you, Liss," he said to her. Then he turned toward Cristin and gave him a pat on the back of the shoulder while saying, "Welcome to Ideclan," as he walked out of The Fox's Hypothesis.

"Your room is up those stairs and down the hall to the left, room number five," Alis told Cristin.

He grabbed the blankets and key as he thanked her and started walking toward the stairs. Elasus was still talking with the old man by the fire but by now they were both laughing.

When Cristin reached the base of the stairs, he said, "Let's go, Ryker. It's time to sleep."

The boy jumped up and ran toward his father. As he came close, he jumped again and Cristin caught him.

"Goodnight to you, sir," Cristin said to the old man.

"And a good night to you, Raddox of Edemar," he replied in a voice only they could hear.

Cristin started shaking because of his adrenaline as he looked closer at him.

It isn't anyone I know. I've never seen him before.

"Why do you think my son and I are from Edemar?"

"Well, your son, I'm not so sure. He speaks like he's from all over the place. But you have a distinct dialect. You hide it well, but it's distinct."

"You're drunk and hearing things. Have a good night," Cristin said in a stern voice as he turned and started up the stairs.

Fool! I should have camouflaged more! he scolded himself.

"Raddox, I didn't mean to offend you," Kandros said sincerely. "Fight well tomorrow."

The Edemarian continued carrying his son up the stairs and down the hall toward their room without reply. When he got there he set Elasus down, then put the key into the iron lock and opened it. The room was dark but the light from the hall showed Cristin where the candles were located. With one of the candles from the hall he lit a candle in his room. Then Elasus ran across the small but spacious accommodation and jumped right onto the bed.

"Off, child," Cristin commanded while he closed and locked their door.

"Yes, father."

Cristin walked over to the window and decided they could make it out if they needed to escape. Then he looked at their bed. It wasn't wide but it was long and it would fit them both, and it was a bed. When all the blankets were set, Cristin unsheathed his sword and set it close, then both of them climbed into the most comfortable thing either had slept on in half a year.

Cristin could fall asleep at any moment but Elasus' mind was full of all the thoughts and curiosities he had for this new land. And one question more than any other was at the forefront of his mind.

"Father?" He waited but got no response. Cristin's breathing was low and calm. "Father!" he said louder.

Cristin shook as if he'd been awoken by the sensation of falling. And it took him a moment to gather himself.

"Oh... what is it?" he asked as he shut his eyes again, hoping Elasus' question wouldn't be too difficult.

"Do you know what a synchronicity is?"

Far to the East, an army of over one hundred and sixty five thousand acted out their restlessness into the late hours of the night. Drunkenness, brawling, and defilement dominated the activities for the bulk of Camulus Erra'Aulius' men. The Emperor drank wine as he walked through it all with his General, Fenric, and others of his elite and noble.

The air was filled with putrid smells of liquor and urine. And the sounds dominating the camp were that of laughter, belches, and farts whenever the roar of a fight would die down, or the tortured would die.

Camulus kept his men vicious and battle hungry, giving them advancement when one challenged and killed another of higher rank, so long as that challenge was in accordance with his rules. His men were disciplined, professional, and ruthless.

All those not slaves loved Camulus for his ability to bring them battle after battle, constantly feeding his and their bloodlust. The Emperor enjoyed the fact that his men shared the same want for war as himself. His father, Berrinus, had made sure they were all seasoned veterans by the time the army was passed down to him. And he made sure they stayed that way.

The fear of those who went against him were his five hundred Lancers, masters of horse and lance. Many Lancer Horses, all groomed to perfection, stood next to one another while some slept and others ate. Each horse's saddle and tack were made with the utmost care. And the steel plated armor in front of them was of the finest in the empire.

Camulus inspected them proudly as he walked past. All horses in his army were strong and worthy in their own right, well fed, maintained, and trained throughout their lives. But Lancer Horses outdid all others. And they showed no signs of fatigue as Camulus, by his own calculations, was only five and a half days away from reaching Saddeye and taking the Orakal's ancient city.

He smiled at the thought, then drank more wine while rubbing the various claws on his necklace.

"Cypria's been challenged!" the Emperor and his entourage heard someone yell.

Camulus looked at General Fenric, then they walked quickly over to where the crowd was forming.

Everyone wanted to see what would happen with Cypria, especially Camulus who promoted him partly to observe how his men would behave. For the Emperor, it was interesting watching his soldiers' hate for Cypria play out. They hated him because he was Camulus' slave and still a higher rank than they were, and also because his skin was as dark as night. Yet they followed his orders during battle without hesitation because of his martial prowess. The Emperor was intrigued by the two opposites surrounding this one man.

By the time Camulus and his elite reached the challenge, one soldier was already on the ground with his arm bent the wrong way while another circled the unarmed Cypria at the center of the savage mass. Most cheered as they stood, but a few Lancers rode around the group, allowing them to see over everyone else.

The soldier still standing attacked Cypria and the slave dodged his strike, then reached in quickly and grabbed his sword arm. He spun the arm up and around, popping it out of its socket, then the man shrieked as he fell backward while Cypria kept his sword.

Two more ran in to attack the slave with swords drawn, breaking the rules for challenge but Camulus didn't interject. Cypria hacked an arm off one then pierced the heart of the other. He let out a deep lion like growl as three more ran in for him, all of them irate that their friends were now dead or dying by a dark slave.

Cypria picked up another sword from the ground and charged one so they couldn't surround him. He swung down forcefully, burying the second sword deep in collarbone, then pulled at it but it wouldn't come free.

He turned and brought his forearm up to block a strike to his neck while at the same time swinging the sword he still held to keep the other man away. His arm protecting his neck was sliced to the bone as he brought the sword back and into the gut of the man who sliced him.

A soldier from the crowd stepped out into the clearing and produced a small sleek throwing axe. He positioned himself, preparing to throw it at Cypria.

A mounted Lancer threw a javelin at him, and it went through the man's chest before the throwing axe left his hand, just as Cypria savagely struck the last challenger down.

To make it appear as though he hadn't helped Cypria, the Lancer in blue and white yelled, "Follow the rules of challenge or I will kill you myself!"

Then he galloped off and the crowd dissipated in disappointment as Cypria grabbed an iron poker from a fire and started closing his wound.

"I told you, Fenric," Emperor Camulus reminded his General. "Keep an eye on those two. This is on course to become *very* entertaining."

"She is courageous to face her own torture," Nakuta of the Shogin said.

"An act of courage I'd prefer she not have to demonstrate," Captain Higada added.

They and the thirteen others stood along a pathway leading into one of the many smaller courtyards at the palace of Saddeye.

"Is there anything we can do?" Nakuta continued.

"We can do as she commanded," Rokomu stated.

"Even if we hear her scream as she's tortured?"

"Especially!" Higada yelled with frustration. "You heard her words. We must wait until our path crosses the Ravenborne or she dies."

"What if we leave now? We could kill Camulus within the week," Nakuta suggested.

"Our Forty Third Law prevents any Shogin from becoming assassins," Higada told him. "I've looked for a law that'd allow us to leave and be rid of this threat, but have found none."

The Orakal, Binc, and Hrija walked by at that moment, and the Shogin bowed to the ground.

"Hrija, Binc, I'll meet you there," the Orakal said.

Hrija and Binc slightly bowed and then walked off quickly. They knew the Shogin had been unsettled, and that unsettled everyone else.

"Rise. You all look troubled."

"Forgive us, my lady," Higada replied as they stood. "We're resolved to do as you will."

"I know you all think my having to go through this is sacrilegious. But understand it's still nothing compared to what others have had to endure. And they've endured it without the knowledge they'll live through it. I know I'll live through it. So I can rest assured knowing there's an end. Can your minds rest knowing this?"

"Yes, my lady," a few answered.

"You stay silent, Higada," the Orakal observed.

"My mind will rest when you've returned with us and are safe."

"You think I'll be safe afterwards? Why?"

He had no answer.

"Banish all thoughts of security from your minds. After we're reunited is when the true danger begins."

"What danger is that?" Nakuta asked.

"That depends on certain events soon to pass."

Chronicle Eight

At a very young age I brought Prince Cael to the Council of Ten and Seven. The boy exuded masterful bearing as he walked across the smooth stone floor toward them with myself in follow. Many would break the kingly demeanor in which they greeted such a collective, but Cael could not. The council studied him for a few rare moments, then went off the normal course by asking Cael this riddle instead of beginning with the customary questioning.

When the desert touches sky as high as mountains rise,
the journey of the monk takes the seeds of growth,
on her journey to internalize the seed she gives it to the sage.
If the monk's journey ends before it can be internalized,
the sage will nourish the seed and protect it,
but eventually the seed will destroy the sage,
and the seed will take its place.
What has taken the sage's place?

All riddles have numerous answers worth contemplating. But to my delighted surprise, Cael said:

"It is the high desert environment of which you speak, when a chipmunk takes the seeds from a tree and places them under the sagebrush for storage and protection. If the chipmunk dies they'll not be able to retrieve the seed and it may be forgotten. If the seed opens then the tree grows under the protection of the sage, eventually killing the sage and taking its place. That is why, at the high desert there are often trees growing out from sagebrush."

To this day we still discuss his answer, and observe the

truth of it while walking through the high desert.

Written by Segais not long after accepting Cael as a protege,
and inserted like many other papers in a book full of Philosian
Riddles found at The Fox's Hypothesis.

Chapter Nine

THE IDECLAN NIGHT WAS CALM AND THE MORNING calmer still. The Sun hadn't risen yet and a fire burned strong in the upstairs hearth at the O'Ronan household. Acillus kept the fire going throughout the night and thus his and the Queen's room was quite warm. The fireplace was one of three in the three hundred and thirty three year old home. And though the house was old, the Cedar trees used at the time of its creation were still alive and well. The five Cedars grew tall over the years and their canopies were now nowhere near the roof, and had also been woven together so that they'd grow together to form a shelter over the house.

Acillus and Andraste slept throughout the night without any disturbance. And even though the Sun wasn't up yet it was still light enough to walk around without aid. The roosters were greeting the day out at the farms and dogs could be heard barking here or there. But Andraste began stirring at a low whirling sound, moving fast and then slow, then fast again. It stopped suddenly and that was what brought her to the fullest form of awake.

There it is again, she thought when she heard it once more. And her husband started moving around as well.

"Is that our boy?" she asked him.

"Yes. Cael's thinking with his new staff. Makes a sound like a Hilernian Storm when he gets it going," the King answered with his head still under the covers.

Andraste got out of bed and put on her heavy sunil robe, then went to stoke the fire.

"What place is the Sun?" he asked her.

She walked over to the middle window facing East, raised a heavy cloth and pushed open large wooden panels to look for the Sun.

"Just below the ridge. Not long before it shows itself."

Acillus jumped out of bed while saying, "I have to be quick. We won't get to spar again this morning. Forgive me."

"You're forgiven," she said with a fierce but playful look.

The tournaments would begin in a few hours and Acillus needed to be at Ideclan's Hall before they started. He dressed in his sunil tunic, wraps, and new cloak with Oak and Corvid over his Ideclan Amulet before heading outside to talk with his son.

"Acillus!" the Queen called to him from upstairs as he reached the downstairs back door leading out into the courtyard.

"Yes?" he called back up to her.

"I'm wearing your warm leather pants today since I know you're not. I was cold all day yesterday and will not be so again today."

"Of course my wolf," he said. "Bring some extra blankets so I can be warm beside you."

"Of course my lion."

Acillus turned and headed outside through the back door to join his son.

All the snow had been removed from the courtyard where Cael spun his broad staff. The courtyard was large enough for him to swing the staff at full length without hindrance while still leaving enough room for trees, stone tables, and other furnishings at its outskirts.

The staff had always been one of Cael's favorites to practice with. It was natural to transition a great many staff skills into the spear. The spear was his father's favorite weapon and a specialty of his mother's lineage. And it was known to those who knew him that when Cael spun his spear or staff, he was thinking.

Acillus didn't want to interrupt him as he knew the staff replicated the speed of his thoughts, but he didn't have to as Cael spun around on the ball of his foot and stopped when he saw his Da. He stood up straight and both walked toward each other before greeting the Clanii way. Cael kept his staff in his left hand through the greeting.

"Ahroo, vying with the wind for supremacy?" Acillus asked.

"Not in the least. Are you ready for the tournament?" Cael taunted as he started spinning the staff at his father.

"My wraps are on," Acillus answered in the same fashion.

The wraps were lengths of soft sunil cloth roughly three inches wide and nine feet long. They were wrapped around forearms and shins to pad the skin and help armor fit.

"Did Segais say anything about being at council this morning?" the King continued.

"He did, said he'd be there, so he might be already."

Acillus nodded before saying, "Good. Many irons are in the fire. Will you be at the practice fields before the tournaments start?"

"I will."

"Okay then. Are *you* ready for the tournament?"

Cael guffawed.

Acillus nodded and smiled, then exited the courtyard that they shared with four other houses, as the Prince leaned his staff against a tree and pulled the bit sticks from underneath his dark green cloak.

I've been ready, he thought.

Cael wasn't pleased about having to be deceitful by competing under a false identity in the tournament. And the aggression in his movements proved it as he trained. But he trusted Segais.

The sleep was well appreciated but the night too short for Cristin. He was half awake as he ate breakfast with Liadine and his wife Sylla on the main floor of The Fox's Hypothesis, while Elasus ran around all over the place. The night before had been calm at the inn compared to this morning, so Cristin wished his son wouldn't dash about so much as he kept an eye on him. But Liadine told him not to worry as the young child wasn't causing any trouble.

"So how does it all work? Will you be in the fights today?" Cristin asked.

"Not now, Raddox. I'll tell you on the walk there. Eat up, you'll need the energy," Liadine answered with a mischievous grin. And his wife Sylla gave him a little laugh to go with it.

When the food was finished, Liadine and Sylla paid for the meal while Cristin went to corral his son.

Something's gotten into him, he thought.

Elasus hadn't stopped running around all morning aside from pausing to talk to the old Philosian by the fire again. Cristin trusted his son's judgment. Elasus saved their lives a few times by his reactions to strangers. So when Cristin heard him laughing with the old man this morning, he thought he might be alright. But that synchronicity question he'd gotten from his son the night before almost disheartened him.

His murdered wife once loved a poem that used the word synchronicity, with a rhyme Cristin thought was tortured, but his wife had still loved it and said it often.

Better to think of fighting this morning than that one.

The word brought the possibility of tears whenever he thought of it.

"Ryker," Cristin said loudly.

Elasus heard his father call to him and before abiding, ran over to the old man and each did hand gestures Cristin couldn't have replicated on first try. It was the Philosian greeting and farewell. And the Edemarian smiled when he saw it. The

Philosians were always teaching and he thought it well his son was already learning.

"Did he teach you that?" Cristin asked when his son got close.

"Ya."

"Ya?" he corrected.

"Yes. Sorry, father."

"Did you ask him about synchronicities?"

Cristin couldn't help himself.

"I did and all he said was, 'later little one.'"

He thought that'd be the answer his son would get. Kandros wasn't so full of ale this morning as he was late last night.

Liadine and Sylla, as well as Cristin and his son walked out of The Fox's Hypothesis together and headed toward the practice fields. And despite it being a significant morning there weren't many people on the roads just yet.

Four festivals were held each year and everyone from the city grew up with the festivals and tournaments. They all knew the three hundredth and thirty third year of Ideclan would be seen in their lifetime. And now to add to that lifetime of building excitement, the three hundredth and thirty third Festival of Four Fires would also be a Prince's debut. A dynamic that always made the Declanii brackets interesting. Not every month had a festival but every month did have a tournament. When a tournament and festival were combined it made the event all the more grand. And when the festival was a milestone like this one; it was spectacular.

Only a few people were seen walking on the roads and most had that fighting look about them. Like they were about to contend in the tournaments as well, young lads like Cristin, fighting lads.

"Does it cost to enter?" Cristin asked suddenly, remembering he and his son had few coin left.

"Not a single copper piece. Just wait in line for the first time recruits and when you get to the front, tell them your name and fighting style, from there they'll pick which Talon's tournament to put you in. Make sure to get a wooden weapon that matches the overgrown one you left in your room. And don't forget to grab some of the protective leather armor as well. There's thick wool underneath and it's what you'll fight in."

Cristin had reluctantly left his sword in their room because it was an Edemarian Sword. And in the tradition of their homeland, Elasus kept the key to their room.

"What about a helm? Do you have one?"

"I have none."

"They have spares. We do all training and tournaments in our battle helms. Have to be comfortable fighting in them when the real time comes."

Cristin nodded.

"After that, you fight. This first day will be group fights.

If your group wins or you stand out, you advance. You'll be wearing that padded armor but people *will* be swinging so watch your head. Kill strikes are what take you out so watch out for those and give plenty in return. Remember to stay in control and don't lose your temper if you have one. If the Commanders or Declanii see you out of control in any way, you're disqualified. We work with precision and accuracy, we do not flail about."

"I'll remember," Cristin assured him.

The group of four came to a road where they'd part ways. Cristin decided to trust Liadine and Sylla with watching Elasus while he fought for the day. Liadine was Captain of one hundred scouts, and Elasus and Sylla were getting along well.

Liadine didn't have to fight during the first day. His rank put him in the brackets for the second day, but he was still going to continue on and show Cristin the way while his wife took Elasus to grab blankets and snacks.

Cristin and Elasus embraced as they said farewell. Then Elasus walked with Sylla down the road between homes made of living trees, thick planks, and stone while holding the old woman's hand and trying to skip. As the young boy and elderly woman walked happily away, Cristin watched them. This was the first time since leaving Edemar he'd be farther than a sprint away from his son, and he felt more than a little apprehensive.

"Come lad, he'll be fine. My wife's a good woman. Between her and all her friends, Ryker won't get a moments peace," Liadine told him for encouragement.

Cristin nodded and then started following the old scout toward the practice fields again. As they made their way, the streets grew busier. It wasn't just fighters heading there anymore. Now there were carts and wagons and all manner of people. Cristin noticed some of them were merchants. Foreign travelers were easy to spot. And the others he saw were those going to secure good views at one of the twelve practice fields, all of which surrounded the original field. There were far too many people for Cristin to continue distinguishing which would be fighting and which wouldn't.

"When Ridec and the Thirteen of Old founded this city," Liadine began as they went. "They only needed one field for training, which they created outside of the original walls that are now Old Ideclan. But as the city expanded and its inhabitants multiplied, so did the army, until each of the twelve families who followed the O'Ronans were responsible for not only a file of Declanii, but also a Talon of one thousand soldiers, along with their scout and archer contingencies, each needing its own practice field. The O'Ronans have never had a contingent of Declanii or a Talon of their own. It's part of the symbolism that they're for the people. So instead they started funding the four Supply Talons some time back.

At the center of all practice fields is the main field. It's the first and will always be the oldest, the field reserved for King and Declanii. That's where the last fights of the tournament will be held. The fields have been enveloped by the city over the years much the same way we've been enveloped by the tournaments," Liadine finished.

They smelled fresh meats and stews along with other aromas as they made their way. Almost every shop they walked past was closed. A barber, a book store, the music shop, the tailors, a large textile warehouse, the jeweler, a gem store, a sculptor's studio, a saddle and tack expert: all these shops that'd normally be packed with activity were as empty as though abandoned. Cristin saw a nice sign on the sign maker's door that said, 'Gone to Tournament.' He also saw a toy maker closing up his shop after grabbing a large bundle of wooden swords to sell on the fields.

"Which Talon do you think I'll fight for?" Cristin asked as they paused to let a cart go by.

"Pray it be the Tenth!" the old scout exclaimed. "But that depends on openings in the ranks. It'll also depend on how many new rooks there are. All things the Tournament Master and his criers will know."

When they reached the tournament grounds, Cristin's eyes grew wide. The streets and fields were filled with people, including a female Declanii; her heavy sunil cloak, unmistakable. The young man from Edemar was taken aback by how big the city really was.

The Sun wasn't two fingers' width above the mountains and already there were flutes, lyres, bodhrans, and other instruments being played while people danced to the music and warmed themselves by fires.

When they got closer to the lines, Liadine stopped them and pointed the rest of the way for Cristin, as well as filled him in on which field he himself would be located.

"Alright, that's it Raddox, right over there is where you go. My youngest is fighting today, Enay, for the Sixth Talon. So that's where Sylla and I will be watching Ryker. It's the farthest field middle North. And I'll bring Ryker over to watch you fight as well, just find me and tell me which Talon you're in."

"Please look after my son with vigilance, as if he were

your own," Cristin asked from his heart.

"It is done. Under Sylla's and my watch, no harm shall come to your boy."

"On your honor as Captain of all Scouts for the Tenth Talon?"

Liadine laughed before saying, "On my honor you young giant."

Cristin thanked him, then walked over to the lines that branched out from one very long table. Thinking all lines led to his destination, he chose one of the middle ones. He was at least twenty five fighters back from the front and it was about the same for each of the twelve lines' length.

There were conversations all around and he could still hear the music. But over it all he heard the Pathplacer Criers at the front taking names and asking which area of the tournament they'd be challenging: archery, combatant, or scout.

Earlier at breakfast, Cristin learned from Liadine that the scouts' actual tournaments and initiations were held outside the festivals up at the mountains of Caibre Pass. But the old Ideclaner told Cristin no more when the Edemarian said he'd be challenging for a combatant position.

Cristin had to ponder how he'd handle the Pathplacer Crier's question.

If I tell them my fighting style is Edemarian Sword then all will know where I'm from. So I'll tell them instead I'm a one handed longswordsman and simply hold the Edemarian back from the way I fight.

Shortly after he joined the lines, Cristin became grateful Liadine had brought him there as early as he did because they grew substantially behind him. Not everyone in the lines would make it into the army, but many always tried.

Of the twelve tournaments held every year, only four were for induction and rank, the four that were held during festivals: two for the King's Army and two for the Queen's Army. The Queen's Army held their tournaments and festivals during the new moons instead of full ones like the King's.

Cristin waited patiently as the lines moved. Most people he thought were likely Ideclaners but many were from other lands as well. He was looking to see if any were Edemarian. None as far as he could tell were. But as soon as he began relaxing, those at the front gradually looked his way, and then a few more. They appeared to be speaking in hushed tones and looking straight at him. Suspicion almost overcame him until he realized they were looking straight past him to a group of four who'd stopped walking toward the lines a ways behind, and were speaking to one another.

Two of them had long blonde hair though one was more of a golden tint. One had very long black hair in neat braids, and the other Cristin recognized as the man with burning red and yellow hair from the night before; the one with the Philosian innkeeper. His hair looked like it was on fire with its color variation, hence the Fianna's hair was often referred to as burning red. Cristin deduced they were all descendants of the thirteen families from Clanii. And judging by how much everyone payed attention to them, he presumed they were well known.

Cristin picked out the leader of the four. He wasn't as tall as the man with burning red hair or as broad as the shorter, blonde haired man. He bore a slight resemblance to the black haired one, but there was something distinct about him. Cristin sensed the other three were very protective of him by their body language.

The Edemarian began staring at the man along with everyone else as he tried figuring out if he knew him or not. There were a great many descendants of Clanii around his age and well over one hundred thousand people who lived at Ideclan.

And still... Cristin was beginning to think the leader looked a lot like an adult version of someone he met a long time ago at Edemar.

Cristin realized he was staring at the man as the man turned his head and looked at the lines.

Prince Cael then turned back toward his friends and said what looked like 'fight well,' before walking off through the practice fields. Cael wouldn't have to sign in this morning and his false identity already had.

Cristin turned around with many others when the Prince's three friends made their way to join the tournament lines.

Soon, the large Edemarian walked up toward the table to declare admission. At the table were many of the Pathplacer Criers, and on the table was a bowl with silversage burning within it. The smoke was starting to billow through the lines and bathe the contenders.

Cristin reached one of the criers at the middle of the table and without looking up from his quill and paper, the crier asked, "Name?"

"Raddox."

"Two d's like the hero from Lore?"

"Yes," he answered with a hint of reluctance.

"Archery, combatant, or scout?"

"Combatant."

"What's your weapon?"

"One handed longsword."

"Do you have a wooden one?"

"I do not."

"That's not a problem. So, Raddox, are you prepared to join this busy and experienced army?"

"I am."

"You'll be contesting for the Sixth Talon; farthest field in the middle to the North. They're in need of one handed longswordsmen."

Cristin gave his thanks and walked to where they handed out the padded leather armor and tournament weapons. The criers had a less frustrating time finding a wooden weapon for the Edemarian than they did a leather suit and helm that'd fit him. But after searching they found some, and then Cristin was off to the Sixth's practice field. Which was where Liadine would be watching his own son, Enay, fight. And his wife would be watching Elasus. Cristin was thankful he'd be next to his son.

There was hardly any room to maneuver as he made his way. People were everywhere, making it difficult to differentiate road from field. And it took more than a few Ideclaners pointing him along for Cristin to continue heading in the right direction.

It was taking him longer to get there than he thought it should, but he was able to save time by sneaking through a portable store holding someone's wares.

He began jogging through the tight mass after noticing folk forming up on the fields he passed, and soon he could hear rules being shouted. His jog turned into a run as he angled around people, carts, and campfires. There were more humans here than he'd ever seen at any one time in his life. Not even at the great Summer Festival of Fwynndarlanai were there this many people. He'd never forget that festival. It was the one where he was attacked by a group of four assassins and received the large scar down his chest.

Finally he arrived at his field, made certain by the six wolves running in a circle on the banners stuck in the ground. Then he began searching for where Liadine and his family had set up because no one was forming on his Talon's field just yet.

Cristin noticed the many looks he received from the people he passed. He was bigger and taller than everyone and everyone appeared to notice. Until at last he found his son and Sylla.

When Elasus saw him he ran to his father and began talking about all the different experiences he'd already had during that short while. But then stopped his speech at his father's command.

"Tell me later, when I can concentrate on what you say. My mind is preparing for the tournament right now."

With a big hug, Elasus left his father and ran back to Sylla. Cristin noticed Liadine and Enay walking toward him as he watched his own son run up to Liadine's wife. The old scout's son had many of his father's features, but he was easily recognizable as a warrior and not a scout.

"Raddox, fighting for the Sixth! Not bad. This is my youngest, Enay," Liadine told him.

"Hello, Enay. Good to meet you."

"Well met," Enay said as they shook hands. Enay had braided brown hair as long as his father's shoulder length white hair.

After greetings and introductions, Cristin followed Liadine's son to the practice field proper. And as they joined the group now forming, they heard a Tournament Crier for their Talon start to call out rules and instructions. He showed them a bag of sticks. The end of each stick in the bag was painted one of four colors. And among many instructions, the crier told them which part of the field to go to depending on what color of stick they pulled.

Cristin felt the anticipation growing within him. Some of the other fields were already alive. Loud shouts and cheers permeated the air. It was Mard, the Fifteenth of Midwinter, and the Three Hundredth and Thirty Third Festival of Four Fires had begun.

In moment's time, Cristin was standing off to the side with a large group of warriors who possessed the same color stick as him. A Tournament Crier counted out ten men and separated them from the rest. Cristin was among them. And the crier had to yell so they could hear above the roar of the crowds.

"All right, you know the drill! You ten fight against ten from each of the other three color groups! Either your group wins or you stand out singularly to advance! So better chances if you become a team! You heard the crier on how matches are scored! There are four Declanii as well as eight Tournament Criers judging this Talon today! We'll be looking for precision and control! Don't disappoint!"

Cristin smiled. He was ready.

The four groups of ten were called back onto the center of the field and each advanced, shoulder to shoulder from the cardinal directions. Cristin was the farthest man West in the Southernmost group and he felt as though he were water crashing over a dam as they continued walking toward one another.

"Fight!" the crier yelled.

Cristin didn't charge like an Edemarian and stayed in formation. He wanted to advance but not stand out.

The four teams clashed at the middle.

His one handed longsword wasn't familiar but he still held the line, staying close to his team and keeping anyone from reaching their backs via his flank. A clumsy block almost caused him to trip over a teammate but they recovered. And their unified actions won the round.

"Fought before, have we?" Liadine asked him with his mischievous grin as Cristin reached them after the fight.

"Leave him be you old coyote. Well done young man. Fight like that and you'll be protecting the people in no time," Sylla told him.

Liadine pointed out one of the Declanii who'd been judging Cristin's fight.

"You see that man in sunil?"

"Yes."

"He'll be who you fight under, Ainnileas Shymurrow, Sixth Talon Commander. He's a good lad, Clanii lad, has a good head on his shoulders, really turned the Sixth around. You have a good Talon, Raddox, but not as good as the Tenth!"

Cristin smiled. Eleven more fights would happen before his next round so there was time to relax. That was when he noticed how dry the fields were. And it surprised him how there wasn't a single sign of mud.

When it became time for Cristin to fight again, Elasus wished him well as he walked back onto the field.

"Fight!"

The Edemarian stayed with his team, resisting the urge to run at his competition. Cristin was in the middle of the line when the four teams broke apart and clashed. He became embroiled in single combat with a veteran who wanted to win. The longsword felt light in his hands and it was difficult to use effectively. He was almost taken out, but a teammate helped by slashing the veteran in the back and fortunately his group was victor.

The next round he fought in went well with his team defeating the other three by working together. And Cristin smiled while walking off the field with Liadine's son.

Liadine cheered for both him and Enay excitedly, as they were on the same team that round.

"Not bad!" he said to them as they neared.

"When's the next fight?" Cristin asked.

"After the rest of the fights for this round, the Sixth takes a break. Gives us a chance to see what all the other cheering is about. So let's go."

Elasus walked as the group made their way around the fields, but Cristin ensured he stayed close because he kept getting distracted by all the numerous children running everywhere.

For the first time in his life, Elasus didn't feel a constant state of urgency or worry from his father. It was also the first time the young Edemarian had seen his father relaxed and talking freely with strangers. And that led Elasus to know he liked Ideclan.

"What would you like to see, Ryker?" Liadine asked as they walked. "Archery, or combat?"

"I'd like to see the flight of an arrow."

"Archery it is then!" the old scout bellowed.

"Liadine," Cristin said as they walked. "Who was that man from the inn last night, the one with red and yellow hair talking to the innkeeper? I saw him again this morning."

"That was Irhanach Fianna. There's some Ideclaners with red hair but none in all the lands have hair like the Fianna's. They're one of two families not originally from Clanii who left with Ridec and founded Ideclan."

"Who's the other family not originally from Clanii?" Elasus asked. He was enjoying piecing together the histories he was learning.

"That'd be the Mullquanes. But where they're from is a closely guarded secret of theirs."

"Why?" the child continued.

"You're gonna have to ask one of them. And don't be afraid to. They won't take offense, they just won't tell you."

It didn't take them long to reach the archery fields since they were located not too far from the Sixth's. But by the time of their arrival the first day's contest was almost complete.

When Liadine and his group got there it was down to the final three archers. Two of them the old scout had never seen before and the third was a young man named Ohelathe Mullquane. Cristin recognized him as one of the four who everyone paid attention to at the sign up lines, the one with long black hair in small neat braids.

The Mullquane lad was next to let fly and it appeared he was last as he nocked an arrow.

The Tournament Crier gave the signal.

Ohelathe drew back and let loose quickly. His arrow hit dead center. He loosed his second and it hit one finger's width away from the first. Then the young lad loosed his last, and it hit just above the other two in equal distance, forming a small triangle and the crowd cheered.

"Whoa! That was tricky tree!" Elasus proclaimed, using a Fwynndarlanai expression.

The old scout grinned as he said, "Come now. This contest is over. If we hurry we can watch another fight before your father must again."

The small group tried making it to another field but all were too crowded and time was running out so they headed back to the Sixth's.

When they reached the Sixth's, they heard a Tournament Crier calling the next combatants back onto the field. Cristin picked up his wooden longsword, donned his helm again, and headed out. This would be the last fight of the day for him and if he won, he was guaranteed a place in the brackets for the second day, which guaranteed him a place on the army.

Cristin got into position with his teammates.

"Fight!" the Crier yelled.

The warriors on his team formed a shield wall but Cristin had no shield. To the Edemarians a sword could protect you better than a shield ever could. And the bigger the sword the more protection it gave. The words of his old masters flowed through his mind as he thought of two choices.

He could fight with his teammates or go out alone and draw many his way.

Hide the Edemarian from your style, he thought.

He stepped back to the rear of the shield wall and attacked from behind its protection.

His team almost became enveloped as they did their best to defend. But half were taken out before the other half became aware of it.

I have to win to advance!

Cristin made his move and broke away. The longsword went from its defensive maneuvers to vicious strikes. His speed and ferocity were like that of a viper. He felt the need to win so he unleashed his Edemarian fury, and two men were taken out swiftly.

Cristin looked to see if any of his teammates were still fighting and it saved him. He was just in time to block a downward strike barely coming into view before pushing the fighter away and repositioning himself.

He ducked quickly underneath the next swing and then deflected another's strike. Cristin blocked an attack to his left and dispatched the man across the chest with his sword, then swung his sword back the other way to ward off more attackers.

Some of the others stepped back and formed a shield wall, and one of them was Prince Cael in disguise.

The Prince had put extra padding in his leather armor

to make him look heavyset. His full helm covered his disguised hair and face. And he fought nowhere near to his ability.

Cristin ran for them and as he did he felt a sharp sting travel across his leg. He knew one of them had snuck behind him and when he turned he got jabbed in the back fairly hard by someone else.

The other team had won and they wasted no time in celebrating. Cristin looked around and realized he'd been the last man standing to oppose them. Prince Cael noticed it too. He also noticed the Edemarian in his style.

Cristin stood tall but his head was slightly down. He didn't know if he'd get to advance.

"Hey, you," a demanding voice called to him.

Cristin turned.

"You advance," Ainnileas the Disciplined said, then the Commander of the Sixth Talon walked away to talk with a few Tournament Criers.

"Thank you," from under his breath was all Cristin could muster past the relief he felt.

As he walked off the field he had a big smile on his face, and it grew bigger when he saw his son's smile running straight for him

"Did you make it, father?" the boy asked when he reached him.

"Yes, son! Making it to the second day gets me a spot

on the army. I think we're here for good," he said with great happiness as he took off his helm.

Elasus let out a cheer that was dwarfed by the rest of the crowd, then the boy and his father walked off the field together. Cristin was met with much applause and congratulations by spectators, especially Liadine and Sylla.

They all stayed for what would be the final fight of the day for that field. Liadine and Sylla's son, Enay, was one of the combatants and he did well, helping his team advance. All around it was a good first day for the little troop, and both Enay and Cristin put their names in for the second day.

Everyone started leaving the fields but they'd be back shortly after they ate. During the first night of each festival, but especially the Festival of Four Fires, most went back to the fields and gathered around the fires that kept them warm all day, and listened to their favorite stories or news from other lands. Many people liked moving from fire to fire, listening to different tales as the night went on, changing the style of storytelling and mixing up the conversation.

Before that however, the first dinner of every festival was eaten at home with friends and family, and this night, each family was given a portion of the deer hunted by the Declanii.

Cristin and his son were of course invited to eat with Liadine and his large family; and they agreed. On their way back to the fields after dinner they stopped by The Fox's Hypothesis so Cristin could grab their wool blankets. Then they were off to the fields again.

A friend of Liadine's was a storyteller and performing this night. So the scout led them to the fire where he practiced his craft. All took seats as close to the fire as they could. The group around the bard wasn't the largest on the fields but Cristin could tell right away he was skilled. And the Edemarian found himself looking forward to a good story.

The bard was in the middle of a tale which Cristin had both heard and read. It was the story of Arashrillian pirates during the Seventh Age, about a few hundred years before the True City of Arashrill was founded, who tried attacking a fleet of slower Gisspor ships as they embarked on a trading expedition. By all accounts the Gisspor traders should have been overrun. But their supreme knowledge of the weather and seas enabled them to bait the Arashrillians deep into a storm. And every pirate lost their life in the encounter.

Cristin enjoyed a tale of smarts over strength but looked at the faces in the crowd as he enjoyed this one, discerning if any were Arashrillian. The story was from long ago and those of Arashrill had long since been an intrinsic part of The Kinned Lands. But he still imagined it might offend a few.

As he looked for Arashrillians he caught sight of a man walking their way. He recognized him as the Clanii lad from the tournament lines, the leader of the group of four who'd grabbed everyone's attention. The lad was wearing a heavy dark brown cloak and now that he was getting closer, Cristin started thinking he really did know who this Clanii was.

Cael was just about to reach them when the bard finished. Then the crowd gave their applause and started talking to one another.

Cristin was going to ask Liadine who the man was so he could be sure. But before he was able to, the storyteller yelled, "Prince Cael!"

The young Ravenborne stopped and looked at him. His heavy dark brown cloak was bundled warmly around himself, as well as what now appeared to be a brown blanket matching in color that served as a mantle around his shoulders.

"Would you like to hear a story?" the bard asked with a grin.

"I would," Cael answered, and then moved in to sit down beside them all.

"What would you like to hear?"

"How about: The Youngest Clan of Woodrats," he said while taking a seat on a bench next to Elasus and Cristin. He gave the two he sat next to a slight nod and then the bard his full attention.

"This story begins," the bard said as he threw a piece of wood on the fire, and many embers flew up. "Long before the Ages were ever recorded, during a time when the natural and movable would still combine, when the Ancients walked in force and the animals we know today were first rising in number."

The children forgot the cold as they drank hot chocolate and listened to the tale, with the crackling fire adding to the ambiance.

"There was a clan of woodrats during that time. Woodrats themselves had been around for many cycles, but these were the youngest of the entire tribe. They were unique in that they befriended other animals of the forest. The elder woodrats were against this, but the young ones didn't change their ways because of it. They appreciated the knowledge learned from their forest friends.

One day a rabbit came and told the young clan of an impending danger. The young clan went to their elders with this news and were shunned away, dismissed as disobedient children for trusting a friend not of the woodrats.

And so the young woodrats set their own clan in motion. Their best scouts gathered all the information they could and learned of a threat never seen by the likes of anyone they knew… turtles!" the bard said humorously serious, and Elasus thought that was funny.

"But these were no ordinary turtles. These turtles were large, they had black shells, and were very smart. They were among the oldest clans of the Turtle Tribe. The rumor of their terror had already spread far and wide through the low forest creatures and the woodrats were among the last to know. The young woodrats tried finding survivors of their battles but none would talk. Until finally, one scout happened upon an old mole from far away.

'Ya, I seen 'em,' said the old mole. 'They march as one, snapping and biting as they go. Their shells are as armor where it covers them. Their formations allow none to get past. They're fast for turtles and can maneuver if you get behind them. There's no hope.'

The young scout thanked the old mole and brought back his report to the clan. The woodrats devised a plan, and when they brought that plan to their elders, the only answer they received was, 'no, we need the help of no others.'

The young ones weren't dissuaded and continued on. The first part of their plan consisted of seeking out the local prairie dogs for help. Does anyone remember why?"

"I do," a six year old boy said.

"Yes, young one?"

"They needed the prairie dog tunnels to hide and scare the turtles."

"Correct. The prairie dog clan had vast tunnels running under their territory, a territory that was reportedly next to be attacked by the black shelled turtles. Their plan was to use these tunnels to ambush and encircle the turtles. Does anyone remember who else they enlisted to help them?"

"The crows!" another child shouted.

"The crows indeed. The crows were asked to make spears out of sticks for the woodrats. For the crow can whittle wood with perfection. They often make hooks to hunt bugs from trees. And the ends of the sticks they made for the woodrats were all pieces of artistry in their own right, viciously carved to do the most damage.

But the prairie dog tunnels were also for another part of the plan, does anyone remember that?"

A four year old girl shouted out, "The tunnels were too small fer the turtles to get in ta!"

"Exactly, young one! Their safety was, when pursued by the turtles, they'd run back into the tunnels and another woodrat would come up from a different tunnel to continue the attack. Once they confused and surrounded the turtles, they'd pierce them from all sides using the spears the crow clan made.

After much planning and preparation, the morning of

the attack finally came and the black shelled turtles could be heard marching through the mist. The woodrats listened to the vibrations of their march rumbling the forest floor as they waited in the underground tunnels.

The other animals started scattering in the face of the turtles. Few stayed to fend off the intruders. A badger stayed to fight that day, but even her presence didn't deter the black shells.

Woodrats waited below tunnel entrances, listening for the signal that would call them to charge. The marching grew louder and more of those who stayed behind began to flee in panic.

When the turtles arrived it looked as though there was little resistance so they charged in without pause.

A badger's snarl was heard and the signal given.

Woodrats poured from the tunnels and attacked with spears in their mouths. The turtles were startled and broke formation. When a turtle chased a woodrat, the woodrat went down a tunnel and another woodrat speared the turtle.

They did this, staying within the plan until the turtles found themselves overwhelmed. When the black shells realized they were close to defeat they tried fighting wildly to break free but it was too late. The woodrats closed in on them, and vanquished them."

The bard paused for effect before continuing.

"The young clan knew it was unwise to waste anything that lasts. So they stripped the dead turtles of their shells and brought them home. For many moons, they tried figuring out how to make use of these shells as armor for themselves, but none could make them work.

Until years later, a few that'd been working on them got frustrated and broke two shells when they were slammed together in just the right way.

The woodrats picked up the pieces and started experimenting. Soon, they were able to form the shell shards into overlapping segmented plate armor, form fitting to their bodies. When they showed these new creations to the rest of their clan, they were told to shatter all the shells and make suits of armor.

Those very suits have been passed down within their clan's families ever since. And since that day, those young woodrats have become known as the tribe we call: armadillos."

The crowd cheered. His story didn't disappoint.

"What's your name, lad?" Prince Cael asked the boy he sat next to.

"Ryker, and yours?"

"I'm Cael," the Prince told him before looking up at his father. "And this is your father, Raddox, is it?"

"Yes, Prince," Cristin said, trying not to look directly at him.

He thought he was caught. Cristin had known he knew him ever since the bard called him by name. They went on a royal hunting trip together at Edemar when they were younger.

"Your son speaks well. And I hear you fight well. I'll be sure to watch a match of yours."

Cristin nodded.

If he does remember me, he isn't acting like it. Or maybe that's why he wants to watch one of my fights.

"Fight well tomorrow," Cael said as he got up and walked off.

Cristin's body was completely tense from the conversation. And he slightly jolted when Liadine put a hand on his shoulder.

"Second night at Ideclan and you're already talking to our Prince," the old scout said with a grin.

Cristin's edginess subsided as the small group left the fields and walked back toward The Fox's Hypothesis. On the way, he noticed there weren't many people drinking ale at the inns compared to the night before. The more he looked around he realized he didn't see anyone drinking ale at all. And this he thought unusual, especially for a festival.

"Liadine, why is there no one drinking at the inns like last night?"

"Traditionally, Ideclaners don't drink on the first night of any festival. And you won't find many combatants willing to give opponents an edge during the next part of the tournaments. The first nights are for the families to spend with one another. But tomorrow night, everyone will be having a loud time again. You can be sure."

"And what of the four years of training new recruits have to go through? I just remembered about that today when I overheard some of the combatants talking."

"That's only for the descendants of Clanii, never you mind about that. They have to follow the path Ridec O'Ronan and their ancestors took on the Clanii's second exodus."

"And what of the women?" Cristin continued.

"They have to pass the four years of training as well."

"I meant, why did the women not fight in the tournament today? I've read that Clanii man and woman fight together."

"The women mostly fight in their own tournaments. There's only one tournament a year where men and women fight together. But I know what you're getting at as it's a common misconception. The men and women are not part of the same army. They are two armies. Acillus leads one while Andraste leads the other."

"One more question then."

"Ask it, lad."

"What's done with all the snow that's been taken off the training fields? I noticed they were incredibly dry for Winter."

"Some of it's melted and given to the animals, some is used to build snow mountains throughout the city for kids. Ideclan flourishes because it wastes nothing, not even snow," Liadine said with satisfaction.

Cristin didn't ask any more questions on the way and neither did Elasus. Both were tired and focused on their bed back at The Fox's Hypothesis. When they got there, the boy and his father said farewell to Liadine and Sylla, then went straight into their room and fell fast asleep.

Declanii

Chronicle Nine

I write this knowing full well it may be the last time I ever touch ink to parchment, as it is only hours before many shall be touching blade to blood. Therefore I'll spend my last free moments with what has always brought me peace, the uniting of word and paper through thought and quill.

For four years now, we've been battling the Runidareeans, fighting, skirmishing, driving them North into their own lands, diminishing them down to their weakest point. And yet they are still many. What's left of them have rallied against us at the valley below, forty thousand to our ten thousand. Four to one. Troublesome numbers surely, but more troubling are the lack of possibilities for any kind of retreat, as to our backs are sheer cliffs formed by the Quenie River below. And were any of us to consider running toward either flank, the Runidareean horsemen would simply ride us down. We are trapped.

I trust our Lead General, the young Prince Acillus, I sincerely do. I know the swiftness of his thought firsthand. And it has become quite apparent to me he studied the arts of war with the same vigorousness as he did my lessons. I know this because the Prince took command at the very beginning of this campaign, when his father, King Ailither, was stricken use of an arm by arrow for the rest of his days. It has been Acillus who's led the army to victory these last four years, so I trust him when he says this piece of land is exactly where we want to be. Though, it has tested the depths of my trust completely. If it hadn't been for these last four years, I know not whether my faith could handle such a test. More than once I nearly put to use my knowledge in service to save my life, but thankfully, the true moment never arose due to the dashing of Acillus, and so the masquerade is still intact.

As I look back and consider those moments where my long life was almost brought to its end, I must face one more fact upon reflection, one truth I have come to realize by being a part of this campaign. I know now that we of The Kinned Lands have truly been at peace, because Ideclan has been at war. This is most peculiar since those who founded Ideclan, the Clanii, were never warriors or fighters at origin, but poets and sailors with a bit of adventure in their hearts. And it was many years ago when the ancestor of Prince Acillus, a man named Ridec O'Ronan, made a choice that would change this.

More than three centuries ago, Ridec was in a position of leadership among the Clanii when friend turned foe bid him choose migration as the wisest path for their posterity. After the reasons for his decision were brought to a council of his kinsman, only twelve of the seventy seven families chose to follow him and his, and not the entirety of the families, only specific lines of them. One of these families, the Fiannas, were from an island just above and to the Northeast of the Clanii's island. And another family originated far from the area all together, the fierce and proud Mullquanes.

The rest of the Clanii, not thinking the threat Ridec foresaw was legitimate, or that he was trying to sow seeds of division through intrigue, mocked and laughed at the once respected families as they readied for their voyage. This was unexpected within the Clanii culture. Never were they completely divided and at no time did they belittle one another. Something had changed in them and Ridec knew what the catalyst for that was.

The island the Clanii inhabited then is the smallest and most Southwesterly among an archipelago of four. Morrigan, the largest island of the archipelago, enlisted the Clanii in an alliance much against their preference. This generation like most generations of Clanii before them had never picked up a true weapon and were reluctant to go to war. Even so, they did extremely well for Morrigan and the archipelago during their battles with invaders from the North, and so many riches and praises were given to them. Which blinded all except Ridec and a few others to the fact that because their external threat was removed, Morrigan was now about to wage war on them.

The riches obtained from Morrigan hadn't rendered Ridec sightless, nor made him forget the ancient Clanii Tenets. So he led those who chose to go with him down to the boats prepared for their voyage, and the thirteen families sailed West in hopes of finding more land, another island perhaps. But a long lasting storm brought them far East above and then beyond the Impassable Straits.

Some would argue that the next part of their voyage is a myth, that Treewolves and other Ancients don't exist. But sagas, writings, and earthly evidence suggest otherwise. Ridec himself had a very close connection to this ancient past, he was of the Ravenborne himself, as have all O'Ronans been since him. It is widely accepted that because of this connection, Ridec and the thirteen families landed within the realm of the Treewolves after the storm. For countless have tried to find these Ancients without success. Few things are truly known about the wise Treewolves, and since the Ages have been recorded even fewer humans are known to have come in contact with them.

The best account of an Ancient during recent times is that written by Ridec himself. He articulates very comprehensibly and at length the experience he and the thirteen families had with these massive tree beings. In his account he also records the nifu ellwulle, or prophecies, as they've become known. But this phrase's original translation from Old Clanii roughly means willed intentions in the Common Tongue. And this may be more accurate to their nature indeed. The nifu ellwulle were shared with the Clanii by a Treewolf whose name is written as Wardolf. The conversations exchanged with Wardolf were the primer to change Ridec and everyone with him, to alter them in such a way that they'd be willing to accept these, willed intentions, as others have done so in the past. All of whom have failed. These other cultures who failed were all chosen for the nifu ellwulle based on many aspects. But the most similar reason to the Clanii for being chosen was how peaceful they were, and for a very important reason.

It is said that accepting these prophecies magnifies the energies and abilities of they who accept them, that the decisions they make begin to affect more than their immediate surroundings. That they forever grow stronger and wiser as the strength and wisdom of the entire line is held within the youngest of that line. That their actions build upon themselves and what they do returns to them exponentially. It is said they shape the very world. However, the setback with which the Treewolves have encountered when sharing the nifu ellwulle throughout the Ages is that one of two things has always happened to the culture who accepts.

The first is, even though the energy and ability around they who accept is expanded due to their own choices, their culture is still not capable of defending itself and therefore its ways, values, and ideals do not continue. Or two, they lose sight of their peaceful, equal ways, and become so immersed in war that it destroys them from within. And now the once unified people lack all resemblance of what they were, having fallen into patterns of dominance and destruction. Either way, each is considered unsuccessful.

I think what the prophecy bearers are seeking is to walk the balance in between, so that a culture of peace may prevail and the true reasons of being be sought without fear.

Ridec was reluctant to accept the nifu ellwulle during his stay with the Treewolves. It would mean that he, along with his brothers and sisters of the sea, would properly learn of war and then have to put that knowledge to use; for those who accept such things as the nifu ellwulle gain much attention from others. Having been from Clanii, Ridec read many books and scrolls about the Treewolves and societies they interacted with in the past, so he knew all too well the dangers that awaited after acceptance. The council taken with his kin that day however, guided him to accept, showing that all of them accepted. And so once again they set out to sea, this time, to fulfill an old prophecy.

After leaving the Treewolves, Ridec and his companions spent four years along the path suggested to them by the Ancients; sailing, walking, battling, and especially learning, before they came to a small outlet of land my people have called home since the Fifth Age. Little more than three centuries ago, Ridec and the thirteen families came to my people at the close of their voyage, asking for the privilege to build a city so close to our own. For the small peninsula that is still our home, and the calm bay just to the West of it, and much more mind you, matched the exact description given to Ridec of their destination. As did we Philosians who inhabit it.

There was a malicious threat to my people at that time, a lethally corrupt King from the East who drained life force from all the land, and his name was Tarkin Erra, a truly brutal being. Because of him and many other reasons, the wisest of Philos known as the Ten and Seven aligned with Ridec and the thirteen families that day.

Declanii

The Philosians knew the Clanii to be peaceful and enjoyed profound words in the prophecies shared by Ridec. Striking an accord, our two cultures banded together and rallied a third, Teker Ren, to our cause. The three peoples formed a rebellion which they soon referred to as the Tribellion.

Setting out to make the land safe to inhabit once more, the Tribellion Alliance defeated their foe, and Ridec O'Ronan himself slayed the invading King, Tarkin Erra. Which created a blood feud between the O'Ronans and the Erra that has lasted to this day.

When all returned to the peninsula after that campaign, the Philosians were more than willing to help their new allies with the rock work to build a city. The Clanii chose to call their new home, Ideclan, a very sacred word in their ancient language.

Since the official founding of Ideclan on Winter Solstice of the year Seven Hundred and Sixty One of the Eighth Age, we've recorded time as the Ninth Age per the Treewolves' request. And to this day, Clanii and Philosian cultures have grown intricately and wonderfully interwoven together, while still retaining their strong individualities.

But the Clanii are something different from what they once were. In Ridec's day, just after accepting the nifu ellwulle, they were a relatively simple people wielding crude weaponry, secondhand items mostly familiarized to them by the lands they just traveled through. They were a peaceful and thoughtful people who wanted nothing more than to live their own lives and be left alone to do it. But over the years they've changed the way in which they manifest this. Before the nifu ellwulle were accepted, they chose to flee for the sake of keeping their ways alive, and now, they stand for them. The Ideclaners led by the descendants of Clanii have immersed themselves in the school of war, only to become its finest students.

The young Acillus himself, descendant of Clanii, leads the Declanii, apex of what their new ways have become. They are one hundred and fifty six of the most inimitable fighters among all the lands. It is they who when at the center of the formation lead and inspire all others. And it is these men who share Acillus' sentiment that we're on good ground, cut off from all retreat and surrounded...

But alas... the Horn of Ravenborne has just been sound, calling all ranks to muster and I too, must go. I promise never to cease putting thought to paper if my eyes see Sun tomorrow.

Yet before I part I wish to record one more thought. As I reflect upon this situation I must think about that fulcrum which keeps the line level between a peaceful people and a warring people. The line that separates a peaceful people who cannot defend themselves from a warring people who have no choice but to implode. And I ponder where our fulcrum is along this line. We're not voyaging on the side of peace to the point of defenselessness, this is certain. Which leaves only two other options: either we've not tipped the balance in either way, or, at some point we've become too much of a warring people and are already marching down our own path of destruction.

Written by Arakkus of Philos
Rone, the Thirty Second of Latesummer, 306th Year of the Ninth Age
Just before the Last Battle of the Runidareeans

Declanii

Chapter Ten

"Are you ready for the Moon Race, dear?"

"I am," Ashnayn said as she fixed her shark tooth knife to her diving vest. "This is my favorite race of all."

"It's the hardest race of all!" her handmaiden exclaimed.

But the Princess' mind was only on the competition ahead.

"Will you grab my water gourds please?" Ashnayn asked, and the handmaiden left the room.

If I win this race again, everyone of all Twenty Tribes will know I'm the best. Then with the Champion's Request, I can get the people to help change the chiefs' minds about me marrying Gowgluni.

"I have them, dear, but it sounds like," the handmaiden began as she came back.

The eight guards assigned to Ashnayn then barged into her room without permission.

"All Chief Daughter, come with us."

"To the Moon Race?"

"No. It has been declared under teeth and bone that now is the auspicious time for the making of your wedding gown."

"Now! That takes hours! I have a race to win!"

"No one may defy the rights of teeth and bone. It's been declared. Come with us."

"It was declared so I couldn't race! You have to see that! Or are you eight blind like everyone else?"

"We see what we must. And now we must see you to the wedding grounds for your gown making. The makers are already there."

After thinking it over she said, "Give me a moment and I'll go with you."

"You have one moment," the leader acquiesced, then left with the rest to wait outside.

The handmaiden rushed to Ashnayn and said, "He doesn't want you to race."

"I know," Ashnayn agreed frustratingly.

"What are you going to do?"

The Princess looked at the water gourds strung around her handmaiden and pointed at them, saying, "Bring those to the starting line. I'll be there when the conch is blown."

"How?" the handmaiden asked nervously.

"Do it!" Ashnayn commanded, and the elderly woman bowed before leaving.

The All Chief Daughter left the house and was escorted

by her guards. As they walked to the wedding grounds, every step filled Ashnayn with disgust. When they arrived she saw the makers already spreading their fabrics, feathers, and other equipment. Then she looked to the moon to judge the time.

Not long until the race starts, but I have to play this role so the guards let their awareness down.

Ashnayn stepped up onto a small platform at the center of brightly decorated trees and allowed the makers to start their measurements without saying a word. The eight Hobaru guards stood in a circle around them and Ashnayn liked how far apart they were from one another.

The makers took a small bit of time before finishing with their measurements and when they reached down to grab fabric and other materials, that's when Ashnayn made her move.

She dashed in the direction of the race through two of her guards. The Princess passed between them before any alarm was raised and none were fast enough to catch her. The starting line was roughly two miles away and she ran vigorously to be there on time.

When she arrived, the grounds were packed with people from all Twenty Tribes. The Moon Race was the hardest and most popular race. It was one of only two races that included all four Hobaru activities: running, swimming, climbing, and diving.

At the starting line and out in front of everyone was where the contestants who qualified for the race were located; the best three of each tribe. Ashnayn was supposed to be among them, fifty nine were out there, she was the sixtieth.

And when the Princess stepped out with the contestants she was immediately recognized by Gowgluni.

"It has been declared under teeth and bone! You must be at the wedding grounds this instant!" Gowgluni yelled. Then he looked for her guards but they were far behind.

"You dare come between the Hobaru and their Moon Race?" she yelled back while grabbing the water gourds from her handmaiden.

Ashnayn instantly had the support from many. For the Moon Race was declared sacred under teeth and bone long ago.

Gowgluni looked around and realized the situation was lost. "Of course not, let the race continue."

He quickly pulled a contestant aside and close to himself. The contestant was a man he trusted, a man known as Chief Son Huaddu.

"Take this knife and give me the one in your vest. Do *not* cut yourself with it. Cut the All Chief Daughter on her outer arm only. Throw the knife in the sea when you're done. And do it after the swims, during the last run."

"I will."

"You will. And every day your father's Chief Seat for your tribe looks more and more yours."

Huaddu smiled as he attached the knife to his vest and blended back in with the others. Gowgluni looked to see if any were suspicious as he hid Huaddu's knife on himself and none were the wiser. He made his way back to the chiefs and nodded. Then one of them blew a conch.

The contestants set themselves. Ashnayn was ready to pounce.

The conch blew again and they were off, all running at a fast yet sustainable pace.

The first leg of the race was a ten mile run through rough and rocky territory around the outer edge of the island. And no one tried pulling ahead. All stayed within talking distance. Huaddu watched Ashnayn from the back of the group while the Princess ran at the front. Huaddu was almost always the best swimmer and he knew after the climb and dives he could pass her during the second swim. And when she passed him during the last run…

Yes, that is the best time to cut her. Gowgluni is always right, he thought.

The group ran in silence under the light of the full moon, dodging rocks and slipping past trees until they came to the first dive site ten miles from their start. A Hobaru was there to oversee the contestants and Ashnayn waved to him as she jumped from forty spans hands first, then broke the water gracefully. After surfacing she immediately started swimming the course around the island.

The second leg of the race was a ten mile swim and Ashnayn enjoyed the water as she put forth her effort to keep up with the great swimmers. But because of his skill, it wasn't long before Huaddu was ahead of everyone.

I will win! the Princess affirmed.

After nine miles of swimming she was feeling strong. The water invigorated her and the third leg of the race, the climb and dives, were only a mile away. Ashnayn was ready. Many of the great swimmers started going their fastest so she wouldn't get too far ahead of them during the climbs.

There was a Hobaru overseeing every climb and dive, and sixty spans was the height of the first one. The climbs went higher until the final one which was the tenth, and near two hundred spans.

Ashnayn reached the first climb and started her ascent. The climb wasn't difficult with prominent hand holds and the course was becoming familiar. When she neared the top, the best swimmers had already dove but she wasn't far behind. At the top, she wasted no time and dove immediately, making the smallest splash of any Hobaru.

They didn't swim far before they were climbing again, and this climb had less handholds but were still prominent. Halfway up, Ashnayn passed fifth place. At the top she dove once more and swimming put her back in seventh.

During the third climb she passed fourth place and first place Huaddu was diving a minute before she was. The next swim put her back in fifth place but the fourth climb was tough with little handholds and lots of technical difficulty. Ashnayn flew compared to the others who had to think and plan. She passed Huaddu and when she dove at the top, no one was right behind her. While diving she checked her vest to make sure the stone figurine was still there, and the Princess was confident as she landed with little splash.

During the next swim, the greatest swimmers caught back up but she wasn't worried. The rest of the climbs were difficult and the last three often killed people. If one fell at all it was likely they'd hit a rock in the water below, which was why the dives were so important.

By the time she reached the last climb and dive, Ashnayn was in the lead and beginning to feel the effects of the race. At the top she stretched for the briefest of moments; then dove again. She glided between two crags as she landed, then kicked to the surface and swam.

The next leg of the race was another ten mile swim and Ashnayn swam fast but not her fastest. She stayed steady and consistent, never slowing or breaking form.

If the others catch up I can burst ahead during the run. But I have to conserve energy for the run.

Huaddu was the first swimmer to pass her. His flawless technique made him a native of the water and he looked as though he were a merman gliding over its surface.

Ashnayn thought to go faster when she saw him but knew better.

I'll pass him when we get to the run.

Huaddu and four others pulled ahead during the final swim, but the Princess stayed calm and continued her sustainable pace.

After ten miles in the water the last climb came into view, which led to the last leg of the race, the twenty mile run. The five greatest swimmers were already running by the time Ashnayn reached the top and she wasted no time in assuming her apex pace.

The final run of twenty miles changed between smooth paths and the outer rugged terrain of the island, and Ashnayn ran through it all like wildfire. The Princess of the Twenty Tribes passed fifth and fourth place within the first mile and third and second place within five miles. At the seventh mile, Ashnayn came around a large bend and saw the first place Huaddu.

Chief Son Huaddu heard her coming and looked ahead. He saw a patch of thorn bushes and quickened his pace so she'd pass him by those. Then he discreetly pulled the poisoned knife from his vest. Her steps grew louder as Huaddu planned his attack to make it look as though it was the thorn bushes that cut her.

He could hear her breathing more clearly the closer she came. Then as she passed him, Huaddu acted like he tripped and pushed Ashnayn into the thorns while falling on top of her.

"Sorry, Princess, I didn't mean to trip," he said as he got up by covering her eyes while pushing her head deeper into the thorns with one hand, and that's when he sliced her outer arm with the other. Then Huaddu ran fast once more while con-cealing the knife until he could toss it.

Ashnayn yelled with rage as she stood up and ran to catch him. And when she passed him she said nothing but curses and taunts. But after another mile of running the Princess felt more fatigued than usual. It was a different kind of fatigue, a sick feeling. Her pace slowed even though she put more effort into it. And the low level of water from her gourds was quickly used up.

"What's happening?" she asked out loud. And that's when she noticed her mouth was numb.

Ashnayn pushed through the poison as long as possible, holding off the other runners until she finally had to slow to a jog, and quickly found herself in tenth place.

No!

The Princess had little strength left. Soon Ashnayn was in twenty second place. By the time she reached the finish line she was delirious and dead last. Her pace was a quick walk and all Hobaru still there looked at her with uncertainty.

Gowgluni walked over to her and said, "Here, drink this. It's water."

He lied, it was the antidote.

She gulped it thinking it was water and the way it refreshed her caused Ashnayn to thank Gowgluni.

"Thank you," she said.

"It's my pleasure."

Declanii

Chronicle Ten

Enough time has passed and I think the wisdom of the experience has finally set in, allowing me to write about what has become known as The Last Battle of the Runidareeans.

Fear, as the emotion is known, gets in the way of life. This is one thing I've learned. Fear, as it is known, also preserves life. This is another. Nowhere have I seen these two opposites manifest more than at that battle, and my mind still returns there easily.

I remember a slight but long hill sloping upward toward us. The cliffs dropping down at our backs with the wide and swift Quenie River below. Raging wind battering away at everything in its path. And the army of the Runidareeans outnumbering us a heavy four to one at the base of the slope below.

After four hard years of fighting that is where we found ourselves. Acillus organized the Talons so that we assumed three battle lines, one behind the other, each battle line ten men thick. The first line had long pole spears laid before them, hidden and ready for the cavalry charge. Up until that moment we'd only used standing trees to mitigate a horse charge, which was one of the reasons why Acillus was as calm as a Clanii at sea. For when that charge came, not only did the uphill momentum slow them but the raising of the pole spears halted their charge in place. When an unstoppable force meets an immovable object we are bound to find out which is more true to their name. And that day, the army led by the Declanii could not be moved.

I profess I did little more than hinder those around me.

Declanii

There was hardly any room to maneuver during that battle. I couldn't go anywhere. We were so tightly packed in formation with enemy all around, cliffs to our backs, and no possibility of retreat, that I thought I'd breathed my last. But this situation has its advantages, I suppose.

Where Acillus got the notion to fight this way is well beyond me, yet here I am, able to write this. After the battle there was much feasting. I pulled the young man aside to ask him specifically why he thought fighting like that was a good idea. I must confess I had a hint of, 'Are you mad boy?' in my tone. But he only looked at me and smiled.

'It's called death's ground, when there's no room for retreat,' he said. 'People fight their hardest when it's the only chance they have of survival.'

And with another sip of ale he was off to rejoin the foray of feasting. I stood there momentarily perplexed, questioning myself on this concept. Acillus marched us specifically to that location so we'd have no other choice but to fight or die. Which shows either utmost trust in his fellow man, or an extreme case of madness. I've not yet been able to discern which.

Excerpt from Arakkus' Journal
Dated Mard, Third of Earlywinter, 307th Year of the Ninth Age

Chapter Eleven

Alistriana told her father she'd be taking work off from The Fox's Hypothesis for the festival. She wanted to be at the fields for Irhanach's first tournament. The days off were arranged without question and now, during the early crisp Midwinter morning of the Sixteenth, she walked hand in hand with Irhanach through their favorite park toward the practice fields. The conversation shared between them served well to calm the young man's mind as they walked through the trees. If she hadn't engaged him this early in the morning he'd have been thinking of nothing else but the fights by now.

Both were warm as they left the park and walked along one of the main streets of Ideclan. Alistriana wore on top of her winter clothes a heavy black cloak that engulfed her. She looked cozy as she peeked out from underneath the hood with her dark brown almond eyes. Irhanach was just as warm in his white cloak. He was tall and his burning red hair made him stand out even more above a crowd. He was lean, fast, and possessed more strength than he was ever credited. He could be loud and boisterous at times but never around Liss, and anything he said he was able to prove.

"Ahroo, Irhanach! Fight well today!" an Ideclaner called out to him.

"Ahroo, good man," he called back.

Many descendants of the thirteen families were well known at Ideclan and Irhanach made sure he was. He was fond of saying, 'Being a red haired Fianna makes me rarer than the rest.'

This was the only thing Alistriana allowed him to vaunt in her presence, his Fianna descent. She enjoyed how it made her smile. And she loved his hair. But this morning more than any other, Irhanach's confidence uneased her.

"As you know yourself, this is unprecedented! When we fight our way to the top they'll put our entrance to a vote. And after that's sealed, we'll be full Declanii and won't have to go on the four years abroad. This is a great honor, Liss. None of the other descendants have ever had this opportunity unless they're an O'Ronan."

Alistriana was worried about why they wouldn't have to go on the four year journey. She was a Philosian and looked at every angle she could comprehend, then searched for angles that she couldn't.

"Why not?" she asked after some silence.

"Why not what?" he asked back. His mind was starting to fixate on the fighting ahead.

"Focus, Irhanach. Why won't you and the others have to go on the four years of training? You're a descendant, it's mandatory for you."

"Now, Liss," he tried to interject.

"No, Irhanach, why not? Why would they want you in the Declanii so soon that the tournament council is willing to let you forgo four years of valuable training, extremely valuable training that could save your life?"

He knew if he didn't tell her the truth as he knew it right away, she'd eventually get it out of him through questioning.

And after that, she'd be mad at him all day for not telling her from the start.

"Didn't I already say it's what Cael wants?"

"I know that. But what does that mean?"

"It means… it means that for some reason, Cael wants us to be with him and the army and not off training."

"You're still not answering the question. Why does Prince Cael want you to stay?"

"I might think from your line of questioning *you* don't want me to stay," he said, trying to make her smile. It didn't work and Alistriana was getting upset.

"That's *not* why I ask. If he wants you staying instead of leaving then he must want you to leave for somewhere else before you'd return from training. Are one of the armies marching East?"

"I don't know, Liss."

"Don't follow your passions blindly," she said as she caressed his cheek while they walked. "Why hasn't Prince Cael told you? Are you not one of his best friends?"

"I am," he answered assuredly.

"And what of Anrahan, or his cousin, Ohelathe?"

"You know how Cael is, there's probably many reasons why he requested this. And people talk all over of Camulus and his plans to invade so who knows, Liss. And it still isn't for certain. A vote still has to be held. We still have to fight!"

All the conversation did was worry her more. But she stopped questioning him so he could get into the mind set needed for the tournament. And after a short time later they arrived at the practice fields.

Both Irhanach and Anrahan were given the same Talon on the first day by the Pathplacer Criers; the Second Talon. And as the young couple reached the Second Talon's practice field they found Anrahan next to one of its banners with the insignia of an Ideclan sword crossed by a river.

"Where's Ohelathe?" Irhanach asked as they joined him.

"Archery started early," Anrahan answered.

Anrahan was five and a half feet tall and thicker than an ox with a deathly mobility about him. The Aenenay Family blood joined with the Elemarian blood was quite evident in his strong and powerful frame. He had blonde hair worn in many braids and his brown eyes were fierce. Anrahan had hard features with high cheekbones and spoke little, especially when not spoken to. He was well known among the Clanii and throughout Ideclan for having the second most strength among the living descendants of Clanii. The strongest was his father.

"What about you, Anrahan? Do you know why Cael wants you three to forgo the four years of training and join the rank and file right away?" Alistriana continued. Unrelenting was her personality.

"All right, Liss. Anrahan and I have to warm up. Where are you gonna be?" Irhanach interrupted.

He wasn't lying when he said his pals didn't know either.

Alistriana sighed before giving her answer. "My friends and I will be at the South side of the field today, so the Sun isn't in our eyes. Both of you fight well," she said softly.

"We will," Irhanach replied.

He and Liss kissed before she looked into his green eyes and then walked away.

Irhanach turned back toward Anrahan and both smiled. They understood Alistriana's worry but for them this was one of the greatest honors. The fact that Cael believed in them enough to make the request had given them added confidence.

The young men donned their heavy padded leather armor and helms, then with sword and shield, proceeded to warm up for combat.

The second day of the tournaments promised more challenging contests. The first half of the day would still be group fights, until the one hundred and twenty eight best from each Talon were asserted. Then, those one hundred and twenty eight would fight one on one during the second half of the day until the top ten of each Talon were asserted. First and second place would become First and Second Sword for that Talon. And the top ten combatants along with the top three archers from each Talon would advance to the third day.

The fields were filling with spectators again. Merchants sold wares and cooks had special recipes grilling over fires for which others chopped wood. A roaring was heard over at the archery contests and both Irhanach and Anrahan knew who that was for.

The fighters for the Second Talon were called onto the field and colored sticks were passed out, separating them into groups. Irhanach and Anrahan met after they each pulled a stick.

"What color did you get?" Irhanach asked his lifelong friend.

"Green," he answered while showing him.

"Ha! Again the same as me, brother! What luck! We stand back to back and the tournament is ours!"

Anrahan smiled and nodded.

The Tournament Criers for the Second Talon started separating the combatants into who'd fight first. And both Irhanach and Anrahan lined up so they'd be called out together.

The crowds were in a frenzy across the grounds. The fights on their field hadn't yet started but the cheering from all around got everyone going. And the anticipation surrounding the Second Talon built to a crescendo as the combatants who wouldn't be fighting in the first group started walking off the field.

Irhanach smiled. The thrill of the crowd excited him. Anrahan's face was stern, resolute to the task at hand as they stayed on the field, shoulder to shoulder.

"Fight!"

All combatants charged for the center. Anrahan remained silent as he ran, Irhanach shouted his battle cry. The four teams crashed into one another and what was commonly team battles turned into a tavern brawl and the crowd loved it.

The mass of combatants dwindled as many were defeated. When the group was small enough, everyone saw the two Clanii boys fighting back to back at the middle. The rest of their team had been eliminated and the other teams knew that if they wanted a chance at winning this round, they'd have to join together to defeat the two stalwarts at the center. And there were only seven combatants left after joining together.

"What do ya say, Anrahan?" Irhanach yelled out in the middle of a laugh.

"Ha!" Anrahan grunted a laugh in return, his eyes full of ferocity.

They knew not to charge and separate. They'd been doing this since childhood, back when it wasn't seven men but thousands of imaginary ones trying to defeat them. And it felt like a normal circumstance for the two boys.

Four of the seven charged in while the other three moved around to attack from behind. Irhanach and Anrahan took the attackers as they came, swinging and stepping gracefully, blocking and striking effectively. And the four assailants were taken out with ease.

Then the two Clanii turned together and locked their shields, facing the three that were now in front of them, all of whom were from different teams but didn't think to fight one another.

Irhanach and Anrahan advanced. Anrahan bulled into two as Irhanach used his momentum on a sweeping sword strike. The strike took out one fighter while Anrahan's shield knocked the other two to the ground. Then the Clanii boys reached them and gave killing strikes before they could recover. And the crowd cheered for both while they walked off as victors.

Leaders from The Kinned Lands had been arriving over the past few days and many were pleasantly overwhelmed by the magnitude of the festival and the fights. For the Daeadaks and Gisspor it'd been a long journey sailing across Trader's Strait and then the rest of the way close to land because of how treacherous the sea could be.

The Arashrillian leaders arrived the day before, along with those from Teker Ren who were just a boat ride up the river away. The Arashrillians were a hearty people and enjoyed the festivities. The Teker Ren were a forest people who lived up in the trees and they too, enjoyed the events around themselves. The Elemarians would be arriving later that day, and the Edemarians within the next few.

Hinturan didn't count itself among The Kinned Lands, but Cael had spent time there with Segais when he was younger and built good relations. So they'd be arriving within a few days to partake in the war council as well, a fact that was to be kept in utmost secrecy by all who knew; a stipulation of the Hinturan for them to even come.

The group matches went on as the morning warmed. Both Irhanach and Anrahan were counted among the victors of their last three fights and it looked promising for them to be first and second seats for the single's tournament. They were taking off their padded leather armor while waiting for the placings to be posted for the next phase when they noticed Cael approaching them.

"How'd it go?" the Prince asked.

He showed no signs he'd been fighting all morning as well, disguised as Segais wished it.

"You should have seen Anrahan throw this guy! Near ripped his leather off as he did! Where were you?" Irhanach asked.

"I went to watch another fight. I wanted to see if this lad would make it into the single's matches and he did. Big lad, newcomer named Raddox, fights with a longsword."

While disguised, Cael had tested Raddox to see if he could draw the Edemarian out of his style again and it worked. Because of this, the young Ravenborne started his plans to make a wooden Edemarian Sword for him in secret. For the Prince had a feeling he knew who this newcomer was.

"I think I heard about him. He did well then?" Irhanach questioned.

"Yes," Cael answered while nodding. "Very easily."

"Why did you watch him?"

"I think I recognize him. And I believe I know where I recognize him from. But I'm not certain yet."

"Did you get to see any of Ohelathe's rounds?" Irhanach continued.

"Aye, and he's still in the lead."

Cael sat with his two friends and relaxed while waiting as the tournaments went on around them. When the Second Talon's single combat brackets were completed, the three got up and walked toward the boards upon which they were posted. And on the way, Irhanach jested with Anrahan about the likelihood of himself being the first seat.

Cael stayed behind the crowd as his two friends made their way through to see the placings. And the Prince could tell by his friend's yell that he'd gotten the seat he thought he would.

"Doesn't matter," Anrahan said after seeing he got the second seat. "It only prolongs your confrontation with me."

Irhanach slapped him on the back and said, "Too true my friend!"

Cael smiled as he slipped away to disguise himself for the single's combat of the Sixth Talon.

The first phases of the tournaments were always exciting but single combat drew more spectators. There was almost no room to maneuver around any field. People were packed shoulder to shoulder so all could glimpse the best of each Talon.

These were the fighters with experience. Many had drawn steel up at Caibre Pass and some of the old veterans fought during the Last battle of the Runidareeans or the Second Siege of Ideclan, as well as other engagements on land and at sea.

The only three still among the Talons' tournaments who hadn't yet proven themselves in battle were Irhanach and Anrahan for the Second Talon, and Ohelathe for the archers. Everyone assumed the newcomer, Raddox in the Sixth Talon, could be defined this way. But none of them had known the extensiveness of his struggles over the last three years.

The biggest surprises of the tournaments thus far were how Irhanach and Anrahan secured the first and second seats for their Talon as rookies. And that news spread like wildfire. Cristin found himself lower in the bracketing of his tournament but was still fighting nonetheless. And he'd made it while using a sword roughly one fifth the size of his own Edemarian Blade.

The single fighter tournaments started shortly after the brackets were posted. And everyone fought hard to contend for either Talon Command, or what was likely on most hearts, to join in on the third day's tournament, knock a fighter out of its brackets, and wear the sunil.

There were only one hundred and fifty six slots in the Declanii and thirty six were for archers. A few at this stage had made it before and were fighting to regain their position. Some of these men still wore their sunil. For once one officially donned the sunil during a battle, they wore it for the rest of their career. And filled in on rotations and duties if need be.

Irhanach stood ready for his first single's match, peering above his shield at the veteran he faced.

"Fight!"

Both attacked. The young one tried his luck with a gambit that allowed the veteran a serious opening to Irhanach's chest if the fiery haired lad failed. The combatant saw this and went for it, causing Irhanach's gambit to work as his sword found its way up to the throat of the veteran.

"End!"

"Congratulations, Irhanach," Anrahan said as his friend returned from his victory.

"You're up next!" the Fianna declared with elation as he sat beside him.

Three other fights had been going on the field at the same time as Irhanach's, but his was the most watched.

Anrahan got called up next and Irhanach cheered as he proceeded onto the field. All combatants they faced were capable and still proved little match for the two descendants of Clanii who'd been training with Cael their whole lives. And all on the fields were excited to see how well Cael would do.

Irhanach and Anrahan tore through the ranks with increasing speed. In this phase of single elimination, both advanced to the top with neither losing a single match. And there were two more fights to go that'd decide who'd contest against them in the semifinals. They sat next to each other and watched their future targets.

At the Sixth's field, Cael prepared to lose his next match lest he become one of the top ten and make it to the third day in disguise. He'd fight to the greatest ability allotted for this persona, and lose. Cael walked onto the field with extra padding in his suit and a full helm on his head. Under the helm he wore a wig of coarse black hair that completely covered his golden locks.

"Fight!"

The young Prince had fun staying within the bounds of the style he created, never utilizing his true ability. And he lost with grace. Segais caught up to him as he walked off the fields to change back into himself.

"What did you learn?" the old wizard asked when he reached him.

"I thought the deception would gnaw at me, but it proved more educating than expected. People really don't pay attention to everything that goes on around them. Most just focus toward a few things and let their minds fill in the rest."

"Indeed. Now apply that to yourself. You did well. No one ever suspected you."

"They did not."

"The exercise is complete. Enjoy the rest of your tournament."

Cael nodded and continued walking toward a hideout of his at an old woodshop, Hoireabard's Woodshop, because it held his livery he'd change back into. It was also were he'd make the Edemarian Sword for the newcomer, Raddox. He'd make it fast, not spending any time on detail because if he needed it, it'd be by tomorrow.

Irhanach and Anrahan kept watching the matches that'd decide who they fought. The same thought raced through their minds. If they both won their next matches then they'd fight against each other for First and Second Sword of their Talon in the first tournament they fought in, something that had only been done a handful of times by a Clanii before.

In a tournament full of big happenings, each imagined if they did this it'd be talked about forever. Though the thought raced through Irhanach's mind more than Anrahan's as the Fianna joked about it with a few spectators, while Anrahan stayed quiet and studied the possibilities for his next opponent.

When those fights concluded it was time for the semifinals; fought one at a time. Irhanach was called out first and he walked onto the field while crossing his sword and shield over and under to keep limber.

His opponent was well known and working his way into the Declanii. He was tall, strong, and lifted his sword and shield while yelling to the crowd after his name was called. Many cheered back as Irhanach stood calmly at the center.

"You know," the boy started as his opponent got closer. "It really is too bad you won't be making it into the Declanii."

"Quiet yourself," the man said, annoyed that a young one would think to taunt him.

"You've worked so hard at getting here and now your unluckiness has caused you to have to face me. I promise I won't embarrass you," the fiery haired Fianna goaded.

The man looked at Irhanach with anger.

"Fight!"

Irhanach's opponent charged, shield up. The Fianna boy moved forward while shuffling left then right. His opponent followed right. Irhanach sidestepped left as he dodged an attack, then angled his sword up into the man's throat, slipping it over his shield and forcing him backward.

"End!" the crier yelled.

Irhanach walked off the field amidst plenty of cheer.

Anrahan and his opponent were called next and they each walked to the center.

Irhanach saw Cael returning as he returned from his own fight. And both cheered for their friend.

Anrahan's opponent was a well known scout for the Second Talon and always counted among the top fighters. Both he and Anrahan crouched and stared above the tops of their shields.

"Fight!"

The scout lunged forward with a sweeping strike. Anrahan shield blocked and then stepped forward while attacking overhead. The man blocked as he stepped back. Anrahan stepped forward again, raising his shield parallel to the ground and punched the rim into the scout's shield, pushing him back. Anrahan crow hopped and bashed his shield rim into the scout's shield a second time, breaking the top clean off while knocking the man off balance and when he saw his opening, the young Clanii quickly thrust his sword at the scout's chest.

"End!"

Pawdar was pleased with the tournament's proceedings, and looked forward to the final fight of his Talon. Pawdar was a man who hailed from the Western lands across the Great Ulfinn Ocean. He had no blood ties to anyone of The Kinned Lands and yet he worked for those lands with great love. He served as Second Talon Commander, and was a Veteran of the Sunil.

All on the Second Talon's field gathered closely for the final fight, leaving only a circle thirty paces across for the fight to take place. Those among what were considered the first forty rows sat down or crouched so more people could see. The fields around them sounded off with loud cheers and yells but theirs was silent. All wanted to hear the Lead Crier for the

Second Talon call out the last fight of the day.

"Alright, everyone!" the Lead yelled to reach maximum range. "Fighting for Sword One and Two of the Second Talon: Second Seat fighter, Anrahan of the Aenenay Family!"

The crowd cheered while the young man walked toward the center of the fighting circle. He had a smile on his face as he looked back at everyone.

"Also fighting: First Seat fighter, Irhanach of the Fianna Family!"

Irhanach smiled too as his name was called. And he walked onto the field.

The moment was theirs. Neither felt singular glory. Both had a strong sense of brotherhood toward each other and in turn to Ohelathe Mullquane and Prince Cael O'Ronan. Cael was known far and wide but his brothers knew him best. They were proud of the training he'd been giving them, and they knew this was a victory for their young coterie no matter who won.

Both set their stances and Cael smiled. Not because he saw Alistriana across the field shaking her head; she knew she wasn't going to hear the end of this. But because he'd seen these two fight countless times and knew what was in store for the crowd.

Anrahan always fought stronger of the two while Irhanach was the faster fighter between them. He fought with almost the same swiftness and grace as Cael, except he had nowhere near the amount of power as the young Prince. And Anrahan out powered them both.

Cael was a ways back standing behind those sitting or crouching. His heavy black cloak with white hood did well to keep him warm. And he looked on proudly at whom he knew would one day be two of his best leaders.

"Fight!"

Both stepped back and Irhanach grinned at Anrahan.

"Not going to charge, eh?" the Fianna asked.

Anrahan leapt forward with a shield bash. Irhanach crouched low and brought his shield up, forcing Anrahan's above his, then stepped to his right while trying to corral the young Aenenay's shield away before thrusting his sword. Anrahan used his strength to bring his shield back and blocked. He threw his own strike and Irhanach blocked. Back and forth they went.

Anrahan impressed with his strong and fierce strikes while Irhanach awed with his maneuvers and reflexes.

In little time, they each breathed heavier as neither appeared able to best the other, while both tried hard to win. Cael had a look of true interest as he watched his friends fight the finest they ever had. The three in sunil judging the match, constantly kept moving to stay out of their way. Cael reckoned this was the longest he'd ever seen either of them take to defeat the other.

The two Clanii circled, slightly fatigued but resolute. Irhanach lunged low with a shield punch parallel to the ground. As Anrahan bashed his own shield down on top of Irhanach's, the fiery haired Fianna pulled back fast, raising his so he could force it down on Anrahan's. Irhanach knocked Anrahan's shield down with his own and as he did he brought his sword up and over it, straight to Anrahan's neck.

"End!" the Lead Crier yelled.

There was no circle in the middle anymore as everyone rushed for the center to celebrate. And the cheers were immense.

With the end of the match, the Second Talon's tournament finished earlier than usual and the crowd started to dissipate. All were off to see if they could catch another Talon's final fight.

Irhanach and Anrahan congratulated each other while taking off their helmets and padded leather armor to cool down. And their sweat billowed from them as steam in the cold.

"What was that?" Cael asked with a big grin.

But before either could answer they heard a familiar voice call to them.

"Hey, lads!"

"Ohelathe!" Irhanach yelled back. "How'd you fare?"

"I fared well. But the whole city could hear the crowd during your fight!"

Ohelathe was a Mullquane. Not even Cael knew where the Mullquanes were originally from and they were cousins. The secrets were passed down with the Mark of the Mullquanes and neither Cael nor his cousin had earned the Mark. The

Mark was a large part of Ohelathe's life. He'd thought about it a great deal, and wondered what he would have to do to earn the coveted secrets of his family.

Ohelathe was somewhat tall, lean, broad shouldered with stout arms, and slightly tan like his mother. He had the dark black hair and ice blue eyes of the Mullquanes, and was every bit a warrior of that family as his ancestors. The Mullquanes began as spear and shield wielders but over the years, many of them had taken to the bow.

"You gonna tell us or what?" Irhanach asked Ohelathe, referring to his faring at the archery tournament.

"I made First Arrow of all the Talons!" he exclaimed.

They congratulated him with cheer. The day was theirs.

"You lads want to see if we can catch Raddox, the newcomer, see if he's still in the fights?" Cael asked his friends.

"What Talon is he fighting for?" Irhanach asked back.

"Sixth," the Prince answered with a smile.

All four looked at one another.

Anrahan was the first to grab his gear and run toward the Sixth's field. The other three followed, weaving through the crowd. Cael kept his hood high while following in the back where his friends had already cleared the path so he wouldn't bump into anyone and have the whole area take notice.

They ran fast, dodging people as they made their way

toward the Northern part of the fields. For how stout Anrahan was, he was very agile as he led them through, until they broke out of the massive crowd into a somewhat open area at the North, open enough for them to run in a straight line directly for above the Sixth's field.

Their destination was a salt storage building not too far to the North of the field, and before they got close, Cael threw his hood back and turned the running into a foot race. When he passed each of his friends, they knew all too well and joined.

After they reached the building, Irhanach was sure he won the race while Anrahan led the way in. The structure was typical of Ideclan engineering. It was made from large trees that grew to envelop the long wooden planks and stones forming the walls. Once inside, the boys dropped their gear and went toward the Southward wall and up the stairs, something they'd done hundreds of times before.

Phaedrus was now a Declanii Commander, but when he first came from Gisspor he fought in the Sixth Talon. He was one of the boys' favorite fighters growing up, and they made their way to where they used to always watch him.

When the four young Clanii got to the second floor, Anrahan grabbed a chair and stood on it to open the thatched coverings of a specific window. The window was for repairing the roof and pruning the living trees, but none of them ever used it for that. To them it had always been their secret doorway. Once all were on the roof they sat in the same spots they sat in for years, and looked out at a not so high bird's eye view of the Sixth Talon's field.

On the Sixth's field, everyone got into position for the final fight while the two fighters readied themselves. One of those fighters, who almost no one at the festival recognized because of his disguise, was approached by an old wizard who spoke so only the fighter could hear.

"Commander Rallin, of the Vanguard, I presume."

Rallin's heart jumped until he turned to see Segais and said, "I thought it was someone else who saw through my deception."

"Not likely. Though I must say it's daring of you to go this far. Will you fight under both yourself and this other persona tomorrow?"

"Possibly. I like throwing sticks in the wheels of the ongoings around me."

"So I've noticed," Segais said with a smile. "Perhaps you can help me throw a stick of my own?"

Rallin looked at the wizard while wrapping his wrists. "What are you thinking?"

"This boy you're about to fight." Segais pulled a two handed longsword from inside his robes. "Give him this."

Rallin grabbed the sword while asking, "Why?"

"I want him to defeat you. And I want him to reach the top tomorrow."

"Is this the real weapon he fights with?"

"Somewhat. Tell him if he doesn't accept it then you'll reveal his secret."

"What's his secret?" Rallin asked with a grin.

"If you can defeat him, you may know. Will you do this?"

"I will."

"Good, and fight your hardest," the wizard commanded before melding back into the crowd.

Rallin walked over to where Cristin warmed up.

"Hey Raddox," he called to him.

"Yes?" Cristin answered.

When Rallin reached him, quietly he said, "Fight me with this sword or I'll reveal your secret."

"What's my secret?" Cristin asked defiantly.

Rallin shoved the sword in his hands. "Fight me with this or everyone will know."

And then the Commander of the Vanguard walked back to his area. He was pleased to see Raddox start practicing with the blade he gave him, and also took note of how proficient he was with it.

Cristin was on an edge. He discreetly scanned the crowd for threats while warming up and looked to make sure Elasus was still safe with Liadine and Sylla.

Cael and his friends wouldn't have been able to watch the fight from the ground had they tried. Everyone was either sitting, kneeling, or crouching in the front rows and all were crowded together.

There was now one combatant at the center and it wasn't Raddox. They weren't able to tell the Edemarian apart from the crowd until he started walking toward the center.

"Hey, I've met that lad!" Irhanach said with surprise.

"You've met him?" Cael asked.

"No one could forget a man that size. I met him two nights ago at The Fox's Hypothesis when I was seeing Liss."

"He's the lad I told you I think I might know," the Prince informed.

"How?" Ohelathe asked.

"I'll tell you when I'm sure. Look, he's using a larger sword."

The four boys fixed their attention on the field to watch the fight.

"Anyone recognize who he's fighting?" Irhanach asked.

None of them did.

"Fight!"

Cristin and Rallin circled while trying to find each other's weaknesses. Cristin's fear of this man knowing his identity quickly turned into anger, and it'd been a hard day for those trying to find a weakness in the Edemarian's style. His journey through life, first through politics and then on the run from them, had caused him to be a hard man. None so far had succeeded and Rallin was no different now that Cristin possessed the longer sword backed by growing rage.

But Rallin wouldn't let Cristin find a weakness in him either. The brute of a young man knew how to use the longer sword to his advantage, and yet the Vanguard Commander guarded himself well, moving with incredible agility.

Rallin tried gaining the initiative by maneuvering through Cristin's reach but couldn't. Cristin was too swift at using the whole sword to block. The hilt of an Edemarian Sword was often up to two feet long, then there was another one handed hilt above the large handguard with another handguard above that. And then the double sided blade extended up to five feet or more. The two handed longsword Cristin held wasn't near that size but the hilt was still long enough for him to perform a few Edemarian techniques.

Cristin stepped back while swinging the wooden blade, keeping his opponent on the defensive and creating space. Rallin moved away as Cristin began spinning it around like a staff, not taking any liberties that a real sword wouldn't allow. He spun the sword gracefully, speeding it up with the now encircling steps he took while switching hands, corralling his opponent with long arcing strikes. Rallin had to think quickly on his feet to keep blocking and dodging. Faster and faster Cristin spun the sword between attacks, bringing his weapon around himself in every angle and direction to keep his opponent defending.

The four young lads sitting on the rooftop watched the fight in attentive silence.

Cristin lunged forward with a thrust and Rallin parried. The young Edemarian continued forward, bringing his sword all the way around in a sweeping strike. Using his full strength he slammed it into the Vanguard Commander's shield, forcing Rallin to step to the side in order to absorb some of the force. Cristin struck for his sword and knocked it out of his hand. And his own sword never stopped as it came back around again and finished on Rallin's shoulder, blade to neck.

"End!"

The four heard the crier yell it from above the silent crowd. Then everyone cheered. And a number of veterans recognized the Edemarian in Cristin's style.

"You don't know cac," Cristin told Rallin with a vicious stare after removing his sword from his neck, and the Vanguard Commander smiled.

Eventually the fields began emptying as the tournaments ended and everyone went home to prepare for the evening. The second night of each festival was always a joyous one. It was the music night. Just as the first night how everyone gathered around a storyteller, this night, they'd gather around those playing music and dance to their heart's content.

Declanii

Chronicle Eleven

You are correct, my son. And these are my thoughts
on the matter. King Acillus is enthusiastic about Edemar being
a nation among The Kinned Lands. The problem is that not
even the Edemarians consider themselves fortunate to be. Most
believe it was out of fear for the Runidareeans that they even
joined us. But to prove this, those of Edemar would have to
speak truth and I know of none who can.

I know that Edemarians torture, are fond of assassinating one another, and have been questing for the return of slavery ever since the end of the Wars of the North. The level of
political intrigue among all their ranks is revolting. They are the
polar opposite to what we work to achieve. They are incredibly
vicious fighters and superb is their talent with the Edemarian
Sword. All of them are deadly to a definite degree.

The Treewolves chose the brothers Edemar and
Elemar for the nifu ellwulle to start the Eighth Age. They must
have been very different from what their descendants have become. I worry that because they failed their attempt at the nifu
ellwulle, Acillus wishes to see them succeed as a people. How
the Edemarians are still around and haven't annihilated themselves from within is another perplexing trait of theirs. They
are survivors I suppose, vicious like badgers in their tenacity to
continue on. We must take all precautions that their ways do not
grow among The Kinned Lands.

My greatest fear is that Edemar secretly seeks to destroy
our attempt at the nifu ellwulle. I think they endeavor to sow
seeds of doubt among Ideclan and its people to accomplish this.
And it's already working on me. If Acillus can bring wisdom

from within them then we'll laugh at my fears. But there is a gnawing within me, telling me to be ever vigilant when it comes to Edemar and so I will. At best they are ruthless and untrustworthy.

Reply letter by Conail Cailian, Advisor to Ideclan
To his son, Lorcan, Seventh Talon Commander
Dated Pard, the Twenty Fifth of Earlysummer,
Year Three Hundred and Thirty Two of the Ninth Age

Chapter Twelve

As the Sun set behind the Rywinn Mountains, lively music was heard resonating from the fields of Ideclan. Everyone there or heading that way was dressed in their Winter warmest. The Clanii loved Winter and a great many Ideclaners had grown to love it as well. All were looking forward to the evening's festivities. Fiddles, tin whistles, flutes, variations of drums, and more were played as people danced and walked to the fields with excitement.

Merchants sold their wares. Carts filled with jugged ale or barreled mead could be found across the grounds and they were the first to sell out on the second night of any festival.

The second nights were also the best of the year for the inns and taverns. All were at capacity since Sundown and would stay that way for the rest of the evening. The main contingent of the Ideclan Navy was at port as well, greatly swelling the ranks of social activity. Loud songs were sung at every inn or tavern, and shouts accompanied by foot stomps burst from their doors.

Long tables were set out on the fields and many brought a dish such as sweet meats roasted with personal marinades, smoked jerky, special topped potatoes, stuffed onions, dilled turnips, Winter salads with berries, cheeses, gravies, bread, rolls, honey, and the Ideclan favorites of sweet cakes and cookies.

Cael, Ohelathe, Anrahan, Irhanach, and Alistriana, walked together through the crowds, buying food and goods from different merchants and enjoying the music.

Then they strolled past one of Alistriana's favorite songs and she persuaded the four boys to stop and dance. Irhanach never missed a chance to dance with Liss but it took a little more convincing for the others. And it didn't take them long to start enjoying themselves once they did.

Irhanach and Liss danced together while Cael and Ohelathe joined in with the larger group. And Anrahan found a lady to dance with.

The five danced the night away with smiles stuck on their faces. And the troupe of bards if at all possible, became more heartfelt with their songs once they noticed who danced before them. Everyone at Ideclan knew who Cael was and most of The Kinned Lands knew what he looked like. The Prince was well traveled before he finished education, having visited every nation among The Kinned Lands and a few that were not.

The scene livened as the band picked up the tempo and dancers started shouting with them. They interlocked their arms at the elbows and spun each other around. The four young Clanii often danced at the festivals throughout their lives, but once Alistriana joined their group it became almost unavoidable.

The troupe of bards played their favorite songs so no one thought to leave. Ohelathe was the first to sit down for a break and Cael and Anrahan followed while Irhanach and Alistriana stayed out dancing. One of the tables near them had barrels, bottles, and jars of different ales and spirits. But the four boys surrendered themselves to water for the night while Alistriana drank wine.

"When will you get your Marks, cousin?" Cael asked.

"I've been asking my Da the same thing my whole life. And not once has he ever given me any hint as to when I'll be tested or what's involved. I still have no clue," Ohelathe answered with frustration.

"Setting the example for when your children ask you *their* whole lives," Anrahan told him.

Ohelathe nodded as he thought about it. He felt more than ready to receive his Marks. A Mullquane boy or girl didn't fully become adults and learn the knowledge of their family until they earned their Marks. His Da Quinnlan had them, his Aunt, Queen Andraste had them, his Woda, Aislin had them, his Woma, Saraid, and Granwoda, Laisren had them too. He grew up seeing them on all of his elder kin.

Ohelathe knew from the moment he understood what the Marks were that he wanted to earn them. And for much of his young life he thought about what he'd have to do, and if he'd be able to.

"Hey," Cael said, snapping him out of it. "You know you'll earn the Mark, cousin."

"You're as much of a Mullquane as any before you." A bold statement by Anrahan but he meant it.

Over the centuries, the families who possessed the best fighters and commanders among the Declanii continually changed. Each family was at the top of this side contest at one point or another. But the Mullquanes had been the best all around for a long while, only to be eclipsed by the O'Ronans some one hundred years back. Whatever Ohelathe would have to go through to get the Marks, he knew it would be tough. But his resolve grew by the day.

"I will indeed, thank you lads," the Mullquane stated.

"Cael, what'd you find out about tomorrow?" Anrahan asked after nearly drinking his entire cup of water. He was referring to the likelihood of them having to face the Prince in the tournament before the end of the day.

"Nothing. They were too busy and didn't have the bracket structures fine tuned yet. So I'll just choose whichever file you lads don't get drawn into. We're going to catch everyone unawares," he said firmly.

Irhanach and Alistriana joined them just in time to hear him.

Cael and his Clanii friends grabbed their cups of water and lifted them in salute while Alistriana grabbed her cup of wine and did the same. She'd known them closely for almost two years now and was very much a part of their coterie.

They all delighted in the festivities as they continued conversing. And then the course of the night changed.

"Well, well, look who's coming our way… and *with a cup!*" Ohelathe stated with elevated excitement.

All of them looked.

The woman walking their way was of such a beauty that many at Ideclan would challenge a Sandlion for the chance to be her husband. She'd refused over one hundred suitors by the age of twenty five. Her name was Aveline Hafrana, daughter to Marchann and Maebh Hafrana, granddaughter to the Admiral Finn Hafrana, who possessed her mother's dark hair and brown skin with blue eyes. And as she walked toward them with a cup in her hands, her purpose became quite evident.

Cael was the only one in the whole area not staring at Aveline the Enchanting.

And before she reached them, Irhanach grabbed Alistriana's hand to go out and dance again. The Philosian expected this so she quickly took a sip of wine before putting her cup down and letting herself be taken.

Both Ohelathe and Anrahan got up and walked off in conversation as though they were too busy for anything about to happen at that table.

And three strides later, she was there.

"Prince Cael," Aveline said loudly enough to be heard, but softly because of her voice.

Cael stood and looked at her once more. He knew what her intentions were by how she held the cup. The back of her right four fingers rested flat on top of her left four, and they served as a base for the chalice while her thumbs held the cup in place.

The giving of spiced cider in this way was from the elder days of Clanii, when the fishermen would return home from braving the ocean and their wives gave them hot cider to warm them. This act of love had become tradition over many centuries and during the years before the founding of Ideclan, it had become the common way that women proposed marriage.

Aveline looked into Cael's ice blue eyes as she stood there. Her dark hair billowed out from the hood of her green cloak and her pear colored dress form fitted to her brown skin.

Cael continued looking back. They'd been friends all their lives. But the Prince was often traveling to different lands and Aveline had been on the four years of training abroad that almost all Clanii had to go through, which never let them grow into anything more than a friendship.

"I want to give you this, Cael," she told him.

"No you don't," he said back with a grin.

Aveline burst out laughing before tossing the cider inside the cup onto the ground.

"Who talked you into this?" he asked.

"I told my Woma I would, just to ease her mind. She made the cider as well."

"Don't be too happy when you tell her I said no."

"She might come after you when I do."

"Indeed."

"Get your rest, Prince. I'll see you tomorrow."

Cael nodded. And then Aveline walked away toward Old Ideclan. He finished his water and decided she was right, he did need his rest, so he ran to catch up with her and they walked back together.

There was a lot on his mind, starting tomorrow, everything he did would be recorded and for all to see. He'd be an O'Ronan in the army; the next King. And his conversation with Aveline did well to focus his thoughts.

They reached the edge of the fields then started walking down gravel roads toward Old Ideclan. And the Prince decided to visit his ravens once more before going home.

While walking, Cael greeted those who greeted him. And as they strode past a tavern, the song emanating from within it sparked his joy enough for him to recite a poem written by Tayg Shymurrow; a poem which had given birth to the song he heard.

"To fare across the sea is bold,
We can bring the winds within our folds,
But to live a life and not get old,
Now that is a tale that should to be told.
With that life we'd sail the seas,
Soar across with the ocean breeze,
Greet new lands with bended knee,
And make sure all are completely free.
With this titan task we run,
The labor will be less of the Sun,
All can be in its light as one,
When man's last fight is finally done."

It was getting late. Cael wanted to see the ravens then get home quickly so he'd be well rested by morning. Tomorrow he and his friends would fight the very best. The population on the streets lessened as Cael and Aveline neared the oldest part of the city, and the people mostly minded their own business while trying to find home after a night of heavy drinking.

The two young Clanii walked through the time worn gate into Old Ideclan and then parted ways as she went home and he to the roost.

There were much fewer people as Cael neared the

roost. He breathed in the night air deeply before letting out a sigh. It wasn't too cold and as of yet, nothing a heavy blanket and cloak couldn't handle.

The roost was like many buildings at Ideclan with trees for corner posts that grew to envelop the long, thick, wooden planks connecting each tree. There was no roof but the corner posts had grown their canopies to interlock with other trees throughout the roost, creating an accommodating shelter.

There was still snow on the crowns of the trees from the last fall, and some of it came down when a light breeze went through their branches, giving the appearance it was snowing inside.

The roost was open for all to enter but almost no one other than the Ravenborne ever did. The ravens weren't known to attack but due to their size they were a frightful sight. And much legend surrounded them.

There was no door to the roost, only an opening at the center of the North wall. Four feet beyond the opening was a stone wall as tall as the outer walls, it was one foot thick, twelve feet wide, and the middle four feet of the stone wall centered on the four foot opening of the North wall. This was to give the ravens privacy by blocking the view directly in.

To enter into the roost one had to walk toward either side around the stone wall and Cael walked to the left as he'd done countless times. The roost was one of the larger housings at Ideclan with well over two thousand ravens calling it their home. But many were off scouting when he arrived.

Cael chuckled at the snow coming down while walking toward his friends' favorite roosting spot. As he made his way, many ravens cawed a greeting and he returned each one with a nod until he reached them.

Cael had known his raven companions since he was a young boy. The male's name was Roxgrin, and the female's was Binneen.

"Hello, Waldron," Roxgrin thought to the Prince.

Waldron was Cael's raven name given to him by them.

"Ahroo, Roxgrin, Binneen. How's your roost?"

"Calm. But this is not the way of your mind," Binneen thought to him.

"I'm thinking of tomorrow. Nothing a good sleep can't take care of," he thought back.

The ravens liked this. They often told him a good roost could improve almost any troubling thought.

"I just came by to say good night before I headed home. I'll see you both tomorrow."

"Tomorrow then, Waldron. We'll be there again for one of your many beginnings," Binneen said.

Cael nodded and put his hand on his heart as he turned to walk out of the roost. Roxgrin snuggled back up to Binneen and fell asleep while more ravens greeted Cael as he exited. He couldn't understand their thoughts but he could understand their intent. And after learning from ravens for almost his entire life he could understand their caws. He bid them all farewell as he left.

The Prince wasn't in the roost long but when he walked out it felt considerably colder to him. So he wrapped his heavy blanket tighter and smiled because he could still faintly hear the music from the fields while walking the rest of the way home.

It didn't take him long to get there and when he did he found his Da still awake at almost one hour after midnight. He was walking up the stairs with a big brass pot in his hands, containing burning logs from the downstairs fireplace, transferring them up into the fireplace in his bedroom.

"How was your night?" Acillus asked his son when he walked in, stopping halfway up the stairs to ask him.

"Eventful."

"How so?"

"Aveline proposed."

"Did she?"

"Her Woma put her up to it."

"I see. Now I'm not surprised. Your Ma says Aveline is favored to wear the sunil after their next tournament."

Cael nodded before saying, "We talked about it on the walk home."

"Try to get some sleep. Tomorrow is your debut."

"I will. Tell Ma goodnight."

"I will. Goodnight, son," Acillus said, then he turned

and continued up the stairs.

Cael walked through the front room and grabbed the lit candle his father had left for him, then went through the hall leading toward his own room. As he reached it and went inside, he pushed aside the large blanket of fur hanging in the doorway.

Cael had accidentally broken the door by piercing a spear through it when he was eight. He'd made a fairly large hole and afterwards put up the fur blanket. He never put a wooden door back on because he liked the fur so much. It'd been there for twelve years and as Cael let the blanket go it fell back into perfect position, sealing the doorway in the exact corner of his room.

The hearth to his right was in excellent condition for over three hundred years old. It'd been built by Ridec himself. It was much wider than it was tall and it came up to Cael's stomach. The fireplace started a few paces from the hide covered corner door and went almost all the way to the other end of the wall because Ridec mistakenly made it longer than planned. It was fashioned from stone bricks placed together with no mortar. Many of the bricks, especially the top ones forming the arch, were curved to make them fit and stay together without falling to the floor.

Above the hearth was a shelf traversing the length of it. On the shelf there were numerous golden coins from different lands Cael had traveled. Thick candles with three wicks were on either end of the shelf and a ceramic bowl for burning silversage stood at the middle. He lit some of the sage with the candle and blew on it, causing the dried herb to smoke profusely before setting it back into the bowl.

Above the shelf, running horizontally on the wall was an old spear. It was one of Acillus' first and he gave it to Cael when he was younger. A few feet above that were two crossed swords with their tips pointing down, displayed behind an old shield. The shield and one of the swords were Ridec's while the other sword was Jossilan's. Ridec and Jossilan had put those weapons there themselves and they were only removed for maintenance.

Angled from the hearth and near the corner of the room was a tall wooden easel hanging on the wall which held many maps: maps of the city of Ideclan and all The Kinned Lands, maps all the way from the Western and Northwestern kingdoms, as well as maps of the far Eastern and Southern empires Cael had picked up from Gisspor Traders.

To the right side of the hanging easel and next to the stone hearth in the very corner of the room were several different spears and unstrung bows leaning up against a weapon holder that nestled in the convergence of the two walls.

To the left of the easel was a door leading out into the courtyard. Cael had a heavy wool blanket covering the doorway to keep out the cold, but this one's wooden door was still attached.

To the left of the door leading outside, at the corner opposite of the door Cael just walked through, was one of the Cedar Trees that made up the house, and right up against it was a large wooden desk made to fit in that corner perfectly. Shelves extended up from the desk all the way to the ceiling and there was no space available for any other book on them. Candles with three wicks waited to give light on the desk. And above where he wrote, hanging from his bookshelves, Cael had the Clanii Tenets carved on well made wooden plaques.

He kept stacks of paper, phials of ink, and fresh quills stored inside one of the drawers. In others he kept more maps and writings of his own, as well as writings of a few city projects he'd proposed; such as a duplicate of what he'd presented to get the underground aqueduct approved.

In the corner adjacent to his desk and along the wall was his bed. At the foot of his bed facing his desk was a chest. In between the desk and the chest was a tall wooden post with many long arms spiraling out from floor to ceiling. Most of Cael's clothes were hung from this Clanii Clothes Tower, and he folded his blanket and cloak over one of its wooden arms.

On the fourth wall opposite the wall with the door leading out into the courtyard, Cael had placed his collection of weapons he'd amassed throughout his life. There were at least ten staves lying on the ground or leaning up with pairs of bit sticks strewn about them.

Many swords were sheathed and hanging on the wall surrounding a beautiful Sravan Axe displayed at their center. He had three different shields propped up and seventeen spears waiting in weapon holders. Quivers filled to their fullest hung from wooden pegs and a number of unique bows accompanied them. Cael could've supplied a small warband with the weaponry in his room. He was proficient with all of them and a few were handmade by himself.

After glancing at them, the Prince was inspired to bring out his practice swords he'd prepared for the tournament tomorrow. He knelt down to get under his bed and moved both a medium sized wooden chest and a smaller locked metal chest before pulling out the bundle of blankets with his weapons wrapped within. He untied the leather lashings and unwrapped them carefully so they wouldn't clang together, unnecessary but such was his respect for them. Cael unwrapped the blankets all the way and then lifted up his two wooden swords, one in each hand.

They were identical and double edged with their shortest width not far up the blade and their widest width two thirds up the blade; each ending in a long, sharp, point. They were also widest right where the blade met the handle, giving them a design that was often referred to as leaf shaped. Cael learned of this design from a book far beyond the Eastern lands belonging to a kingdom called, Gal Gahma. The rare book was one of the most expensive things he ever traded with a Gisspor for.

Cael was weaponly diverse by his twelfth birthday, and never did he shy away from the bit sticks Segais had taught him. He developed a method with the help of Segais as a practice opponent, turning that method into something he could use with two swords. No one other than Segais had seen him do this. Neither his friends nor his family had any idea about the dual wielding system he'd been cultivating.

Cael worked with the Master Armorer, Corrick, for nearly two years developing his true swords into a reality, getting the mix of metals just right, the temperance exactly so. Corrick enjoyed helping him keep them a secret and loved working with the young Prince. He'd have Cael's true swords ready shortly, a few days at most. All he had to do was finish the edges and attach the hilts, then present them to Cael.

The Prince had finished making his wooden tournament swords a few months earlier. They were the sixth set he'd made, they'd taken three months to make, and were exact replicas of those tucked away at Corrick's forge.

The Edemarian Sword he'd made for Cristin, or Raddox, earlier that afternoon before the dancing, had nowhere near the amount of detail and was quite crude in comparison. He was only able to spend a little more than an hour on it between the tournaments and the dancing, and so it wasn't much more than an outline.

Cael stood with his two swords and walked to the center of his room, then started practicing. The Prince maneuvered all around, striking and defending in silent arcs while being careful not to hit any of his walls, load bearing pillars, or doors. The Prince swung harder and moved faster through the soft candlelight. He heard his breath escape him as he let forth more force. And when he neared the end of his practice he picked up the pace until the wooden swords sounded like wind.

He stopped at the part of the room he'd started, breathing slightly more, then wrapped his two swords and carefully put them back under his bed next to the wooden Edemarian Sword. He stretched, changed into his nightclothes, then climbed into bed feeling ready for tomorrow and fell fast asleep.

Cael dreamt of sitting at a large desk he recognized but didn't know. He looked around as if awake in the dream, realizing he was himself yet realizing he was in a different body while looking at himself. He looked at the desk and on it were many stacks of papers as thick as great books. He picked up the lone piece of parchment directly in front of him and brought it closer to his eyes until words were legible. 'The List,' it said at the top. And below were many names.

Declanii

Chronicle Twelve

My correspondence wasn't expected for another month but Segais says writing to you about what just happened is more important than itineraries or plans.

We were ambushed by pirates not too far from Daeadak. Our route ahead was cut off and one look aft showed me the same circumstance. Both directions had two ships and each ship had more men than mine. My instinct was to head North and West toward the Impassable Straits, as for some reason the straits were a comforting thought at that moment, and they continued to be for all of yesterday while we outran them with our rowers.

But today brought wind with it that allowed the pirates to catch back up. How they were able to follow us through the night I cannot tell, even Segais is suspicious. As they neared I saw how massive their sails were, and though we had unfurled ours they were no match for those fine pieces of engineering.

We labored mindfully to make our ship faster. I kept the rudder true and ordered almost everything thrown overboard. All sailors available threw out kite sails for extra pull. And even though this helped we watched them gain until they were close enough to hear their taunts. If the straits had been any farther away they'd have had us, but we narrowly made it to the Sea of Crags. They were so close we were knocking away their grappling hooks by the time I directed our vessel between the first two rocks.

These rocks were giant crags spearing out from the sea and the passage between them was narrow. As I intended, the closest ship ran into the crag on the right, smashing their hull, and the sailors from that ship had to climb onto the crag to survive. Many of them are probably still there.

The three ships remaining maneuvered around and continued following us deeper into the rocks. I saw another set jutting out from the water, not as narrow at sea level but possessing odd formations that stuck out around their peaks. I directed us through these crags and the ship after ours snagged its fore starboard boom sail against the crag to the right. The rock pulled the ship sideways and the next vessel crashed into them. Neither was sailable afterwards.

The last ship moved around and continued its pursuit. As we'd first made it to the Impassable Straits a fog was setting in, and the farther we went in the denser it became. When the fog was so dense we couldn't see the last ship nor they us I had the wind spilled, the anchors thrown, and the oars plunged to stop us. It broke many of the oars but I knew that'd happen. I used Roxgrin and Binneen to time their approach so as not to damage our ship as much as possible, and their ship bumped into ours. When they did, myself, Segais, the twenty Declanii, and sixty sailors boarded them.

Their number was close to two hundred and the battle brutal. The pirates had nowhere to go as we cut them down. Blood made the deck slick and the wind elevated their screams. I've known I'd have to end breath but to do so is something different. I feel sadness yet not remorse, for to let them live would've been to kill myself. The men I killed are connected to me now, and I them, I see the truth of that as you both have explained. And now I know the turmoil of having those I'm responsible for, die in a battle I've commanded. Thank you both for preparing me for this.

Sagas of the Ravenborne

Upon exploration of their craft it's quite evident they hailed from one of the coastal cities of Arashrill. We took what was worth saving, including oars, burned their bodies with their last ship, and have returned to our previous course.

Post Script: I see now why Segais wanted me to write this letter. I love you both and will write more soon.

Letter from Cael O'Ronan to his Mother and Father
Dated 28th of Earlysummer, Year 327 of the Ninth Age

Declanii

Chapter Thirteen

THE THIRD DAY OF EVERY TOURNAMENT WAS ALWAYS the most grand. And at the Declanii field there was much that needed to be done. Volunteers picked up what was missed from the night before while carpenters worked to assemble already made parts of wooden bleachers and wooden cubes. The cubes were used to form a foundation for the bleachers, and they elevated progressively as they went back to form a large stadium.

There had been far too many spectators at Ideclan for everyone to pack around the Declanii field, so the stadium had become quite extensive over the years. For the carpenters it was worth it when they heard the crowd's hurrahs, and also because they were paid by Ideclan's Treasuries for their time.

What they did was make frames of collapsible wooden cubes one span in height. The wooden frames were oak sturdy and when the workers stood the cubes up, placed them next to one another and linked them together with wooden pegs, then tacked them together with thin iron strips and nails, it formed a solid platform for the next level of planks and bleachers to be set upon. There were thousands of these and every single cube in the structure was linked to all the cubes around it. And then the entire structure was braced with beams to the ground.

Carpenters continued their routine in the early morn-ing darkness. The cubes and stands were set at the same place every three months and this had been done for so many years that the workers were now comfortably efficient. Skilled laborers climbed to the highest points with cubes tied to themselves and stacked those cubes on top, pegging them into place while others worked from the ground angling up to them. There were extra tasks that presented themselves as they went, and all were handled with ease.

At the beginning of Ideclan, when this field was the only field, Ridec had dug a hole in the ground at the East end and buried a log end up. He did the same many paces away and connected the two logs with a long beam. He did this so the ravens could perch while they watched the Declanii. As the years passed and the number of ravens calling Ideclan home swelled, many different poles and logs and even living trees were added to the roost so they could watch and preside over the fights.

The roost on the East end had become wider than the field, and close to each end of the roost started a set of bleachers with the cubes to elevate them. Both bleacher stands traversed three quarters length of the Declanii field and would be parallel except they curved outward starting at the roost and then curved back in at the other end, allowing for space in between the field and the stands.

The third and last set of stands was placed perpendicular to these on the Western side, across the field from the roost. It also bowed outward to allow space in front. And over two and a half thousand people worked to get it all ready for more spectators than ever before.

When the Sun rose to barely over the Philosian Range, people started arriving to get good seats. Lot drawn merchants set up their carts between the Southern stands and the Western stands at the Southwest corner of the field. And on the other end of the Western stands, between them and the Northern stands, stood the archery targets. They'd be shot at from the field.

This arrangement was outgrowing itself and barely able to accommodate all who came. Engineers and architects were working on a way to build a permanent stadium but this idea was still in the planning phases and a site not yet voted on by the city.

It was two hours before the fights would begin and already their were people starting to fill the stands and catch up with the carpenters. Kids played hide and seek underneath and all around the stands, making their parents frustrated because they kept getting in the workers' ways. Fires were tended as Tournament Criers ushered the people so every seat and all standing room could be taken advantage of.

Many in attendance grew up watching these tournaments and all were filled with excitement. There were always contestants who'd become crowd favorites, always talked about, and this morning was full of discourse.

But Cael O'Ronan was at the forefront of every discussion. It had long been a marvel to see how well the O'Ronan Prince would do in his first tournament. A Prince's Debut was a grand event for the city and in many ways a revealing. It had been a mark of proof for each O'Ronan that the son was a greater fighter than their father as he advanced further in his debut tournament than his father, a testament to the truth of the nifu ellwulle.

As the Ninth Age progressed, Ideclan's population grew. As the population grew, so did the army and the challenges to get to the top, and still, each O'Ronan son progressively placed higher than their father. Coming into the two hundredth year of Ideclan's history the O'Ronan's stopped entering at the Talon level and started entering in the Declanii. Acillus' Da, Ailither, made his way to the top of the Declanii his first tournament. King

Acillus fought all the way to the General of the Talons, Arkben Rorourke, in his. Arkben defeated Acillus then, the only to do so in single combat.

For Cael to continue the trend he'd have to defeat his father's General of the Talons, Seamus Weynahar. Many debated over who'd win that fight, the young Ravenborne or the old bear. In the people's minds, for Cael to continue the path of the nifu ellwulle he'd have to defeat Seamus and then face his father. And that was at the forefront of everyone's hushed speculations. Would they get to see the Prince challenge the King during his debut for the first time in Ideclan's history?

The old scout, Liadine, did his best to explain some of this to Elasus, or Ryker, while they and Sylla sat on a lower section of the stands and watched Cristin warm up for the day's events. Liadine talked about all he could with Elasus, answering every question he was able. And Elasus very much enjoyed the way Liadine told stories.

"Where was I?" the old scout asked after losing his thought from speaking on a side tangent too long.

"You were talking about Prince Cael's deeds when he was young," Elasus reminded him while eating a sweet treat.

"Ah yes, thank you. I already told you about the pirates he faced when sailing through the Impassable Straits."

"You did."

"And what of his answer to the riddle at Philos?"

"That was the first story you told."

"Oh, right. Did I tell you it was Cael's idea to tunnel the underground aqueduct? He petitioned for it when he was seven, I think, not much older than you are now. After he suggested that we knew we had a bright young mind for our Prince. Needless to say, Ryker, we've been looking forward to this festival for a long while."

The Festival of Four Fires had been celebrated by the Clanii for Ages. Every year it was held on the full moon after Winter Solstice. The four saplings for Ideclan's Hall had been planted during Spring before the Tribellion was formed, but Ideclan was officially founded at the beginning of the Seven Hundredth and Sixty First year of the Eighth Age on Winter Solstice, which changed the year to One and signaled the beginning of the Ninth Age.

During the first month of Ideclan's existence, the Thirteen of Old decided to continue the festival and it took on an even deeper meaning as it began symbolizing the birth of Ideclan with the birth of a new year. And the four fires retained their representation of the four seasons, but added to that was also the four saplings given to them by the Treewolves.

The number three was important to Ideclaners because it took an alliance of three cultures called the Tribellion that allowed for Ideclan to be founded. But more fundamental was the Clanii Calendar which had to be studied to grasp the level at which the number three weaved throughout. The fact that there were three threes in this year's title made everything more significant in the minds of the people.

Stragglers filled any space left on the stands. Aromas of different snacks and treats drifted through the crowds. The twenty merchants providing goods for this festival were chosen at the end of the last festival by lottery and all were busy keeping their tables and carts full. The first Declanii combatants hadn't yet taken the field and apprentices were already running back to their boss' shops to refill their stock. They'd known for three months that their names were pulled and had been preparing ever since.

Back at the baker's shop, bread was piled on ceramic trays stacked to the ceiling. One of the butchers had eight hollowed tree stumps hauled in on two wagons. And inside them he smoked different preparations of meat. Another merchant had an ample supply of fresh fruits wrapped in paper and shipped up from the South.

But no matter what the people were preoccupied by, everyone hurried when they saw the Tournament Master take the field and the combatants gathering off to the side while being organized by Tournament Criers. It was frigid and more than half of them wore their Winter cloaks in the deep blue of sunil.

Criers cleared the field of children and people trying to get across, which meant the fights were only moments away. And the Tournament Master raised his hands, signaling his request for silence.

A rustling of wings grew loud. Caws became audible and all looked to see a murder of Ideclan Ravens flying for the roost at the side of the field. They flew over and came down in circles, landing on the many perches. Over one hundred ravens, including Acillus' two friends, Dugan and Fey, and Cael's two, Roxgrin and Binneen, came to watch the proceedings of the day.

It took the crowd little time to quiet down and all became still.

"Now, we are ready to begin," the Tournament Master declared with a smile and the crowd erupted as the fighters went to their camps.

The people stayed in the stands but the fighters had their own camps at the outer parts of just three sides of the Declanii field, as the roost had no camps in front of it. At their camps were anyone from helpful trainers, cutmen, squires, or selected friends and family members. All of whom quieted down in unison to hear the next statement made by the Master.

"First Talon Commander, you are challenged!"

Commander Corbin, who wasn't of Clanii descent, stepped out to the center amidst plenty of cheer. Corbin was fifty three with long brown hair, brown eyes, medium height, and average muscle. And his skill with the spear set him apart. The First and Twelfth Talons were on the farthest flanks in most battle formations so only those who wished to fight with spears joined the First and Twelfth.

Corbin spun his spear as he approached the center of the field. The Declanii tournament had no padded armor regulations. Instead, the fighters dressed in their sunils or regular clothing and helm. Corbin wore no sunil, he was one of the few Talon Commanders who'd never joined the Declanii. Rather, he fought for Talon Command, won it, and kept it.

The First Talon was under the first unit of Declanii, or First File, which was headed by the Mullquanes and command-ed by Quinnlan, Cael's uncle. Staying a leader under the Mullquanes was a heavy task but Corbin had been up to it. He was dressed in a simple brown tunic with no sleeves and a pair of black pants underneath. And his brown hair was tied behind him.

The man challenging Corbin was a capable combatant. He came close to fighting his way into the Declanii the last tournament held for rank and that had made him somewhat recognizable. As he walked onto the field he received a good amount of cheers as well.

The two fighters stood across from each other with shields and spears at the ready.

The crowd started getting louder as their anticipation built while waiting for the Tournament Master's signal. He knew he'd have to call it soon or even the contestants wouldn't hear him.

"Fight!"

The challenger charged while thrusting his spear. Corbin had his shield in left hand and spear in right. He lunged forward and to the left, parrying the thrust to his right with the spear, and then lunged with the other leg past his opponent. When he landed he spun toward his right to face the challenger who'd been turning around after charging forward. Corbin thrust his spear at him while he turned, and the challenger finished turning to find the spear pushing at his chest.

"End!"

Corbin's head was high as always but his challenger's wasn't. The young man was named Rakas Sal. He hailed from a small village West of Teker Ren, and seemed just a boy next to Corbin the Quick.

There were no more Talon Command Challenges after that and next came the Declanii tournament. Each of the twelve files would now fight up their ranks in a series of three tiers until the fourth tier, where the champions of each file would fight one another for the right to challenge Finnian U'dinry in the fifth, then the old bear, Seamus Weynahar in the sixth, and then the King for the seventh and final tier.

Four sections were cordoned off at the middle of the field so four fights could go simultaneously. And shortly after, there were four sets of fighters vying for placement.

It was difficult for anyone to hear over the crowd until the foreign upstart with the longsword walked onto the field. The talk was that he hailed from The Gray Forest, though, many thought that was just a joke because of the size of him, since The Gray Forest was the largest forest known. The other three fights went on but many in the crowd discussed the prospects of his next fight as they watched Raddox walk toward his area.

Cristin kept it as hidden as possible but on the inside he was a raging torrent of nervousness. Even when he was young and stood next to his father, Kaldranos, as he spoke to the masses of the city of Edemar, or when his grandfather, Paxinrios, schooled and disciplined the Edemarian Swordsmen, there were never this many people.

All I wanted to do was join the army so I could provide a life and learning for my son and not have to live in the wilds. But no, I had to be foolish and see how well I could do. I should have just loved the forests. This is too dangerous.

He was fearful of Edemarians recognizing him and angry for drawing this much attention toward himself. He'd heard his people's Generals and diplomats would be in town soon, if not already, but that didn't exclude any other number of

Edemarians from already being there. It'd been almost exactly three years since he fled. That amount of time had put a lot of stress and worry on him. But anyone who noticed his worry now just took it as nervousness for the fight.

The young lad snapped out of it when he saw the Tournament Crier looking at him, asking if he were ready. He nodded and set his position. Then the crier asked the man in sunil facing Cristin, named Ruan of the Lahanbrey Family, if he were ready. He was of Clanii descent, a member of the Declanii, and turning sixty this year. He nodded and set his stance as well.

"Fight!"

Cristin realized he was tense and relaxed as Ruan charged in while raising his sword to strike. Cristin brought his weapon across to parry, then brought the sword back to attack and slammed it into Ruan's shield as he blocked, breaking the strapping that held it to his arm. The strike sapped much of Ruan's strength in that arm and it burned. Cristin immediately swung his sword around to strike again. Ruan tried blocking with his own sword but it was knocked from his hand. Raddox continued his weapon's motion, bringing it all the way around himself in a full arc and then stopped the wooden blade just short of Ruan's neck.

"End!" the crier yelled with verve.

Loud cheers rang for Raddox as he walked back to his camp where an old scout many knew waited for him. It wasn't unusual for Ideclaners to cheer on a foreigner. Every family that called Ideclan home was at one point from somewhere else, including those who founded the city. Indeed, Ideclan was a steady stream of successful immigrants.

As the fights went on another seized the attention of the entire crowd. Irhanach Fianna walked onto the field. His burning red hair caught the light of the Sun as he swung his arms to keep them loose. He wore a suede leather tunic that was a deep maroon and held close to him by a braided rope belt.

Many who considered themselves authorities on tournament fighting believed Irhanach's flash and flair to be his downfall. It had gotten him into the Declanii tournament but a number of side bets were now placed against him by spectators.

He peered over his shield at his opponent, Dulkas. Dulkas was from a small city called Hastu, located one hundred miles North of Arashrill on the coast. He was also a scout for the Ninth Talon. The scouts were well known and sometimes more difficult to beat. It was harder to stay alive as a scout and they trained more often at one on one combat.

"Fight!"

Sword and shield clashed as they moved around each other, blocking and parrying, striking and dodging. The match lasted longer than most so when the other three on the field finished they didn't continue, allowing everyone to watch the contest.

The two fighters had that uniqueness about them; when another's style is perfect against their own and likewise theirs to the other's. Watching them fight was like watching something choreographed rather than improvised.

The scout swept his leg forward, trying to trip Irhanach. As Irhanach backed away from it, the fiery haired lad brought his sword down, striking Dulkas' shin and the scout jumped back in pain, becoming off balance. Irhanach bashed his shield into the scout's shield, knocking him back more, and then moved in aggressively to prove a kill strike at the scout's neck before he could recover, ending the match.

The young Fianna returned to camp amidst the cheers, and joined Anrahan and Ohelathe as they prepared for their challenges. Cael was off talking to his Da at the side of the Declanii field with an unusual bundle of fur and cloth underneath his arm. Within it he had his two wooden swords and the crude Edemarian Sword made for Raddox.

Anrahan's fight was shortly after Irhanach's. He pulled as an opponent one who was considered a Veteran of the Sunil. His name was Alaois of the Shymurrow Family. Ten years back there'd been a great naval battle between Camulus' forces and Ideclan in which this veteran valiantly partook. He was considered a veteran back then as well; a worthy adversary for Anrahan and indeed the toughest fighter any of the young lads would have to face for their first tier.

"Fight!"

Alaois charged. Anrahan crow hopped with a shield punch. He struck the veteran square in the face and blood came gushing out of his nose and mouth as he fell backwards like a tree, unconscious before hitting the ground.

Criers rushed in to perform aid while Anrahan stepped back like he was supposed to. Alaois didn't wake up after a short span of time, so he was disqualified and carried off the field where he did finally awaken.

Anrahan advanced but he wasn't happy as he walked back to camp.

"I didn't mean to bloody the lad," he said as he got close to his friends.

"You advance," stated Ohelathe, a very Mullquane way of looking at it.

"Aye. But it's not going to look good when it comes time for everyone to vote. They want precision, not brutality."

"You'll be fine," Cael said as he approached the group. "Everyone knows it's real war that has to be fought and not just the flair of our tournaments."

Irhanach and Anrahan were doing well. Ohelathe's archery would start before the third tier. And Cael prepared himself. He chose to fight in the Eleventh File. The Prince was the only one who could do this. All others except the Declanii Commanders and Talon Commanders were drawn by lots to determine which file's tournament they'd fight in. Cristin was pulled by lottery into the Second File's tournament, Anrahan was pulled for the Fifth, and Irhanach pulled the Tenth.

Cael chose the Eleventh, that way he wouldn't have to fight any of his friends unless they made it to the top with him. And also because the Eleventh division of the army, Declanii File and Talon, were commanded by the Weynahars, a fierce family.

Seamus Weynahar was General of the Talons. His son, Tomass; the Eleventh Talon Commander. And their relative, Finnum; Commander of the Eleventh File of Declanii, one of the fighters in the King's front Ravenline. A worthy family for Cael to make his debut with.

The Prince walked onto the field proper with his

bundle underneath an arm. Except for the First and Twelfth Talons there were no restrictions for what arms one had to use. Drills incorporating many different weapons into the support of a shield wall had long been in place and interesting tactics ensued. Yet still, many wondered why he didn't have a shield.

As Cael walked toward one of the four sections on the Declanii field he was accompanied by a young boy. Each section had two squires, one for each combatant. Cael's squire was eight years old and excited to be with the Prince for a fight.

Cael and the boy reached an outer edge of their section and continued conversing while waiting for the fight before his to end. The young O'Ronan could see his opponent on the other side. His name was Vonder. And he was a second generation Ideclaner.

When the fight in front of them ended, Cael knelt to the ground and carefully set his bundle down, then began unwrapping the outer layer of fur and inner layers of cloth. Many in the crowd leaned this way or that, trying to get a glimpse of what he had.

After Cael stood back up, the squire grabbed the cloth and fur wrappings still covering the Edemarian Sword, then stepped back. The large bundle was a bit heavy for the young lad.

Everyone had a reaction to Cael's weapons. There were cheers, whistles, claps, and jesterly boos. He moved them fluidly as he walked to the stance marks, not paying attention to any of the crowd. And when he got there, Cael nodded at Vonder. And Vonder nodded back.

The Tournament Criers for the other three sections let

their matches finish, then didn't keep them going so all could watch the Prince.

"Fight!"

Cael thrust each sword at Vonder. Vonder blocked with his shield. The young O'Ronan stepped forward with a feint and Vonder stepped back, then attacked with his own straight thrust. The Prince stepped to his left and with his right hand sword pointing down he parried the thrust to his right. With his left hand, Cael snuck the other sword just above his opponent's shield and then under his chin while stepping forward. And Vonder was forced to stand up and walk backwards while Cael's sword pushed at his throat.

"End!" the crier yelled.

Ravens cawed and the crowd cheered.

As Cael got back to their camp his friends had many questions about the new swords.

"They're shaped like this so I can hack," he answered while hacking with one. "And pierce," he said while thrusting the other. "The design allows for both."

"Where'd you learn of that?" Irhanach asked.

"A weapons manual from a land far past the Eastern empires. I traded a Gisspor for it."

Before the Sun could move one more finger's width in the sky, the second tier fights began. Cael's name was called first and he jogged to the stance marks with vigor. As the Prince made his way he saw his opponent and smiled. It was

Declanii

Tomass Weynahar, the eldest of Seamus' children.

Cael and Tomass squared off at their stance marks. Tomass was strongly built but the Weynahars were known for their strategic minds. Cael knew it was one of the reasons why Seamus and his Da had been best friends their whole lives.

"Fight!"

Tomass shield bashed and Cael crouched completely underneath, then thrust each of his swords into Tomass' ribs while shuffling forward. And the Weynahar's own momentum dug the swords in farther.

"End!"

Cael stood with a smile and shrugged as Tomass laughed. It didn't bother him that the match was brief. Then they shook each other's forearms, half of the Clanii greeting or farewell, and walked off the field together.

Next it was Cristin's turn to fight. And he and Cael nodded as they moved past each other on the path.

Cristin was fighting a Veteran of the Sunil named Scannac Fianna, a distant relative of Irhanach's. And there was much talk of this being the end for the newcomer. If there was anyone at Ideclan who came close to matching Cristin's size, it was this man. He'd worn the deepest blue in the black of a raven for more than twenty years. And his scowl was sinister.

Cristin felt pleased with how well he was doing but hated being out in the open for anyone to recognize him.

The night before, while celebrating with the city on the

fields, Liadine had introduced him to the woman in charge of Housing and Planning. Cristin almost jumped for joy when she said she'd talk of available houses with them after the tournament.

A worry now troubling Cristin though, because of talk he'd heard over the past few days, was finding someone to watch Elasus if he had to leave with the army. But Sylla was getting along well with his son and said she'd take care of the child if and when they went somewhere. So that seemed to solve itself. Yet he still didn't want to leave his son behind.

What choice do I have? This is the game I have to play if we want to live here. And why did that Philosian have to tell Elasus about synchronicities? he questioned himself.

The word still returned to him. And reminded him of his wife. But he pushed all this from his attention and focused on the match.

"Fight!"

Scannac walked aggressively toward Cristin as if nothing could get in his way. Cristin stepped back, bringing his sword up from behind himself, then stepped forward while swinging the weapon over and forward in a full arc strike. The veteran blocked and the powerful strike combined with the forceful block splintered his shield while breaking Cristin's longsword in two.

When the Edemarian felt his sword fail he dropped it, then moved in and punched Scannac square in the jaw from up under his helm. Scannac fell backwards on his rear and felt the sword rip from his hand as Cristin stomped on his chest, forcing him down. Then the Edemarian put the wooden blade at Scannac's neck.

"End!"

The crowd erupted.

And Cristin couldn't help but smile through all his worry while walking off the field.

Irhanach and Anrahan ended up fighting at the same time not long after him. Both were victor at the end of their matches and each caught the other peering across the field to see if they were still standing for advancement, and they grinned at each other.

At the end of the second tier there was an intermission before the archery tournament. During the interim, many had time to make it home or stand in line and grab something to eat. This was an occurrence for much conversation as the fighters and crowd intermingled. Cristin spent the time with his son. Ir-hanach went for a walk with Liss. Ohelathe and Anrahan ran to grab soft taters. And Cael spoke with his father.

"What does that foreign lad, Raddox, make you think of, Da?"

"Two things," Acillus said to his son. "His fighting style reminds me of Edemar. And I've come to the conclusion he's more the product of selective breeding rather than the realm of happenstance. Something to come out of Hinturan, perhaps," the King joked.

It was close to the answer Cael had sought. He was growing more confident he knew who this man was. The Prince was now almost certain he remembered him from Edemar.

"That new Commander General of Edemar's, the one

who's here or will be soon: I forget his name?" Acillus continued.

"It's Kemish."

The King leaned in to signal he hadn't heard over the crowd.

"Kemish!"

He heard it then, but also failed to pick up the disdain in his son's voice. Cael certainly remembered Kemish from his travels at Edemar when he was younger.

"Be wary during this council, Da. The Edemarians are going to be their same old selves."

"We'll see. I know they can move past their failings. They only have to know that as well."

"They'll have to *want to* as well," Cael returned, and his Da laughed.

The archery tournament began shortly after the intermission. There were thirty six Declanii archers and thirty six challengers. Their tournament would be conducted in two parts. The first was distance and the distances were always different for every tournament. There were five distance targets and each contestant started from the closest with three arrows. If an archer missed and the next archer hit, then they who missed would have to hit their next target or they were out.

All contestants let fly their first three arrows and made it to the second distance.

Then they flew again and made it to the third.

Tristas Rorourke, son of the former General of the Talons, Arkben Rorourke, was one of the most renowned archers in all The Kinned Lands and known for his three bottle trick. He and two of the Mullquanes, Aislin and Ohelathe, were unquestionably in the lead.

During the next distance, competitors started falling out while others began to shine. Among those who shined were Crin Rorourke, Paidraig Brogan, Raniel and Galladan Hafrana, and Diarmuid Shymurrow.

After the fifth and final distance, they, along with Tristas, Aislin, and Ohelathe, were the only ones left. These eight waited as criers took their positions to throw targets for the second part.

A crier stood on either side of the archery range, and at a nod from the archer, they threw a paddle no larger than a good sized pumpkin across.

Each archer took turns putting an arrow through one paddle for the first round. Then they took five paces back and so did the criers.

In the course of the next round, Crin Rorourke hit his target. Then Paidraig Brogan went after him and missed.

Galladan, youngest son of Admiral Finn Hafrana, went next. As the crier threw the paddle he let fly. Everyone could hear the twang of his bow and the thud of the hit. And his target toppled over while it fell.

Paidraig stepped forward once more and nodded. The target was thrown then the arrow let fly and the miss so close that only his arrow's feather hit the paddle. Paidraig's shot eliminated him and he finished eighth overall.

Now the criers would throw two paddles per turn. And if an archer missed, then the next would have to miss as well or they'd be out. And then the next would have to miss or they'd both be out. There were no second arrows from this round forward. All six archers could be eliminated if they missed and the final archer hit their paddles.

Raniel Hafrana went first and was eliminated by Ohelathe; seventh place.

Crin was then eliminated by Galladan; sixth place.

Galladan was eliminated by Diarmuid; fifth place.

The last four left were Aislin, Tristas, Diarmuid, and Ohelathe. Three rounds past and no archer missed. So they advanced to the next phase where criers on both sides threw targets for each archer. Now they'd have to hit two targets from both sides of the range, totaling four.

The archers held four arrows in their draw hands, enabling them to nock the arrows in succession rapidly. They trained for this extensively. During battles they grabbed bundles from their quivers, not one at a time, and this greatly affected their rate of release.

The archers went one round and none of them blundered. Then in the next round, Aislin missed his last paddle. His grandson, Ohelathe, went after and pierced all his, eliminating his Woda and dropping him into fourth place.

Aislin had been counted among the top three archers for over ten years. And the elder Mullquane gave his Wosri a smile and a pat on the shoulder before walking off the field.

Shortly after, Diarmuid was eliminated by Tristas. So only Tristas and Ohelathe remained. They each went another two rounds with no misses and the difficulty advanced.

Ohelathe was first and hit them all. Then Tristas did the same.

Tristas went first in the next round. The targets flew up and across the field and each were pierced by his accuracy. It was rare that archery tournaments made it this far and the crowd expressed their appreciation.

Ohelathe stepped up and nodded. The criers threw their targets fast. He hit his last three but missed his first one. And after Tristas' next turn, the Rorourke was victor.

The crowd let all the archers know how much they enjoyed their display by giving them a standing ovation backed by raucous cheers.

"Next time," Tristas told the Mullquane with a smile as he started off to collect his arrows.

Ohelathe pointed his bow at him and nodded. He hadn't won the tournament but he made it further than any other archer ever did, displaying skills that took men decades to master. When the Tournament Crier held up Ohelathe's hand and announced second place, the crowd roared. And as he returned to his friends they congratulated him.

Criers then prepared for the third tier. The winners of the second tier would now fight until one combatant from each File remained. Then they'd face the Commander of that File, the member of the Ravenline, to complete the third tier.

For the First File of Declanii it came down to Corbin, Talon Commander, against Quinnlan Mullquane, First File Commander. Quinnlan was a Mullquane who never took to the bow and focused on the spear. The Mullquanes were consummate spear wielders, hence, they fought on the flanks for Ridec so long ago, and then controlled the First Talon, a spear Talon. Corbin put up a courageous fight but Quinnlan defeated him in a masterful display.

For the Second File, Pawdar, Second Talon Commander, and newcomer, Raddox, squared off to see who'd face Awley Rorourke. Cristin had an intact wooden longsword that had been found for him. He wore dark green pants and a long sleeved gray coat. Both his pants and coat had rips from the long years on the run. Pawdar was a Veteran of the Sunil and wearing the colors. It was interesting to see the contrast between sunil clothes and ripped rags so high up in the tournament. Artists and sketchers would make many renderings in the months to come.

"Fight!"

Cristin attacked. His strikes were strong but Pawdar deflected them off his shield before beginning his own counter attacks. He baited and frustrated Cristin with odd angles and movements, then sidestepped to get him to trip. But the young Edemarian recovered and was able to let go of a surprising swing of his own. Pawdar blocked with his shield and took advantage of an opening by thrusting his sword at the top of Cristin's stomach. Cristin turned his body just in time to dodge, then grabbed Pawdar's wrist that held the sword and pulled him in close, elbowing him in the face with his other arm. The blow stunned Pawdar but his helm took most of the force. Then Cristin's longsword hit him in the neck just after.

"End!"

Very shortly, the Edemarian found himself facing the Declanii Commander, Awley Rorourke.

"Fight!"

Cristin swung hard and the Commander used his shield to block. Then Awley swung low and Cristin brought his sword down to parry. The Edemarian followed through with a step forward and a shoulder lift into Awley after the parry. The Commander was lifted off his feet then thrown to the ground, and Cristin finished with his blade ready to pierce Awley's sternum as he landed.

"End!"

Raddox had won and would advance, much to the surprise of everyone.

The Third File went like most others with the Talon Commander facing the Declanii Commander for the next tier. The Talon Commander was Hasufal and the Declanii Commander, Ayson of the Brogan family. And Ayson defeated Hasufal.

For the Fourth File it was the Fourth Talon Commander, Colman Lahanbrey, against his Declanii counterpart, Noa Nirowin. Noa was the oldest fighter in the army at one hundred and two, and subsequently the most experienced. He looked as though he could be Colman's Great Grandfather. But age and experience dominated the fight with Noa advancing.

The Fifth File pitted the upstart, Anrahan, against one of his childhood heroes. Anrahan had just beaten the Talon

Commander, Fergus Hafrana, and would now face Phaedrus of Gisspor, the man who all the boys used to climb on top of the house to watch.

Phaedrus was born from a land known for its Master Navigators, merchant traders, large cargo vessels, and knowledge of the paths of planets and stars, not sword and shield fighting. He kept his black hair cropped at two fingers width and it spiked on its own. He was the kind of man who looked like he was in a bad mood even when he wasn't. And the scar that caused one of his brown eyes to droop didn't help.

Both he and Anrahan walked onto the field next to each other.

"Hello, lad," Phaedrus said in his deep voice.

Phaedrus knew he was many of the Ideclan boys' favorite. He was a testament to non Clanii lineage being able to contend, keep up with, and defeat the descendants of Clanii. And Anrahan had emulated a lot of his fighting style from him, Clanii or not.

"Fight well," Phaedrus said as he tapped his wooden sword against Anrahan's shield before walking over to the stance marks.

Phaedrus wore a sarong the color of sunil and a vest the same hue. Gisspor always traded with far lands so their clothes were often as varied as their travels.

"Fight!"

They charged and collided shield to shield. Before they broke apart, Phaedrus swept his sword across. Anrahan ducked and shuffled back. When he came up, he lunged forward and shield jabbed at Phaedrus. The veteran pushed Anrahan's shield down with his own and attacked over the top with his sword, stopping it right at the conjunction of Anrahan's shoulder and neck.

"End!"

The crowd showed their respects for the young one, but it'd be Phaedrus who'd advance. Anrahan walked off the field completely frustrated. Irhanach had defeated him in almost the same manner, and now he was resolved to never get into that position again.

The Sixth File was fought by its Declanii Commander and Talon Commander. The Talon Commander was Ainnileas Shymurrow, one of the best. But he lost to Marchann Hafrana, eldest son of Admiral Finn Hafrana, and father to Aveline.

The Seventh File was won by Declanii Commander Corcc Lahanbrey, who defeated Talon Commander, Lorcan Cailian.

The Eighth was won by Aymond Aenenay, Anrahan's father and Declanii Commander. He fought his Talon Commander, Liamm U'dinry, for victory.

The Ninth was won by Coilin U'dinry, Commander of the Ninth File. He fought one of his subsidiary lieutenants who'd just defeated his Talon Commander, Arrann of Arashrill.

The Tenth had one of the best Declanii Commanders, Eilidir Shymurrow; the best Talon Commander, Crastinus; and the young one, Irhanach Fianna. As it went, Irhanach faced Crastinus first.

Crastinus was another in a commanding position whose family wasn't Clanii or even from Ideclan. He originally hailed from the far Western lands that interacted with Gissporian traders. Something happened to him during his youth so he bartered passage with the Gisspor because of it. He asked them where a swordsman might go, and they brought him to Ideclan.

Crastinus was the Commander at the gate who'd let Cristin and Elasus into the city on that cold night before the festival. The young family reminded him a little of himself when he left home all those years ago.

"Good to see you, Irhanach."

"And you, Crastinus. I trust your whole life has led you to this point and now that you're here, you're finally ready."

"Oh yes lad! I've been training for you since I beat my first whelp!"

"The only thing age will do in this fight is slow you down."

They both grinned and set their stances.

"Fight!"

Crastinus moved to his left, putting himself between Irhanach and the Winter Sun, which put the Sun in Irhanach's eyes. He tried mitigating this but Crastinus was like a shield wall he couldn't get around. It frustrated Irhanach to the point of trying a foolish overhand strike. Crastinus took advantage and knocked the boy off balance, then came in with an upward pierce into his stomach.

"End!"

The crowd cheered for Irhanach's performance. And shortly after, Talon Commander Crastinus defeated Declanii Commander, Eilidir Shymurrow, to advance.

The Eleventh File's fight was fought by Finnum Weynahar and Prince Cael. And before it was called, a few ravens cawed.

"Fight!"

Finnum charged with furious strikes. The Prince took both his swords while stepping left, angling around Finnum, and struck down from left to right, attacking Finnum's sword and shield. After bringing his swords up rapidly he brought them down again, attacking right to left this time, striking Finnum's sword and flank as he continued angling around him.

The Prince walked slowly yet sidestepped fast, moving in a way that made Finnum appear as though he were stuck in molasses. As Finnum kept turning to face him, Cael kept sidestepping around him while leaving one of his swords horizontal at waist level. As Finnum turned he pressed his stomach against the horizontal sword and Cael did a slicing motion, pulling his sword through Finnum while continuing to step around him, one step ahead of him. Then Cael put his other sword point at Finnum's lower back and pushed him forward.

"End!"

Cael advanced.

The Twelfth File was fought by Banna Cailian, the Talon Commander, who was defeated by Declanii Commander,

Lochlann Fianna. And Lochlann advanced to the next tier.

The twelve now left, plus four honorable mentions, fought the fourth tier to see who'd face Captain Finnian U'dinry in the fifth. These were fought one at a time and the first eight to be eliminated were the honorable mentions, as well as Noa Nirowin, Ayson Brogan, Coilin U'dinry, and Lochlann Fianna, Irhanach's distant relation.

Next, Quinnlan Mullquane fought Cristin, known as Raddox.

"Fight!"

Quinnlan lunged forward and thrust his spear at Cristin's face. Cristin caught the spear and split it in two with a tremendous strike. He kept the part with the point and Quinnlan turned his part around so the counterbalance was now like a mace. Both attacked aggressively until Quinnlan knocked the half spear from Cristin's hand. Then Raddox held his longsword with both hands and kept Quinnlan on the defensive.

Quinnlan watched for an opening and found one, then bulled into Cristin, knocking him to the ground. On the way down, Cristin swung his longsword to keep Quinnlan from getting on top of him, then hurried to a knee with a powerful swing, slamming the longsword into Quinnlan's shield. The Mullquane kicked for Cristin's face but missed, then went to slam his mace into Raddox's weapon and knocked the longsword from the Edemarian's grip.

Cristin instantly pushed up with his legs and punched Quinnlan square in the jaw, dropping him to a knee. Raddox punched again but hit his shield. Quinnlan got up with a shield bash and Cristin moved back, then ducked underneath and grabbed Quinnlan by the waist. He picked him up and before Quinnlan could counter, he was taken to the ground. Cristin scrambled on top of him while moving his shield out of the way, then raised his fist to strike.

"End!"

They got up from the ground and shook each other's hands.

"You fight well, young lad" Quinnlan said. "I daresay you've done it before. Are you truly from The Gray Forest as the city talk would tell?"

"*Junag.*"

"What was that?"

"It means, 'I am,' in one of our native tongues."

"Ah," Quinnlan answered with a smile that stretched the Mark of the Mullquanes.

Next, Phaedrus of Gisspor fought Marchann Hafrana. And Phaedrus advanced.

Then Crastinus defeated Corcc Lahanbrey.

Anrahan's father, Aymond Aenenay, the strongest living Clanii, was then defeated by Cael shortly after.

When that fight finished, Cael went over to Raddox with the fastly made Edemarian Sword.

"Hey, Raddox," the Prince called to him.

Cristin turned to see Cael holding the sword with its point going all the way down to the ground, roughly cut but still close to the correct size and style. And the young Edemarian froze for the briefest of moments.

"I'm only here to assist you in making it as far in your debut tournament as possible; that's all. You'll need this." Cael let the sword fall to the ground before Cristin. "I'm impressed you didn't need it for my uncle."

"I..."

"Fight well," he interrupted before walking away.

The next combatants were Cristin and Phaedrus. Both walked to the center of the field and faced each other. Cristin didn't know how to feel; fear of being caught seemed reasonable. But instinct took over as he held the familiar weapon.

"Fight!"

The Edemarian quickly realized distance was key as Phaedrus worked to let no distance between them. Then a smooth sidestep got the Gissporian around Cristin's defense as Phaedrus moved in to strike. Cristin rotated the sword from its center to block. Phaedrus struck again and the Edemarian Sword blocked again. Its blade was five inches wide and Cristin treated it like a wall he could hide behind.

Then the Edemarian swung fast at Phaedrus. The Gissporian blocked with his shield before lunging in. Cristin stepped forward and used his own hip as a fulcrum and the Commander's own momentum to throw him off his feet. Then he put his Edemarian Sword right at Phaedrus' throat as he landed on the ground.

"End!"

Liadine looked over at Elasus and said, "You know, Ryker, I think your father is one of the more talented fighters we've ever seen in our tournaments. Where'd he learn all that?"

"Protecting me."

The next fight was fought by Cael and Crastinus.

As each stood at their stance marks, Crastinus said, "Well, after twenty years of watching you grow, we finally get to see how all those years have fared you."

Cael smiled before saying, "You get to experience it."

Crastinus laughed as fight was yelled.

Both combatants attacked. Cael parried Crastinus' attack while his own continued unabated. Crastinus ducked. The Prince sidestepped to force his opponent to reposition. As he did, Cael struck again and Crastinus knocked the sword from his hand with his shield. The Ravenborne held his lone sword with two hands and Crastinus sneered as though he'd cornered his prey. He charged the Prince with a thrust. Cael corralled Crastinus' blade with his own, maneuvering it in the direction he wanted. And then with a flick of the Prince's wrists, Crastinus' sword flung from his hand and Cael's blade went to his neck.

"End!"

The crowd and ravens cheered. The young O'Ronan performed as expected and would now face Raddox, who was astounding everyone. Their fight would close out the fourth tier, and the winner would face Finnian, Captain of Declanii.

After a brief intermission, Cael and Raddox were out on the field while waiting for the crowd to find their seats once more.

"I see you know that weapon," Cael said to him.

"I hear you know many weapons," Cristin answered.

"Yes, but the Edemarian Sword is one I have little experience with. I was at Edemar once, when I was younger. Is that where you learned to use it?"

Cac! I should have just lost but no! I had to see how well I could fight!

Thoughts of worry and escape grew in Cristin's mind. He looked for Elasus, and his son still appeared safe with Sylla.

"I remember a young lad when I was there," Cael continued. "He was about my age then. He's supposed to be dead now. But back then he did a kindness for me when no one else would."

Cristin looked at Cael in the eyes, for the Prince was referring to himself.

Cael could see how anxious Raddox had become and therefore knew this was him.

"My friend from back then could never do the things he was accused of, even if he grew up at Edemar. I'll always be in debt to him."

Cristin eased slightly and looked at Cael with curiousness.

The Tournament Master appeared and bid them, "Take your stances please."

The crowd quieted as they saw this. And some of them began to smell smoke.

"Fighting to advance," the Master yelled, "is Raddox of the Gray Forest!"

Cristin set his stance.

"Also fighting to advance; Prince Cael O'Ronan!"

Cael set his stance.

Both looked at each other, ready for battle.

"Wait…" the Master continued. "What is that?" he asked, and the two combatants looked up to where he pointed.

"Fire!" someone shouted from atop the stands.

"Fire! Fire!" more people yelled with vehemence.

The backs of every stand holding the bleachers had been set on fire with an accelerant. And the people at the tops started rushing down, creating chaos. The accelerant caused the fires to grow rapidly and screams began permeating the air as whooshes of flames climbed up the stands, leaping to great heights on three sides of the Declanii field.

At the merchants' station, across from where the archery took place, a carriage door burst open and a Vord, nine feet tall and wearing all bearskins, exited with violence and rage. He charged for the center of the field toward the Prince and Cristin.

In the confusion, only a few saw him at first. And those in his way were run through like a plow in the ground. Then many saw the Vord and some ran to attack. Ohelathe let fly an arrow that hit the giant in the throat but bounced off.

Cael and Cristin stood side by side with their wooden weapons, ready to face the Vord. At the same time, each broke their weapons against the ground in the correct way to give them sharper points, and they grinned at each other before looking back at the charging attack.

A group of warriors reached the giant and tried stopping him but he wasn't slowed. The Vord picked up Ayson Brogan by the back of his head with one hand and caved in his face with an elbow, then slammed his dead body into Seamus, knocking the General unconscious. Rallin, the Vanguard Commander, tried piercing the Vord but his sword broke on the giant's skin, and he was knocked back several feet by a backhand as the Vord kept running and killing.

The King, Queen, Aislin, and Quinnlan, ran over and stood by Cael and Cristin. Finnian, Captain of Declanii; along with Ainnileas and Crastinus; tried slowing the giant before he reached them. The Commanders went for his legs as Finnian jumped to get a hold of his neck. Those who went low were shaken off within a step and the Vord grabbed Finnian and slammed a fist down on his head, then stomped a foot into his face after dropping him to the ground as he continued running.

The Vord was now only four giant paces away.

Then Segais arrived, his movements unnoticed by everyone. Time slowed for the old wizard as he maneuvered behind the giant and put a hand on his back.

He said the ancient healing words, "*Palratas seero yunovik, kalratas heerlox sunovrim.*"

Then time returned as the Vord took two more steps before falling to the ground, dead.

Chronicle Thirteen

"Know you about the Vords, young one? Know you about the race of giants who walk this earth?"

"No one has seen a Vord for a thousand years," the child answered.

"True, but why do you think that is?"

"The Vords are gone."

"Gone? And what could make them gone? Vords live longer than any human and are incredibly tougher. It's said it takes a Vord to kill a Vord."

"Then why train for them? Why build castles the way we do if we can't kill them?"

"We do what we must."

"Tell me about the Vords, please."

"The men are bred for war, eight to twelve feet tall with bodies as strong as bulls. The women are just as tall, and many practice dark majic that turns their eyes red. All Vords are tough as anvils. And few have punctured their skin with weapons. They take the heads off their enemies and offer them to their ancestors. They're not to be trifled or reasoned with. All they understand is their axe."

"Is it possible they could return?"

Declanii

"The histories say, seven times the Vords have disappeared and six times they've returned. I see no reason why they won't return for a seventh."

"What do they do? Where do they go when they disappear?"

"Some say to an island far up in the North. But only a Vord knows for sure. All we can do is be ready."

An old servant tucks in a Royal Grandson at the Marble Palaces
Of the Five Kingdoms in the Western Lands

Chapter Fourteen

THE ORAKAL'S CRIES REVERBERATED OFF THE ANCIENT palace walls of Saddeye. Both Binc and Hrija heard her wails and ran up the stairs to assist her. They arrived to find the Orakal sitting at a window with her head in her hands and tears falling to the floor as she sniffled.

"My Lady?" Binc called to her.

She turned to see them.

"What saddens you?" Hrija asked as they stopped four feet before her.

Much made her cry but all she could say was, "The Vords will return soon."

"The Vords?" Binc questioned.

"One was tricked off their island and has murdered many who would've been as kin to me," she sobbed.

Binc kneeled down to be at eye level with her.

"We knew this day would come," he said apologetically.

"I know the people in my Walks better than if they were kin. I know things about them they have yet to perceive for themselves. And now their pasts, presents, and futures, are gone from my sight! Paths I can no longer Walk! Bright and honorable people, killed! One Vord murdered so many... and only one could stop him."

Binc searched for comforting words while Hrija felt compassion for the young girl that she worked hard not to show. But neither understood the child and the Orakal was aware.

"I haven't told either of you about this Walk. Please, meet me at my Stone Throne. I'll be there shortly."

Both bowed before making their way to the Orakal's garden.

The Orakal collected herself, then donned a heavy winter cloak the color of burgundy and went as well. She arrived quickly and walked straight to her Stone Throne past the Reflecting Pool. When she turned and sat, Binc and Hrija bowed completely, then stood.

"What do you wish to tell us?" Hrija asked.

"It is now likely that it won't only be me who Camulus takes prisoner."

"Who else?" Binc queried.

"You," she answered while looking back at him.

His breath stopped and fear captured his face.

"The Emperor will not harm you. He wishes to be named. Be steady and you'll survive."

"Oh my," Binc said while dropping slowly to a knee, feeling a little lightheaded.

Hrija put her hand on his shoulder. Then asked the Orakal, "There's more, isn't there?"

"When Emperor Camulus returns for his army, as I've said, he will give me over to be tortured. This is when the Shogin go through a great test of patience. And after they've rescued me with the Ravenborne, I'll not return here until my Seventeenth birthday."

"What!" Hrija exclaimed.

"My Lady!" Binc said astonished.

"When I'm seventeen we'll be reunited again. But I must go on a quest with the Ravenborne and Shogin. You'll both stay here and prepare."

"Prepare for?" Binc asked.

"I'll know more as time goes, and send messengers. In the meantime, you must keep Saddeye open as a place of pilgrimage for all people after Camulus leaves with his entire army."

Bink started, "My Lady, that'll be difficult without you here. Several nations are now displeased you won't lend them war aid, or the Shogin. They'll..."

"You'll stay true to our ways and be successful because of it."

"Yes, my Lady," both answered.

"Orakal, what is this quest with the Ravenborne of which you speak?" Hrija asked.

"I know very little myself. I thought there was such a slight chance of this quest happening that I haven't Walked through any of it. I made a mistake. And now all I know and can say is: When the deer are dying, the crow are gone, and the wolf has lost its way; the Thirty Three will expand as a Fifth Breath is breathed."

Chronicle Fourteen

Hardolf is dead. The eldest of all Treewolves has been slain by my intent. He was my friend, my ally. I trusted him with his council and he trusted me with mine. But that trust has killed him along with my wife and son, the last of their lives taken by my majic. This leads to the question I must ask. And when a question is asked it must be answered. Why do the ancient healing words now kill?

Written by Segais during a time he refers to as,
The Dark Age of his Soul

Declanii

Chapter Fifteen

When the final count came in, twenty three people had died because of the Vord and over two thousand were injured from the fires. Those of the healing craft engaged themselves to great lengths. The fires were contained but still burning hot. And the water wagons ran their courses with efficiency. The chaos had subsided but fear drifted throughout the city as King Acillus addressed those standing next to himself and the dead Vord.

"Forget whether or not Vords exist. How did one slip through our city, and why?"

"It appeared to be charging for Cael," Councilor Conail suggested.

"Then it fell, and Segais was behind it," Aislin stated.

"Where is Segais?" Queen Andraste asked.

Everyone looked around and no one saw him.

"The Home Guard have taken up positions and are patrolling the city," Acillus said with sadness. "But we must decide how to continue this day. We can have the funerals after the sword dance tonight. But what of the rest of the tournament? Finnian is dead…"

Cael thought for a moment. And tears welled up in his eyes for Finnian as he said, "We can't continue this tournament without a Captain of Declanii, so let's continue the day as if we just finished the tournament, and later we'll pay our respects during the sword dance and the funerals."

All agreed.

After each tournament held during a festival, every King since Tressach O'Ronan, led the Declanii aside and away from everyone else. Acillus led only those who'd already been Declanii and this time, Cael, to just outside a large warehouse within Old Ideclan. None who still needed voting to become Declanii could go with them. And when they arrived, Acillus promoted Dennus Brogan to Third File Commander, then called a vote for Captain of Declanii.

"I nominate Quinnlan Mullquane for Captain," Phaedrus of Gisspor proclaimed.

"I second," Eilidir Shymurrow said.

"I third," Noa Nirowin agreed.

"All vote," Acillus called out.

A hand was put into the air for a yay vote, or pointed toward the ground for a nay vote, and all votes were yay. Next, he put to vote the matter of the three boys, Irhanach, Ohelathe, and Anrahan, becoming Declanii.

"What say you lads?" Acillus asked.

Most approved because it was what the Prince wanted, and also because their talent couldn't be denied.

"There's one more thing then," Cael interjected. "If they are voted for, what says everyone to the same for Raddox and his longsword?"

"An Edemarian in the Declanii!" someone shouted, and more than a few laughed.

"What is true for one is true for all," Cael stated, reminding them of the Clanii Tenet. "He has defeated some of our best."

The question raised much deliberation but they voted to let the young man in as well. Raddox's skill couldn't be denied either. And Acillus smiled. He saw in his son's actions what he might be setting up for the future.

Then it became time for the real reason why everyone was led aside. And the King directed them all into the large warehouse they were standing by.

Inside it was cold, and had only an uneven dirt floor to stand on. Rays of the late Sun shone through slits in the walls but it was still dark. And the Declanii formed a circle with no one at the middle.

Acillus stepped to the middle and remained silent.

Then Cael stepped toward the center and said to him, "I call to gather the Tournament of Silence."

"My Prince!" General Seamus spoke out with haste. "The Silent are always in peril."

"He's right. Are you sure…" Eilidir started.

"I hear what you say, lads," Cael interrupted. "But the sword and spear do not dictate my future. It isn't the arm that wins wars, but the mind. I call to gather the Tournament of Silence."

"Alright," Acillus nodded. "The tournament begins."

The King resumed his place in the group, giving Cael the center of the large room.

There were two entrances to the building and each now had three Declanii guarding them. The rest began walking in opposite but concentric circles around the perimeter of the room, some going sunwise, some countersunwise, alternating each row. And the noise of their shuffling feet was quick to overpower other sounds.

The Silent were masters at drifting through moving crowds, and it was difficult to see.

One darted in to attack. The Prince became aware just before and blocked, then swung but missed and the attacker disappeared back into the crowd.

Someone assailed again and the young O'Ronan crouched quickly. Before he was up the assailant was gone.

Cael started moving around so he wasn't a stationary target, feeling for his pursuers as he glided over uneven ground.

Another stormed in for him at the group's edge. He parried with a practice sword while striking down with the other, and the man let out a grunt of pain before slipping away.

Cael dodged the next attack and just missed with his own. He heard fast footsteps coming from his left and spun out of the way while striking with a sword, hitting the man across the chest and trapping the wind in his lungs. It brought the man to one knee and he crawled back into the crowd.

Immediately Cael was attacked by another. He dodged and felt the wind from the wooden blade caress his face, then the attacker was gone.

Cael jogged alongside the group as they walked and another jumped out at him. The Prince sensed it and struck the man before he could exit the crowd, then the moving mass swallowed him back up.

Cael ran through the middle of the large room to the other side.

Aislin Mullquane started humming. Then everyone began humming in unison, one long tone over and over, making it difficult for Cael to hear anything but that.

The Prince slipped into the group of walking Declanii and disappeared. Two charged in but they only met each other at the center of the room. Cael charged them, knocking one away with his shoulder while striking the other. The one who was struck, slunk back into the crowd while the lad who was shoulder bulled charged again. Cael tripped him and slammed him into the ground in the darkness.

Three more bolted from the crowd simultaneously. The hums were loud as Cael ran forward and thrust a sword into one, then grabbed him and threw him into one of the others. He attacked a lad but missed, dodged a strike, then hit. The last swung downward and Cael sidestepped to make him miss, then hit the man across the head with a strike of his own. The lad stifled a yelp of pain as he quickly moved back into the crowd.

"End!"

The Declanii stopped walking and humming while

Declanii

Aislin stepped out to the middle with his grandson.

"Prince Cael, you're accepted into the Silent," he said, and then rejoined the crowd.

Acillus stepped forward and yelled, "Dismissed!"

With the order, everyone exited the building and went to prepare for the evening. And the King and Cael spoke as they walked home together.

"How long have you wanted to be Silent?" Acillus whispered.

"Since before I knew about them."

The King smiled but it was a sad smile. His mind was heavy with the day's losses.

"How'd you know when to call the tournament?"

"I ferreted it out. The Declanii do a good job of keeping who's Silent a secret. And their cover stories are impressive."

"You're going to need a cover story for when you leave now as well."

"I've always traveled throughout the lands," Cael said with a shrug. "That should be enough."

Acillus nodded knowingly. He loved his son very much and trusted his skill, but was worried for him.

After a short time, the streets of Old Ideclan started

filling with Clanii descendants dressed in their finest. Many women wore their light leather armor in the same fashion as Jossilan O'Ronan, the first Queen of Ideclan.

The women who could wore their sunil with full battle dress. And all women brought with them shoes made of completely wooden soles to change into once they reached the fields. Those men who could wore their sunil tunics and cloaks with full battle dress. And both women and men wore their Ideclan Amulets in the shape of the city's fortifications.

They in sunil all wore the same armor. Their shin guards protected from just below the knee to four fingers width above the ankle. Corrick's expert skill had been poured into each. The shin guards had the appearance of steel ravens. And at the top was a small spike protruding forty five degrees forward. Directly below the spike was the raven's head looking downward. The raven's wings wrapped around the calves for protection, and on the outer edges, real raven feathers were attached for tonight's sword dance.

Their right bracers protected from elbow to wrist and were like a raven as well, except instead of the steel beak pointing downward along the armor it protruded outward in a curve at the elbow for puncturing enemies, catching weapons, and manipulating shields. The left arm usually carried a three foot in diameter circular shield layered with wood, linen, and thin steel.

The shield's design was four ravens with their tails meeting at the middle. The ravens' heads reached the rim of the shield and certain beaks protruded forward for grabbing and manipulating enemy shields and weapons, while wolf heads filled the spaces between the ravens. And all of it was masterfully manipulated from the outer layer of steel by

Corrick. The wooden practice shields they carried for tonight's festivities were but replicas of these fine items.

The helms worn by the men and women Declanii were the signature craftsmanship of Corrick. They had the appearance of a steel raven folded down and molded around the head. The tail came down at the back and flared slightly outward at the top of the neck. The tail was connected to, but more appropriately one with, the two wings that came down either side of the face protecting to the chin. At the ears was a small hole which funneled sound, formed by a conical shape the wings and tail made where they met. The raven's head and beak came down the front of the face, with the beak ending at the tip of the nose.

Every helm had thirteen raven feathers traversing across the top, representing the thirteen families, but the King and Queen's helms alone were known as The Helms of Thirteen. These helms possessed an extra pair of steel wings sweeping back across the top sides of the head, almost meeting just past the tops of the backs of their heads. These wings stayed close to the helms and didn't protrude far. The ravens' eyes for the King and Queen's helms were finely cut sapphires that reflected light brilliantly. During the tournament, no Declanii helm had feathers in them, but now, each had thirteen Ideclan Raven feathers traversing laterally across the top.

Out on the main field, the workers who'd built the stands for the tournament were now connecting many long and wide pieces of planed flat wooden boards. Because of the assassination attempt, they set the boards down between the smoldering piles of bleachers and stands. And many workers paused here or there to watch them burn with frustration or sadness.

After the boards were set, the people either took their places among one of the formations forming on the fields or moved into one of the spaces designated for spectators. The sword dance was about to be performed. There were a number of sword dances, and this festival's dance payed homage to Jossilan and her courage during the quest of the Thirteen of Old. Sword dances were dedicated to many things like the Tribellion or the Ancients; but this one dedicated to Jossilan was the most well known and loved among the Clanii, as well as the number of Ideclaners who'd learned them.

Acillus and Andraste stood at the center of the Declanii field facing each other. All Declanii and their husband or wife, lined up the same way in expanding spirals radiating out from the King and Queen. Two straight perpendicular lines were also formed and intersected at the King and Queen. This formation repeated itself on every field and they all interlocked together, but only the Declanii field had the planed flat wooden boards set in place. And since there were already three large fires, the workers only had to start one more to symbolize the Festival of Four Fires, which they started East of the roost.

All Clanii women in this arrangement wore their wooden soled shoes, as well as Alistriana who danced with Irhanach, and Aveline who danced with Cael. It was dark and what they were about to perform was complicated. But they'd grown up doing these dances the third night of every festival.

The Declanii started with shields up and swords crossing the sword of the person dancing with them. Andraste, with her back straight and her sword held to her husband's, began tapping her feet in a smooth and even rhythm, then finished by clacking her sword against Acillus'. The wives and women Declanii mimicked her exact movements, followed by the rest of the women doing the sword dance. Three times they did this, starting at the center and moving out like a wave.

Click Clack Clik Thwaaak!!!

Acillus began next, fighting with Andraste, making music as they clashed with each other. Then all the Declanii repeated the rhythm, then everyone else, again expanding out like a wave, three times.

Clik Clack Thwaak Claaackak!!!

Each of the fields flowed into the choreographed battle, blocking, striking, counter striking, making beautiful rhythms of music that harmonized with the clacking of the women's feet. As they continued, the tempo quickened and everything made of wood produced harmonious sound. Swords banged against shields and other swords, feet stomped the ground.

Thrack Clik Thwaak, Clack tik Throoom!!!

Everyone inside the city heard the booming of music made by sword and shield, foot and wood. Different sections danced different steps to harmonize with each other. And the formations they made were as beautiful as snowflakes. Leaders from other parts of The Kinned Lands were stilled with amazement, many not taking sips from their drinks to have no interruptions.

Thrunck Daak Thraack Whaaakak!!!

Then the tempo slowed and abruptly changed. The slower pace became multiple rhythms across the fields until all joined into one pattern again that started from the outer edges and moved in toward the center, instead of center to the edges as it had begun. They did this three times until all were silent save the King and Queen going back and forth in a violent rage, fighting with no preplanned movements until Acillus' sword broke because of Andraste and flew off to the side, skipping on the ground. The sword dance dedicated to Jossilan wasn't over until the Queen broke the King's sword.

A brief silence was followed by many roars and clashes from wooden weapons. Everyone on the field, including the King and Queen, yelled and made as much noise as possible so their kinsmen's souls could hear them.

Then the festival was over. There wouldn't be another sword dance for three months or the same version en masse for a whole year.

Fehurin Cailian, the man who challenged Acillus at every council on his use of coin, and a leader of the growing movement among the Clanii to return to more peaceful ways, looked at his wife and said, "It is this kind of behavior that takes us away from the Old Tenets. I swear, my love, the Clanii are almost finished. We waste more money on this nonsense than anything else."

"We'll bring us back on the right path. Away from this violence and to a more prosperous course. Of that I'm sure," she said knowingly while grabbing his hand. Fehurin's plans were just as much hers.

Soon the funerals began. And after the last words were spoken and the pyres burned down, Cael walked back to Old Ideclan with Aveline and his friends. It took them a long time to get home because they made a few stops along the way, one of them was the park Alistriana and Irhanach loved to frequent. And after reaching Old Ideclan they all parted ways to their own homes.

When Cael arrived at his, he found his mother and father by the downstairs fireplace. Acillus was reading books of strategy and theory while Andraste looked over notes concerning her city projects.

They greeted their son as he moved over and knelt by the fire to warm himself. And it wasn't long before a loud knock rasped at the O'Ronan's door.

"My King, my Queen, it's urgent!" they heard from outside.

Cael recognized the voice so he stood up, walked over, and opened the door to see the Tenth Talon Commander, Crastinus, standing before him.

"Prince Cael," the Commander acknowledged with a nod.

"What is it Crastinus?" the King asked as he stood.

"Sire, at the front gate there was a man from Teranim trying to enter the city. He seeks an audience with you."

"Did you take his weapon?" Acillus asked.

"First thing. I also put the lads on double patrols and Old Ideclan's walls are being reinforced right now. We have him well guarded outside the main city in one of the small store houses by the chicken coops. Liadine's called up every scout to scour the city so neither he nor any other Teran can slip by. He won't be a diversion for another Vord if that's why he's here either."

"I don't think he's here to assassinate," Cael stated. "If so, we wouldn't have known of his arrival until it was him knocking on the door."

"I agree," Acillus spoke. "I doubt Vords and Terans are working together. Yet this is still unprecedented. Summon Seamus," the King paused while he thought of Finnian, "Quinnlan, Conail, and Aislin if you can find him. We'll all meet where you have the Teran detained, Crastinus. And I want you personally seeing to the patrols tonight after you get a few men to alert the other Captains and Commanders to our new situation."

"Yes, my King!" Crastinus said, and then mounted his horse and rode off.

The O'Ronan family donned their warmest clothes and placed an iron screen in front of the downstairs fireplace before leaving. Cael left the house first and then Acillus held the door open for his wife. With a smile she walked past him and caressed his side while kissing his cheek. Once outside, all of them moved briskly over to the stables and mounted their horses. They used rope bridles and reins with no bits or saddles, as the Daeadakian training had survived over the years.

The ride was cold but fast and when they arrived it was just after midnight. Their destination was a small store house out on the agricultural fields next to the chicken coops. And there were more than a dozen guards around its perimeter. After dismounting and hitching the horses, Cael opened the door for his Ma and Da and all entered.

The building was simple. Vertical wooden planks made the walls while thatching created the roof. Inside was unadorned except for a desk at the far left corner which held four burning three wick candles on it, and a square table at the opposite corner which held four burning three wick candles as well. And stacked against the wall to the right were piles of sacks of chicken feed such as grain and corn.

Aislin had somehow made it there before them and was leaning against a wall while he waited.

The old scout, Liadine, and three of his best guarded a small man who sat politely in a chair at the center of the room.

Seamus, Quinnlan, and Conail could be heard as they rode up and dismounted, then entered the building.

He was a short man in his nineties who sat in the chair, not strongly built yet nothing about him seemed frail. His skin was an olive tint and his head had black hair that didn't go past his ears. He also possessed long braids of hair, obviously not his own, that were tied around his arms and one around his head.

Teranim was an unfamiliar place. And the Terans were widely feared because of their ethos and ability to assassinate. Part of their belief was an affront to one of their own was an affront to all; and this could only be rectified by assassinating the foreign offender, along with the ruler of that offender as well. For more than five hundred years it was commonplace for Lord, Potentate, Sultan, Shah, King, and any other form of leader to be assassinated by these people simply because a Teran was offended by a subject of that leader.

The Terans became so renowned for assassination that rulers passed laws banning their citizens from ever going near Teranim or dealing with its people. Their weapon even put fear into the ruthless King, Tarkin Erra, many years ago. The Terans were hierarchal with their weapon and never did a Teran affront one of their own, or anyone else. This was meant to be a reflection of their discipline and leadership. Assassinating the other ruler was meant to show them the lack of theirs.

The laws forbidding people to go to Teranim stayed in

place and soon there were fewer assassinations. Over the last two hundred and seventy years, they'd been completely left in peace because of it, save for the cunning King, Tressach O'Ronan, and his voyage there.

This man alone who sat at the center was no threat, but with his weapon, everyone in the room could be in danger. They were all scattered about and only the King now stood in front of him. The man wasn't bound because he wasn't a prisoner, and he didn't have his weapon. It was locked in a box held by Liadine.

"What can we do for you?" Acillus began. "You have our attention."

"Great King," the Teran said, "There was much discussion as to who we should seek. And since the Terans and Clanii have had respectful dealings in the past, we chose you."

Acillus and Aislin knew of what the Teran meant. He was speaking about Tressach O'Ronan. But Aislin, Captain of the Silent, knew more concerning the Silent's inception than anyone else alive. And only from Aislin's reports did Acillus have any idea of what the Teran would speak of next.

"Nine years ago, after the great land shake, a wave came in from the sea and decimated us. But we rebuilt our home. It took years to do this. And it was all in vain because this last year, the Erra'Aulius Empire, as they call it now, brought their whole army to our city during Midfall in the middle of the night. More than five thousand of them trapped us within."

Everyone except the Teran knew that if there were only five thousand, then it was just Camulus' Western Army and not all of them. But no one thought to correct him. It was then that Crastinus entered the room quietly enough not to disturb the conversation.

"They didn't allow anyone out of our city while they ate the wheat and green from our fields, plucked all the fruit from our trees, and wantonly wasted the harvest and hard work of this last year. We had not yet brought it in."

His voice broke and a tear ran down his cheek as he continued.

"Our Grandmaster tried arranging a meeting with the army's command, and after two messengers were killed, he gained the commander's ear. He convinced him that Teranim had amassed wealth from the rulers we've assassinated. And that we keep it hidden. He proposed the elderly, the women, and our children be set free, and then he'd show him where the treasure was. The commander agreed to just the elderly women and children and even though they were famished, they had smiles on their faces as they exited the gates."

The Teran now held back no emotion as tears fell freely from his eyes.

"The army cleared a path for them to walk through. When our families walked out, they sealed us back in and lined up to attack. They charged them! The jousters used their heads for target practice! My wife! My grandchildren!" he cried while putting his head in his hands.

Andraste moved over and knelt beside him to give him strength. Tears escaped her eyes as well, running down across the Mark of the Mullquanes.

"What did you do?" Crastinus the Ferocious asked.

"We fought and more of us were killed. The same Grandmaster who lied about the wealth, had traded our weapons away for a small amount of food after the beginning of the siege. That Grandmaster has been assassinated according to our ways. We didn't have our weapons," The Teran said disparagingly.

He gathered himself and sat up straight, then thanked the Queen directly before continuing.

"The Kinned Lands are well known. We wish to keep our individual identity and not lose it to the East. We think this can be done if we kin with you. I know we've come after we need help. But we ask you to consider it. Liberate us, help us reclaim our weapons, and we'll serve The Kinned Lands from then on."

Acillus took a moment to think, then asked, "How did you escape?"

"There's a river that flows underneath our walls and runs through the city. It's not shallow but neither is it wide. Metal bars go from the bottom of the wooden palisade to the bottom of the river. This is an easy Winter, and the river hasn't frozen, so I made it deeper and swam underneath the bars. That is also where I found the weapon you now hold. It may have been left there from the great wave nine years ago."

"Crastinus," the King said.

"Sire?"

"Would you mind if Liadine went on a mission?"

"I'd prefer it," he joked with a wink at the old man.

Liadine smiled and stepped forward to receive his orders, with the Teran weapon still locked in a box underneath his arm.

"Pick a small force and infiltrate Teranim. Have your report ready when we arrive."

"It is done," the old scout affirmed.

The King turned back to the Teran. "Your acceptance into The Kinned Lands doesn't rest on my decision alone. But either way, the Declanii will come to your aid."

The Teran bowed his head in thanks.

"I've called a war council of The Kinned Lands. The vote for your acceptance will happen then. Attend my scouts to your city, help them infiltrate. And I'll sail there with the Declanii when this council is over."

"I will. And the Terans shall be in your debt."

"It is Camulus who owes the debt."

The man smiled in agreeance. Then Acillus nodded and left the room with most of the others.

"Quinnlan," the King started once they were outside and walking toward their horses. "We leave right after the council so get the lads in the know. Seamus, while we're away, organize the Talons for march and sail. As you know, it'll take the Northern armies some time to get here and when they do, they'll need to be organized for sail as well."

"You think the other lands will agree to send them?" Quinnlan asked.

"I do, especially after the assassination attempt. No one has a choice. Camulus is coming and our window for time closes."

"The lads will be ready," Seamus stated.

Crastinus stayed with the Teran while Liadine and his preferred scouts gathered their gear. And the descendants of Clanii rode back to Old Ideclan at a brisk pace.

"Sire," Quinnlan Mullquane yelled.

"What is it, lad?"

"You were quick to offer aid to the Teran."

"I was. I want Camulus looking there instead of Caibre Pass."

"Acillus, you know Admiral Finn..." Seamus started but was interrupted.

"I know, Seamus. He's already voiced his displeasure about the armada sufficiently. And as for the Declanii sailing to Teranim, we'll stay close to shore."

"Camulus will get what's coming. Expect an earful from the Admiral is all I'm saying," Seamus told him, and the King smiled.

Neither the Hilernian nor Immramman Seas were known for their calmness during Winter and the Admiral liked to remind them of it.

"Aislin," the King called out. "Tell Quinnlan the current knowledge on Camulus."

"The Emperor is near Saddeye. After he takes the city he plans on camping his army there for the rest of Winter, then marching for Hinturan by Latespring. His known plans are to take out Hinturan using onagers protected with sheets of iron that also protect its crew. He'll use flaming ammunition to burn them in their trees while safe from their famous bow range," he told his son.

"Know also that the Hinturan are coming to this council," Acillus added.

"Which I'm still uneasy about," the General informed.

"Why is that?" Andraste asked.

"Their breeding programs. They breed their men and it twists my bones."

"Be sure not to let your feelings live on the surface during council. Another's ways are theirs to have and ours to respect so long as they threaten neither us nor the balance of nature," the Queen continued.

Seamus bowed his head.

"And as you know, they breed their men well enough to rise against them if they wished. But for some reason, I think those men enjoy being bred to their beautiful women," Andraste said, and the men laughed loudly.

The conversation made Cael think of his trip to Hinturan when he was younger. And the smile on his face was broad from the memories.

"The Hinturan should be arriving soon, right son?"

Acillus asked, hoping he was correct.

"Aye Da, they're on schedule. The ravens say two mornings and they'll be here."

Cael knew what ship they were aboard because he kept in correspondence with a young Queen he'd met there. And she was one of the delegates on their way for the war council.

"Then the council will be held as planned. Let's ride and be away from this cold."

Each commanded their horses faster and cloaks billowed as they raced home. When Old Ideclan was reached, all stabled their horses and went back to their houses except for Cael, who, shortly before arriving, felt a rise of energy.

"I'm going to visit the ravens. You want to come, Da?"

"Go ahead. And tell them ahroo for me." he answered as he held open the door for Andraste. Then his father said, "See you in the morning," before closing the door behind them.

Chronicle Fifteen

Language is perhaps the greatest tool we inherit from our ancestors. It's what binds us in complex ways, allowing us to communicate and perform great accomplishments. I daresay there are an extreme number of languages on Terr'ah today, but at their beginning, each of the Thirty Three had their own tongue. Those Thirty Three are the originators of all language spoken by humans. And though only some remain intact, I believe all can be regained through study.

Throughout the Ages, these languages have ebbed and flowed with one another to produce many wonderful dialects. Aneuu, in his memoirs of traveling around to teach the Common Tongue, lists and catalogues many of these. The book is titled 'Languages of Terr'ah,' and to my heart it is a fine accomplishment.

The Common Tongue taught to all is derived from eight of these thirty three ancient languages. But the simplest ideas of each were used. Aneuu and many others were successors in a long line of people who worked to make this a possibility. And it was Aneuu who had the pleasure of teaching the Common Tongue to Terr'ah. By the time the Fifth Age was well underway, so to was the effort to make communication for everyone possible.

For the first decade of the undertaking, this idea didn't take root, but communication through pigeons kept all instructors of the Common Tongue on the path. During the second decade of the quest, Aneuu had a breakthrough in that he persuaded two great empires to learn the uniting language. And then he started receiving letters from his associates of how well they were beginning to do. The word was spreading. And when Aneuu and others cultivated masters among those they taught, they sent them out to teach as well.

The language has taken root in some places more than others, but with command of the Common Tongue, one can pilgrimage to many lands and communicate. Ambiguity however, is ever present, and eliminating that from language is a true study.

Excerpt from 'The Life of Aneuu'
Written by Siras of Philos

Chapter Sixteen

As Cael walked to the roost, he looked up at the stars and marked his favorite constellations like Ravhenru, and the three star isosceles triangle representing the Tribellion. He pondered them briefly and wondered what they looked like up close. And then he looked ahead as he continued walking.

The Prince reached the roost and made his way in to find his two friends. The ravens were resting with many others, but only they awoke for the quiet steps of the Ravenborne.

"Roxgrin, Binneen, staying warm?"

"Indeed," Roxgrin thought to him. *"It is good to see you do well in the tournament. And you didn't run from the Vord, either. We are pleased, Waldron."*

"What is your path now?" Binneen asked.

"We'll be traveling soon. In two days I'll know more. But I'm fairly sure we're going across the sea before everyone else."

"We'll be ready," Roxgrin thought.

"We're flying far in the morning. Come visit when it's afternoon," Binneen told him.

"I will. But right now I'd like to know something."

"Waldron wishes to know about the hawk feather I gave him."

"That's right, Roxgrin, I do."

"I'll speak of it now. How did I acquire the hawk feather?"

"You either found it, or took it."

"I took it, from a hawk who attacked us. We had no food for it to take. It had no young we could threaten. We were able to feel its thoughts. And it did this because it was trained since birth to think we ravens are its only food."

"We felt these thoughts, and thoughts of other hawks growing up with it, and many more being born. Each forced to live this way," included Binneen.

"Who does not like we friends of the Hra'ahven'kuern?" Roxgrin asked, using the Clanii word for Ravenborne.

"The Emperor from the East, I think."

"The man we go across the sea to face?"

"Yes. But whoever is behind this will be stopped," Cael declared.

"That is good. Now we must rest," thought Binneen.

"I'll come by during afternoon when you've returned, sleep well."

"Goodnight, Waldron," they both said to the Prince.

Cael exited the roost and walked home, listening to the sounds of the freshwater fountain as he walked past. The fountain's pool, supplied by one of the aqueducts, was starting to freeze at the surface. But wooden clubs waited to break the ice off the busy supply in the morning. The overflow drained into the sewages of the city. And both the sewages and the aqueducts had flown enough not to freeze so far this Winter.

Camulus is devious, Cael thought as he walked. *Nothing fights harder than when it fights for survival. I must tell this to Da.*

Cael continued on while breathing in the cold air as he thought it through. He passed by Ideclan's Hall with its four massive trees for corner posts, and the Rockraven symbol of Ideclan on its large oak doors. He knew the fire inside would still be burning strong, kept ablaze by attenders. He also knew the war council wouldn't be held in there this particular time. The building was open for all to enter and part of Hinturan's agreement to attend this council depended upon keeping their attendance a secret.

As Cael walked he looked up at the sky again, and stopped to observe a shooting star. It was then that an unseasonably warm breeze hit him. And he felt odd as he started walking again, realizing he couldn't escape the warmth the breeze had brought.

A sudden and spherical golden light lit up around Cael. And the light grew brighter as he took two more steps.

The Prince stopped and looked around, realizing he could see everything through the golden light that enveloped him. He could see every needle of every pine tree, and every pebble on the road.

He looked at the sky and became aware of innumerable

amounts of stars and clusters of lights he'd never seen before. The Ravenborne stared in wonder for a length of time he couldn't tell. And then he felt the hairs on his arms raise and pushed back a sleeve to look.

When he looked up from his arm he saw a man standing before him, enveloped in the golden sphere with him.

"Where'd you come from?" Cael asked, half startled.

"The same place as you," the man answered in a deep voice, and his words vibrated the golden light around them.

The stranger had golden hair, golden robes, and bright blue eyes set within skin the color of tan to the point it was almost golden as well.

"What is this?" Cael asked.

"An initiation. You've prepared yourself well, Ancient One. You are ready."

"Ready for what? What…?"

Cael's voice trailed off as he noticed this man's golden hair flowed into his golden robes continuously. There was no end or beginning to either where they met. Then he realized the man wasn't touching the ground, but levitating slightly above it, and Cael stepped back while looking at him with wide eyes.

"It has begun."

With those words the man was gone and the golden sphere with him, as well as the warmth. Cael wrapped his robe and two cloaks tightly before quickly walking away. Then he started running for the place Segais stayed while at Ideclan.

Throughout the years, Segais had dwelled at one of the finer inns at Middle Ideclan while he taught Cael. And after the first few years of this, he'd taken the room above, the room below, and knocked out part of the ceiling and floor to make a separate three story wing for himself.

It didn't take long for Cael to reach the inn and when he did he burst through the door and shut it quickly, waking up the lone attendant. Then he ran for the entrance to Segais' wing.

The Prince took no caution in being quiet when he entered the old man's abode. He knew Segais would still be awake and located him by a deep but faint humming sound.

The first floor Cael walked through was full of chairs, couches, desks piled with papers, and bookcases as high as the ceiling. At the middle of the room there stood one square table with a board game taking up nearly the entire surface. The board was sixteen squares wide by sixteen squares long. It was Segais' favorite, known to the Philosians as kijgin. And this board's pieces reflected a game still in progress.

The young O'Ronan walked across the room and up the spiral stairway to the second floor which was cluttered with worktables of all kinds. Segais often had experiments going. And Cael walked by one with an assortment of herbs steeping in the tiniest iron pot he'd ever seen. The smell was revolting so he backed away as he moved on.

There was another mixture steeping on a workbench that was completely foreign to him. It looked like melted rock. And next to the melted rock he saw a glass whose liquid appeared to be climbing up the sides. It was luminescent and intrigued Cael as he continued on.

Detailed maps, charts, and diagrams of mathematics and stone masonry, covered the walls of this floor, and Cael enjoyed them every time he was here. When he reached the other side where the staircase was, he walked up in circles following its spiral design.

He'd only been to the third floor once since Segais commandeered this wing for himself. It was the old man's personal quarters and Segais always preferred his privacy. But Cael figured the curiosity he'd just experienced was far too important to wait for the Philosian to finish humming.

Going up the stairs he started distinguishing the different tones Segais was making. And when he reached his private quarters, the Prince decided to wait since now he could tell the old man was almost finished.

Segais was at the very top of his wing, just underneath the cap of the roof. It was a small room in the shape of a pyramid, walled with special wooden slabs reverberating his humming back to him.

As Cael looked around the spacious top floor while waiting, the Ravenborne grew bewildered at the plant life he saw. It wasn't the forest of ten year old evergreen pines or the other indigenous trees and shrubs about the room. It was the varieties that required a much warmer climate that caught his attention, for none of them could have survived outside.

Everywhere around the room there was life: oaks, manzanitas, orchids, succulents, philodendrons, ferns, and vines that climbed up every space on the wall and up across the truncated pyramid ceiling. He also noticed an ambient glow and after searching, Cael still couldn't pinpoint its origin.

How is he keeping these alive? And where is this light and warmth coming from?

Segais stopped humming and exited his upper pyramid room by ladder.

"Well, boy, why the disturbance this late? And in my private chambers no less," he asked on his way down.

"Apologies. But you have to hear of what just happened."

"Go downstairs and we'll make some tea while we talk," the wizard bade him as he stepped off the ladder.

"Let's also talk about this room."

"Go."

Segais gave Cael a light shove toward the stairs.

Cael left for the first floor and started a small fire in the hearth once he got there, then went to collect the water. Segais was down not long after, wearing his heavy black robe. His long and thick bronze hair and curly copper brown beard were both oiled and braided. And his gray eyes were calm and reflective.

"What's this that has you excited?" the old wizard asked.

"I'm not entirely sure," Cael answered while hanging the pot of water over the fire.

"Start with what you know," Segais instructed as he put his focus on the kijgin board now in front of him. Then he made his move while sitting in one of the chairs beside it.

"What I know, is that a man appeared and disappeared right in front of me, accompanied by some type of golden light. A light that's similar to the light upstairs in your personal quarters," he stated while walking toward the kijgin board.

Segais stopped studying the game and turned to look at him.

"A man?"

"A man with golden hair and robes all flowing together. A warm wind preceded him and the warmth didn't leave until he did. He floated at least one hand's width above the ground, and his presence made my hair stand up like that energy you experiment with," Cael finished as he plopped into the other chair next to the kijgin game.

While in thought, Segais stood up and walked over to the hearth and shredded some ginger before putting it into the water with a few pieces of strange bark. Then he walked back and sat down again, still deep in thought.

"One of them materialized here, right in front of you," he said with a hint of amazement, and more to himself than his young protégé.

"He said it was an…"

"It spoke too. This hasn't happened in Ages. What was said?"

"He was a he, not an it, Segais," Cael thought to correct him while he made his move on the board.

"*It,* is beyond form as we know it. If it wishes, boy."

"How do you know of what I speak?"

Segais took out his pipe and told him, "Keep focused," while loading it with sweetflower.

"At first I asked him where he came from, and he said the same place as me. Which I must confess, I know not what he meant."

The Ariek grinned before saying, "Your ancient Clanii culture calls it First Breath. What is First Breath?" Segais asked while making another move.

Then he got up again to stir the tea at the fire. And brought back with him a small tin plate with a lit candle and a bundle of rope wick upon it. After sitting back down he lit the rope wick with the candle and then used it to light his pipe.

When Cael decided how best to answer, he said, "The Clanii belief is that First Breath is everything, and everything is First Breath."

Then the Prince made another move.

"So you see, we are all formed from First Breath. Hence, we all come from the same place. What else was said?"

"That the encounter was an initiation, and that I've prepared myself well. He also called me Ancient One."

Segais sat back and lit his sweetflower again. An intense expression formed on his face but he was able to hide it from Cael.

"Interesting. What else?" he asked with a mouthful of smoke.

"Just that I'm ready. And after I noticed he was levitating, he said; it has begun; then vanished."

The old wizard continued puffing his pipe while Cael took in a deep breath, thinking everything through as he gazed down at the board.

Then Segais made his move and said, "When it called you Ancient One…"

Cael looked up at him.

"Did it say it just like that or did it speak to you in another language and you were able to understand?"

"It said Ancient One," Cael answered questioningly.

"Of course. How would you know if it were in another language? You'd simply understand," Segais affirmed quietly to himself. Then he closed his eyes and searched his mind.

As Cael watched him, he saw Segais go through a shift, as if he found the answer to an internal question he'd long been struggling with. And then the Philosian opened his eyes.

"I fear I've long withheld far too much knowledge from you."

"How so?"

"I'll show rather than explain. Move your chair over here, and face me."

Cael moved his chair and sat back down to face him. Segais' posture was perfect as he took a few deep breaths. Then the old wizard formed a triangle with his hands by connecting his thumbs and forefingers, then slowly brought his hands up so that the triangle centered on his forehead.

Cael watched a triangle made of light form within the triangle made by Segais' hands. Once it was formed, Segais moved his hands apart, and the triangle started spinning and arcing above head level toward Cael, before stopping exactly between them, spinning and throwing off very small strands of brilliant light.

The O'Ronan was struck with wonder and Segais chuckled, remembering what it was like for so many to first see something of this kind. With his intent, the old Ariek continued the triangle on its path toward Cael.

"Do not fear," the Philosian said.

As the triangle approached him, Cael started grinning. And when the triangle reached his forehead it assimilated into his mind.

The majic resurfaced for the Prince many things Segais had taught him, and the lessons came flooding back. So much more of what he'd been taught now made sense; many things he'd pondered were becoming clear.

And then in an instant, Cael went from feeling like he was swimming in a sea of awareness to being slammed back into his chair. And the first thing he noticed after the few moments it took for him to be fully present, was Segais' smile.

"You know majic!" Cael declared.

"Don't be too astounded. There's knowledge out there beyond all of us."

"Like what?"

"How could I describe what is beyond me?"

"In any matter, you've kept a profound secret." Then after a short pause, the Prince asked, "Do all Philosians know majic?"

"Each in their own way."

"Why didn't your people used it for their troubles in the past? Surely this could've helped when the Halendak invaded, or during the Tribellion Battle. Why did they use staffs and bits instead?"

"Listen to me. I got caught up in the moment and should have warned you first. You must tell no one of this. Understand?"

"Yes, but…"

"This is a guarded secret of Philos for reasons you cannot fully comprehend yet."

"What about the old Clanii Tenet, Eradicate the guarding of Knowledge?"

"Yes, well, that one I don't specifically agree with, and for good reason."

"Then because of your reason, I will keep this secret."

"Of course you will. It's time to bring you into the folds of Philos."

"Indeed," Cael agreed with a grin.

"You won't be grinning much longer, boy. This isn't an easy thing to learn."

"What will you teach me first?" Cael asked.

"The first lessons will be slow and the amount of practice between them great."

"I'm ready. And they won't interfere with my other lessons."

"Are you ready? Because you've lacked the patience before."

"What do you mean?"

"What were the few lessons you were never good at?"

Cael threw his head back after remembering the frustrations Segais was referring to.

"To do this you must quiet your anger, and calm your impatience," the old man told him.

"Anger seems to be a tenacious part of me."

"When you were younger, I backed away from this issue because indeed it must be you that shapes you. But now it's time to conquer these emotions. Because overcoming them is a vital aspect to developing the concentration and will necessary for majic."

"Alright, I'll try to meditate again."

"Try?"

"I'll do."

"One of three techniques you'll do first is the quieting of the mind. Simply sit where you'll not be disturbed and focus on your breathing."

"That's it? Am I supposed to breathe from a specific place like you taught me when I'm injured?"

"No, just focus on the breathing itself, until you can do that for quite some time without being sidetracked.

The second technique is the running of the mind. Again, sit in a quiet place and instead of focusing on your breathing, watch your thoughts without trying to influence them, and observe what paths they take."

"I'll practice this as well."

"And thirdly, you'll practice the focusing of the mind. Choose an idea you have for the future, one that brings good emotions, and envision it as though it has already happened. Solely focus upon this thought and think of nothing else. *Feel* as if it were real, and live inside that imagination.

Do these three practices and you'll be well on your way. Oh yes, and one more thing. I know we've spoken of them before. But now I want you watching for them on your own."

"Watching for what?"

"Synchronicities."

"Coincidences that are no coincidence? I'm not so sure, Segais."

"Watch for them. They are signs of a destiny created by yourself. Pay attention to their subject matter. And follow them if the feeling is strong."

"Alright, I will."

"I expect nothing less. Now... it's your move," the old wizard told him while gesturing toward the board.

Then the two stayed up late into the night, enjoying each other's conversation while drinking ginger tea and playing kijgin.

Declanii

Chronicle Sixteen

Sarna,

I need your help. I've been promised to Gowgluni but I will not marry him. Someone might even be sabotaging my efforts to stop the wedding. It is now my responsibility to make sure Hobaru rule stays in Hobaru hands. Will you hide me on your island? Please tell no one. We can meet in stride when the moon and tide are one, at the place where I first told you my secret.

A letter written by All Chief Daughter Ashnayn, intended for Chief Daughter Sarna

Declanii

Chapter Seventeen

Ashnayn's handmaiden burst through the door with more force than she meant, and startled the young Princess who stood at her desk.

"I apologize, dear. I didn't mean to frighten you."

"That's alright," Ashnayn calmed while slipping the letter she held into a small cylindrical envelope. "I'm glad it's you and not one of those guards."

"How are you feeling?"

"Better, I don't feel nauseous anymore."

"I think the scrape from that Moon Race was the cause."

"Perhaps, or maybe it was something else," Ashnayn stated suspiciously.

"Either way, I'm glad you're better. What do you have there?" the handmaiden asked while collecting clothes from the bin.

"A letter to Sarna."

"Such a bright young lady, she'll make a fine Chieftess for her tribe someday. What's the letter about?"

Ashnayn hesitated before answering, "I'm asking her for help."

"Oh, how so?"

"I'm not going to marry Gowgluni. And I'm not going to stay on this island so they can force me to. This letter asks Sarna to hide me on hers."

"Now, dear, I don't think that is…"

"I don't want your thoughts! I want your help! You're the only person who can get close to me that I trust. So will you help me?"

"What help would you like?"

"Gowgluni's mercenaries watch me at all times when I'm outside this house. They watch you too when you're with me, but not when you go home. Take this letter to Byl. Tell him you're not feeling well and ask him to bring it to the pavilion for you at dinner. Have him send the letter and no one will know the difference."

"I don't know, Ashnayn."

"I do. Please?"

She nodded and the Princess gave her the letter. Then the handmaiden left the room quickly and Ashnayn looked back at her desk, wondering if her plan would work. Sarna's island was large and it held the greatest forest of all the islands.

She has a hut in the thick of that forest. Perhaps I can hide there.

Ashnayn walked out of her room and down the main stairway, then out the back toward her exercise area. When she got there, she jumped up to the pull up bars and did a quick forty in perfect form before walking to the dining pavilion with her guards close behind.

Upon arriving, Ashnayn didn't see Byl while making her way to grab a plate. At the plate table she caught the sights and smells of buttered birds and honeyed hams and her stomach growled. When she reached the food, Ashnayn filled her plate to its fullest and then walked to a dining table with joy.

The food was more than deliciously satisfying because it was the first of it she'd been able to eat since being poisoned at the race. And while she ate, Ashnayn peered around for Byl but didn't see him.

The Princess got up for seconds and after her plate was full again, the young Hobaruan turned back for the dining table. A quick glance told her Byl still hadn't arrived and that uneased her. She ate the rest of her food nervously, scanning the pavilion as discreetly as possible, and she tried eating slowly but Byl didn't arrive by the time she finished. So Ashnayn cleared her plate and put it in the dish basket as sluggishly as a snail.

I don't want to leave yet. I have to see Byl put that letter in the box. Where could he be? Did he tell on me? Is he caught? Oh!

Ashnayn almost burst with joy when she saw him, but was able to hide her emotion while walking over to fill her gourd with water to keep an eye on him. As Byl walked to the letter table, Ashnayn's excitement grew. And when he slipped a few letters into the biggest box she thanked the Currents and gulped the water she grabbed, then began strolling out of the pavilion. She glanced to see if her guards were suspicious and they weren't, so Ashnayn simply sauntered at a normal pace, thankful Gowgluni was too busy to eat dinner with her this evening.

At least the letter got out. If this doesn't work I'll swim if I have to. I will not marry that man. What!

Ashnayn turned a corner and was startled to see Gowgluni standing before her. To his left and right were his personal guards and behind him was the Princess' handmaiden. And her own guards looked more alert after seeing them.

"I'm sorry, dear," the handmaiden said. "But this *is* helping you. You'll see that in the long run."

Ashnayn shook her head in disbelief.

"Your handmaiden apparently has more wisdom than I thought," Gowgluni began. "I was curious as to her loyalty for you. But now I know she is completely devoted to your best interest."

"Loyalty to me, is measured by me. Not you. She lacks as much wisdom as you do."

Gowgluni laughed to hide his anger before saying, "Grab her."

Ashnayn's guards seized her quickly so she couldn't run.

Gowgluni continued, "There are many things you need to be taught. Ego isn't one of them." Then he turned and said, "Follow me. The Princess isn't to leave her estate until I say otherwise."

Then the guards followed Gowgluni to her home, with Ashnayn tightly in their grasp.

Later that night, a small fleet of Ideclan Diving Ships furled their sails and dropped anchors roughly sixty nautical miles South of Ideclan's Harbor. The Diving Ships were on their way home, but with this one last stop. And many aboard the six ships searched the sea for signs of shark.

"Alright Divers! The sea is calm enough! Drop the lines!" Cathalain of the Aenenay Family yelled.

Cathalain was Admiral and Captain Diver of this fleet. He was a tall, lean man with long arms and legs. Like most divers he kept his black hair short. And a distinguishable feature he possessed were his large hands and feet, which many of his friends jested with him about how well they served for swimming.

All divers were covered in animal tallow and strips of felted wool to keep them warm in the water. They also wore linen wraps around their waists and linen bands around their chests to keep knives close, each with wool underneath as well.

And all free hands went to task at constructing what had become known as diver decks.

The six ships worked as teams of two. As the two ships came alongside each other, they each used ropes to send over long reinforced beams to secure themselves together. These vessels were designed for this with locations to lock the thick crossbeams in place.

Two small boats, one from each ship, were then

deployed between them. They were made so that when they connected, they formed a broad deck with a large square opening at their center. And after they attached together, these two boats sent back ropes and beams to their ships so that all were securely fastened, rendering it one vessel.

With that completed, two divers from each ship grabbed a rope that'd been tied to a heavy rock. And with their other hand, they held onto a linen net. The divers dove into the water, one each at the bow and one each aft, all on the inner side facing the other ship, letting the heavy rocks pull them down.

After the four divers reached the sea floor, which at this location was roughly fifty spans, they opened the nets and set them, then searched for more rocks to fill their nets while keeping their rocked ropes close.

At certain locations across the Hilernian Sea, there was an abundance of rock piles due to the Ideclan Navy hunting for pearls there. They'd accumulated over the centuries, and were often reused. Cathalain was a superb navigator and the ships had been stopped amidst plenty of them.

The bottom of the sea was dark and it was difficult to see. Almost everything needed to be done by feel but that didn't slow them. And the first divers of each ship had their nets filled halfway before untying the rocks from their ropes and then pulling on those ropes thrice to be raised.

When they aboard the ships felt the tugs on the ropes, they went to the outer sides of the vessels and sent rocks attached to those same ropes overboard. The counterweight pulled those ropes across the ships along pulleys and hauled the divers up.

Once they were aboard, two more divers from each ship went down with ropes tied to rocks as well. When this second set of divers made it to the bottom, they proceeded to fill their nets. And after their nets were full, the divers untied their rocks and pulled on their ropes thrice, then were lifted by counterweight.

A third set of divers dove once the second set were up. And these searchers of the deep, held onto a rocked rope with one hand, an iron pulley in the other, and had one end of another rope tied to a foot. When they reached the bottom they attached the edges of the linen nets to the pulleys, closing the nets, then untied the ropes from their feet. They thread the ropes from their feet through the pulleys, then untied the rock that brought them down and pulled on that rope thrice.

The divers were brought back up while keeping hold of the ropes they'd thread through the pulleys. And when they surfaced, each diver handed that rope to those on the deck formed by the boats between the two ships.

While the divers had been constructing the rock net and pulley system, others brought a diving bell from one ship and a long air channel from the other over to that same deck between the two ships. The diving bell was made from an iron skeleton wrapped by a hardened leather skin that was oiled and covered in beeswax. The air channel was made from the same material with an iron hexagon frame at specific intervals so that it stayed open to let the air flow. They connected the air channel to the diving bell with a simple style of nuts and bolts and an oiled cloth between them, then sealed it with beeswax.

The divers on the diver deck who'd grabbed the ropes, swam underneath the boats and connected them to the diving bell through the square opening in the deck. Then they prepared to watch the bell on its way down. Two groups aboard each ship, all who'd trained for this, held the other ends of the ropes that went down through the pulleys on the nets and back up to them.

"At your ready!" Cathalain yelled to those holding the ropes.

They called out in unison, "Ready! Pull!"

And the diving bell began to lower slowly and equally on all sides. They continued doing this while the spotters watched its level, sending signals topside by tugging ropes of their own as the air channel was helped down by other divers watching over it. The delicate process took time as the bell was pulled to the sea floor. But it wasn't long before they had the apparatus close to the nets and the spotters, who'd been breathing through the bell the entire time, pulled their ropes to alert everyone to stop. Then those back aboard tied off securely.

"Alright! Keep shark watchers at every direction! Bell watchers and air watchers are set! Standby and rescue divers be at the ready!" Cathalain called out.

A number of both male and female divers dove in while using rocked ropes and weighted vests to pull them down.

"Strig, I want shark watchers doubled."

"Doubled, Admiral. Aye, aye!"

Cathalain watched his divers go about their profession. He thought they had a good chance of finding a pearl tonight. This spot was always known for its relative abundance despite its depth, and it hadn't been hunted in quite some time.

"Tea, Admiral?" a sailor offered.

"Ah, thank you."

Cathalain took the cup of ginger tea and continued watching his charge.

They'd been diving for about an hour when Strig walked back to him and asked, "Are you going to dive tonight?"

"The ginger has warmed me, so yes," the Admiral replied happily, and prepared to dive.

He doffed down to his diving wraps and donned his chest strap with knife, then started walking across the quarter-deck before hearing a lookout yell, "Shark! Shark! Eight marks off starboard bow!"

"Up the divers!" Cathalain commanded, and immediately the divers were notified and brought back up by counterweight. The Admiral looked at the ropes and saw one wasn't moving. "What's the delay?" he yelled.

"It hasn't been pulled back by the diver, Sir!"

Cathalain ran as nimble as a cat from ship to ship across one of the beams that connected them, then grabbed a rocked rope and dove into the water where the last diver was supposed to have surfaced.

He descended quickly, pulling his knife as the rock dragged him to the bottom.

Those on the ship immediately prepared his rope to be extra counterweighted and sent over the other side.

When Cathalain reached the sea floor he didn't have to feel far because the diver was unconscious near his rope. The Admiral cut his own rope and the rock fell while he wrapped his legs around the diver and his rope around his own arm, then pulled it thrice.

A sailor pushed the heavy counterweight over the other side and Cathalain held on tightly while the rope pulled them up. And as it did he saw the shimmer of the shark coming toward them.

The Captain Diver held out his knife horizontally from himself and aimed for an eye as the shark attacked. He missed its eye but slit its gills instead. And the force of the impact almost caused him to lose hold of the rope, but he was able to keep his grip as the shark swam away with his knife still in it.

The Admiral continued being pulled up by counter-weight with the diver between his legs, and from the pain in his side, he knew some teeth had touched him.

"I got the lad," he yelled while hoisting him as they surfaced, and the divers from the diver deck grabbed the unconscious man and lifted him onto it.

Cathalain pulled himself up and checked where he'd been cut by teeth. He'd live, so he watched as a veteran diver felt for a pulse on the unconscious one.

"He has a heartbeat! Turn him on his right side!"

The divers put the unconscious man on his right side, then the veteran slapped his back in such a way as to push the water from his lungs.

Within moments, the man vomited water as he was brought back, then looked around to get his bearings. When he fully came to, he looked at his hand and chuckled as he realized he still held the oyster. He gave it to Cathalain and the Captain Diver smirked when he felt it was of the rare variety. Cathalain grabbed a knife from the veteran, opened it slightly, then smiled when he saw the black opalescent pearl within it.

Emperor Camulus Erra'Aulius, rode at the head of his vast column of Lancers, Knights, foot soldiers, chariots, onagers, supply wagons, and slaves. It was early in the morning and he felt refreshed from the night's rest.

Cypria was at the back of the long column with the other slaves. And chains weighed their march. Fresh wounds from the many challenges for rank covered Cypria's body. He was thankful none of the recent challenges had broken the rules, so Lancer Merrick hadn't had to intervene. But the chains still chafed his new and old wounds with every step, causing him consistent pain.

The Lancers and their horses up at the front were dressed in draped livery and plate armor; every set worth more than enough to feed an entire village for a year. And each horse was cared for more than they at the back of the long column.

The Emperor smiled as he thought of how much he loved riding at the front of some one hundred and sixty five thousand of his men. He was a young and handsome man in the lands at forty five, but he also carried an old family hate within him. He kept his brown hair short and his green eyes were often full of rage. He possessed a strong build having been trained his entire life. And he rode comfortably in command at the front of his marauding men.

Camulus remembered well when he was younger, watching his father ride at the head of this army with supreme control.

Berrinus would often tell him throughout his childhood, 'Someday, Camulus, these men will be yours. You'll command them into farther lands than I. And when you do, take Saddeye and have the Orakal there name you the one of their prophecies. Fulfill this, and Ideclan will be yours.'

Camulus' smile widened.

Only two more days till Saddeye, he thought. *And that little oracle will name me.*

Chronicle Seventeen

It's been some years since I left that wondrously beautiful place and yet long into the night do I still yearn for a voyage back to Daeadak. Philos is my home but Daeadak is my Heaven. The roaming hills and giant boulders cut by wandering waters and boundless winds stretch as far as one can ride. To experience this is well worth the almost unbearable trip by sea to get there.

The freedom by which the Daeadakians express with their horsemanship has simply surpassed almost all else. Why everyone does not ride as much as they can is a mystery to me. The sheer thrill of racing around on one of those powerful animals, and I daresay the Daeadak know how to breed them, has been the hardest thing to banish from my mind. And the skills they demonstrate with this partnership, far surpass anything I've seen with other animals, except of course the Ravenborne.

I must sound somewhat like a sheltered cub coming out of the cave for the first time when it pertains to this subject. But it's true. I find living in this stone city more unaccommodating to my taste as every day passes. Not due to a dislike for this fine and thoughtful abode but due to my ever growing fondness and love for horses. To watch a free roam of hundreds is the most beautiful thing I have ever seen, and to ride on one of them is the most thrilling thing I have ever done.

At a young age the Daeadakian is taught to become family with the animal, and they treat their horses better than family in some cases. Familiarity with their steeds is at a level which allows them to perform more masterfully than anywhere else I've been. They can maneuver completely around their mounts without falling off, ride every horse without saddle or bridle if they wish, and the level of accuracy with bows from their backs is something to be studied.

During my two year stay there, the people were more than welcoming and included me in their customs. Every morning, those who wish it go for a ride along their coast. My first morning was my first ride and I rode every morning for the rest of my respite. These rides are a mainstay of their ways like festivals are to others. For they go on hunts or journeys across their wide hilled and open lands with all the celebration of a grand event.

One of these rides is an annual hunt for their sacred ram. I am no hunter. One would be hard pressed to find a hunter among the Philos, so I only spectated when it came time for this event, and thankfully it arrived after some time of my be-ing there. For if it had been at the beginning of my stay I know not whether I'd have had the skills to almost keep up with them. These rams which are only allowed to be hunted once a year on this sacred hunt, and only one is allowed to be taken during this hunt, are among the finest specimens known. It is my theory they descend from the Ancients. The animals are treated as such, and are protected by all from Daeadak.

The Bighorns are magnificent in a way that can only be known through experience. They wear pure white coats of long hair and are able to climb anywhere with their strong and pow-erful frames. It is said by the Daeadakians that this ram is the hardest animal on their lands to hunt, and judging by the efforts it took I might have to say so myself. Yet I cannot speak on the methods they employed because to witness their methods is to be sworn to secrecy. Every part of the ram is used. The meat is eaten that evening at the site of its departure and the hide is reserved for the King. The ram's two horns are ceremoniously removed and cleaned, then given to the King as well. These two horns will be presented as gifts by the King to his Generals and others of the sort. The horns produce such a sound as I have never heard, and they can easily be perceived above the rumbling thunder of a full Daeadakian ride.

Ridec O'Ronan participated in this hunt on his journeys there, and proved an excellent horseman that day by keeping up with those of Daeadak. He even saved the King's life after a lion took his horse. In thanks, the King gave Ridec one of the horns from that hunt, which is now known as 'The Horn of Ravenborne.'

The Daeadakians themselves are small in stature and weight, very agreeable to the horses, I'm sure. They wear mostly leather and furs and have hats that curl up over their eyes and ears. Their eyes are more narrow than mine, and usually take on the hues of brown and dark green, but the latter are more rare. Their skin is a lovely light tan or in some cases even an olive color, and with all these features together, they are a beautiful people. I look forward to making a return journey there someday, perhaps very soon.

Written by Philip of Philos during the Sixth Year of the Ninth Age
A Parchment found among the things he left behind after moving
to Daeadak

Declanii

Chapter Eighteen

"Tell me it's almost over with. This trip is nothing like those on our rivers," Biewren groaned, half sick from the tossing of the Hilernian Sea.

Her older sister, Biethwren, wasn't bothered by it while she sat next to her younger in their ornately carved tallship, with a wood burning stove going strong at the center of their cabin.

They'd been voyaging from Hinturan, staying close to shore the entire way, sailing for the narrows of Trader's Strait so they wouldn't have to brave the open sea, then staying close to shore once more as they made their way to Ideclan. It caused the trip to be considerably longer, but it was worth it since the two young Hinturan Queens were on board.

"Go out and breathe the fresh air if you like. Signs of Ideclan are in sight so gather yourself. The Prince will be there to greet us."

"The Prince? Why didn't you tell me that sooner? I look as though I've ran into a tree."

"You're presentable, little love," Biethwren told her younger.

Then the elder checked her appearance once more, and grinned as she thought of seeing the Clanii she'd stayed in correspondence with over the years.

"Are you going to command the Prince to be under your dominion of marriage?" Biewren asked with an innocent smile.

"I must engage Cael differently. Our ways are not theirs. These men won't listen to everything we say, or do as we command."

"I'm no child. I know the men out here are practically wild like animals."

Biethwren grinned again.

"Do you remember anyone else from Ideclan besides the Prince?" Biewren asked.

"The only other I truly remember is that old Ariek, Segais. Did you meet him? The one that had Mother in tears with laughter."

"I wasn't allowed to be with all of you, remember? I had to stay and watch the small children," Biewren said curtly. She was still upset about it.

"He's Philosian though. Tell me, where is Philos?"

"That's ridiculous! It's just East of Ideclan! Mother didn't send us on this trip so you could give me history lessons!"

"If that were a lesson it would've been geography. Why don't you give me the history lesson," Biethwren suggested without playfulness.

"I have nothing prepared, and I don't want to!"

"When we return home you go before the Habra'Mahd. Are you prepared for that?"

"Yes."

"Then tell me, in brief, the history of our lands, especially the part about our specific branch of Queenship and how it works to strengthen the Matriarchy."

Biewren stared at her older sister in disbelief. She couldn't stand that Biethwren was telling her what to do right now.

"We're almost at Ideclan," she said quietly.

"We have time."

"And I'm not feeling well, remember?"

"You're not being punished. But if you aren't prepared for the Habra'Mahd, what do you think your punishment will be?"

Biewren bolted up from the cushioned plank and stood in front of her sister while assuming as rigid a posture as possible on the ship. She began reciting their people's history, and after hearing her perform correctly the part she always messed up, Biethwren had her skip ahead.

"…And so because of this, the men didn't give the power back to the Habra'Mahd. Many things happened during that time, but the most atrocious were the Acts of Savage, when the men exceeded all power and took everything from the women, and the women had nothing left of their own."

"That's fairly short and barely peels at the bark. Tell me you know more, or…"

"Of course I do! I just…"

A loud knock rasped at the door to their cabin, interrupting Biewren.

"Enter," Biethwren commanded.

The captain of their ship, a broad, stout man with a bald head and red brown skin, opened the door.

"We've almost arrived and the men make ready for port. What are your commands, my Queen?"

"Port for medium duration. All Sailor and Guard Breed stay with the ship. Ten of the Rishee Breed accompany us. Is this so, Hakran?"

"So this is, my Queen," he answered, and then began shouting orders before shutting the door.

Biethwren looked back at her younger and asked, "What is the dominion of our branch of Queenship?"

"We are the deciders. We choose what a man gets bred for, and what lines are suitable for continuation of that breeding. We keep watch and guard over the ancient bloodlines. And the success of everything depends on us; for the surety of our people depends on skill, and if we breed skill, we will thrive."

"That's one way of saying it. And not the worst. We'll talk more on the way back. Our trees surely know Mother will have my skin if I don't help you."

"Mother knows I don't need your help!"

The two young Queens began making ready for their arrival. It was warmer at their homeland to the South, but they were well prepared with many folds of elegant silk garments and black, concealing cloaks over top. Biethwren and Biewren exited their warm cabin and though prepared, they were instantly grateful for the extra blankets and furs draped around them by the Rishee.

It was then that two ravens flew over their ship and Biethwren smiled to herself. Despite the Winter's chill, she was in high spirits to see Cael again.

Both Queens stood tall and proud on the deck as the Sailor Breed brought them into port. Each Queen had auburn hair with red brown skin and gray eyes, traits indicative of their family line, and evidence of their genetic skill to pass these traits on to every daughter. Though they kept these traits well hidden under their deep dark hoods.

Even though Biethwren was only nineteen, she held much stature and respect in the matriarchy that was Hinturan. She was one of the youngest Queens on the Queensdrin. And her family's particular branch gave her a great deal of influence and responsibility. Her family was also the reason why Hinturan was just as strict with its selectiveness of its women as they were its men.

The men of Hinturan did have power among themselves, and those with mental wit were able to gain esteem. A few even held positions that had them telling some women what to do. But no man ever told Biethwren, Future Lady of Lineage, Queen of the Right Seat of House Handorlyin, what to do.

The captain of her and her sister's ship, patrolled the deck while giving commands and tying onto the dock at Ideclan's Port went smoothly. When that was completed, ten of the Rishee escorted the Queens off by way of a gangplank, then surrounded them in a wide octagon once they were on dry ground and looked at this new land with wariness.

All Hinturans preferred their tall trees, and their cities high up in them. Every floorboard close to a tree was notched into that tree. This was the same technique taught to Ridec and his companions by the Teker Ren when Ideclan was first built. Though, Ridec was only taught how to create walls based on the ground, not extremely high platforms strong enough to support a matriarchal society of over two hundred thousand people.

"On second thought, I don't know what's worse, the rocking of that sea or the cold of this land," Biewren declared while wrapping her blankets tighter.

Biethwren smiled again, and was pleased to see the Prince with ten others, all wearing unassuming cloaks while walking toward them.

"Biethwren, Queen of the Right Seat of House Handor-lyin, you and yours are welcome here," Cael said with respect as he reached them.

"Ravenborne, from the House O'Ronan, we thank you," she replied in the same manner, and then parted the Rishee while walking toward him with her sister in tow. "It has been too long since our trees have branched together. Tell me what news the leaves bring."

"They bring whispers of cooling shade," Cael returned as she reached him. "How was your voyage?"

"The sea was mostly calm but the trip too long. And the weather here, is it always this cold?"

"It's usually colder. What of Hinturan? Your trees never seem to lose their warmth."

"As they never should."

Cael gestured toward three carriages and they all started walking together.

"Do you have full say for the Queensdrin?" he asked.

Biethwren became annoyed he shifted to business so quickly.

We haven't even finished the greetings to my satisfaction, she thought.

"I have full say for the Queens of Hinturan. You remember my younger, Queen Biewren, of the Left Seat of House Handorlyin?"

"I remember as the rings do. I also remember that House Handorlyin is the Second House, second only to the First House, House Hinturan. Is this as true as the pinecone's fall?"

"It is, Prince Cael," the younger Biewren replied.

She grinned at his Hinturan phrases. Not many were allowed up in their tree cities so it was highly uncommon for others to use them.

"Everything is in order, and our presence has not been alerted to. Is this so?"

"Indeed it is, Lady Biethwren," Cael told her. "The

council is being held where we can drive the carriages right into an enclosure and no one will see us."

"That is acceptable. It appears our appeal for secrecy is understood."

After a short bit of walking they reached the carriages with six horses each, and the Queens commanded their Rishee to get into the second one while the Declanii, in unassuming cloaks, got into the third. Then they climbed into the first with the Prince and marveled at how warm it was.

Cael gave them a smile and said, "Made special for the Hinturan Queens," as he motioned with his hand toward a small cylindrical wood burning stove fashioned by Corrick, the Master Smith.

"It's so small, yet feel the heat!" the younger Biewren exclaimed.

Their ride to Ideclan was brief but the day fully underway by the time they climbed up the switchbacks while traversing the road from the docks to the city. The guards at the South gate knew the routine well, and when each carriage driver gave them correct hand signals in succession to one other, they let the caravan in and closed the gate behind them.

Prince Cael and his guests went straight toward Old Ideclan where the council would be held. Leaders from all The Kinned Lands were already there: twelve from Daeadak, nine from both Edemar and Elemar, thirteen Arashrillians, seven Gisspor, three from Teker Ren, and five Philosians.

A multitude of Clanii and Ideclan Council Members were also in attendance. But besides the King and Queen,

Aislin, Seamus, Quinnlan, Cael, Conail, and now the Declanii who were at the docks with the Prince, no one at the entire city knew of Hinturan's arrival.

The three carriages pulled into a large barn connected to the half living house where the council was located. As Cael exited from the first, he heard a familiar raven's caw in the distance and smiled as he started leading the two Queens inside. The Queens ordered their Rishee into the warm carriage while they waited. And the Declanii moved to guard the perimeter.

Two other Declanii stood just inside the doorway, and nodded at Cael as they entered and walked by.

Within the house it smelled of a sage, which the two ladies were immediately fond of.

"Silversage," the young O'Ronan told them after noticing their delight.

He led the Queens down a hallway where much clamor and commotion was heard coming from a room at the end. Halfway through the hallway, he walked into another room designated for weapons. The Prince set his bits and swords down, the swords were just presented to him by Corrick the day before. And Biewren looked questioningly at her sister concerning their Honor Daggers. The elder nodded and both placed them down delicately on the table before following Cael out.

The commotion caused by rearranging the room at the end of the hall stopped as they walked toward it, but the clamor caused by debating nations didn't. The Kinned Lands were bonded by Ideclan, but that didn't stop old rivalries from springing up.

Cael was sure some of the arguing he heard came from Edemar and Elemar, sworn friends and then enemies since long before joining The Kinned Lands. He also heard his Ma and Da, along with a few others. But there were at least eighty men and women in the large room standing around the blazing central hearth in the shape of a hexagon, the same shape as the room. And many were trying to speak. The council had not yet began or there'd be more order.

As Cael led the two Queens down the hallway he was stopped by Rann who'd arrived just before. Rann was a brother to the Daeadakian King, Rowin, and a man of sway in the horse lands.

"Prince Cael. Strong strides to you."

"And to you. How fare the flanks?"

"They fare well. But I must ask a King's Question: when will you return to Daeadak and ride on our sacred ram hunt? Rowin has not forgotten your promise."

"Tell him neither have I, and we will ride after Ideclan has solved this problem with the East."

"I will, young Prince."

"How fare the troubles with Aguptah to the South?"

"They're a concern. But many of us are available for this quarrel with Camulus. Good ridings to you," Rann said before making his way into the room.

"And to you," Cael replied, then continued leading the two hooded Queens into the large room behind him.

"What's this, Prince Cael? More surprises?" a man named Kemish from Edemar yelled as they entered. It'd been his voice heard most from the room. "If Edemar isn't treated equally in this manner!" Kemish continued, returning his attention toward the King.

"Edemar will be treated as fair as it always has," Acillus told him with calm authority. "Now that everyone is here, we may take our seats and start this council."

All in the room quieted as they sat down, except for Kemish who continued on as he sat.

"Well, Prince? I know almost everyone here except for your two mysteries there. Who are they?"

"They are friends, Kemish. Hold your tongue for council," Cael told him, and it angered the Edemarian more.

"Let all nations here be recognized," Acillus immediately declared before their conversation could go further.

Cael and Kemish had old history. When the Prince was nine he went to Edemar and during his stay there, he partook in a hunt where by wonder the young O'Ronan was separated from both Segais and his Declanii bodyguards. While separated, a spike trap made for boars sprung on him and nearly punctured Cael when he thought he was by himself. Cael knew it was Kemish he saw off in the distance afterward, riding away from the event, but he only saw his back. Because the Prince was alone he couldn't prove it, but he knew it was Kemish. And ever since then he'd been harboring revenge.

"Ideclan," Seamus Weynahar began.

"Philos," an old man with white hair and black robes said after. He was accompanied by four others dressed the same. His name was Ganpur, currently the most senior member of the Philosian Ten and Seven.

"Teker Ren," one of three by the name of Ban Sring called out. All three wore buckskins with loincloths that went completely around them. And long sleeve tunics and cloaks made from leathery leaf, a plant that makes its home without dirt in the large y's of the trees at Teker Ren. Their clothes were made by overlapping and sewing these leaves together.

"Daeadak," the man named Rann engulfed in furs said. He was accompanied by eleven others. All who had the same black hair, small short statures, and wore multiple furs along with fur caps that curled up over their eyes and ears. It was these people's ancestors who taught Ridec and his companions how to befriend horses with grace.

"Gisspor," a man called Sahndrose pronounced. He was accompanied by six Master Navigators, all wearing flowing robes. Each was well groomed and adorned with multiple bracelets, necklaces, rings, and other jewelry from across Terr'ah. Their ancestors taught Ridec and his fellow Clanii the paths of many stars, and how to navigate by them.

"Arashrill," a broad man named Urian said among thirteen, all of whom were masters of the spear. Their ancestors carried out a tragedy for Tarkin Erra during the Tribellion War, and were almost destroyed by Ridec and his army afterward. But the Arashrillians had proven their loyalty since then, and became a valuable member of The Kinned Lands thereafter. The clothes they wore consisted of soft cloths folded, draped, and sashed around themselves, each in the colors of their different Factions, with the insignia of the pirate crew who founded their Faction embroidered on the outer most cloth.

"Elemar," Rayde, one of nine said. All nine were fit and strong and wore mostly blankets for warmth. The Elemarians specialized in fighting with a sword in one hand and grappling with the other. It was their ancestors who taught Ridec and his followers how to wield the sword. They wouldn't teach them their grappling techniques however, so the Mullquanes taught them how to wield a shield along with the sword instead.

"Edemar," Kemish grunted, surrounded by eight others who looked just as unpleasant to be around as himself. Their homeland had tremendous while tragic history. It was these men's ancestors who Ridec and his companions fought against with Elemar, so that Elemar would teach them the sword.

"All lands are declared. This council is sealed and commenced," Acillus said.

If it were any other kind of council then next there'd have been turns taken for each nation. But this was a war council, and so Acillus threw a few logs on the fire before continuing.

"Many centuries ago, during the zenith of the Fourth Age, there were seven brothers who were sons to a King. This King didn't achieve the throne through succession. He rose to it by noble acts. His deeds were simple at first, such as caring for peoples' animals while they were away, feeding those who had nothing left from his own supply, or bringing a letter from one friend to another.

He'd done so many things for so many people that the King before this man, heard of him and his kindness. This previous King wanted someone he could completely trust among his company, and so he summoned the man with seven sons, and asked him to perform a few tasks in order to ascertain whether or not he was indeed as true as the tales say.

Over many years the man with seven sons proved trustworthy and wise, and he earned a seat next to the King, and the King consulted with him on many things. The only area of state the kind man didn't involve himself with was the army, and he didn't have to with how deft he was at handling foreign policy. His eldest son however, involved himself greatly with the military."

All in the room focused on Acillus' story. The large fire warmed them and most were relaxed. Many thought they knew who he was speaking of, but only a few Clanii and the Philosians knew about them this far back. So everyone listened keenly, even the two young Queens.

"Some years later, the King passed away and there was a festival held in his honor. Because the King had no sons, at that festival, his will was read aloud to all. To most of the nobility's surprise, but not to the commoners, the King had written down this kind man with seven sons as his successor.

Now it was this kind man's turn to rule and because of his wit, he was able to solidify his right with the nobility's support. In the end, the nobles all realized they prospered because of him as well.

When it came to his seven sons, this new King put nothing before them, not even the affairs of his country. The eldest was strong but had no full brothers because his mother died giving childbirth. The next two eldest were full brothers to each other but their mother had also passed. The next four were all full brothers but their mum went mad and left them some time before their father became King. So the seven young men never had a real mother, and the Kind King always felt they were lacking love because of this. And so he never withheld any of his own from them, and too often let them get away with things that he shouldn't have.

This man was King for twenty years before his kindness became corrupted like his sons. And that was when he decided to show his heirs they were loved by giving them more. He saw in his realm eight major provinces, the greatest being controlled by himself.

He called for his Princes and in a grand event, stripped his nobles who were previously governors and bestowed those titles on his offspring. Each now had cities of their own on which to supply and pay for their warbands.

Under this system of rule, their territories grew greatly, and it wouldn't be for another two thousand seven hundred years before their realm would grow again. This man and his sons controlled more land than they thought possible, and the deeds they now performed, out shadowed any good deed the old man ever did.

The sons were never known for their honor and they loved each other less as the King grew old. This was his one regret. He didn't care about his deeds, good or bad; he was concerned that his sons didn't care for each other. He knew that eventually to gain power, they'd war. As his days grew few he'd call them into his chamber and work to make them grow a stable relationship. But all they'd think about was how to acquire more of the empire for themselves once he was gone.

It became so contentious that once he did pass, there wasn't even a funeral for him before the war started. The four youngest brothers allied against the other two and the eldest. The other two of course joined together, but they also sought the eldest. He'd been with the military when his father was just an advisor, and had the realm's true veterans at his command.

Their civil war waged for years with the original alliances being broken and new ones forged in numbers too great to count, crossing and double crossing each other until not even their Faights can get it right. What is certain, is that betrayal caused there to be four kingdoms in the empire instead of seven, and that didn't last long. The seven brothers would be nothing but bones, yet their lineage would still carry the hate and once again, war would be upon them two centuries later.

They fought until all that was left were the eldest brother's line, and the second eldest's of the four. These two lived in relative peace for the next four Ages and most of this one. The name of the empire stayed the same, but the two Kingdoms had their own names as well. The side led by the younger lineage took its name from their mother; which they called the Aulius Kingdom. The side of the eldest son who'd been with the military, they called the Erra Kingdom.

Both sides of the empire started expanding their territory again at the end of the Eighth Age. Until little more than three hundred and thirty three Clanii years ago, when a King from those lands named Tarkin Erra, decided to venture West.

The Tribellion Army stopped him and sent his army back to their own lands. But the King, Tarkin Erra, was slain by Ridec O'Ronan. And this has created a blood feud between the Erras and the O'Ronans.

The Aulius didn't share the blood feud with the Erra,

but thirty years ago, the two that were side by side for so long, became one. The Erra led by Camulus' father, Berrinus, decimated the Aulius. Within eighteen years, the vast empire came under the rule of one man, who joined the names Erra and Aulius.

And now, their empire under Camulus has stretched to five times the land as The Kinned Lands. In Camulus' very own words; he's taken enough of the East, to take the West. We're not certain, but we think the assassination attempt involving the Vord was orchestrated by him as well.

You all must know, Camulus has also recently captured Teranim," Acillus informed them.

The council flew into a number of mixed reactions. As no one had ever taken Teranim. The way they developed their weapon over the centuries and their ability to assassinate with it, frightened nations' leaders to the point of insanity.

"Natural causes weakened them and enabled Camulus' Western Army to siege them outright and by surprise," Acillus continued, causing everyone to settle.

Biethwren greatly involved herself with the Hinturan spies and was curious to know how the King was aware of Teranim, because not even she would risk her agents going near that place. It comforted her to know that no one could see her curiosity through the deep dark hoods she and her sister wore.

"Camulus now has his main army, combined with the North, South, and East armies, all together numbering near one hundred and sixty five thousand, possibly surrounding Saddeye this very moment," Acillus let it be known.

"Is he there for the Orakal?" Urian of Arashrill asked with concern. He was a follower of the old ways and grew worried for the child.

"What a shame," General Seamus put in. "Keeping that young girl locked up the way they do, never showing her any sort of love or friendship. What kind of oracle do you think that will raise?"

Urian had long since shed his Arashrillian temper, but was already done with Seamus' disrespect for his faith and about to speak, when Queen Andraste noticed and quickly spoke first to dissipate the situation.

"Another's ways are theirs to have and ours to respect, Seamus."

"Indeed, my Queen," the General agreed while bowing his head.

As Acillus watched Urian calm, he became aware that some in the room weren't following them.

"I see there are a number of us who don't know this prophecy. It's important to Camulus. And Ganpur of Philos is more versed than I, so I ask you, Ganpur, to give us the short of it. I've already taken too much time with the histories."

"Indeed you have," Ganpur poked fun. "Krig brana nag kriskta. Who's heard this?"

A few hands went up, Urian's was among them.

"It means: The Walks of Life. And that is what they at Saddeye call their faith, which centers around some very long prophecies. The short of it is, when the ninety ninth daughter is born, the child is to be brought up with no love or physical contact of any kind. Special measures were taken to make sure her physical self was never touched by another human, not even by midwives during her birth. From the earliest age, the Orakal has been self sufficient.

Imagine what that must have been like, crawling and then walking, trying to reach those around you for contact but never could, only to find out why you can't once you've learned the language, and then having to adjust to that as your reality.

She has now reached the age of twelve and is by all accounts most perceptive. Two Philosians pilgrimaged there to see if this were true and indeed it is. They say she is completely sovereign unto herself.

The lands at Saddeye, those surrounding it, and many areas all throughout Camulus' empire, believe in a prophecy that says someone will be named by the Orakal and return the love the father held for his seven sons, then there will be no more civil wars. During that time when the Kind King first became ruler, his people prospered so greatly it became almost a Golden Age for them, and they've wanted to return to that ever since.

If Camulus takes Saddeye, and he will, he can make it look as though she's named him by lying, threatening her, propaganda, or who knows that man's mind. If The Walks of Life think he is named, he will have another one hundred thousand fighters rallying to his banner. And with it looking like the prophecy has been fulfilled, his people will start to love instead of fear him."

"I don't quite follow," Seamus said.

"How so?" Ganpur asked back.

"Why would the people have need of that prophecy? It was thirty years ago when Berrinus combined the last two kingdoms of their empire. There should be no more civil wars."

Ganpur looked at Acillus.

"I'll answer, Seamus. Recent intelligence says Camulus has been using his own men to terrorize the civilian population into believing there are other lines of the seven brothers, seeking to usurp his throne once more. He's deliberately keeping the fear going so he can fulfill that prophecy."

Not all conversations between Aislin Mullquane and Acillus were shared with the General. But Ganpur had already known about this, as well as Queen Biethwren.

The King continued after a short pause.

"From Saddeye, he's certain to leave by Latespring and march across The Hot Sands to take Hinturan."

"How will he do that?" Sahndrose of Gisspor asked.

"Siege engines with flaming ammunition."

The Master Navigator sat back in his chair. He knew Gisspor would be next given its proximity, and went to his notebook to make some estimations based on the Gissporian thirteen moon calendar.

"Camulus' engineers have made onagers with iron protection that can reach confirmed distances of at least three hundred spans. They'll hurl fireballs at Hinturan until their forest is no more," Acillus said.

It was then that Kemish decided to stand and give Edemar's opinion.

"Let it burn! What do we care about that immoral den of harlots and their weak men? They can all die before Edemar will go to their aid!"

Cael started speaking so Biethwren couldn't, and it almost didn't work.

"This concerns more than just Hinturan, Kemish. Get past yourself to see that."

"Hold your tongue, boy!"

Biethwren stood up from her chair and pulled her hood back.

"You hold your tongue before I take it! No one speaks of Hinturan that way! And no one commands a Ravenborne! Now sit! Do as I say or bring forth this Queen's wrath!"

"What's this? A girl? What's going on?" Kemish asked as he sat with a mocking laugh.

Cael started speaking again before the young Queen could continue because she was ablaze with rage.

"This is Biethwren, Queen of the Right Seat of House Handorlyin, from the trees of Hinturan, Future Lady of Lineage, and member of the Queensdrin. Heed her well, Kemish. They bring information that may make the difference."

"When the forest is on fire, the wolf and dear run together," Acillus interjected. "The council will now listen to Queen Biethwren."

After calming herself, the young Biethwren began by saying, "Hinturan first wishes to acknowledge The Kinned Lands for keeping other nations away to our North. And since you've been a peaceful people, proven through the centuries, you've therefore guarded our North. And because of this, we seek what can be done together."

"Sounds like the true reason is now you need someone guarding your East," Kemish remarked.

"Let the Queen speak. I will hear what she has to say," Urian the Fearsome told him.

Urian was First Spear, the highest rank one could achieve at Arashrill. And Kemish wasn't quick to rebut him, so Biethwren continued.

"Siege equipment, prophecies fulfilled, one hundred thousand extra warriors, all of this matters little when looking at what Camulus already has. If we do not work together, he'll crash into us like a falling tree.

There's a council to be held by Camulus in one to two months' time. Most of his five hundred Lancers will be there for a jousting tournament, and every advisor surely will, as it's his last council before heading this way.

It will commence in the Tower of Ohengus at the Twelve Lakes of Lareen, the closest major city to Saddeye with an arena. The information in this meeting will be of vital importance. Not only because they'll discuss plans for their campaign, but we know Camulus has kept secrets as well. And we need to uncover these truths.

The Tower of Ohengus is said to be greatly tall, and at the top on the Eastern side is a room where the meeting will be held. This chamber has a large window open to the elements. Scouts will climb up the spire undetected and hide at the top while listening in, then climb back down and sneak out of the city."

"Good luck," a man from Edemar sneered.

"We will not perform this mission. One of you will."

"And what of Hinturan?" Kemish asked. "What's your part?"

"Hinturan cannot commit its scouts. But we will commit our army to the command of the Ravenborne King: twenty thousand men bred for the sole purpose of fighting."

Biethwren stood proud while declaring this. She was the one who'd talked the Queensdrin into sending their troops in the first place. But her statement was met with the sounds of shifting in chairs and uneasiness. It was the word 'bred' that did it.

"The Kinned Lands are grateful to have Hinturan as an ally, we thank you. And Ideclan will take on the scouting task," Acillus responded.

Biethwren continued, "Have your scouts stop at the principal island of Hobaru. The climb up the spire is not one for a novice, and enlisting those who are skilled is always wise."

"I'll pass the word, thank you," Acillus said before turning back toward everyone else. "Now it's time for votes. The matter of Teranim is first. They have requested to become part of The Kinned Lands."

He gave the council time to talk about the abruptly presented matter before calling the vote. Normally, there'd have been many days or even months of discussion before a matter like this was decided upon. But this was a war council. And Acillus could call to vote whatever he felt necessary.

"All in favor, stand, those not, stay seated."

Only four men and two women chose to stay seated.

"Teranim is with us. The next vote is: are The Kinned Lands at war with Camulus and do we march to face him? Or do the Northern Armies stay and wait behind our walls while Daeadak, Gisspor, and Hinturan are destroyed?

As we all already know from previous councils, if we don't leave and engage him before he reaches The Hot Sands, then there is no terrain in or West of the Sands beneficial for fighting his army at the South.

What say you to march forward?"

Everyone stood or stayed standing. Even Fehurin Cailian knew the truth of what Camulus' Lancers and Knights could do on open ground. If Camulus controlled Hinturan, Gisspor, and then Daeadak, that would create a multitude of problems. Not to mention cut off the valuable trade Gisspor did for all nations of The Kinned Lands. So Fehurin was pleased to see everyone on their feet.

"All nations, send homing pigeons and command your armies to mobilize," Acillus ordered. "Armies North of the Hilernian Sea, sail for Ideclan's Port, then get designated and manifested transport ships for the crossing."

"The Edemarian Army already prepares, and will sail soon," Kemish told him.

"That was prudent, thank you."

Kemish nodded.

"Sahndrose," Acillus called out.

"Surely, the armies need our ships and they shall have them. As planned, there are enough at dock and not out trading to accomplish the maneuver."

"The sooner they're here, the better."

"Indeed," Sahndrose agreed while looking in his notebook. "Will we be sailing through the Immramman Sea?"

"No, we'll land between Hinturan and the Hobaru Mountains. Camulus has many patrols in that sea and if he gets word of our march too soon it could fail us. The navy will patrol the strait so Camulus can't sail his army out in case he tries. And if need be, the navy can come in, clear the Immramman of patrols, and pick us up."

Acillus then addressed the entire room again.

"After the Northern Armies land at the location made secure by Hinturan and Daeadak, that will be when our next council is held."

"Who will guard Caibre Pass while we're away?" Ban Sring questioned.

Queen Andraste answered, "Some of the scout contingent will stay behind with five hundred of the Homeguard. And upon any word of an army marching for the pass, I'll march the women to defend it."

Andraste had a look on her face that dared anyone to challenge her ability to do so. And the Mark of the Mullquanes intimidated many.

"Would it help if the Northern Armies left troops for the pass?" Urian suggested.

"Then we wouldn't have the strength to face Camulus. I know most of the women from your lands don't fight, excluding Daeadak; but here you all know it's celebrated. They'll hold the pass," Acillus affirmed.

"They better hold it!" Kemish yelled. "If Camulus does send an army and they don't, then it's free reign on all our lands! Everything will be burned!"

"The women here aren't weak like the ones you prefer, Kemish," Cael taunted the Edemarian while staring at him.

For the second time, this time to end the council instead of beginning it, Acillus spoke quickly so their conversation couldn't continue.

"Since votes have been cast and we're all in agreeance, that concludes this council. Scouts will bring dispatches for further information."

"One more thing," Biethwren put in. "There is a man who risked much by bringing us the information regarding Camulus' council: all costs must be paid to spare his life should his path be crossed. He is very tall, his voice is deep, and he has many scars across his body."

"May we know his name?" the King asked.

"You may not, for he was smart enough not to give it. But you will know him from this: along with his burgundy eyes, his skin is as dark as night, a gift from the hot lands he's from."

Then Kemish said something he would soon regret.

"That's no gift! You mean he's of the Black Tribes from the South! The Arieks! The ancestors knew it as a curse and so do we! Edemar will fight and die alone long before it saves slaves!"

Before anyone could react, Cael was across the room with his left hand cupped around Kemish's throat as he moved forward. And without slowing, he lifted Kemish up from his chair, tipping the chair backward, and gracefully slammed the large Edemarian against the wall with enough power to startle him.

"Cael!" his father yelled. And the force of the yell snapped everyone's attention toward himself.

The young O'Ronan released his grip and stepped back when he heard his father, but the look on Cael's face made Kemish think twice before doing or saying anything.

The King walked over to Kemish and spoke so all could hear.

"If you withhold your martial protection from someone, simply because of where they're from or the color of their skin, then you have no business being in this council and indeed, no business with The Kinned Lands. Now, make your decision, is Edemar with us, or not?"

Nothing about the King said he was joking.

"Edemar is with you, of course, King Ravenborne," Kemish answered while straightening his clothes.

"Council is concluded!" Acillus yelled.

Everyone quickly went to grab their weapons and leave. The only people who stayed in the room were the King, Queen, Cael, Seamus, Quinnlan, and the two young Hinturans.

"Fool boy! Here I am talking of uniting against an empire and here you are dividing us! You've made an enemy for life!" Acillus yelled.

"We were already enemies for life!" Cael returned.

"Explain!" Andraste commanded.

"While at Edemar he provoked me to look a fool in front of their whole court, which I know was planned by their whole court. And then on the festival hunt he attempted to take my life."

"Why have you said nothing of this?" Acillus asked.

"I can't prove it."

"Edemarian scum," Seamus said, then spat on the fire in the hexagonal hearth.

"You've proven many things, young Ravenborne, and will prove many more," Biethwren declared while looking at them as though it was her house they were standing in. "Hinturan now wishes to speak further about the task that will take some of your scouts to Hobaru and the Twelve Lakes."

"What is it?" Andraste asked with a hint of shortness.

"To whom will you be assigning this mission?"

"Our best," Acillus answered with equal shortness.

"They'll have to be your very best."

"Indeed," the King agreed.

"They'll have to be your Silent," Biethwren said, and all looked at her with surprise. She'd anticipated this response and had hers prepared. "Ideclan knows of our Denzage, and Hinturan knows of your Silent. If our two peoples are to work together then we must be honest, lest one think the other is hiding something from them when they are not. Hinturan won't commit its army unless we're promised it'll be the Silent who perform this task. And we'll only accept the promise of a Ravenborne."

"Can we trust Hinturan?" Seamus asked everyone else in the room.

"Let this be the first test," the elder of the two young Queens suggested.

"Why are you specifying who must perform this scouting task?" the General continued.

"Because if you don't send your best, then we'll have to send ours, who are already engaged elsewhere. This mission is of the utmost importance."

"You have my promise," the King said.

He was slightly suspicious, but also not oblivious to the looks she'd been secreting toward Cael, and so he didn't think it was a trap. And he also wasn't worried about anyone getting the best of Aislin Mullquane.

"Now tell your Silent this: Hobaru has five islands, each of them with few pathways up. Most of the islands are sheer cliff all the way around and the paths, well guarded. But there is a word that barters entrance onto the main island: svudarh. It means, 'I'm peaceful.' They also speak the Common Tongue so no interpreters are necessary."

"Thank you, Queen Biethwren," Acillus said. "Information is always appreciated. I know you're eager to get back to the warmth of your homeland, so if that is all, your carriages await and will take you both to port when you're ready. But please feel free to make yourself at home while here for as long as you like."

Two men and two women wearing plain clothes and no sunil walked out of the hallway and into the room they were in.

"These four will accompany you back to port when you choose."

Biethwren nodded before saying, "Hinturan's Army will join with Ideclan's at the battle camp. Rest assured, the landing for your ships will be secure."

"I have no doubt."

Each Hinturan Queen started following the Declanii out and before leaving the room, Biethwren turned toward Cael.

"Farewell, Prince. May our trees branch together soon."

"Indeed," Cael agreed as he nodded.

Then the two ladies retrieved their Honor Daggers and left entirely.

"Seamus, you'll handle the armies, the supplies, and the scout dispatches. Andraste has the city. Quinnlan, the Declanii are gathering on the field. Bring them to the docks. We leave for Teranim when I arrive."

"Aye," Quinnlan said excitedly.

Then they all grabbed their weapons and walked outside.

Seamus and Quinnlan said their farewells, before the Prince and his parents walked home while the two elders continued their conversation with the young one about his actions during the council.

"Your intention was in the right place," Andraste told him. "But your action was not. A true King helps guide the people to grow so they can guide themselves. What you did today only demonstrates that you don't know how to guide your own self."

"What Kemish said wasn't right."

"It wasn't," Acillus carried on. "And neither is forcing another into thinking as we do. What Kemish displayed was pure stupidity. But what you did was worse, not only because you are to be King, but because you treated hate with hate. Hate doesn't lead people, Cael. Your example will. And Instead of making progress with Edemar and changing their minds through patience and wisdom, you slammed their Commander General up against the wall."

"It was reactionary. But he greatly disrespected Segais' people."

"Would Segais have gotten angry?" the Queen asked.

"No," Cael grinned while saying.

Just remember," the King continued. "Kindness is more powerful than rage. I doubt much will come of it while Camulus is a threat. But now you have Edemar to deal with. And the Clanii who say we've become too warlike have momentum with what you just did. Learn to control your rage. And focus on what's coming."

"Speaking of," Andraste said. "Tell your Woda I think it wise you all stop at Hobaru."

"I agree, Ma. At the very least we need an advisor and proper training for such a climb."

Just as the O'Ronans were about to reach their family home, Cael's three friends emerged from down the road. Each was wearing their sunils and prepared for the voyage to Teranim. They'd snuck away from the fields to see what was taking Cael so long.

"Go talk to them, quickly," Acillus said. "And tell them they're in trouble for leaving the others."

Then the King continued on with Andraste while the Prince walked toward his friends.

"You're supposed to be with the Declanii. You think my Da or Uncle aren't going to do anything?" he said when he reached them.

"Nothing we can't handle," Irhanach returned with a grin. "We were wondering where you were. Come on lad, get in your sunils. We're leaving soon."

"I'm not going on this one."

"What, why not?" Anrahan asked.

"This is our first task as Declanii," Ohelathe stated.

"We've been talking about our first mission since we could say the words. What do you mean you're not going?" Irhanach added.

"I'm seeing to other tasks. Just listen to the commanders and keep low. And don't be heroes on your first mission."

"Seriously, Cael, where will you be? How could you miss this?" Irhanach queried.

"We'll meet up at the South. I'm not missing out on the war, just the battle. Now go fight well and watch each other's backs."

His friends reluctantly said their farewells before

returning to the Declanii. And Cael went inside his family home.

Once the Prince grabbed his kit and was done with his own farewells, he slipped away and almost made it out of the city unnoticed, until he heard a most familiar voice.

"Rather rude to leave without saying farewell, bad luck in some lands," Segais said as smoke curled up from his pipe.

"Segais! Where were you? I looked for you earlier."

"My friend Dunuvo returned from his pilgrimage, and we were speaking of the upcoming events."

"Have you decided?"

"Yes. I will take your father's offer. When he gets back from Teranim I'll sail with the armies and meet you at the South. Conail is staying here and rightly so. I'll be your father's war advisor."

"And then mine," Cael said with a smile.

The old wizard smiled in return, but it was to hide his sadness at the truth of it.

"You were right, Segais. You knew it would happen like this a long time ago."

"Resource, recognition, or revenge; all are easy to predict." Then he grew intense as he leaned in and said, "Watch yourself, and mind you go within like we talked. Work on the three techniques: the quieting of the mind, the running of the mind, and the focusing of the mind. They'll prepare you for the next lessons. And also very important, remember to watch for synchronicities, those coincidences that are not coincidences."

"I will."

"Only watch; observe, do not search."

"As you say."

"Off with you!"

Cael smiled at his old friend, then headed toward the docks and boarded the Silent's boat once he arrived.

It was a fast boat with one mast and unique rigging tailored for its small crew. And the fourteen handled it with ease as they sped onward toward Hobaru while planning to use the coastline as much as possible, with Roxgrin and Binneen following them high above, keeping an easy pace.

With worry in their hearts, Acillus and Andraste watched their son and the others sail away from atop the walls of Ideclan just near the Southern Gate, the same place they'd always watched their son sail away from.

Shortly after the Silent's boat was out of view, the King said farewell to his wife and met the Declanii at the docks.

The Declanii boarded three ships always designated for them. Each had a crew of one hundred twenty, and sails the color of sunil. Once boarded, the three ships, along with five other transport vessels, sailed East for Teranim. And two Ideclan Ravens followed them as well.

Declanii

Chronicle Eighteen

It is true. The child known as Krig Orakal nag Kriskta plays a complex role in the structure here. A role which many would fight to eradicate. Nevertheless, what is unthinkable to some has already been lived by others. To raise a child with no love is not thought of by the sane. Yet that is the case for the Orakal. And I know not how this irrational pattern entered the Walks of Life's thinking. But upon further study, it seems to have originated from within the earliest forms of their religion.

To my graciousness, I was given an extensive look at the prophecy scrolls at the temple of Saddeye, and my conclusion is that they are authentic. In these writings, it speaks of many jus-tifications for raising a child in such a way, none of which struck my mind to change its course and agree. And I never would have, until I met the child. I expected to find a snobby, angry little girl when I went to her court, but instead was taken aback by the young Orakal's bearing.

Being raised in such a manner has given the child sharp understanding. How this happened I can only speculate, and my first speculation is this: she possesses a will stronger than most to endure an upbringing like hers. Besides not being loved or cared for, I have confirmed she was completely left alone from age four to age seven, and then again from ten to eleven, these times being spent in complete solitude. So how does she know what she knows? How does she have a bearing that adults still work for? And how can she speak many lan-guages, most mind you, without being taught?

She is truthfully the ninety ninth born of Saddeye, with a different appearance to each who look at her, and some say

Declanii

the one prophesied by their faith to name they who will bring back peace to their lands. But that is all trivial compared to what the other prophecies here suggest. Whether or not she accomplishes any of them, though, only the new tales will tell. I look forward to recounting these prophecies in their entirety to you once I return.

One of many letters written by Ilianak of Philos, to his love,
Talina of Philos
Year Three Thirty Two of the Ninth Age

Chapter Nineteen

"Sire, the men have Saddeye completely surrounded," General Fenric told the Emperor, Camulus Erra'Aulius.

"This is already trite. Just annihilate them. I'm sure the Orakal wont mind naming me after that."

"Surely, but may I?"

"I spoke in jest," Camulus declared.

And his General smiled.

What should be done? the Emperor thought. *If I storm the city then most of them will die. If I wait, well, I'm not going to wait.*

The Emperor and his General, stood at the entrance to Camulus' war tent. It was the first thing set up when they arrived and it sat up top a small hill overlooking the city, its river, and his surrounding army.

"Follow me," Camulus ordered, and Fenric obeyed.

The Emperor wore his armor made of black leather interwoven through steel plates with silver inlay around every edge. His green eyes and brown hair fit his young face well. And he moved with a grace that revealed his lifelong training.

Fenric wore the full plate armor of the Lancers along with a colored sash and cape indicative of his house and rank: green and black. He was almost bald, but what hair he did have was white, tied behind him, and came out from underneath his heavy helm. And his brown eyes reflected the blankness of seeing more war than anything else in their existence.

As they left the tent, ten armed guards snapped to attention, then followed Camulus and his General. A group of representatives from each part of the army followed after, but only in range enough for them to hear if they were called for.

The Emperor and his General, surveyed the terrain and how it associated with the city. Men snapped to attention everywhere Camulus went. Each saluted with two fists to their heart. And 'Honor to the Emperor' was called out by every officer they passed. Camulus walked as if he heard none of them; but paid attention to all.

The two walked until they reached the Northern wall of Saddeye, where Camulus noticed a weakness.

"Ha!" he exclaimed. "Engineers!"

"What is it, Sire?" Fenric asked as a representative from the Engineers ran up to receive his orders.

"These walls are clay and here's a weakness, a crack from top to bottom. Engineer!"

"Yes, my Lord?" the representative said.

"Divert that river into the center of this wall here."

"Yes, my Lord," the man said again as he bowed, and then ran off with haste.

"Very nice," Fenric commented.

"Quite," Camulus agreed with a self satisfactory smile.

Even I *might follow your rules, Orakal,* he thought to himself.

The Emperor and General walked back to the war tent, and were joined by a dozen or so of Camulus' infamous five hundred Lancers, the nobles of his realm, dressed in plate armor and different colored sashes and capes.

All of them watched as one hundred engineers with shovels ran to the river and started digging a canal toward the city, while another hundred ran to the North wall of Saddeye and started digging a canal toward the river.

Up in the windows of the palace, an increasing number of worried faces appeared, including a Shogin in full armor. And it made Camulus and his men roar with laughter.

Within an hour the canals were met in the middle and the berm holding the river was dug away. Then the engineers started blocking the river's natural path so that all of its water went crashing down through the canal. With full force, the wall was punctured in little time and water started spilling into the city.

After a large breach and enough room was created, Camulus and his Lancers entered and encircled the city via perimeter road. Each Lancer had ten Knights behind them, with ten foot soldiers to command behind each of them, which constituted less than one third of the entire army camped outside of Saddeye; all of whom were commanded for the Orakal to remain untouched so as not to hinder the prophecy.

A horn was blown and they moved in. No one interfered with Camulus and his men as their horses' hooves sloshed through wet streets while the army made its way to the center.

At the center, surrounding the palace, were the people who couldn't fit inside, and it was enough for the Emperor not to wonder about the rest who were safe in the caverns below.

When Camulus reached the people, he looked up at the windows and saw some of the leaders of their ancient religion.

"There's no need for discourteousness, great city of Saddeye!" he called to them. "Clear a way to your councils so we may discuss this!"

Within moments, a path began clearing from inside out toward Camulus. A short old man wearing white silk robes was the cause. And he stopped a few steps before the Emperor.

"My lord," the man said awkwardly, while giving an even more awkward bow.

"You have come to take me to your councils?"

"No, my…"

"Then you are the one to be sacrificed?"

"No my..."

"Then you have come to take me to your councils," Camulus recommended.

"Yes my Lord," the man agreed, only thinking of his want for more life.

If this works and I'm named the one of prophecy, all the better.

Fifty of Camulus' Lancers accompanied him and Fenric as they dismounted and followed the man inside. Among them were Lance Commander Gragon, and Lancer Merrick.

When they walked inside, Camulus thought the palace to be nothing special. He noticed it was made from the same clay as the outer walls except painted. And even though the art was pleasing to his eye, it also appeared as though it hadn't been repainted in decades. And many of the walls had pieces crumbling from them.

Frightened people filled every room and hall. No one dared say a word as the feared Emperor made his way to the top of the palace.

Once there, two of his men pushed open large wooden doors. And he walked through to greet the leaders of the ancient city.

"So..." Camulus said as he held out his arms wide while smiling at everyone. "*This* is the Shogin, only fifteen or so left? No wonder you didn't make a stand."

"The Shogin were once many, now few return from the training among the Dokiri," a young girl stated. "Most die from the training, or flee from it. Like all true combat systems, each level is more difficult than the one before it. For the Shogin, this is exponential, and for the duration of their lives. So as for these fifteen, you will need more than your fifty to match their abilities."

"Ah, Orakal," Camulus said as the Shogin parted to

reveal her. When he saw the young girl sitting there, she looked to him as though she could be one of his daughters.

"Why have you taken my city, Emperor of the Er-ra'Aulians?"

"You mean to say an oracle doesn't know the answer to her own question?" Camulus asked mockingly.

"You're not the one of prophecy. I assure you now."

"Prophecies are funny things, often fit into the mold after the fact. But some are real. And all accounts of you claim to be real."

"How can you expect for it to stand, for people to believe you've been named? When everyone here has seen you take this city by force, come into this council uninvited, and now you're all but telling me that *you're* the one of prophecy?"

"Again! How does an oracle not know the answer to her own questions?"

"I'm not amused."

"Force you say? What force did I employ? The force of nature perhaps, but no actual violence was used to take this city, no blood was shed. And as for councils, I asked your fat man there if he went down there to take me up here and he agreed. That specifically, little Orakal, is not coming uninvited." Then Camulus said with a mocking bow, "I had an escort."

The young girl shot a disapproving glare at the man who led Camulus up, and it made him cower behind Binc and a few others wearing similar robes.

"You see, I've broken no stipulations. And as for who is the one of prophecy and who isn't, well…" Camulus' gaze grew intense. "We'll let the Faights decide that."

"The Faights decide nothing, foolish man. Do you know what damage you've done by diverting that river? Many depend on that water. Divert it back!"

"I understand not knowing what love is can make a person cruel. So I won't hold you in death for calling me foolish." Then he looked around the room. "Him however," Camulus declared while pointing toward Binc. "I'll hold in my dungeons."

Two Lancers grabbed the man in light blue and purple robes and held him tightly.

"Leave him be," the Orakal commanded.

"I'll not break any of your laws or stipulations, child. But I will break one of you every time you disrespect me."

Then he started walking toward her, causing many in the room to be nervous. His men moved in to thwart the Shogin from making any attempt on the Emperor's life. And it was a heightened moment.

Camulus sat beside the young girl, closer than anyone else but still careful not to touch her, and said, "Now," in a tone that suggested they were great friends. "Tell me all about yourself. We have a long journey ahead to the Twelve Lakes of Lareen, and it would be unpleasant if we were strangers."

Declanii

Chronicle Nineteen

For anyone who would study language and interaction, the reality of ambiguity should be researched with great interest. For when a sentence or word may be understood in more than one way, it will exist.

An example of ambiguity would be: The healers checked on every other stable horse.

The first instance is, who is referred to when the word 'healers' is used? Another instance are the words, 'every other.' Did the healers check on the rest of the horses, or did they check with every other horse there, meaning they skipped over half of them? The sentence can mean either. Then there's the word 'stable.' Are these horses in stable condition, or are they in the stables?

On all my travels and in every book I've read and written are there these misunderstandings. This is equally true if not more so when it comes to translating text, be it recent but especially ancient, for the more time to have gone by seems to make translation more difficult.

So I say patience is what we must express until we find a way of obliterating this base confusion from conversation. Then we can deal with those who lie.

Written by Siras of Philos
Date Unknown

Chapter Twenty

THE LATE EVENING SKY NEARED DARK WITH THE LAST bit of pastel blue clinging to the West. And a chilling wind brought three Declanii ships followed by five transport ships toward their aim. They were nearing the target site of fifty miles up the coast from Teranim, so many aboard watched for signal lanterns on land. The day was Rone, the Twenty Fifth of Midwinter, and it had been six days since they left after the council with fair goings.

Scouts on land saw the recognizable ships with sunil sails. So Liadine and two others, opened their signal lanterns and used mirrors to reflect the light.

"Thar the lanterns be, me King! Should we beach?"

"Yes, Gardin," Acillus answered.

Gardin was from Athal Mor. He'd visited Ideclan for a festival when young and during then his father took him to see the sea. He fell in love with it. And as soon as he was able he found his way back. After twenty years as a sailor and ten as a captain for the Ideclan Navy, he'd caught Acillus' attention.

"A'ight lads! Bring us ten marks port and make ready for beach!"

The ships were guided flawlessly up the sand. Then planks were set and Declanii poured out of them. The transport vessels anchored a distance from shore and would wait for the ravens, Dugan and Fey, to fly back and signal them to sail for Teranim.

"Ahroo, Liadine, and happy birthday," Acillus greeted the old scout as his feet touched dry land.

"Ahroo, and thank you," Liadine smiled.

"What do we know?" the King began.

"They did fight the Western Army down to about three thousand. But only five hundred remain at Teranim."

"Where are the rest?"

"Heading North for two days now."

"What of the five hundred?"

"Careless. They assume they've broken the Terans but patrols are still maintained; four groups for the wall walks of the wooden palisade and two groups patrolling the paths of the city. The rest stay in the meeting hall near the center. It's the longest and tallest building. And they have no Knights or Lancers with them. All went North."

"Terrain?"

Liadine drew of what he spoke in the sand.

"The city is butted next to the mountain on its East side, and the palisade is close enough to it that it can be jumped on from it. The sea is only two hundred spans to its Southwest. And the river running through the city does so mostly North to South. Right here is where it runs underneath the palisade and that's where the Teran escaped. It's also how Craine slips in and out. He's the only one who passes for local."

"Right," the King agreed. "Is the charcoal ready?"

"It is. And tonight will work. The people won't leave their huts," Liadine told him.

"Lads," Acillus called out, and all gathered to listen.

"We were going to sneak the people out of their city. But the Erra'Aulian numbers are fewer than we thought, and I have a new plan:

We still run for Teranim. But a mile before the city, the combatants doff our armor. Every archer save three will take our armor and stealthily place them in arrow range from their South wall. Make it look as though all Declanii march for the city. Then set your unused torches in the ground so the armor will shine once you light them.

After you've set up and on my command from raven, light the torches and your first arrows, then let fly at a fast pace. With their attention directed South, the combatants will storm the North while covered in charcoal. There are only five hundred of them, good odds when taken by surprise. Does everyone agree?"

"Aye!" was heard all around.

"Grab your kits and prepare. We leave in a few moments. Archers, pick three of you to come North."

Three volunteered. They were Diarmuid Shymurrow, Galladan Hafrana, and Ohelathe Mullquane.

"Alright lads, we run for fifty miles. After the archers set up, all will rest before the assault. One moment," Acillus notified.

Everyone made their final checks and adjustments to both their gear and themselves.

"Declanii!" the King shouted.

"Ravenborne!" they shouted back in unison.

"At my pace," he commanded, then started running.

The sky was now completely dark and the King led them up from the beach so no one had to run through sand. It was a quiet run with most of them concentrating on their breathing or the lapping shore, and the flapping of ravens' wings. Only Cristin breathed hard and fell behind. Some archers stayed with him and gathered many sturdy sticks while they ran.

The pace was such that when they arrived at the splitting point, no one was fatigued save for Cristin the Towering. With final preparations, the King sent most of the archers South and led the rest of the Declanii North.

It wasn't long before all were in position. And by the time the gear was set up while the archers stayed hidden, everyone was rested enough with little more than three hours before sunrise. The combatants covered their faces, necks, arms, legs, and shields in charcoal. Then Acillus had Dugan and Fey fly South and caw three times.

Archers flipped back the sunil cloaks covering the armor held up by sticks they'd gathered on the run, then lit the torches as a few shouted mock orders of "Move forward!" and "Let fly!"

Guards on the Southern wall wiped the tiredness from

their eyes when they saw what they thought to be Declanii. One sounded the alarm as arrows began raining down upon them. And in short time, many were underneath their shields and ready to fight at the South.

An arrow that'd been lit with fire caused a hut to go up in flames. And the Teran family inhabiting it, quickly ran from their abode into their neighbor's.

"Curses! What's going on?" the Erra'Aulian Captain shouted, and then hurried for cover underneath a subordinate's shield after an arrow hit nearby.

"The Declanii are here, Captain! To the South!"

"Form up! I want the entire contingent battle ready now, Corporal!"

"Yes, Captain!" the corporal said, then he ran off. But everyone not on duty was already making their way by the time the lower ranked man reached the meeting hall near the center. And he still went inside to see if there were any stragglers.

Just outside of the palisade at the North, Irhanach looked toward his two friends and whispered, "Initiation through fire, lads," with a wild look in his eyes. They were ready for their first assault as they crouched low.

"Now," Acillus commanded quietly.

The Declanii hoisted three archers and three warriors up onto the palisade. And six enemy sentries were caught off guard when six other men appeared as if they were catapulted there. Three of the sentries were taken out by arrows before the combatants could kill the other three. Then the charcoal and sunil covered Declanii began pouring over the North wall like flood waters spilling over a levee.

Most kept low to the ground and close together until everyone was over, except for the two files who stayed up on the wall walk of the palisade to clear it.

"Silent and swift," Acillus ordered.

The men on the ground separated into three groups: three files down the East flank led by Quinnlan Mullquane, three files down the West flank led by Eilidir Shymurrow, and four files down the middle led by Acillus.

As the Declanii moved through the city, the two files who stayed up top began making their way across the wall walks as well, keeping pace with those on the ground.

Acillus' group reached the meeting hall at the center without hindrance. Just then a man exited wearing corporal's armor. Diarmuid let fly an arrow through his throat before he could yell any warning. And no stragglers were found inside.

"Keep moving," the King directed.

The Eastern group met relatively little resistance. And those clearing the wall walk jumped down to unite with those on the ground once they cleared their side. One of them was Irhanach. And the others had found it difficult staying silent while keeping up with him. He and Quinnlan took out almost every sentry on their side before anyone else.

"Follow me," Quinnlan whispered, then moved his men to rejoin with the King's.

The Western group had to maneuver with caution. Those clearing the wall walk waited for those on the ground. They communicated through hand signals, keeping each other informed about the sixty Erra'Aulians now guarding the Western flank.

Led by Eilidir Shymurrow, they crept toward the enemy, four or five at a time, each group making their way until they were almost upon them.

Then Eilidir bolted from his position, initiating the attack. They threw spikes from the backs of their shields as they ran. Heavy spikes the length of two hands pierced into man and wood as the sixty were rained upon, while Ohelathe shared the sky with his arrows.

Many sentries fell from the salvo, and the rest followed as the pack of Declanii moved through them.

Anrahan was among those at the front of the ground group, and he cut through one sentry's stomach, then shield bashed another in the face.

The Erra'Aulians on the wall walk were taken out simultaneously by the file clearing it. Cristin was up on the palisade and he chopped down two with his Edemarian Sword, then picked up another with one hand and threw him on the spikes of the wall.

Quinnlan's group rejoined with Acillus', and then both waited for Eilidir. Once Eilidir had his sector cleared, he led his men toward the King. When they reached him, Acillus commanded them all to form up in rank and file on the main road North from the enemy.

Declanii

The hut that had caught fire from the arrow was somewhat isolated and though it burned bright, it risked no other buildings and now gave good visibility.

"Forward!" the O'Ronan commanded.

Some of the Erra'Aulians turned to see a ghostly force marching toward them. And the Declanii were deathly quiet as the Horn of Ravenborne was sound by the King, signaling the archers to stop letting fly and join the battle.

"Behind us!" a few shouted as they all turned.

The captain was surprised at the new threat and ordered his men to attack without thought.

"Charge! They have only their shields! The glory of killing them is ours!"

"Close formation!" the King yelled with fervor.

The Declanii pressed together as they walked, forming one solid mass. The first rank known as the Ravenline, interlocked their shields and battled the oncoming enemy who spread themselves apart. Some of the fastest runners were taken out with sword or spear. While the three archers who stayed behind the rank and file, flew arrows at the rest.

The Declanii continued marching forward at the same pace regardless of how many Erra'Aulians came at them, until the captain realized his folly and called his men back into formation.

"Halt!" Acillus commanded.

Studying their surroundings he decided this was the place. They were stopped between two large huts that gave them adequate protection from flanking on either side.

The enemy was now only forty spans away, and fully formed into a shield wall.

"Declanii! Not one of you will leave this cursed place alive!"

None of them responded.

"Forward!" the captain growled. And his men advanced, together this time.

Thirty spans.

Their armor clinked in unison as they marched.

Twenty spans.

The Erra'Aulians started their shield taunt.

Ten spans.

Swords clashed and shields crashed as they met. Limbs were hacked and bodies pierced. But no mortal injury belonged to the Declanii who fought with exact precision, until a battle pulse, which were the brief moments between fighting when they broke apart and moved the dead aside.

Acillus knew the timing to be right and yelled, "Rotate!" then blew a small bronze whistle hanging from his neck.

Upon the whistle, every combatant in the Ravenline,

turned sideways and squeezed between the files toward the backs of the formation, while the rest of the ranks moved forward; the next front line interlocking their shields as they did.

It was then that Acillus heard it, the whirling of the weapon. He looked from his position that was at the middle, between the second and third ranks, to see the Teran who'd come to Ideclan, with a large hut burning behind him. The King could see the shine of his weapon, and he knew it well from books.

The handle was one and a half feet long, collapsible, and cylindrical like a staff. From the top came an intricately woven chain that was twelve feet long. At the end of the chain was a small sphere, completely smooth. The entire weapon was made from a metal known intrinsically to the Terans and secretly to the Philosians. It shined like silver and was famous for never breaking.

The Teran swung it in precise strikes, whipping armor and skin away from those he attacked. Five charged him and Acillus watched as the chain sliced them, the arcs reminding him of Philosian geometry. The Teran swung with great velocity. His accuracy was flawless and his speed hypnotizing. Tears fell from his eyes and screams came from his soul as he showed everyone why that weapon was to be feared. It shattered blades and eviscerated bone.

Then Acillus saw what he waited for. The archers came over the walls and stayed on the palisade as they took out sentries before flying arrows at the backs of the enemy. It wasn't long until panic overtook the Erra'Aulians and their formation crumbled.

"Free fight!" Acillus commanded, then blew the whistle.

Declanii charged into the confused mass. It was a slaughter as the last few threw down their weapons before putting their hands in the air. And a few who'd surrendered died in the haze of battle. Cristin was the cause of one and in the end, only fourteen were left.

"We only wanted ten to survive. Should I kill the others, my King?" Marchann Hafrana asked with a vicious grin.

The young man at the tip of his sword sobbed when he saw blood dripping from it.

"No. Fourteen will do."

"Too bad," Marchann said to the young man while disappointedly moving his sword away from his throat.

Then Corcc pierced the chest of the man next to the frightened young one. And as its lifeless body fell to the ground, throwing knives fell from its hands.

"Thirteen will do," Acillus said. "As you can see," he continued, directing his speech toward the Erra'Aulians. "Teranim is now part of The Kinned Lands, and as such, is under protection of the Sunil."

"What will you do with us?" the captain, who cowardly managed to stay alive, asked.

"Go back to your army and tell your Lancers we wait for them here if they wish to dispute claim over this land."

"We are five thousand! How do you expect to live out the week if you let us leave?"

"I challenge every one of you to come back and find out."

With that, the thirteen were set free at the Northern end of the city. And the last of them was seen running through the first light of day.

"That should be enough to bring the Western Army back down here," Acillus said to Quinnlan.

"Aye," he agreed.

The archers collected their raven fletched arrows while some of the combatants starting piling the bodies. And a few minor wounds were tended to.

Irhanach, Anrahan, and Ohelathe gathered together at the outskirts of the groups of Declanii. Each had killed his first man, and were beginning to feel the after effects of the experience.

"A lot more intense than our childhood adventures," Anrahan said.

"Indeed," Ohelathe agreed.

Then Irhanach dry heaved.

"Are you alright?" Anrahan asked.

"I'll be fine."

"How are you lads?" Marchann questioned as he walked by. A dead body hung over each of his shoulders.

"We'll be fine," Anrahan answered. Then both Ir-hanach and Ohelathe nodded.

"You all did well for your first. How are your minds?"

"It isn't easy taking life," Irhanach stated.

"As it never should be. Talk to Noa Nirowin if your minds stay troubled. He's good with words of this nature, and knows how to achieve a balance."

Each nodded they would, and then went to task with everyone else as the archers and a few others made their way to pick up the gear that'd been set out.

Many locals started exiting their huts. And the Teran who'd joined the battle, walked over to Acillus after regaining his composure and said to the King, "It is done. We are now, Terans of The Kinned Lands."

"Indeed you are. But I must apologize because now we all need to leave," Acillus insisted.

"We've been prepared to leave since they salted our land."

"They salted your land?" the King asked with surprise while he looked around and smelled the air.

"They did so with joy. We are prepared to leave."

"Then what are your people's wishes?"

"Those not of the weapon we ask be brought to Ideclan until a suitable home may be located. Those of the weapon, we ask be put to service against the Erra'Aulians. We have stores of our metal hidden, and means to make more sa haRi."

"Agreed. What's your name?"

"I am now, Grandmaster Muann."

"As it should be," the King said with a grin.

"It is the leader's role to lead," Muann stated.

Before the Sun climbed much higher, the Erra'Aulian dead were burning strong and the Terans were all aboard the transport vessels sailing toward Ideclan alongside the Declanii and a few Tenth Talon Scouts.

On Acillus' ship, in his quarters; Quinnlan, Grandmaster Muann, and two Teran elders spoke with the King over hot tea made from something the Terans had never tasted.

"It's ginger," Acillus told them. "Too much can be hard to drink, but just right and it warms the stomach. May I ask you some questions?"

"Please," the Grandmaster answered between sips.

"The braids you all wear around your arms and heads, the hair is not your own, correct?"

"Correct. Teran women have an understanding we men do not. When a woman loves a man she cuts her hair off if she chooses, and then gives it to the man. This helps the man be closer to that woman's understanding," Muann answered.

"Intriguing. And, have your people discussed where

they'll look for a new home?"

"We have not. It took time for us to accept that we would have to leave our ancestral home. Soon, I'll bring up the discussion for a new one."

"This presents an opportunity. There's an island just South of Ideclan's Harbor that's been uninhabited since the Tribellion War. It became a retreat for the O'Ronans some two hundred years ago. And I've walked it many times. There are no buildings, it has revitalized itself over the last three hundred years, and is quite beautiful. It's also fertile with many fresh water springs and good fishing. And if the island were to become the Terans' by their choosing, they'd be in perfect position to protect Ideclan and its port, should the need arise."

"Yes they would," Muann agreed.

"Would the Terans consider this?"

"The Teranar will have to walk this island with you before deciding. But it is a good proposal, and we will discuss it with all seriousness."

"Do you prefer I call you Grandmaster Muann?"

"You may call me Muann, Acillus."

"How many, 'of the weapon,' do you have?"

"All that is left are myself, the two masters beside me, thirty intermediates, and six beginners. The weapon you saw me wield is for our beginners and intermediates. Proper sa haRi will be crafted with the metal we brought."

"Thirty nine of you?" the King affirmed.

"Yes."

"I beg your forgiveness," Quinnlan interjected. "But didn't you say your Grandmaster was assassinated while we were back at Ideclan? Does that mean you were promoted?"

"It does. It is I who assassinated the previous Grandmaster that traded our weapons in for food, and let the elder women and children go."

Quinnlan Mullquane grinned with a slight forward nod.

And then the Teran smiled into his cup of ginger tea.

Chronicle Twenty

Our husbands have proven they can fight, but this isn't enough for me. If we are to raise a nation that can survive then the women will have to fight as well, because I know the strife ahead is going to be more difficult than anything we've faced so far.

As you know, for most of our stay at Daeadak, the women of that land taught me their way with the sword. And I intend to use the sword with my utmost ability on Ridec. He's just as new to the weapon as I am, practically, and this training from the Daeadak that I have, no one else among us has.

I'm going to fight Ridec with all of my heart, so that my heart returns to me every day. He'll be fluid and graceful yet vicious and aggressive so that no man may take my husband from me, because the harder I fight him, the stronger he'll be. I'll teach every woman to do this, including you, and throughout the greatness that our will people become, the women will always train with the men.

Letter from Jossilan O'Ronan, First Queen of Ideclan,
to Lovandri Weynahar,
during Ridec and the Clanii's Quest

Declanii

Chapter Twenty One

Ashnayn stood defiantly at the center of a bamboo temple residing at the middle of one of many sacred groves on the Islands of Hobaru. This specific grove and temple she now hated. It was the grove her father had dragged her back through so she could be promised to Gowgluni. And now it was the grove she was forced to walk through again this morning, before being forced to enter the temple and stand at the center again.

Every chief currently on the main island was there. As well as Gowgluni and forty of his mercenaries who blocked the doorways so there was no possibility for her to escape.

The Princess showed nothing but anger. The thought that these men could make her stand there, made her wish she was the greatest warrior among all the histories.

Her father stood off in the shadows making his presence as little known as possible, and she'd long since cast aside any hope for his help.

The All Chief's cowardice is beyond forgiveness. And the rest of these men never deserved it in the first place. All of their caring words toward their wives and daughters are lies wrapped in a manipulating love, she thought.

Then one of the chiefs stepped toward her with the wreath of shark teeth and bones. And her posture sank slightly when she saw it.

I hate that wreath, too.

"All Chief Daughter Ashnayn of the Twenty Tribes of Hobaru," Gowgluni began.

The fact that he was leading this council showed her just how much influence he'd really gained.

"You've broken the laws of the people."

"You're not one of the people," she resisted.

"Enough!" he yelled. "You're to be my wife! You will not speak to me with insolence! You've already shown enough disrespect when you ran out on your being declared to me. Then you showed me *even more* disrespect when you tried so hard to win the Moon Race and gain the Champion's Request to end our betrothal. And then you attempted escaping me all together by leaving this island and hiding on another! Put her under teeth and bone!" he ordered.

The chief with the wreath stepped toward Ashnayn and held it above her head.

Gowgluni continued, "It is declared under teeth and bone that the All Chief Daughter Ashnayn will no longer participate in any race."

"What!"

"Nor shall she retain any royal privileges. She's no longer aloud outside her family's pavilion. And all meals will be brought to her. It is declared that their royal family ground is sacred for the making of the wedding dress and work on it shall begin immediately. The All Chief Daughter is forbidden to talk to anyone outside her family's pavilion. And she may neither receive nor send letters nor correspondence of any kind."

"This is tyranny!" Ashnayn yelled.

"She will also have respect on her mind and in her voice when she speaks to those of authority. If the Princess fails at any of these declarations, she will spend an appropriate amount of time in the cliff cages. It is declared under teeth and bone."

Ashnayn's jaw dropped. The people of Hobaru feared the cliff cages and she was no exception.

"Instead of your usual amount of guards I thought these forty would suffice. They will take you back to your grounds now. And you *will* prepare for the making of the wedding dress." Then Gowgluni directed his orders toward the forty. "Take her back."

"Yes, Master," the leader said before corralling the Princess with his men.

During the walk back, Ashnayn did everything she could not to cry, and held her head high as she thought of what to do. It was still early in the morning and when they reached her family home, her heart grew angry again after seeing everything was already prepared for the making of the wedding dress.

Ashnayn walked up to the platform and let the dress makers start taking their measurements for a second time.

I will not wear this on my wedding day, she declared to herself.

The Sun had almost reached its zenith by the time the Princess was allowed to step off the platform. And Ashnayn felt rigid from having to stand there for so long, so the young Hobaruan walked over to her exercise area.

The forty guards continued surrounding her as she moved, which frustrated the Princess completely.

She hopped up to one of her pull up bars and began doing sets of twenty to warm up. As she exercised, her guards started relaxing which Ashnayn noticed, and it gave her an idea similar to the one she'd had when she escaped for the Moon Race.

The All Chief Daughter continued exercising. Not because she felt like it but because of how complacent they were becoming.

Then during a pull up, Ashnayn hoisted herself up so that she crouched on top of the pull up bar with perfect balance, then bound like a frog over a few of her guards, landing in a somersault, and was up and running at top speed before any of them could start after her.

When they did it was like a pack of hounds after a hare.

Ashnayn weaved through huts, houses, and palm trees. Some of her guards were fast but they lacked her agility and when she reached the forest, the Princess began losing them in the thickness of the trees and their narrow paths.

I can make it to my lake on these paths. They won't keep up with me through here. It'll take them time to figure out where I've gone and that'll give me a few moments to think. I have to figure out what I'm going to do. This isn't what I wanted. Perhaps the lake will bring me clarity.

And with the lake on her mind, she picked up her pace and lost the guards.

Chronicle Twenty One

The Ravenborne are some of the most feared entities to ever walk Terr'ah. Right from the onset of their discovery, they were met with suspicion and violence. But thankfully this world seems to be crawling back into some sort of sophistication. For no longer are they hunted or subjugated as in Ages past.

One thousand years before the Ages began was when the Ravenborne first started becoming hunted and exterminated. Those who didn't have the ability to communicate with ravens drove those who did underground. Over time, especially during the Second Age, the Ravenborne were hunted to an alarmingly low rate, seemingly vanishing from the tales all together. Until a light shines in the Third Age when we read about Lenias of the Lands of Unnba; the most famous Ravenborne of days past, who mystified and made spectacular what many were raised to believe a curse.

Acceptance of the Ravenborne wasn't immediate after that, but they were no longer hunted so fiercely once the story of Lenias was widely circulated. Yet there were still many rulers who'd place prices on the heads of Ravenborne. And so they, for the most part, stayed underground for five Ages.

When the Eighth Age began, tolerance for the Ravenborne was more present. Within their own families and societies they were far more accepted than in the past, but to outsiders it was still a source of uneasiness. Until the Ninth Age, when Ridec O'Ronan became the first Ravenborne King since the days long before the Ages. Because of this, among The Kinned Lands the word Ravenborne is now common place. But everywhere else it may still cause suspicion or in a few places even reverence.

Declanii

It has been my joy and privilege to have the descendant of Ridec and a Ravenborne himself under my tutelage. I've been in position to witness firsthand the wonders a pair of ravens and a human can achieve.

I don't know if anyone can cultivate this ability like some of the old tales say, it seems to me, to be intrinsic to birth. But it's evident that the number of Ravenborne appear to be growing. And with warriors like the Declanii behind a family of them, I do think it's safe to say they are making something of a return.

Chapter Three from the book: 'Intricacies of the Ravenborne'
Written by Segais of Philos

Chapter Twenty Two

It was the early morning of Mard, The Thirty Third of Midwinter, and two days into the third Clanii week of the Silent's voyage. For much of the way they'd traversed the Eastern coast of the Hilernian Sea, thankful the weather stayed favorable by not sending any storms as was custom for this season on the great water.

Knowing the custom, Aislin Mullquane still chose to sail straight for Hobaru from off the coast of Braknar. It was a bold choice but necessary given the time restraints. And now that they were past the deep waters South of Braknar, it seemed a beneficial one as well.

The elite group numbered thirteen with Aislin commanding two squads, each consisting of four combatants and two archers. Muirenn Brogan was Captain and combatant for Silent One. And Cael had earned the right to become Captain of Silent Two.

In Silent One besides Muirenn there was his second, the combatant Rander Hafrana, an expert in handling spies and counter spies. Third was Faolin Lahanbrey, known for his tracking skill. Then there was Ainmere Shymurrow, the youngest at forty seven until Cael fought his way in. The archers for Silent One were the famed Tristas Rorourke, the tournament's champion; and Hanlan Mullquane. Hanlan was Aislin's nephew and a son of Alisander.

It was Alisander's position Cael occupied. The old Mullquane had planned on lightening his duties with the Silent for some time, but was looking for the right moment. And he felt the Prince taking his position was such a moment.

Alisander excelled at espionage and had developed numerous contacts over the years. Instead of leaving with the Silent, he left to gather more information from those contacts. And by the time the Silent would reach Hobaru, he'd be deep in Erra'Aulian territory, alone.

Cael was now Captain of Silent Two. His second was Connor Nirowin. Third was Caston Cailian. And fourth was Astraeus Fianna, Irhanach's Da. The two archers for his group were Aidan U'dinry, son of Finnian, the former Captain of Declanii murdered by the Vord at the festival. And the best kept secret in the Silent, Cathasaigh Aenenay, Anrahan's Grandfather.

These thirteen plus two ravens and one extra human to Cael's surprise, voyaged onward toward Hobaru. The wind was steady from the Northwest and the oars were in the boat as they broke good water.

Roxgrin and Binneen flew above, drifting with the air, while the Silent were either resting or attending tasks, and Aislin stood at the bow, looking ahead. All wore cloaks and clothes the colors of gray, green, or brown. But the cloaks were open and their blankets long since cast aside due to the warmer climate.

Cael was on the starboard side. He'd just gotten his hands wet from pulling in a fishing line and was drying them on his cloak when he became aware of something in an inner pocket he hadn't noticed before.

What's this? he thought.

"What's what?" Binneen asked.

"You heard me? I was thinking to myself."

"Your thoughts are strong, Waldron. We heard them."

"There's something in my…"

Cael didn't pull out the sunil wraps from his pocket. There was a standing order for no sunil or Ideclan Amulets on any Silent mission. But the Prince couldn't bring himself to throw them overboard either. He thought they might have belonged to his Grandfather, Ailither, because the cloak once belonged to him. So he kept the wraps hidden in his pocket.

Since he was as by himself as could be for on a boat, the young O'Ronan decided to sit down, close his eyes, and practice going within like Segais had taught him. He started concentrating on his breathing. But training with these techniques showed Cael why the old wizard had said to find a quiet place where he wouldn't be disturbed. Because whenever the Prince practiced he was always interrupted.

"Hey Cael! Tell us what's going on with you and that Hinturan woman!" Rander yelled. He wore a gray cloak whose hood came over his short dark hair but stayed above his blue eyes.

"What are you talking about?" the Prince asked as he let go of his meditation.

"The Queen lady, what's her name, Biew, no, Biethan?"

"Biethwren," Cael said.

"Listen to how he even says her name," Rander joked. And many laughed, including Cael.

Declanii

The Prince stood up while smiling and shaking his head, then walked aft toward the surprise addition to the voyage.

"Woma?" he said to Aideen, the mother of his father, when he reached her.

"What is it, Wosri?" Aideen O'Ronan asked. She'd been Queen before Andraste and almost everyone called her Aidee.

"Why are you here?" he queried as he sat next to her.

She chuckled before answering, "Ever since your Woda crossed I've been out helping whenever I can. It's advantageous to have an old woman around you know. And if you weren't always off doing your own adventures, you would've noticed I've been off doing my own as well.

And when will it be that you have someone to train with?" Aidee asked, changing the subject. "Ailither and I were already in love by the time we were your age. So why did you refuse Aveline Hafrana's proposal?"

"Who told you of that?"

"These old ears hear everything. This will be fun, having your Woma along on your first task."

Cael smiled at her drollery.

The voyage went on for not much longer before the lookout caught sight of land off in the distance.

"Land!"

The Prince whistled a high tune. Then Roxgrin and Binneen flew down and landed on the oak railing next to him.

The Silent only saw Cael point. But in his mind he asked, *"Will you both scout that land please?"*

"Indeed, Waldron," they both thought back, and then flew off for the task.

"How does that work, Cael?" Ainmere asked him.

"They can hear my thoughts and I can hear theirs, as if our voices are inside each other's heads."

"Can you see through their eyes like the old tales say?" Cathasaigh questioned.

All Silent were paying attention, save Aislin. He'd already asked Acillus these questions many years ago, and continued watching the small speck of land on the horizon.

"Yes. I've seen through them, but certainly not intentionally."

That grabbed Aislin's attention as well.

"When?" Tristas requested.

"I've never told this to anyone, not even my Ma or Da, or Segais."

"I didn't mean to pry, forgive me," Tristas retracted.

"That's alright. The clearest time I can recall is on the voyage to Daeadak. Remember those sails, Faolin?"

"I do indeed."

"And the pirates who ambushed us?"

"I told the tale not too long ago."

"That's how I knew which part of the Impassable Straits to sail for, so we could trap their larger vessels. And where not to sail so we wouldn't hit the rocks underneath. The ravens told me with their sight."

No one asked him another question as they all went back to their tasks after that. And Aidee smiled wide, which the Prince didn't see because he looked down, encompassed in his own thoughts.

The ravens returned after scouting and their cawing grabbed everyone's attention once more as Roxgrin and Binneen land next to Cael.

"We need to avoid that island, Waldron," Binneen thought to him.

"What'd you see?"

"No life, no energy," Roxgrin added.

"No energy?" he asked.

"No colors from the other planes touch it," Binneen continued, and Cael nodded. He knew the ravens saw colors he didn't.

"There are islands past that one with great colors. But they are in danger from the first," Roxgrin informed.

Then Cael looked at Aislin.

"Something isn't right with that island. It has to do with colors they can see and we can't. I've learned to trust them on this, and I think it wise we steer clear. They say more islands are beyond that one."

Aislin and a few others went to the rigging and shifted their sails so they'd pass by the island. As they passed it, all felt a sense of dread well up within them. It looked scorched, even the rocks. No living thing could be seen upon it and the smell was foul.

"Wouldn't have stopped there if we wanted to," Rander stated.

Not long from then the lookout caught site of the islands.

"Land, islands!"

All prepared to dock at Hobaru.

"I still don't think we need to make this stop," Hanlan declared.

"None of us can climb like they can," Astraeus Fianna said to him. He had the same burning red hair with slight tinges of yellow as all Fiannas.

"So we trust them to climb and gather the information for us?" Hanlan continued.

"At least one of us has to climb," Aislin answered.

"What about the ravens, Cael?" Muirenn asked.

"We'll see. Camulus might have mitigated that."

Cael thought of the hawk's feather Roxgrin gave to him, and to what he and Binneen had said concerning the hawks being raised to eat ravens. Then he scolded himself for forgetting to tell his Da about it.

"Cael, if you could, I've been curious my whole life; please tell us why Ideclan Ravens are larger and live longer than any other," Ainmere requested.

Aidee looked at the Prince inquisitively. *Will he tell them?* she wondered.

"That one will have to wait for another day."

"Eradicate the guarding of knowledge," Rander said, reciting the old Clanii Tenet.

"It isn't up to me."

"Who's it up to?" Ainmere asked.

"The ravens," Cael pronounced.

As Hobaru grew closer, Tristas pulled in his fishing line disappointed, and Rander counted his bribing money.

"Remember," Cael spoke. "Svudarh is the password. It means, 'I'm peaceful' in their tongue."

"Can we trust the Hinturan to be truthful on that?" Caston questioned.

"I'll tell you shortly," Cael remarked, and some in the boat chuckled.

The Silent started sailing between two of the islands, but much nearer to one than the other. And they noticed each island jutted from the sea, leaving only cliffs on the way back down. The Hobaru Islands were an archipelago of five, with five to twenty miles between each island. And all were covered with boulders and trees around their outskirts, very much like they were placed and planted there intentionally.

"Look," Tristas directed while pointing toward a section of cliffs.

More than fifty Hobaruans were halfway up and all of them climbed at an impressive pace.

"How tall is that?" Aidee asked.

"Around sixty spans," Muirenn answered.

"They're not wearing any ropes," Ainmere noted.

"Watch the farthest one on the left," Aislin told them.

Everyone turned their attention toward the climber. The others ascended continuously while the one on the far left vaulted, jumping from hold to hold, straight upward every time.

"I wonder if they're some sort of sentry," Cael questioned.

The vaulting climber reached the top first and the rest shortly after. Then a few started pointing down toward the Silent's boat, and Cael waved at them.

The Hobaruan woman who'd been vaulting, yelled a command, then the climbers dove off the cliff in unison. The Silent noticed each of them now had a spear in their hands as well.

"They can dive too," Aislin remarked. "Furl the sails. Let's see what they want. Everyone be ready if words are of no use."

"Don't say the password unless they attack us," Cael said.

"Why so?" Muirenn asked.

"A feeling."

The leader of Silent One nodded. That was all he needed from his future King.

The Hobaru were excellent climbers and divers but also masterful swimmers as well, evident by the speed in which they displayed in reaching the boat. And when they arrived, half of them stopped with their spears pointing at the Ideclaners while the other half went under the boat, then surfaced on the opposite side and also tread water with their spears pointing at the Silent.

Ainmere smirked when he noticed each of their spear tips were made from large shark teeth.

The Hobaruan woman said something none of them could understand.

"Common Tongue?" Aislin asked.

"Common Tongue is for common tongues. And ours are not common. Why are you here?"

"We are climbers, my dear!" Aidee suggested.

Then Aislin gave her a sidelong glance.

"You climb?"

"Of course! We've been traveling to different lands looking for the best climbers. And everyone says Hobaru is home of the very best."

"They are correct."

"That's why we're here. Because we wish to challenge you to a climbing contest!"

The Silent wondered if she were mad while the woman told her companions about what Aidee had just suggested, and they laughed.

"Get out of your boat and let's climb the walls now," she taunted. And each of the Hobaru's body language was that of, follow us.

"I'm sorry, but there are procedures for this."

"What are those?" the Hobaruan asked with suspicion.

"The ways things are done, my dear. It's unfair to challenge us on your home walls just as it would be unfair if we challenged you on ours. So that's why we've been traveling. We're not all from the same land, but we are all the best climbers from our lands. And we've stopped here on our way to the tallest walls in the world in hopes of gathering the very best of you. So that they may come with us and we can finally find out who is the best among all on Terr'ah!" Aidee said theatrically.

The Hobaruan woman thought for a moment before saying, "Our All Chief, Nuadhu, will want to know of this. I'll send swimmers with you."

At a command in Hobaru Tongue, half the sentry group tied their spears to themselves before swimming in front of the boat.

"Follow them," she said.

Then they started swimming toward the main island.

"Oars," Aislin commanded. And everyone on board manned an oar and began rowing.

The pace was such that again, they impressed the Silent.

As they approached the main island, the Ideclaners discerned boats and ships from at least a dozen different nations both importing and exporting. The others they saw were transport vessels carrying goods from the outer islands to the main one.

"Look at that one," Aidan said while pointing.

"Are they pulling it?" Aidee asked.

Aislin put up his oar and then so did Aidee. The Captain pulled out two lenses of different sizes that he procured from a Philosian craftsman and wrapped them in a leather skin to form a hollow cone with one lens at each end. Then he gave the eyeglass to Aidee and she put the smaller lens to an eye.

"They have special harnesses tying them to the boat," she told everyone.

"Training," Cael said. "I'll wager they climb with rocks tied behind them as well."

When they neared the main island, the swimmers began slowing because of all the activity and the rowers followed their example.

"Aidee takes lead. Hanlan and I will stay with the boat. Muirenn has command," Aislin ordered.

"You're staying with the boat?" Aidee asked.

"The woman was paying attention to you for the conversation but the rest of them were glancing at him and me. Our Marks make them uneasy and it'd be wise for us stay with the boat."

"Roxgrin and Binneen will fly high and scout," Cael told the Mullquanes. "But if we're coming fast and need to leave the same, they'll let you know. Three caws means we're coming fast, two caws we're captured, and one caw to follow them."

Aislin nodded and then said to everyone, "You're climbers now, take only secondary weapons."

Cael tied his bits to his belt under his cloak. The Philosian favorites were the only weapons he'd carry off the boat.

The Silent slowed more while approaching an elaborate docking system coming off the island. Tied to the docks were numerous vessels. And there was also a busy market on the quay that continued wrapping around the island to the East.

Many took notice of the foreigners as they approached, but returned to their business once they saw the Hobaruan swimmers climbing up onto the quay before them.

The Silent slowed to a crawl and then stopped to dock. When they finished, their escorts motioned for them to follow and all but two complied. The swimmers tried getting the Mullquanes to follow as well but Aislin and Hanlan's demeanor quickly persuaded them to let it go.

So they led everyone else to a wide set of stairs cut diagonally up the cliff. At the inner part of the stairs was a worn path for animals. And as the Silent were led up the stairs, they saw mostly goats and pigs being herded on the path.

Once they reached the top, all became surprised. The outskirt of the island was a strip of rock and forest, but inside where they were was a bustling city.

Every building had been made using thin trees with designs more elaborate than most would have built with the same resources. And the intricateness of the interweaving at the corners of the buildings and the edges of their roofs were art in themselves.

But the farther they walked through the city the more apparent it became that few outsiders were allowed up in it.

"I'm not so sure I like this," Muirenn proclaimed.

"I see spears and a few daggers but no swords or bows," Tristas spied.

"All indications say these are a peaceful enough people," Astraeus remarked.

"Peaceful enough to let us into their rather large city,

surrounded and outnumbered by them," Aidan added.

It was then that Cael became aware of a flying magpie as he walked at the back of the group. He watched the bird fly up and around in circles above them, then back down in front of him as he strolled. The young O'Ronan felt a sense of wonder and became transfixed to it.

Suddenly the bird stopped in mid flight right in front of him, looking straight at the Prince. No one else noticed the magpie as it stopped behind them and after one step, Cael halted and stood face to face with the flyer.

"Waldron," it thought to him and his eyes grew wide. *"Waldron,"* it thought again and then flew Southeast, away from the Southwesterly direction the Silent were being led.

Without thought he followed the bird, not noticing where his companions went nor they noticing him. No one in the entire city saw him follow the magpie with a large smile on his face. He walked by hundreds of people and not one of them became aware of the odd pair.

Cael followed the magpie out of the city and then for a ways through trees and brush, never knowing how far he walked until he came upon a freshwater lake that was hidden on all sides by trees.

The magpie seemed to vanish when Cael arrived at the tree line. He looked around, shaking off the complete focus of the bird, and then realized for the first time he'd been separated from his group. The Prince tried getting his bearings but he discerned nothing through the wall of trees around the lake.

So he decided to walk down toward the river that fed

the lake. On his way, he thought of how to explain this to the Silent and remembered the password, svudarh, if he needed it to get back to them.

Then he froze when he saw a young woman by the lake's shore, not seven spans from him. She was of middle height and fit like all the athletes on the islands. Her skin was lightly tan and her long blonde red hair was tied behind her. The young woman wore a white sarong and a black linen diving vest with multiple pockets. And a knife made from a shark's tooth was attached to it.

She kneeled down and scooped up a grasshopper into her hand, then stood and threw it into the lake where a few fish waited for the easy meal.

"I wonder what the grasshoppers think of that," Cael pondered, hoping to get a laugh.

She turned and almost gasped but then realized he wasn't one of her guards.

"I… how did you get in here?" she asked with a puzzled look.

"I followed a magpie," he answered while noticing her eyes were green.

That made her smile.

"How'd you get past the guards?"

"I didn't see any. Actually, I don't remember much of how I arrived; just the bird, and then the lake, and then you."

"You're not Hobaruan."

Cael shook his head.

"I am Ashnayn, Princess of the Twenty Tribes of Hobaru, and Daughter to All Chief Nuadhu."

"I am Cael, Prince of The Kinned Lands, and Son to King Acillus O'Ronan and Queen Andraste Mullquane."

"Can you fight, Prince?"

"That would depend on what I'm fighting."

"Forty men with spears and knives. They'll be here shortly."

Cael and Ashnayn started hearing their commotion down the path.

The Prince looked toward the direction they'd arrive, and then back at Ashnayn, who hadn't looked away from him. And as hard as he tried thinking of something else to say, only two sentences formed in his mind.

"I need help at a faraway land. Will you sail away from here with me?"

She smiled a funny smile before saying, "I might. But to get out of this one you'll have to follow me first."

Then Ashnayn darted for the trees, and Cael matched her speed.

Declanii

"Where's Cael?" Cathasaigh asked.

"He's not here?" Ainmere queried while looking behind them as they walked.

"First task and he gets himself lost," Rander joked with a smile.

"Keep walking as if we're here to challenge them at climbing," Aidee commanded.

The main part of the city was even busier than the section closest to the outskirt. And many inhabitants had to move out of their way as they walked.

It was obvious they were being led to a courtyard with a stage at one end. And all noticed the well made chair up on the right side of that stage. The chair was fashioned from the same thin but strong trees as their structures. Palm leaves covered the chair in a beautiful design and were also wrapped around the front of the stage.

As the Silent stepped onto the courtyard, everyone around the area made their way to hear what they were about. The Ideclaners were less than thrilled to now be the center of unwanted attention. There was nowhere to go as they were completely surrounded. And all went quiet as a conch was blown.

The All Chief, Nuadhu, came out of a row of huts with a procession of twenty people behind him. When they stepped onstage, which the Silent were now in front of, they walked across it from left to right, over to the chair according to the Silent's view.

After computing what he saw, Muirenn was suspicious of one. He scratched the back of his right shoulder twice, alerting everyone to pay attention to the second man from the right. His name was Gowgluni, and Muirenn thought that many in the procession followed his orders by their body language.

"*Who are these people?*" Gowgluni asked in Hobaru once Nuadhu was seated on his chair.

A swimmer told everyone their story and that they didn't speak the local language.

"You've come here in the hopes that we speak Common Tongue when ours are not common? Who are you?" Gowgluni asked the Silent with contempt.

Aidee answered, "We're travelers from the Western lands, climbers on our way to the greatest walls in the…"

"Yes, we've been told the story. But what of another part of the story. The two that stay with your boat have marks on their faces."

Aidee interjected quickly.

"A custom from our lands in the West. My husband and son are stubborn as ever. They never leave that boat while we're out at sea. I'm beginning to think they love that thing more than me," she said with a convincing smile.

"That may be. But marks also come from other places. We'll have to discuss this."

The entire group on the elevated stage began conversing, including Nuadhu, who appeared to take second to Gowgluni. Muirenn noted that Nuadhu didn't act as if he wanted to follow the foreigner, it was more as if he had to.

Their conversation continued on the stage while the people around the courtyard began conversing amongst themselves.

"Never been in a situation like this," Connor said, trying to lighten the mood.

"How do you think we're doing?" Aidee asked.

"I'd say we have a half a chance of getting out of this," Cathasaigh joked, and some chuckled.

Then a group of men with spears and knives, ran up to the courtyard yelling in both Hobaru and Common Tongue.

"*The Princess is missing!*"

"The Princess is gone!"

"*We can't find her!*"

Gowgluni turned and pointed toward the Silent while yelling, "Seize them! Search them!"

The Ideclaners had time to say the password but didn't because of an indiscreet command given by Muirenn, who wouldn't use it unless they were attacked as the Prince had wished. And this to him, wasn't an attack. So the swimmers quickly surrounded them. And some of Gowgluni's henchmen grabbed each one as well.

"Is this the hospitality of Hobaru?" Aidee shouted.

"They have weapons!" a mercenary yelled as the Silent were searched.

"Bind them! Bring them to the cliff cages! Organize search parties! I want the Princess found!"

The Silent were quickly bound and brought to the holding cells that were suspended over certain cliffs, known to the Hobaru as cliff cages. The cages could be intentionally dropped to the water but if a prisoner moved excessively, then the thin trees and vines they were made from would break and fall anyway.

Each of the Silent were put in their own holding cell, not too far from one another and easily within conversing range.

"Try to stay still," Muirenn observed after studying the cages.

Then Ainmere quirked a smile when he heard the high and distant caws of two ravens.

Cael and Ashnayn stayed low to the ground, keeping well hidden from the patrols as they searched for the Hobaruan Princess.

"Are you not allowed to go where you wish?" he asked.

"Not since soon after I was promised to Gowgluni. The guards are all under his bidding. I keep losing them on the run.

But that man is cruel. I can't risk your life because of this."

"Can you climb?"

"What?" Ashnayn asked with indignation.

"I saw great climbers as we sailed in, ascending straight up the cliff. Can you climb as they can?"

She looked at him as though he were an ignorant buffoon before saying, "I am the greatest climber on all five islands. I've won over two hundred challenges to prove it."

"That will work."

"What do you mean?"

"I need to spy on an Emperor, and I have to climb an incredibly tall spire to do it."

"Camulus Erra'Aulius?"

"Yes. What do you know of him?"

"A lot of trade is done with his empire. Gowgluni says he's potentially an ally. But I hear the traders talk, and it sounds as if he's bringing his army this way to take more lands. Could he take our islands?"

"It's possible. Your islands have become a center of trade between his lands and the West. But if you sail with me, we can save both our homes if that's his aim."

Ashnayn thought, *A true adventure sounds exciting. And this may be my way off the island.*

"How dangerous?" she asked.

"I'll be honest. The danger is real. But the adventure is fun," he said before feeling as though he sounded like a fool.

Ashnayn thought for a few moments more and then said, "I've never sailed."

"Ever?"

"My father never permitted it."

"You might like it. There are few greater freedoms than the wind and sea."

"Where are you docked?"

"At the Northern part of the island. Can you lead us there without being seen?"

"Follow me."

Ashnayn's strides were graceful. Cael kept up but was nowhere near as fluid. And they paced two miles before becoming aware of another patrol and had to crouch and hide again.

Ashnayn started standing after they passed, thinking they were gone, but Cael grabbed her arm.

"Wait," he said quietly.

And then a few more men ran by.

"How'd you know about them?"

As they both stood from their hiding place, Cael said, "I'll explain…"

Roxgrin and Binneen started flying down and interrupted him.

"Waldron, the Silent have been put in cages. We told the Mullquanes and they've left the docks."

Cael's expression changed to one of concern.

"What is it?" Ashnayn asked, and then backed away as two large ravens swooped down and landed, one on his left forearm and one on the tree limb next to him.

"You're Ravenborne!" she exclaimed quietly.

"I am. Your people have taken my companions captive."

Ashnayn shook her head in frustration.

"I should have never left the guards. All of you are in danger now. It's impossible for us to leave."

"My grandfather and another have been with the boat the entire time. The ravens alerted them first so now they sail around the island, staying hidden. What sort of holding cells does Hobaru keep?"

"Holding cells?"

"The place where you put people so they can't go anywhere."

"That's at the outer edge of the island, on the Western

side. We call them cliff cages."

"How long will it take to get there?"

"Between an hour or two at the pace we've been running, depending on how many patrols we come across."

Cael looked at Binneen on his arm.

"Lead Aislin and Hanlan in view of the cages, then have them hold. Find me when we're near."

Both ravens flew up and North toward his grandfather while Ashnayn followed them with her gaze.

"Do you still wish to come with us?" Cael asked, wondering how she felt about the Ravenborne.

Ashnayn considered it for a brief moment, then looked at Cael.

"Yes."

"Take me there, please, to the Western side. We'll free my friends and then be away from here."

"This way."

She led him through a part of the forest that hid their passage West. Ashnayn was nimble and bound over log and rock like a deer as Cael continued keeping pace, but clumsily compared to her.

Roxgrin and Binneen flew toward the Mullquanes, who sailed a good distance away from the main island.

"What do you suppose happened?" Hanlan asked.

"I have no idea," Aislin answered.

"The ravens are coming back," Hanlan continued as he pointed.

Both looked up and watched them swoop down. Each raven started cawing, one caw at a time, then flew a short distance Southwest and waited there, flapping and cawing.

"One caw, follow," Aislin said.

The Mullquanes adjusted their rigging to sail in the direction of the ravens.

When they reached where Roxgrin and Binneen would fly no farther, it was getting dark. But by using Aislin's eyeglass they could still see the suspended cages imprisoning their companions at the top of the cliff.

"What are we going to do?" Hanlan asked his uncle.

"Figure out a way to free them," Aislin answered as Binneen flew up and off toward the Prince.

Up at the cages, the members of the Silent sat quietly, while Cael and Ashnayn had made it there easily and were not too far from them, but wouldn't go any closer due to the six guards keeping watch.

"Do you know anything about those guards' schedules or rotations?" Cael whispered.

"Nothing," Ashnayn whispered back.

"We might have to wait until the deep dark of night…"

"Waldron, the Mullquanes are near us on the water," Binneen thought as she flew above.

"Keep them there for now," he thought back.

Then she flew to the boat once more.

"My grandfather is down there on the water."

"How do you know that?"

"The ravens."

"Oh, right."

"What's the height of the cliff here?"

"Sixty or seventy spans."

"Do you know how those cages work?"

"No, I've always hated them. But look, over there is a better hiding place."

"Lead the way," Cael told her once he agreed.

Ashnayn led him to where they hid until darkness fully took the land. It was easy for them to hide because no patrols thought to look for her in that area.

When it became fully dark, Aislin and Hanlan started maneuvering closer to the island but the ravens stopped them. Then Binneen flew back toward Cael while Roxgrin stayed.

"Do you think they want us to remain here?" Hanlan asked.

"I do," Aislin answered. "And I think that means Cael has a plan. We only counted eleven in those cages. One of them still isn't there."

In a few moments, Binneen reached Cael again and landed above him in a tree.

"They're still waiting, Waldron, but they wish to act."

The Prince pulled a long, thin strip of cloth from his cloak pocket that he'd forgotten to take out before leaving the boat.

"What's that?" Ashnayn asked in his ear.

"A sign for my grandfather."

Cael threw the sunil wrap high up in the air. Then Binneen lifted off and grabbed it in her talons before flying away.

"A wrap!" Aislin realized once she'd gotten close enough. "I don't think Cael is captured."

Both Mullquanes resolved to stay with the ravens and when the birds were satisfied of this, it was Roxgrin's turn to fly up and assist Cael. Roxgrin knew they'd have to jump from the island to escape, so he looked for a shorter drop as he flew. And the raven found one.

"Two miles South there's a drop half the height as here," he informed the Ravenborne when he reached him.

"Thank you. Direct Aislin and Hanlan there."

Then Roxgrin flew swiftly back down to the boat.

"Anything you can tell me about jumping from high so we don't injure ourselves?" Cael spoke softly into Ashnayn's ear.

"When your hands first touch the water…"

"No, none of us will be diving, just jumping."

"You don't dive?"

"We dive underwater. But not from great heights."

"That sounds sad. Diving is the closest thing to flying."

Cael found that intriguing. Then his attention was taken toward the guards who dwindled down to two as four left to patrol the other parts of the cliff cages.

"What's your fight training like?" he asked, continuing to whisper in her ear.

"Some work with spears, and Gowgluni's guards are starting to train more. But not much else."

The remaining guards got up and walked over to the edge of the cliff. They stood between two large trees and stared out into the dark waters while conversing.

Cael made a pushing motion with his hands and asked, "Would they survive it?"

Ashnayn stifled a laugh and nodded her head while

saying, "Sure, there's no rocks."

Cael ran at the guards as silently as an owl's wings. Before either was aware, he put a hand on each's back and pushed them over. Both were too surprised to yell and all they could do was focus on diving like they'd done countless times.

"Prince Cael!" Muirenn whispered excitedly.

And the Silent turned to see him, and then Ashnayn as she walked up to them.

Without speaking, Cael studied the cages and their mechanics. He started pulling levers which brought them back over land and Ashnayn cut the vine ropes around their cages with her shark tooth knife.

When all were free they ran a half a mile South, then gathered in a tight cluster to talk quietly.

"Cael, that was funny," Rander said softly with a hint of laughter in his voice.

"Good, because you have to do it shortly. A mile and a half South is where Aislin and Hanlan are going with the boat. It isn't as high but we still have to jump, and make sure we're all spread out when we do. Follow me," Cael ordered, and then set a fast pace.

They reached the lower height with no interruptions, but it was evident that back at the cages and growing in the city there was a commotion related to them.

"Is this a safe place to jump from?" Cael asked Ashnayn.

She nodded.

"Jump!" he said as he ran, and then leapt off the cliff.

Ashnayn laughed before leaping hands first into the air behind him. Because Cael had jumped, the rest instinctively followed. And all landed safely, though Ainmere and Rander did so close together.

When everyone surfaced they swam for the boat. In short time and out of eyesight of any Hobaru save the Princess, all were aboard and sailing away from the main island.

"Who's this," Aislin asked Cael.

"Everyone, this is Princess Ashnayn of the Hobaru, and their greatest climber. She's won over two hundred challenges to prove it."

"Greetings," Ashnayn said, both excited and nervous about her newfound freedom.

"Ahroo, dear," Aidee welcomed her.

Then so did the rest, many with, "Ahroo."

"Has Cael told you of the assistance we need?" Aislin questioned.

"He has. And I've decided to help you climb."

The Silent stifled their cheers, for the trip to Hobaru ended up being a success, but they weren't completely away from danger yet.

The ravens flew above them as they moved rapidly on the dark waters of the night while some took turns telling Aislin and Hanlan segments of the story. And all had laughs at the part where Cael pushed two people off a cliff.

After the tale was recounted, Cathasaigh started a potato soup on their stove specifically made for the boat, while the Prince threw dried berries in the air. And the ravens swooped down to grab them as they traveled onward, toward the Twelve Lakes of Lareen.

Ashnayn looked back at the island she was leaving behind and felt the pocket on her diving vest that held the stone figurine her mother gave her.

Freedom will always be mine, she declared to herself.

Sagas of the Ravenborne

Declanii

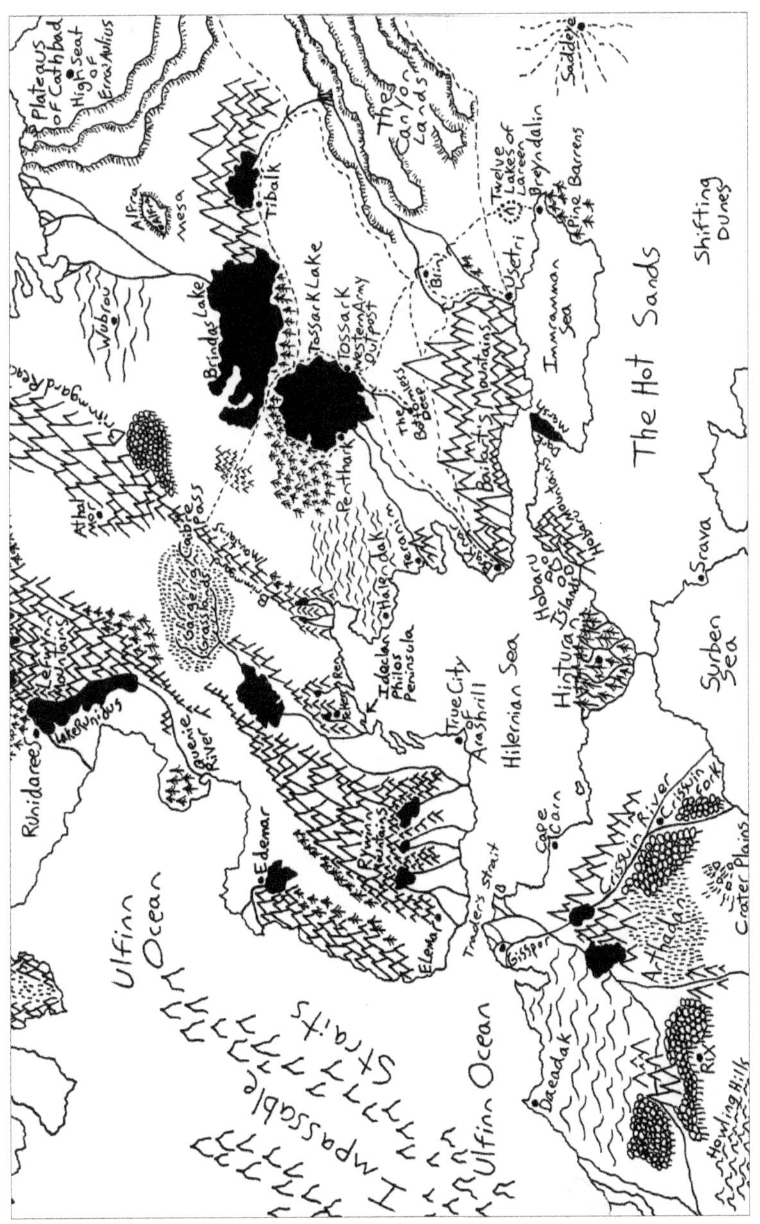

Plateaus of Cathbad
High Seat of Esra'Aulus
Alfra
Alfra mesa
Tibalk
The Canyon Lands
Twelve Lakes of Lareen
Breyndalin
Pine Barrens
Saddleye
Shifting Dunes
Wubrou
Brindas Lake
Tossark Lake
Tossark Western Army Outpost
Usetri
Biin
Inmramman Sea
The Hot Sands
Rinngard Reach
Athal mor
Gage's Cabbec Pass
The Bottomless Deep
Baiket's Mountains
Morketon Mountains
Pentharik
Teranim
Halendak
Idaclan
Philos Peninsula
Fekon Rea
Gaige's Grasslands
Ruhidarees
Lake Rundus
Refyire Mountains
Quenie River
Edemar
True City of Arashrill
Hilernian Sea
Hobaru Islands
Hintura Islands
Hoth Mountains
Scrava
Surben Sea
Ulfinn Ocean
Rivynn Mountains
Elena
Trader's Strait
Cape Carn
Sisspor
Athadan
Crisswin River
Crisswin
Cork
Crater Plains
Daeadak
Rix
Howling Hills
Impassable Ulfinn Straits

Declanii